King Con

Stephen J. Cannell

King Con

WHEELER
PUBLISHING, INC.
ROCKLAND, MA

★ AN AMERICAN COMPANY ★

Published in Large Print by arrangement with William Morrow and Company, Inc. in the United States and Canada.

Wheeler Large Print Book Series.

Set in 16 pt Plantin.

Library of Congress Cataloging-in-Publication Data

Cannell, Stephen J.
   King Con / Stephen J. Cannell.
     p. (large print) cm.(Wheeler large print book series)
   ISBN 1-56895-536-7 (hardcover)
   1. Swindlers and swindling—Fiction. 2. Adventure stories. gsafd
3. Large type books.
I. Title. II. Series
[PS3553.A4995K56 1998]
813'.54—dc21   98-014662
                                                                CIP

This is for Jeff Sagansky,
who liked it first.

ACKNOWLEDGEMENTS

No book is written without the help of many people. As before, Wayne Williams was a tireless editor, along with Paul Bresnick at William Morrow. Thanks to Robert Sulkin for his help with the legal aspects of jury selection; Jo Swerling for his countless reads, giving me first-draft input.

The real heroes of King Con are my two assistants: Grace Curcio, who worked every day and every weekend on the receiving end of my rough drafts, typing and cleaning up my horrible, dyslexic spelling; and Kristina Oster, who imputted everything on the computer and did my countless revisions.

I must again thank my wife, Marcia, who continues to put up with this novel obsession.

"TO DECEIVE IS TO ENCHANT."

—Plato

King Con

Prologue

The poker game had been a card-hustler's dream; the players were strictly in the talented-amateur category and the stakes were unlimited. It was rumored that hundreds of thousands of dollars routinely changed hands in the invitation-only game that commenced promptly at seven-thirty every Tuesday night in the luxurious locker room of New Jersey's Greenborough Country Club. There was an investment banker from Cleveland who was a cautious bettor, and refused to step up even when he held sure winners. He'd also occasionally chase a bluff like a puppy after a pickup truck. There was a fat electronics-store owner who was constantly bathed in a sheen of his own sweat and was a shameless plunger. There were two brothers from Greenborough, who owned a Lexus dealership. They were trying to team play, but kept misreading each other. They talked trash, drank too much, and ended up losing five out of six hands.

Then there was Joseph Rina. He was only five-eight, but there was an aura about him. He radiated power and was movie-star handsome. He was reputed to be a New Jersey mob boss, although he had never been convicted of anything. His nickname on the street was Joe "Dancer." He sat at the green felt table, clothed in perfectly tailored Armani. He remained distant from the others, playing without comment, his magnificently handsome face giving away nothing. Joe Rina joined this game once a month. He would drive down from Atlantic City to the Greenborough Country Club and was generally the big winner.

Seated to his right was Beano Bates. He had been trying to get in this high-stakes game for a month. He was a well-known card sharp and con man, so he was playing incognito, under the name of Frank Lemay. Dark-haired and handsome, he had always traded on his looks and charm.

Although he was a world-class poker player, Beano never depended solely on his card-playing skill. He had two "shiners" working on the table: One was a money clip that he could lay on the table directly in front of him. It was shiny, but only reflected directly back. If you looked at the clip from any other angle, it appeared to be dull and non-reflective. Beano could deal cards over the clip, and the shiner would reflect the cards as they were flipped off the deck, giving him full knowledge of what was in play. The other was a "palm shiner," which he used when it wasn't his deal. It was a tiny, upside-down periscope. He could palm it, or hold it cupped in his hand on the green felt table, positioned so he could look down through the space between his fingers. The palm shiner was low enough on the table to read the cards being dealt off the deck across from him. These two shiner positions, plus his natural skill at cards, gave him an unbeatable edge.

2

By ten-thirty, Beano Bates, a.k.a. Frank Lemay, was eighty-six thousand dollars ahead. The poker chips were stacked in columns in front of him like colorful prisoners captured in battle.

At eleven o'clock they took the main break, and Beano found himself standing next to Joe "Dancer" Rina at the urinal in the over-lit men's locker room of the ornate country club. White tile and chrome fixtures glittered under the bright ceiling lights, while the two men arched yellow streams into the shiny porcelain trough like two teenage boys pissing in a lake for distance.

"You been getting good cards," Joe Rina said without emotion, his movie-star face reveal-ing no hint of danger.

"Sometimes the cards run that way," Beano replied as he watched his urine mix with Joe's and flow into a drain full of bar ice and black pepper.

"You call a lot of six-card optional," Joe said, referring to a dealer's choice game that Beano preferred because, after the fifth card was dealt, the players could exchange any one of their cards for a sixth card before betting commenced. Beano liked the game because it gave him more cards to scope with his money clip shiner.

"Yeah," Beano grinned, "that game's been working pretty good for me."

"You ever hear about Soapy Smith?" Joe said softly.

"Don't think I have," Beano replied, dreading the story, which he correctly assumed would be some kind of ghastly warning.

"They called him Soapy because he marked cards with soap. Kept a little sliver between his index and middle fingers, used it to stripe the cards. Soapy did real good in Atlantic City when I was growing up...drove a big, black Cadillac. All us kids wanted to be like him...lotsa women, great clothes. Always wore the Italian or French designers. Everything was great till Saturday, June eighteenth, 1978....That was the day we all changed our minds about being like Soapy."

"Really?" Beano said, his smile pasted on his face, his puckering dick hanging forgotten in his hand. He put it away, zipped up, and moved to the washbasin, wishing he didn't have to hear the end of the tale.

In a minute, Joe Dancer's reflection joined his in the mirror. "Yeah. Poor Soapy got caught jammin' some players at the Purple Tiger, which was a little card club down on the wharf, by the pier. Those guys he was cheatin' were serious players, and they were real mad 'cause they trusted Soapy, so they held him down and jointed the poor guy while he was still alive."

"I beg your pardon?" Beano said.

"One guy, I think he'd been a medic in 'Nam, amputated Soapy a section at a time, while the others held him down. They had a plumber clamping off veins and arteries so he wouldn't bleed out. Kept him alive for about fifteen or twenty minutes. By the time they took

4

off his left arm, poor Soapy's heart stopped."

Somebody flushed a toilet in the stall behind them.

"That's a damn good reason not to cheat," Beano managed, his insides now frozen like his smile.

"I always thought so," Joe said. And without any expression crossing his gorgeous aquiline face, he walked away from the sink.

The story made its point. Beano figured eighty-six grand was plenty. He decided to just hold even, maybe give some of it back, until the game time limit.

The game was called at exactly midnight, and Beano cashed in seventy-eight thousand in chips. Joe Rina left without saying another word. Beano stayed in the bar talking the losers down for about an hour, drinking and telling everybody it had been the best card night of his life.

At a few minutes past one, Beano walked out of the almost deserted country club and headed to his rental car.

What happened to Beano in the parking lot wasn't as bad as what had happened to Soapy Smith in Atlantic City, but it certainly made the same point.

He had just arrived at his car and was putting his briefcase into the trunk when he was staggered by a massive blow from behind. It hit him with such devastating force at the back of his skull that Beano instantly dropped to his knees, splitting open his forehead on the back bumper. He spun awkwardly around in

5

time to see a nine-iron flying out of the darkness, right into his face. It was a chip shot from hell that broke all his front teeth and shattered his jaw, skewing it terribly. Beano fell to the pavement, then grunted in horrible, unendurable pain as four more horrendous blows from the golf club broke the third, fifth, and seventh ribs along his spinal column, also shattering his clavicle and sinus cavity.

Beano was barely conscious when Joe Rina stuck his handsome face down so close that Beano could smell his breath and mint aftershave.

"You look pretty bad, Mr. Lemay," the mobster said. "You might be able to pull this stuff on that buncha buffaloes in there, but you should know better than to try and cheat Joseph Rina."

Beano couldn't talk. His jaw was locked by bone chips and a break that knocked it badly out of alignment.

"Now I'm gonna take my money back. But let me assure you this has been very helpful," Joe Dancer said with exaggerated politeness. "I've been having trouble with my short game. I think I wasn't keeping my head down and following through like my guy keeps telling me. Thanks for the practice." Joe stood up; then Beano felt pure agony as two more blows rained down onto his body for good measure. He started to cough up blood. Beano knew he was badly wounded, but more important, in that instant he felt something die inside him. It was as if the most critical piece of

6

Beano Bates, his charming confidence, had left him like smoke out of an open window. It was his confidence and ego that allowed him to be the best. As he lost consciousness, he somehow knew that if he survived he would never be the same again.

He woke up in New Jersey, at the Mercer County Hospital. He was in ICU. The nurses told him he'd had ten hours of surgery, that three teams of orthopedists and neurosurgeons had spent the night putting his busted face and body back in place. His jaw was wired shut. There was a large pair of wire clippers next to his bed. When he was conscious enough to understand, the trauma nurse told him that if he felt like vomiting from the surgical anesthesia or antibiotics, he should get the clippers and cut his wired jaw open, so that he wouldn't vomit back into his trachea and lungs and choke to death. It was sobering advice.

He lay in agony for weeks, feeling every inch of his body throb. Even the impressive list of meds he was taking couldn't completely mask the pain.

The New Jersey State Police transcribed his statement from his hospital room. He talked to them through his wired mouth, forming the words like an amateur ventriloquist. Beano gave his statement under his assumed name, Frank Lemay, because there were three Federal warrants out on him for criminal fraud and various other sophisticated con games. He was also currently on the FBI's Ten Most Wanted

List. It was better if the authorities thought it was Frank Lemay who had been beaten up by Joe Rina. He also didn't tell them that he had no intention of ever testifying against the handsome mob boss.

His old friend and fellow card sharper "Three Finger" Freddy Feinberg came to visit him in the hospital. The gray-haired card shark looked down in shock at Beano, who was still swollen and discolored like rotting fruit. "Jeez, man, you look like a fucking typhoid victim," he said. It had been Freddy who arranged for Beano to get in the game. "I told ya, Beano, I told ya, 'Be careful of that guy Joe Rina.'" And then Three Finger Freddy told him about a rumor that was buzzing around in the street. The word was that Joe Dancer was still pissed and had put out a contract on Frank Lemay, because he had not shown the grace and good sense to die in the country club parking lot like he was supposed to. Three Finger Freddy also told him about how the Rina brothers had taken care of disposal of bodies in the old days. It was another story Beano could have done without hearing.

The police told him that a New Jersey prosecutor named Victoria Hart was coming down to interview him prior to filing the assault-with-intent-to-commit-murder charges against Joseph Rina. Because Joe Rina was a popular tabloid star, the press was swarming to get a story. It was only a matter of time until Beano's alias would be penetrated, so he disconnected himself from the tangle of electrodes and I.V. bottles and limped out of the hospital. It was a move that saved his life, but he was now poised on the edge of a cliff, overlooking a landscape of revenge and violence that would change him forever.

Part One
THE VICTIM

"NEVER GIVE A SUCKER AN EVEN BREAK."
—Edward Francis Albee

ONE

Girlfriends, a Dumbwaiter, and a Dixie Cup

Some people simply amazed Victoria Hart. Take Carol Sesnick...she worked as a pediatric nurse at a local children's hospital and had been taking night school courses for a year to become certified, hoping to join the profession as a C.N.P., or Certified Nurse Practitioner. What on earth would possess her to risk her life, to put herself in mortal danger, because the People of the great Garden State of New Jersey wanted to put a piece of pond scum like Joe "Dancer" Rina in the yellow brick prison at Rahway? After Carol testified, she would have to be put in the Witness Protection Program. She'd have to live in some icebox state like Minnesota. Her life would be completely changed and arguably ruined. And yet, here she was, risking it all so Victoria Hart, a New Jersey State Prosecutor, could kick some mob ass in court and convict a short, incredibly handsome little creep who walked on his toes. *The case is going to be close,* Victoria thought, *but winnable.*

The indictment charged that the thirty-eight-year-old alleged Mafia Don had lost money in a card game in the back room of the Greenborough Country Club. The big winner, a man named Frank Lemay, had been beaten almost to death with a nine-iron in the parking lot as he was getting into his car.

13

Seventy-eight thousand dollars in winnings was stolen from him. And then, before Victoria was assigned to the case, the victim had unhooked himself from his I.V. bottles and had walked out of the hospital, never to be seen again. The wallet and credit card he had left in the hospital administrator's office turned out to belong to a man who had been dead for two years, so the name was an alias. Frank Lemay didn't exist. The case against Joe Rina was on the verge of being dropped when Carol Sesnick stepped forward and said she had been waiting for a friend in the country club parking lot and had seen the whole thing. She had become the State's whole case now that the victim had disappeared.

Victoria Hart had on occasion been called "Tricky Vicky" in the Trenton press because she often employed unorthodox legal strategy to achieve courtroom success. Prosecuting Joe Rina, a frequent star of *Hard Copy*, without a complainant got her a lot of ink that she would have rather done without.

Victoria anxiously looked out the car's rear window. "Are we clear?" she said to her State Police driver, who had a weight-lifter's neck that widened like a cobra's hood at the trapezius muscle.

"I'm gonna take one more precaution, but I don't see anyone back there," he said, then slammed down the accelerator and made an abrupt turn through a darkened gas station...shot down an unlit narrow alley, turned left onto a residential street, swung a quick U,

14

then parked and switched off his headlights. Nobody followed. Victoria knew the precautions were necessary, but after two weeks, they were getting damned tiresome.

The car they were in had been selected moments before from a line of fifty plain-blue police sedans in the State Police Motor Pool. This was in an effort to defeat any tracking devices that might get placed if Victoria used the same vehicle more than once. She suspected Joseph Rina would go to any lengths, including murder, to shut down the case against him. The trial was scheduled to start in two days and Victoria had been making nightly visits to her hidden witness to prepare her for testimony.

Victoria's notes for the first day in court were scribbled in her obsessively neat handwriting on a yellow legal pad in her briefcase. She had her opening argument down pat. She was going to give the jury a tour through the graveyard of Rina Mafia tyranny. It would be a morbid history lesson, and she hoped it would redefine that handsome little shit with the perfect white teeth and wavy black hair.

Victoria had been assigned this prosecution by the District Attorney, Gil Green, because Tricky Vicky was popular with the media and had a near-perfect conviction rate, but the voir dire process had been brutal. New Jersey used the "Donahue Method" to pick jurors, which meant that the jury box was filled with candidates and the Prosecution and Defense had to question each one in front of the others. It was hazardous because you ran the risk of offending a juror you would later be forced to accept. Voir dire had already taken a week and they had gone through two complete panels. Victoria thought the composition of potential jurors was extremely unfortunate and had favored the Defense. The panels were loaded with undereducated ethnic males who, she thought, would be her least sympathetic jurors. They were already disenfranchised by the system and would see Joe Rina as a role model who disrespected City Hall and won. In the end, she had broken the cardinal rule of jury selection and used her last peremptory challenge to eliminate a twenty-five-year-old Sicilian street character who, she was almost certain, would vote for acquittal.

After six days of selection, Victoria was nervous about her jury. Defense attorney Gerry Cohen, on the other hand, seemed pleased. All through voir dire, he had his jury selection experts spread around him like card kibitzers, whispering, pointing, and pushing pieces of paper in front of him. As each juror was questioned, Gerry would nod sagely and then decide whether to use a peremptory challenge, dismiss a juror for cause, or accept. Victoria had to rely on gut instinct. She didn't have any background checkers with psychology degrees. She had only David Frankfurter to help her.

David was former Supreme Court Justice Frankfurter's great-grandson. He was a tall, skinny, twenty-seven-year-old Assistant State

Prosecutor known around the office as "Dodger Dog" because of his last name and because he had been raised in Los Angeles and loved the Dodgers.

Victoria and David would study the jurors in the panel, trying to pick them by type. She wanted women more than men. She preferred married, white-collar, educated people with children, people who would see Joe Dancer for what he was, instead of some charming refugee from *Hard Copy* who had looks and romance draping him like Armani clothing. She was very worried about jurors ten and twelve, both young unemployed males who didn't fit her acceptable profile. With one alternate left to pick, and all of her peremptory challenges gone, she could be forced to accept the next candidate, whoever or whatever it was. The last alternate juror would be interviewed tomorrow, and the trial would start the following morning.

Her police driver, who she thought was named Alan, finally nodded in satisfaction, turned his headlights back on, and drove out the way he had come. A surprise thunderstorm had dropped a half-inch of rain late that afternoon, and now sheet lightning lit the horizon like flashes of distant artillery.

Ten minutes later, they arrived at the underground parking garage of Trenton Towers. They whisked by what looked like an empty gray Econoline van without paying much attention to it. They didn't notice that the windows were fogged.

Victoria took the old Otis eight-man elevator up to the fourteenth floor. The building was mid-fifties, but she had picked it because it had several advantages from a security standpoint: The floors were small and could be easily protected; there was only one elevator bank, limiting access; and the building had low occupancy and a completely vacant fourteenth floor, which gave them much needed separation from the other tenants. The old fifteen-story residential building was adjacent to a business district so it had little night traffic, making secure meetings between herself and Carol Sesnick easier to arrange.

The elevator opened on fourteen and Victoria walked out into the "safe house," carrying her briefcase, purse, and a garment bag. She was greeted by two plainclothes deputies whom, over the last two weeks, she had grown very fond of. Tony Corollo was the tall, silent Italian who seldom smiled but projected an easy warmth. The other was Bobby Manning. He'd been a Trenton High School football star. He had a ruddy complexion and a lock of auburn hair that hung in planned disarray on his forehead.

"Evening, Ms. Hart," they both chirped. "Bring us anything?"

She had been religiously stopping at the mini-mart near her apartment, picking up candy and reading material for them. She dug in her purse for some tabloid magazines.

"No Nestlé's Crunch?" Bobby Manning said, grinning his question at her.

She found a package of Butterfingers she'd missed in the side pocket of her purse and handed it to him. "Best I could do, Bobby," she said, and they moved off their folding chairs in the hall toward the locked door that led to Carol's suite.

Victoria found Carol in the white tile bathroom trying a new hairstyle. She had curled it and her soft brown hair was now piled up on her head, giving her a French poodle pouf. She was in her slip, holding a hand mirror, with a disgusted frown on her ordinary but pleasant face.

"I fucked it up, V," Carol said, still looking in the mirror, wrinkling her freckled nose. "It wasn't exactly supposed to come out like this." She held up a picture in *Glamour* magazine that showed a thin-faced model with the same do, only it was subtly different. On the model the piled-up curls seemed to look fresh and perky. The narrow-faced blonde in the picture had her hair pulled back on the sides, tight curls cascading down her back. On Carol Sesnick the look was less effective. "What I got goin' here is pure Brillo pad, ain't it?" Carol said, pouting.

Victoria grabbed a hairbrush and started to rearrange the back of the hairstyle. "Turn around a little more," she instructed as she worked, pulling the sides back and clipping them up higher to better resemble the model in the picture.

Carol and Victoria were both in their early thirties, trim and fit, but the comparison ended

19

there. Their reflections both glittered in the large mirror of the too-bright bathroom. They were a study in contrasts. Victoria was by far the prettier. She had classic bone structure, high cheekbones, and a sculpted face. But she was not a fashion adventurer....She wore her hair cut very short to save time. She would roll out of bed in the morning, jump in the shower, towel her hair dry, and hit it with a dryer while she went over her legal notes propped on the sink before her. She could be out the door in fifteen minutes. Her makeup was minimal, sometimes nonexistent. Despite this lack of primping, she had a radiant natural beauty that had earned her half-a-dozen offers to model by New York agents...sleek, well-dressed men who smelled of aftershave and slipped agency cards in her hand, suggesting she call. She dismissed these entreaties as sleazeball pickup routines, despite the fact that the cards they gave her were sometimes embossed in gold with the names of prominent agencies.

"There," Victoria said, clipping the other side of Carol's hair back with a barrette.

"I don't know," Carol said, studying her reflection dubiously. "I think I look stupid. Makes my face seem round."

"Maybe if you don't pile it up so high...let some of this, up here, straggle on the sides," Victoria said, pulling a few strands down. Since she took so little interest in her own hair-style, she felt ill equipped to give beauty tips to others. She was much better at conducting a withering cross-examination.

"You got the dress!" Carol exclaimed, finally spotting the garment bag Victoria had draped over the commode.

"Yep. Gil Green shit a brick when he saw the bill. But, if O.J. can get Rosa Lopez that ugly blue outfit, you oughta get this pretty tan one." She pulled it out of the bag and held it up.

"Love it, love it, love it," Carol said, as she unzipped it and stepped in, then turned to the mirror. "Whatta you think?"

"You're gonna knock 'em dead, girlfriend." Victoria grinned. Under all the easy chatter she continued to marvel: Why would somebody risk everything just because it was the right thing to do? When she evaluated the tremendous sacrifices Carol Sesnick was making, it took Victoria Hart's breath away.

♠ ♠ ♠

In the back of the gray Econoline van, Tommy "Two Times" Rina and Texaco Phillips were hunched over a Building Department schematic of Trenton Towers. They had computer-accessed the plans from the City Building Inspector's office by using a Rina Family computer technician. He'd downloaded everything.

"Fucking heating ducts are tiny....We'll never get inside them, they're forty fucking years

21

old," Tommy said angrily, looking at the plans and smelling Texaco's horrible odor, which he knew was caused by anabolic steroids. In the front seat, behind the wheel, chewing on a toothpick, was a skinny Jamaican Rastafarian. His dreadlocks were greased and beaded; his dusky skin lacked luster.

Texaco Phillips kept flicking his gaze in the direction of the Rasta. He didn't, for the life of him, understand why Tommy would want a wheel man who looked like a fucking jigaboo street character. Texaco had asked Tommy that question twenty minutes ago when the Rasta had gone to take a leak in the gas station can.

"'Cause he's a Dixie cup." Tommy grinned and refused further comment.

Texaco didn't know what the hell that meant, but the grin had spooked him, so he shut up. Texaco couldn't get away from Tommy Rina fast enough. Tommy was Joe Rina's older brother and Joe had put them together for this piece of work, so Texaco had no choice. Tommy, like his brother, Joe, was short, only five-seven, but that was all they had in common. At thirty-eight, Joe Dancer was much more handsome, and walked on the balls of his feet to gain a little height. He'd been doing it since junior high and the habit had earned him his nickname. Joe had beautiful wavy hair and perfect teeth that glittered like a box of Chiclets.

Tommy had the same wavy hair, but it seemed to grow too far down on his forehead, giving him a simian appearance. He had the same white teeth as his brother, but they protruded, giving him a leering over-bite. His eyes were blue like Joe's, but instead of reflecting intelligence, they were pig-mean. The family resemblance was definitely there, but the recipe was off, the results skewed.

"Take us around the block. I wanna see this here fire exit," Tommy said to the Jamaican, pointing to a door indicated on the plans.

"Ya, we be rollin', mon," the Jake mumbled unintelligibly, as he put the van in gear and pulled out.

"Why the fuck don't you put on some cologne?" Tommy Two Times said to Texaco, who couldn't smell himself and didn't know what Tommy was talking about.

They sat in silence as the van rounded the block. The tires hissed on the rain-wet pavement. With the windows up, it was close and stuffy in the van. Texaco was the kind of odd creature who took up more space than his body was allotted. He carried a lot of baggage that took getting used to. Aside from his pro-linebacker size, he also had a unique personality which included a sense of humor that had never progressed since the eighth grade. He had a huge collection of fart jokes, and a sexual appetite that was criminally short on foreplay. He was in the jump-on, hold-on category and joked that during sex he used the "Honor Method," which instructed: Once you get on her, stay on her. It was a concept that twice got him arrested on date-rape charges while he was still playing middle line-backer for the New England Patriots. After a few midnight phone chats, both victims had a last-minute change of heart. Texaco's body odor and personality could cool a room like awkward laughter.

"Put the fucking window down, Demo. It stinks in here," Tommy said. The Jamaican didn't respond; his hands were busy driving. "Hey, you listenin' up there? I'm talking to you."

"Mickey Mouse is in de house but Donald Duck don't give a fuck," Demo mumbled but finally rolled down the window anyway. Texaco, hearing this, shook his head in disgust. What a moron. The Rasta's name was Demo Williams. What a fucking breed of people. *Who would name their kid Demo?* he thought, forgetting that his parents had named him Texaco. The van circled the block with the window mercifully slipstreaming cold, fresh air.

"Pull up there," Tommy said.

The Jamaican pulled the van to the curb while Tommy studied the fire door; then he started paging through a set of photocopied building plans.

"Gotta old dumbwaiter, goes all the way up. Gotta gas enjin'. It'll be too loud to run the damn thing. If I can fit in the fucking box, you think you could pull it up fourteen floors?" Tommy said, looking up at Texaco, who nodded...glad he wasn't being asked to get in the dumbwaiter with Tommy.

"Okay then, that's the plan. Demo, you stay right here, keep the motor running. And Texaco, once I clear out them brown hats, I want you up there to help sanitize the place. Okay? You'll hear 'em hit when they come down."

"Okay," Texaco said, looking at the cleaning kit in a Gucci leather suitcase beside him.

"I don't know about the garage. Far as I can see, they got nobody in there, but you gotta hold my back," Tommy added. "I don't wanna be up there hosing off these assholes and have the elevator deliver me up a new squad of uniforms."

"Nobody will be coming up the elevator," Texaco assured him, and Tommy looked hard at his huge accomplice, pinning him with blue pig eyes that suggested Texaco was the worst fuck-up on earth. There was electricity in his look but also dead malice and timeless evil. They were the eyes of a prehistoric lizard.

The whole operation had to be fast and clean. Tommy had decided not to use a contracted cleaning crew. On some hits a crew of "sanitation specialists" would follow in right behind to wash the crime scene down with detergents and vacuum the carpets, eliminating trace evidence. The crime scene would be purged...no prints, no blood spatter, no hair or fiber. Problem was, you had to know the cleanup team was solid. It was a new specialty and Tommy had never used one; he would rather not have anybody left behind who could rat him out. Texaco was risk enough. He knew the big, ugly steroid jockey was just smart enough to figure that Tommy would kill him inch by fucking inch if he ever rolled.

Tommy picked the lock on the fire door; then he and Texaco went into the darkened building. The dumbwaiter was still located in its shaft, and once they pried the small door open they could see that the old rope was frayed and dusty with spider webs. Tommy easily fit in the little box. He sat on the metal tray with his knees up under his chin and looked out like a psychopathic child. Texaco pulled the rope, lifting the dumbwaiter fifteen feet, testing the strength of the line. It held. Then he continued to lift the dumbwaiter. Texaco had to grip the rope and ease it up hand-over-hand. By the time the huge ex-linebacker had the box seven stories high, his forehead and massive arms were dripping with sweat. Friction blisters were beginning to form on his palms. It occurred to him that he could make a giant contribution to mankind by simply letting go of the box, sending the little Sicilian maniac on a seven-story ass-pucker ride in the free-falling dumbwaiter. But Texaco didn't have the guts to do it. He knew Tommy would survive the fall, like Wile E. Coyote. Somehow he'd come back and kill Texaco, "inch by fucking inch," just like he'd always promised.

On the fourteenth floor, Tommy slowly

and quietly opened the door of the dumbwaiter and, when he didn't see anyone, slipped out into the hall. The building was musty. Ornate ceilings and faded green-and-red-patterned carpets framed the columned hallway. He could hear the two deputies talking in low tones around the corner from where he was standing. He moved silently to a maintenance closet and slipped inside. He needed to listen to the sounds on this floor to determine how many people were up here. Standing with hanging mops and Lysol bottles, he waited patiently, taking his time, enjoying the intrusion. Killing for Tommy was a luxuriant, tactile experience that rivaled sex. He was in no hurry to end it. He heard a phone ring, and a little later, a toilet flushed. After listening carefully to the sounds and muffled voices, he thought there were at least two women in the corner suite and two men in front of the elevator. The rest of fourteen seemed quiet. The empty rooms talked to him....He could hear no TVs or radios coming from the other section of the floor. He thought the Prosecution had probably chosen the fourteenth floor because nobody else was up here. He was looking out of the maintenance closet through a slit in the slightly opened door.

A beautiful woman he recognized as Victoria Hart left at ten P.M. He could hear her laughing with the cops before she got in the elevator and the doors closed. It was going to be much easier than he had originally thought.

After she left, Tommy "Two Times" Rina

slipped out of the closet and moved up the corridor to where the two deputies were looking at something in the *Star* tabloid. Tommy pulled out his silenced 9mm SIG-Sauer P-226 and held it in his right hand. In his left, he had his 9mm silver and black Israeli Desert War Eagle. They were his two favorite handguns. The Germans and the Jews made the best guns. It was an irony that completely escaped him.

"Evening, gents. Is Liz Taylor getting a new husband?" he said flatly.

Both cops spun, going for their weapons, but they froze when they saw Tommy holding the two silenced 9mm cannons. If they moved, they were a micro-second from death.

"The fuck...?" Tony Corollo said, astounded that Tommy had somehow gotten up there, behind them.

"The fuck?" Tommy mimicked. "Was that the fucking question, you worthless fuck-face?" he said deadpan.

The deputies looked at him and knew they had no chance to get to their shoulder holsters.

"I want you two cheeseburgers to get up and move over to the elevator and stand there with your hands on the door. You, with the brown hair, push the button. Get the box up here."

"What're you gonna do?" Deputy Corollo asked hesitantly.

"Gonna throw you two shitheads a party. Gonna be fun...."

When the elevator arrived, Tommy told

Deputy Manning to reach in and push fifteen, which was the floor directly above, then told him to let the elevator go on up. Bobby Manning did as he was told, and once it was gone, Tommy waved his guns at them. "Okay. Now pry them doors open again; let's get us a look in there." They hesitated, so he re-cocked the SIG-Sauer for emphasis, and the two frightened officers pushed their fingers in and pried the elevator doors open. They both looked down the yawning dark throat of the elevator shaft.

"Officer Krupke, whatta ya see down there?" Tommy grinned.

"Nothing," Tony Corollo said, wondering if he could dive out and catch the cable, slide down it, and get out of the way before Tommy pulled the trigger.

"Nothing? Look again, get way out there...." Tony and Bobby craned their necks but didn't lean out. "What you're looking at down there is the landing zone, fellas. That there's ground zero. Now I want you two bricks to hit right smack in the middle of the shaft. We got cash prizes for that lucky winner." Tommy was really beginning to enjoy himself. "This is 'The Jersey Solution,'" he said. "I get the lady, and you two hemorrhoids get the shaft."

Without hesitation he fired twice, once from each gun. Both silenced automatics made faint hissing sounds like a man spitting out a fruit seed. The first bullet blew Bobby Manning out into the darkness. He hit the opposite wall, slamming against the structure, throwing a spray of arterial blood into the air and all over the brick-walled shaft. Then he fell silently down, palms and shoe soles trailing like streamers as he plunged into the dark abyss. Tony Corollo was simultaneously hit in the mid-back. He flew out into the dark shaft but managed to grab and catch the metal cable. Blood gushed from a huge exit wound in his stomach. He weakly pulled his service revolver and, hanging on by one hand, dripping blood like icehouse beef, he tried to aim at Tommy, but his grip slipped and he had to drop the gun to grab the cable with his other hand. As he hung there, they locked gazes. At the bottom of the shaft, Bobby Manning hit. The sound was faint, like a snowball hitting a brick wall. "Nice try," Tommy finally said to the Deputy, whose intestines were now snaking out of him, blood and stomach acid raining down on his dead partner. Then Tommy fired his silenced Desert War Eagle again, this time hitting the Deputy in the mouth. Tony Corollo's head snapped back and he was blown back off the cable. Little pieces of his teeth recoiled forward and rained ivory chips on the purple and red hallway carpet. Then he too was gone, cart-wheeling freely down the shaft.

On the ground floor, Texaco Phillips heard both of them splat in the oil and shale goop that was in the bottom of the shaft. He gathered up his suitcase of brushes, sponges, bleaches, and hand vacuums, then pushed the elevator button. In seconds he was riding up to join Tommy.

She was in the bathroom, sitting on the toilet, pinning the hem on her new tan dress, when Tommy walked in on her. "Who are you?" Carol said, looking up in alarm. "What're you doing here?"

"Taking care of my brother and having a pretty damn good time to boot," Tommy said. And then he finished the job, right there in the overlit tile bathroom, exploding little pieces of her into the bathtub, covering the tub wall with a fine spray of brain tissue and cerebrospinal fluid.

♠ ♠ ♠

Demo pulled the van away from the building, screeching the tires.

"Don't burn rubber. Just go slow," Tommy said from the back seat. Demo slowed down. "Go to this address." Tommy handed a slip of paper to the Rastafarian.

"We still be chillin', right, mon?"

"You ask a lot of questions. You're gonna be one dead fucking rent-a-nigger, you keep it up," Tommy growled.

Texaco saw Demo's shoulders tighten. But the Rasta didn't do anything; he just drove slowly, heading across town toward the address Tommy had given him.

They arrived at a locked junkyard in Hoboken. Once they parked, Tommy took out a key. Texaco opened the gate and they pulled in.

Tommy looked at Demo and smiled. "That pissed you off when I called you a rent-a-nigger, didn't it?"

The Rasta turned in his seat and looked into Tommy's eyes. He saw craziness and changed his response. "We be hat up, brotha. De work be done. Ain't no need ta be disrespectin'," he finally said.

"Fuck there ain't. You come here, you sit in my van, you drip fuckin' chicken grease all over the seats, you make a fuckin' mess. You're nothin' but a ganja-smokin', voodoo-dancing, low-bone motherfucker who oughta be buried up to his scrawny neck in pig shit and hosed down with donkey piss."

The Rastafarian looked at Tommy like he couldn't believe what he was hearing.

"Now you're probably so pissed I can't fuckin' turn my back on you, right?" Demo said nothing. "So now you gone and give me a big fuckin' problem. Y'see what I'm saying? Now I gotta either watch my back constantly or buy you a fuckin' suit right now."

And with that criminal logic he fired the SIG-Sauer right through the back of the seat. The Jamaican was thrown into the dash. Blood shot up onto the windshield and stained the headliner over his head. Tommy looked at Demo with interest. "Maybe you can help me with something." he said to the dying Jamaican. "That was the Kraut cannon...okay, now here's the Jew gun." He fired two more rounds through the upholstery from the Desert War Eagle. The body danced on the seat as the bullets slammed into Demo Williams, killing him. "You tell me, Demo, 'cause I'll be damned if I can tell. Which one you think got more stopping power?"

Tommy picked up his brass and got out. He looked at Texaco, who was standing, shivering in the cold night. "Fuckin' guy was a Dixie cup, just like I told ya."

Texaco still didn't get it.

"Disposable," Tommy added.

Texaco Phillips nodded; his nerves were badly jangled. There was no doubt in his mind that Tommy Rina was insane.

TWO

King Con

The Florida midday sun cooked the half acre of used cars at Bob's Auto Ranch in Coral Gables. Shimmering heat waves danced along the tops of Beamers and Bent Eights, parked in shiny rows, dressed in cheap new fifty-dollar paint jobs. They begged customers shamelessly with BUY ME and TAKE ME HOME signs propped under the windshield wipers. Faded red and blue plastic triangular flags hung listlessly from guy wires in the stagnant heat like dead balloons after a birthday party. It had been a slow morning...mostly tire-kickers and be-backs.

Because he was sure Joe Rina was still trying to kill him, Beano Bates had dyed his hair blond and had added a mustache, which he needed to lighten constantly. He still wasn't completely recovered from the beating with a nine-iron that had happened six months ago. Remarkably, the brutal assault had not diminished his good looks. If anything, he appeared slightly more rugged. But Beano had been forced to hide, and not only from the Rina brothers....Last week, he had made his second surprise appearance on *America's Most Wanted*.

Beano had been sitting in his fourteen-dollar-a-night motel apartment, feeding Roger-the-Dodger a Big Mac, when his segment had aired. The brown and black fox terrier looked up from his quarter-pounder and barked angrily, perking up his ears and snarling at the TV, as if he knew the whole story was bullshit. Beano looked lovingly at the dog....You couldn't find that kind of fierce loyalty in criminal partners anymore.

On the TV, John Walsh droned on as a picture of Beano with his old dark hair color popped up on the blue screen behind him. "Beano X. Bates," Walsh said seriously, "is perhaps the most notorious and successful con-man operating in the United States today. A gifted actor, Bates can quickly separate you from your fortune. Among con men there is always an acknowledged king of the hustle, referred to in the game as 'King Con.' Beano Bates currently holds that infamous title. If you see this man, don't buy *anything* from him.

Don't let him near your money or bank account, but call us here at *America's Most Wanted* or get in touch with your local police."

"Some con man," Beano muttered in disgust, as he wrapped the rest of Roger's half-eaten burger in a bag, saving it for later.

For the last two weeks, Beano had been selling dead-sleds and junkers to unsuspecting blue-hairs at Bob's Auto Ranch. He was on commission, not salary, trying to move the tired collection of stripped-down preacher cars and ominously noisy cement mixers that Bob was offering "on excellent terms." Despite the depressing inventory, Beano had done well at the Auto Ranch because he could convince anybody of just about anything. Bullshit was his greatest gift. He had made friends with the few attractive women who had wandered in, deciding he was more interesting than the rusting clunkers he was selling. He had dated one or two of them, but Beano was tired and was having trouble putting much energy into anything.

That particular afternoon, Beano was trying to sell a cancerous green Ford station wagon that Bob had taken in trade ten days ago. The car was basically lunched, but the service department had added some lipstick. They screwed beauty bolts onto the engine block and coaxed the tired, mashed-potato transmission back to life. They had sprayed and power-waxed the new green paint. The '86 Country Squire had ninety thousand miles on the odometer. In a final act of criminal camouflage,

Bob's chief mechanic had rocked the clock back to fifty. It now sat dripping oil in the oppressive afternoon heat, a sagging road warrior dressed for its last inspection.

"A great high-occupancy vehicle. Ford sure knows how t'make 'em," Beano said with expansive awe to the mean-spirited old man who was teetering around, looking in the back, trying to put up the fold-down seat that was on broken hinges. "'Course, all those minor defects will be addressed prior to ownership transfer." Beano smiled as the geezer tried to peel up the carpet and look at the floor to see if there was rust.

"Stinks back here," the old man said, looking at Beano and wrinkling his nose. "Carpets all got mildew."

Beano looked at him, not really caring if he sold the wagon. He fired a half-hearted line of bullshit over the dying transaction: "I'm not supposed to say this, 'cause Bob tries to protect all of our famous customers...but this car was originally owned by..." He stopped and looked at the old man carefully. "Y'know what? This isn't the right car for you. There's at least ten others we could look at."

"Owned by who?" the man said, his papery, thin skin reddening with faint interest as he looked at Beano with eyes yellowed by age and a bad diet.

"Well, I'm not supposed..." Beano paused and shook his head. "Can't say...sorry."

"Who? I can keep a secret."

Beano let a silent war of conscience play on

his expressive actor's face, then caved in. "This car belonged to Vinnie Testaverde when he was still playing quarterback for the 'Canes. Reason it's got that kinda funky odor back there is, Vinnie told me he hadda park it at Morris Field behind the Athletic Department there at the University of Miami and people kept breaking in when he was at away games, hopin' to get like, whatta ya call it?"

"Souvenirs?" the old man contributed.

"Right, souvenirs." Beano nodded. "With the back window smashed, carpets kept getting all wet when it rained."

The deal hovered on the precipice of this new fact for a few heart-stopping moments as the old man contemplated driving Vinnie Testaverde's car.

"'Course, you can't tell anyone, 'cause Bob doesn't give out the ownership pedigrees on these cars. I think it's nuts, but Bob, he's got a real thing about it." Beano was starting to get dizzy because he still hadn't fully recovered from the devastating beating and the midday sun was killing him. He wanted to go sit on his metal chair in the shade of the office, drink some iced tea out of his thermos, and curse John Walsh for making him live like a homeless fugitive.

Finally the old man looked up, a crafty defiance in his yellow geezer eyes. "You want fifteen hunnert dollars....I'll go twelve," he said, beginning the familiar dance that used-car barkers call "the grind."

"Even if it wasn't Vinnie Testaverde's car,

Bob won't let it go for twelve," Beano said, wishing he could get to the chair in the shade of the dealer's shed. Ever since the vicious beating, he'd been having intermittent double vision. The old man was beginning to split in two right before him, his whiskery cranial image moving slightly to the right so that he now looked like a double exposure. Despite this distraction, Beano knew the sale was his. Then he had a strange twinge of remorse for his cranky client because he knew the Ford wagon was tired iron. These bouts of conscience had never hit him before....He had never stopped to consider the fate of a mark, but since the assault in the parking lot at the Greenborough Country Club, for some godforsaken reason, he'd started reflecting on the damage he had caused in other people's lives. He'd always told himself that marks were born to be fleeced, that he and Roger-the-Dodger had to eat, but lately these excuses seemed shallow. So he had taken the job at Bob's Auto Ranch, where he could use his charm and gift of gab in a semi-legitimate hustle. It was a temporary rest stop on his road to a new life.

By six o'clock the deal was closed at fourteen hundred dollars and the old man drove the listing wagon off the lot. Beano had promised to try to get him an autographed picture of Vinnie Testaverde, which was not going to be hard at all because he had ten of them left in his desk. He'd written the university and told them he was starting a booster club. He received the photos of the ex-Hurricane superstar in the mail from the Athletic Department ten days later. He'd also spent an extra one hundred dollars and ordered a Vinnie Testaverde autographed football from the Baltimore Ravens, where he was now playing. Beano was now good enough on the signature to fool the old Vinster himself. Beano would mail the picture to the geezer next week with an inscription from Testaverde saying how much Vinnie missed his old rusted-out beater, which had really been owned by an airport yellow cab company before Bob's paint shop had sprayed it green.

That night, Beano took Roger-the-Dodger out for a celebratory dinner of Chicken McNuggets and beer. The terrier sat on the front seat of Beano's newly acquired, low-profile '88 blue Escort and slopped the beer out of an oversized cup while he chewed breaded McNuggets. He was licking his lips, almost grinning. Beano had owned Roger for almost a year. He had been training him to be a shill: to shit on cue and to look expensive, which was often hard for ten-dollar pound-mutts, but Roger had natural talent. He knew how to project attitude. He could strut. Beano had perfected a variety of dog cons. He had a forged Kennel Club certificate that said Roger was a Baunchatrain Terrier and that his name was Sir Anthony of Aquitaine. Roger was also a great ice breaker. While a targeted mark smiled and scratched the terrier behind the ears, Beano would make his opening move. An added plus was that in a bust, Roger would hold his dirt. His pal Roger would never testify against him in court. The terrier was showing real signs of being a world-class sharper, but that was before Beano, using a dead man's I.D., got caught cheating Joe Rina at cards and got blasted onto the path of righteousness with a nine-iron.

"Don't slobber, Roge," he said, and the dog seemed to understand as he slowed down, lapping up his Coors Light with more restraint. "We gotta get us some traction. I know I promised I was gonna try and get Tom Jenner into a golf hustle, but he's an angry bastard when he loses, and with this double vision, I couldn't drop a putt in a wastebasket."

Roger-the-Dodger stopped drinking beer and looked up at Beano like a hold-up man who sensed his getaway driver might be losing his nerve. The dog definitely seemed worried.

Deep down, underneath all of the other stuff, the excuses about his vision and the bullshit about *America's Most Wanted,* there was a lurking realization. Beano knew that the beating by Joe Rina had introduced him to a cold, withering fear he had never known before. He had a numbing, paralyzing reaction every time he remembered the assault. Sweat would cover him like a fearful cocoon. Unreasonable panic wracked him. The most distressing note in this new mental orchestra was in the string section of his recently discovered conscience. He had started to remember the faces of his marks. He pushed his greed aside, and for the first time began to see them as people he had lied to and robbed. He tried to unburden his guilt by remembering the con man's excuse: *You can never cheat an honest man.* It didn't help. In quiet moments after work, when he was in the cheap one-bedroom motel apartment two blocks from the ocean, and while Roger was snoring at the foot of his bed, Beano started to wonder if he should get out of grifting. He had been overwhelmed lately by intense loneliness. His profession had isolated him. He had no friends, only people he knew. A con man couldn't afford to let himself become vulnerable. His problem was, if he went off the hustle, what would he do with himself? He'd been a sharper all of his life. He had no other worthwhile skills.

It had all started when he was six, working for his mom and dad, doing roofing scams. The Bates family was a huge, disjointed criminal enterprise. The National Crime Information Center and FBI guessed that there were more than three thousand Bates family members grifting all across the United States. Beano couldn't confirm or deny that fact, because he'd met only a hundred or so of his cousins, but every major town he'd ever been in had members of his family in the phone book, and his father told him they were all on the bubble. Con games were the family business. Members of his family all used X. as their middle initial, and by simply looking under Bates in any city's phone directory you could find his relatives. Most Bates family members

41

played driveway and roofing hustles. They had elevated these two short cons to an art form.

Beano's parents had been nomads, constantly roaming, living in trailer parks and changing towns to stay ahead of the law. His mother and father would drive down streets in every new town they hit in their rusting Winnebago, looking for houses that had loose roof shingles. Then his father would park the motor home down the street from a prospective mark's house, get out sawhorses and hammers, and send adorable six-year-old Beano back to knock on the mark's front door.

"Sir," he would say in his sweet choirboy voice, "my daddy is down the street putting a new roof on your neighbor's house." It was a lie, but he would point his short, pudgy little arm at his father's Winnebago, now alive with manufactured activity down the block. The mark would smile and crane his or her neck to see. "Anyway," he would continue, always looking straight into the pigeon's eyes to communicate guileless sincerity, "Daddy noticed that your roof has lots of loose shingles. We have more shingles than we need for your neighbor's job. If you want, my daddy could make you a very good price on fixing your roof."

"Shouldn't you be in school, young man?" was a common question, and then little six-year-old Beano would drop the closer...."My little sister has this real bad sickness and we gotta make enough money this summer for her to start her chem...chemo...something."

42

"Chemotherapy?" the mark would contribute, and Beano would nod sadly. This fact would hang over the opening pitch like the angel of death. He rarely failed to "steer" the mark.

His father, Jacob, would come down at lunchtime and look studiously at the roof. He would refuse donations for the nonexistent sister's chemo, claiming family pride. "We ain't much for charity, but thanks and God bless you for your Christian concern," Jacob would say, often finding a tear in his eye and brushing its moisture visibly onto his cheek. Then he would climb up on the roof, rub his chin, and agree to do the whole roof for two thousand dollars, which by any estimate was a helluva deal. New roofs back then went for between five and ten thousand. Now, all thoughts of Beano's cancer-ridden sister were banished by the mark's greed: *These stupid hillbillies are gonna fix my roof for less than the material cost.* With that realization, the mark was hooked.

The next day the Bates family would arrive early. Beano would retrieve the sawhorse and ladder from the top of their motor home and carry it to the house. The homeowners would look out their windows and marvel at this tragic, industrious family, especially that cute, hard-working little boy. By nine A.M., Jacob would be up on the roof hammering loudly, making as much noise as possible to drive the family out. Once they were gone, Beano and his mother, Connie, would join Jacob up on the roof. They would hammer the loose shingles down and quickly paint the roof with heavy number-nine-weight motor oil. When the mark returned home, his "new" roof would be dark brown and glistening. Jacob X. Bates would take the cash from the grateful homeowner along with well-wishes for the dying sister, and Beano's family would get the hell out of Dodge. The next heavy rain might fill the mark's living room with motor oil, but by then they would be in the next state.

As a young man, Beano showed promise for much more. He had learned to run big cons from his uncle, "Paper Collar" John Bates. He ran boiler rooms and bucket shops, Blue River real-estate scams and green goods hustles. He played the pigeon drop and did three Big Store cons. He could dress up and be whatever he needed to be. He had a soft ear and could affect almost any accent or dialect. He was a master of disguises…a scratch golfer, a cardplayer without peer, and he would always find a way to shade the odds in his favor.

Now it seemed, at the age of thirty-four, after rising to the pinnacle of his chosen profession, after having John Walsh dub him "King Con" on national TV, he was about to flounder on the rocks of unreasonable panic. It was unbelievable and it shocked him, but Beano Bates had completely lost his nerve.

"Stop staring at me," he said sharply to the brown and black terrier, who continued to sit on the front seat of the Escort and look at him with canine concern. "At least if I quit, you won't ever have to shit on cue again....You won't ever have to try and look like a five-thousand-dollar Baunchatrain Terrier," he said hotly.

Roger looked disappointed. He glanced out the window at the lighted golden arches. He sniffed at his beer without interest. Then he circled a place on the front seat three times before dropping anchor and putting his chin on his paws. He never took his gaze off Beano, watching him like a concerned parent.

THREE

Scapegoat

"I'll wait for a forensic scan, but I think we're royally fucked in here," the black homicide detective said morosely to the two uniforms by the door. "This bathroom has been scrubbed down. The building cleaning staff uses Lysol, but this smells like some kinda bleach or something. We can probably forget trace evidence too. Somebody went over the carpets with hand vacuums. See them marks on the pile?"

It was Tuesday morning and the detective was Ron Johnson. He'd been "catching" on the homicide table when the call came in, so he was now the Primary on case number H32-35-497. Technically, it was still just a missing persons case, but it had been given a

45

homicide number and referred to that squad. It couldn't be rated as a multiple homicide yet, but everybody knew that's what it was. A high-risk witness and two Jersey plainclothes cops had vanished from the fourteenth floor of the Trenton Towers. The lab techs had been milling around for an hour, checking for blood splatter or cerebrospinal fluid, searching for fingerprints, and vacuuming for trace evidence. The apartment was as clean as the inside of an egg. The crime scene had been carefully sanitized.

Unanswered questions hung in the air and distorted everybody's logic like funhouse mirrors. How did the killers get in? How did they get three bodies out without being seen? How did Manning and Corollo get taken without even firing a shot? Nobody wanted to say that the two cops had fucked up and lost the State's prime witness, along with their own lives, on a high-profile mob prosecution...but that's what everybody was thinking.

Victoria Hart arrived at 8:40 A.M. She'd been jogging when a patrol car found her in the Mill Hill district of Trenton, running the brick sidewalks with their decorative gas lights and iron benches. She was between Jackson and Mercer streets when the blue-and-white pulled over and the two uniforms got out. She was told that when the relief guards showed up at eight A.M., the apartment and corridor on the fourteenth floor at Trenton Towers were empty. Carol Sesnick and her two night guards were missing. Victoria stood in her running shorts feeling a brutal chill, not knowing if it was the unseasonably cold weather or a physical reaction to the devastating news. She showed up at the crime scene in her running gear, which she instantly realized was a mistake. News crews, which constantly monitored police frequencies, were already gathering out in front of the building. She heard shutters click as she ran up the steps, her Nikes squeaking on the concrete. She had been so distressed, she could think of nothing but getting there as quickly as possible. Now she would have to face herself on the six o'clock news, showing up at her friend's murder scene, dressed like a fitness instructor.

Tactical mistake. Fuck it.

She wandered through the small suite of rooms, looking at everything. Her brain had already accepted the worst, but her heart was still trying to deal with the fallout. *Did I get Carol killed?* she asked herself, knowing full well that she had certainly played a key role. She had been in charge, it was her case, she had supervised the security and approved the location of the safe house. The fact that there were no bodies was meaningless and completely offset by the smell of bleach in the bathroom. She looked, for a moment, at the table in the hall...at the tabloid papers and uneaten candy she had left for Tony and Bobby the night before. Her emotions swelled; she felt tears coming to her eyes. *Stay in control, Victoria,* she told herself sternly. She was here to find

47

truth and to seek justice. She could cry for her friends later.

Victoria knew her prints were on the tabloid papers and the candy, so she told that to one of the forensic techs and promised to send a set of comparison prints down to the lab when she got to her office. She found herself back in the spotless bathroom, the smell of bleach clogging her nostrils. The tan dress with the pinned hem was on the tile floor, next to the tub. Like a child's doll at the scene of a fatal accident, it beckoned her, as if it somehow knew the answers, because Carol must have been holding it when disaster struck.

Her boss, Gil Green, called at nine-thirty while she was still walking aimlessly in the room, trading hopeful strained smiles with the hushed detectives. Inside her spinning head, she kept repeating, *I'm sorry, Carol, I'm so sorry,* until the phrase had lost its meaning and had become a mantra to calm her conscience and badly frayed nerves.

They were all gathered in Judge Murray Goldstone's ornate chambers in the huge Colonial courthouse on State Street. The building was in the Victorian section of town, nestled in among residential houses of the maple-tree-lined neighborhood.

Victoria barely had time to run home and change into one of her no-nonsense dark blue suits and a pair of low-heeled shoes. She knew her case was in shambles. Judge Gold-stone had agreed to this emergency meeting at the request of Defense Counsel. Gerald Cohen was, as usual, surrounded by his Yale Law School glee club. They followed him around like rock star groupies. All of them were young Ivy League attorneys who held the lofty title of Co-counsel. They were huddled like cocky athletes on one side of the room. Outnumbered, Victoria was on the other side with young David Frankfurter. Opposing teams waiting for the jump ball.

Judge Murray Goldstone entered from a side door followed by Beth Leeds, the court reporter. He settled behind his desk, looking rested in a pink Polo shirt and tan pants. He had his usual morning Aqua Velva glow. A fringe of gray hair rimmed his bald head like a Greek athlete's laurel wreath. Beth sat in a chair across the room, her Stenograph machine in front of her.

"Where is your client?" the Judge asked, look-ing at Gerald Cohen.

"He should be here, Your Honor. We were up all last night, going over pre-trial briefs. We rented a room at the Hilton. I didn't leave till six A.M. Joe was still there. I called him when I heard about this. He was going to take a shower and try to get here by eleven." He looked at his watch. "We should maybe give him ten more minutes...."

"You were with him *all night*?" Victoria said, looking at Gerry Cohen, her voice shak-ing, barely able to contain her anger.

"That's right, Victoria. All night. All of us were there." He gestured toward his Ivy League back-up singers, who nodded solemnly.

"So you're gonna alibi this killer?"

"I understand that you're upset, Victoria," Gerry said slowly, "but I would appreciate it if you would not make insinuations. I'm an officer of the court and I don't commit crimes in an attempt to win cases. I was with Joseph Rina from six last night until eight this morning...at the Hilton Hotel, room six eighty-seven. There are an ample number of witnesses who can attest to that fact."

"What about his brother, Tommy? Can you alibi him?"

"Tommy Rina is not my client. I don't know anything about Tommy. You got a problem there, take it up with him."

Then the corridor door to the Judge's old Victorian chambers opened. Joseph Rina walked in, dressed in gray slacks, navy-blue shirt, and matching tie. His tasseled loafers danced happily as he entered on the balls of his feet.

Victoria had to admit Joseph Rina was a beautiful package. He was handsome in a way that made you stare. His olive skin was so smooth it seemed almost translucent; his light blue eyes reflected intelligence and were the color of tropical reef water. She hated his guts.

"Sorry I'm late. What's up?" he said, innocently smiling at Gerry Cohen, then nodding at Victoria and the Judge.

Judge Goldstone straightened up, leaned forward, and took control of the meeting. "We have a short menu of issues to deal with and then one complex procedural problem. Let's start with your witness, Miss Hart. I understand from Gil you've got a problem producing her."

"A *problem*? My witness was kidnapped, Your Honor."

"You can prove that?" Gerry said, in his slow nasal whine, looking at her with theatrical shock.

"I lost a witness and two plainclothes cops. They disappeared out of Trenton Towers sometime between ten last night and eight this morning. They have not been heard from. They didn't just wander off for ice cream, goddammit."

"Your Honor," Gerry cut in, "the Prosecutor is obviously alleging foul play. If that's the case, then let her say so. Frankly, who the hell knows what happened up there? All I know is, my client was with me all night and I will so testify. He was also with Trevor St. John, Calvin LePont, and Barret Brockingham...all of whom are present and ready to testify." He motioned toward his chorus of attorneys and, like a Motown singing group, they all shuffled their feet and nodded in perfect tempo. "If the Prosecutor wants to bring a charge of kidnapping against my client, she's gonna have to do better than unsubstantiated allegations and sarcasm about trips to the ice-cream parlor."

51

"Your Honor," Victoria jumped in, "Joseph Rina is a top-drawer mob kingpin. A Godfather."

"I suppose you can prove that?" Gerry protested.

"He sits at the head of the table," she continued. "I had an eyewitness who saw him beat a man almost to death."

"Too bad you don't have the victim," Joe Rina said in his soft, gentle voice. "I always thought that was part of the process. A defendant gets to be confronted by his accuser."

Victoria scowled. She thought Joe Rina had the polished manners of a crown prince, but the sleazy demeanor of a Telemundo game show host. "We don't need the victim," she carried on bravely. "We can certainly substantiate the beating of Frank Lemay, or whoever he was. We have the depositions of the paramedics who picked him up. They will testify to the extent and degree of the injuries. We have the E.R. doctors and trauma nurses at Mercer County Hospital in Trenton. Jesus, the man was in a coma for two days, and we *used to* have an eyewitness who actually saw the beating. She saw Mr. Rina beat the man unconscious with a golf club. That was going to get Joe Rina convicted. He knew it. Gerry knew it. And you know it, Judge. Now the witness and the two cops are gone, and I'm not supposed to suspect foul play? You bet there was foul play. I'm not alleging it, *I'm promising it*. Who cares if he's alibied? He wouldn't do this personally. He can pick up the phone and order a hit-man."

"I think Miss Hart needs to calm down. She's beginning to sound irrational," Joe Rina said, turning his movie-star face toward her, smiling through friendly, aqua-green filters that masked inner ruthlessness.

"Let's cut to the bottom line," Judge Goldstone put in. "Do you think you're going to be able to produce your witness and put on your case, Miss Hart?"

"I don't know. I need Carol Sesnick. Without her or the victim, I can't go forward. I need a two-week continuance," she said.

"Two more weeks?!" Gerry Cohen sighed expansively. "Why not two months, or two years? Hey, Gil Green probably needs more time to milk this thing in the press anyway. Maybe we can string it out all the way to the general election in November. Let's not worry about Joe Rina and his constitutionally guaranteed right to a speedy trial. To hell with Joe Rina. Since it's him, let's just make up new rules as we go along. He doesn't count. He has no rights. Let's call him the Godfather, even though he works every day in the food supply business and has never been convicted of anything. Let's just go ahead and slander him without evidence. We've already been dragging along on this thing for almost nine months. What's another half a month...? It's absurd."

"What do you want, Gerry? Get it on the record," Judge Goldstone said.

"We want to finish jury selection this morn-

53

ing and get started. We have a constitutional right to a speedy trial."

"Okay, I agree," the Judge said. "The court would like to get going too. And that brings us to the procedural question....Once that second alternate is seated, jeopardy attaches."

This was the problem that Victoria had been struggling with all morning. The rule in criminal cases is that once the full jury is impaneled, the double-jeopardy rule goes into effect. That meant that if the last juror was selected and the Prosecution didn't put on its case, Joe Rina would walk and could never be tried again for this crime, even if they later turned up the missing Frank Lemay and Carol Sesnick to testify to the beating. Victoria knew that to gain time, she needed to get Judge Goldstone to grant her a continuance *before* seating the last juror, and not the other way around. She knew it was a long shot, but she had to try.

"Your Honor," she started slowly, "please give us the continuance first. The jurors we have selected, you can send them home for two weeks and then recall them. Once jeopardy attaches, I've got a gun to my head."

"You're the worst time-waster since video games," Gerry sneered. "We've been in pretrial for three months already. They've been dragging it out, Your Honor. This is wrong. My client has been forced to endure harassment in the media, and our District Attorney has been dancing on Joe's forehead every night on the *Evening News*. My client's only crime is he was born with an Italian surname. This needs to end. We want to impanel the jury *now*. If there's a case here, which I doubt, we want to get started."

The dilemma lay before Judge Goldstone like messy road kill. He toyed with the problem in his head while he worked the percentage possibilities of a reversal by the Appellate Court. The old grandfather clock standing in the corner of the Victorian chamber cut slices of time with sharp pendulum ticks until Murray Goldstone finished his silent review and cleared his throat. "I understand your problem, Miss Hart, but we need to get going. The charge against Mr. Rina is attempted murder. If you want to raise kidnapping or Murder One charges with respect to Carol Sesnick and the two police officers, I'll entertain those at a later date."

"I can't prove that yet. The police are just starting their investigation."

"I'm sorry then. We'll continue impaneling the jury this morning, and when that's completed, I'll grant you a seventy-two-hour continuance to get your case back together. Failing that, I'll have to entertain a motion to dismiss."

Victoria was watching Joe Rina very carefully as the Judge said this, trying to gauge his reaction. He was rock-solid. He didn't give anything away. No thought or smile crossed his handsome face. He looked at the Judge with mild sadness, as if he actually cared about the missing witness.

55

He was good. *What a total shit,* Victoria thought.

♠ ♠ ♠

The April sun was bright, but the day was crisp and cold. A light wind ruffled the leaves where the State Courthouse sat.

Victoria's beeper had gone off two minutes ago. She looked at the L.C.D. readout and saw the familiar "911-GG" on the tiny screen, which meant: *Get back to the office, quick.* Gil Green wanted to see her. She knew he must have heard about Judge Goldstone's ruling and was probably about to throw one of his low-key passive-aggressive fits. She had just crossed to her Nissan and put the key in the lock when she felt a presence and smelled mint cologne. She turned and saw Joe Rina standing right behind her. It startled her and she wondered how he had managed to get that close without her seeing. They were almost exactly the same height and she was looking right into his tropical blue eyes.

"You gave it the old college try. No hard feelings," he said gently, as if they were about to become friends and not lifelong bitter enemies.

"Whatta you mean, no hard feelings? I've got big-time hard feelings. Get away from me, you murdering slimeball."

"In that case," he smiled innocently, "I just wanted you to know that I think it was your fault you lost her and the two cops."

"Really? Are you admitting something here, Joe?"

He smiled and took his time as the breeze ruffled his rich black hair. "I've learned that admissions are very much like theatrical concerts. The quality of the music can often depend on where you're sitting."

"Just get the fuck away from me," she said, resenting him so deeply that she could barely control herself. She knew that he'd had her three friends killed and was now standing there smiling and talking about it like a Trenton theater critic.

"You don't need to use abusive language, Miss Hart. That's generally an affectation of people who don't trust their own opinions and need to dress them up with foul language to get them to fly."

"Oh really? Gimme a minute so I can file that under 'Who gives a shit?' You don't become more acceptable because you can form a proper sentence, dickhead. And you're in the food business like I'm in the ballet. You're just a sawed-off oil can in designer clothing who kills people, so get away from me."

"It was your fault, Victoria. The Trenton Towers was a bad choice. If you'd put her in Berlington Place, two blocks away, on the top floor, you could have locked off the elevator. You could have controlled entry and exit. They have TV-monitored security. I've kept a few people safe over there. Maybe next time you should check that one out."

"So, now you *are* admitting something."

"Not really. Besides, whatta you gonna do? Nobody's gonna listen to an unsubstantiated charge from the Prosecutor trying to convict me."

"You're really something," she said with pure disgust.

"As are you, Miss Hart, but as it happens I guess now you're finally out of my hair and on to your next harrowing legal adventure." He smiled benignly, turned, and walked gracefully on the balls of his feet to his car, where Texaco Phillips was waiting for him behind the wheel.

"I'm not through with you yet!" she called after him.

He turned and looked back at her. When he smiled, his ivory sparklers glinted in the cold sunlight. "Yes, you are. If I were a betting man, and your bookmaking detail downtown tells me I am, then you're never gonna see your witness again. So you probably shouldn't even waste your time looking. I'd say 'See you in court,' but that isn't gonna happen either." He got into the passenger seat of the car and Texaco pulled away slowly. As the long, shiny black limo rolled past her, she saw herself momentarily reflected in its glossy surface: The moving car strobed her image, bending it badly.

They met upstairs in Gil's plaque-infested office. But Victoria couldn't get the incumbent D.A. and potential Lieutenant Governor to look at her.

"It was your responsibility to protect the witness," he said, looking out the window at the lazy traffic on State Street. He was dressed in his *Live at Five* attire...his custom-made, gray cashmere suit, his dark maroon tie. The tie was by far the most colorful thing about him. He was ready for the *Evening News*. Gil Green was, in all ways, nondescript. Victoria once thought he should have considered a career as a hold-up man. He was so average looking, nobody would ever pick him out of a lineup. He had no distinguishing features, but his everyman looks masked a ruthless political ambition.

"I had two cops there protecting her, Gil...."

"You are the lead prosecutor. You picked the building. It was your responsibility. I can't cover for you there, even if I wanted to," he said, laying out the usual C.Y.A. office ground rules. That was the way it was in the District Attorney's office. You had to "Cover Your Ass," because Gil always covered his. There were no sacrifices, no shared failures. "Sesnick is missing," he went on. "Even if I had three bodies, I still wouldn't have enough to bring murder charges. Rina's alibied anyway. Without the bodies, it'll go down as an unsolved disappearance. A bullshit missing persons case. With bodies it's better, but without more evidence, still not close to an indictment for murder. He's got a whole troop of Boy Scout lawyers ready to swear for him. We won't get past that."

"What about Tommy?" She asked.

"You won't get anything from him either. He'll probably have the Cardinal from the Sixth Diocese swearing Tommy was stamping out communion wafers all last night." Gil grunted, "We're fucked. Or, let me rephrase that...you're fucked."

"I'm fucked?" She knew she was, but she attempted to at least make him feel bad about it. "All of a sudden I'm out here alone, Gil?"

"We made a big deal outta bringing Joe Rina to trial. The timing is horrible for me with the election coming. If this turns to shit, you're gonna have to wear the hat, Vicky. Sorry, but that's show biz. Around here, everybody's gotta fall on their own fumble."

Sports metaphors from a guy who never played anything more dangerous than bridge. "I'm stunned," she said disingenuously.

"Forgive me for anything I might have to say on TV," he continued. "It's not personal, just necessary."

♠ ♠ ♠

When she saw the six o'clock news, it was hard to forgive him. It was a segment called "New Jersey Talking." Gil Green sat on a set in front of a blue curtain, with the host, Ted Calendar, who had a blond toupee that was so bad it looked like a yellow cat was sleeping on his head. In his soft, non-aggressive voice, Gil told the interviewer that the witness who had been lost would have surely ended Joe Rina's career

60

in crime. He informed the audience that Carol Sesnick had disappeared, along with two brave police officers. He admitted reluctantly that he was personally very disappointed in the security arrangements and only this morning had been brought up to date on the badly chosen safe house.

"This woman's life was in our hands," he said sadly. "I'm afraid this inferior location, picked by a member of my own staff, was a serious mistake and possibly resulted in the death of these heroic people. I'm going to have to conduct an efficiency review on this particular prosecutor. Beyond that, I really can't say much at this time."

Victoria sat in her apartment in front of her TV and silently cursed him, even though she agreed with his assessment. She had been foolish. She had underestimated Joe and Tommy Rina.

In her memory, she saw Carol Sesnick's goofy, playful grin. She remembered her standing in the bathroom with the poodle curls piled high atop her head. She heard Carol's lament as she pointed to the failed hairdo. *I fucked it up, V,* her missing friend's voice echoed ruefully in her memory.

"No you didn't, hon," Victoria said to her empty apartment. "I did."

And then seven hours later, while Victoria was in a restless sleep, the phone rang and changed her life forever.

FOUR

The Connect

It happened in the middle of the night.

"I beg your pardon?" she said, trying to push the fuzzy cloud of deep sleep out of her head and understand the black male's ghetto vernacular on the other end of the phone. "What are you saying?"

"I be trying to hook you up, mama. So cut all the hoorah, we ain't on colored people's time here. Gotta get busy and be workin' it."

"Oh," she said, looking at the clock. It was two A.M. She didn't have a clue what he was saying and was about to hang up, but his next sentence stopped her.

"Dat Jake gangsta gone an' get hisself clipped for sure. Dey go find d'brother in Hoboken las' night. Dat dumb Rasta nigga, somebody go bus' a cap at his ass...leave in a junk yard. Shee...it."

Now Victoria sat up. "Who is this?" she asked.

"Dat nigga be my Ace Cool. Das all how I be fer now. All you gotta know is I done pieced it out....Das why I call you up, on account'a you was tryin' t'splash on dem guinea gray cats."

She could barely pick the words out of the thick rolling ghetto accent. She thought he was saying that he was a friend of the Jamaican the police had found inside that stolen Econoline van in the junkyard in Hoboken yesterday. The man on her phone seemed to think it had something to do with the Rinas. She didn't know how the two cases could possibly be connected. She had heard about the junkyard murder but had paid it almost no attention. Her mind had been reeling from the loss of Carol and the destruction of her case. The police thought the murder was some kind of a drug payback killing because the Jamaican had heroin in his blood. But this person on her phone at two in the morning seemed to be saying the two cases were connected. He sounded high on something. She wondered how he got her home number.

"Can you speak English?" she finally said.

"Hey, don' go disrespectin' my ass. I be tryin' t'drop some good science on you."

"Just say it. What is it?" she pressed, beginning to get frustrated. She reached out and turned on the light in her black and white, minimalist bedroom. She could see a low full moon through the sheer drapes.

"He come here, my Ace Cool, he be zooted up, he say here's de plan, Amp, I gonna work fer dem greaseballs, den I gonna go get me a dope ride, den boom, I be hook it up like I want. He say he gonna be livin' large, but he always been one boned-out nigga, spen' way too much time suckin' da glass dick. He always pumpin' up de volume on everythin', y'know? So I don' pay him much never mind. He say dey gonna go throw dat bitch you was guardin' an' dem two blue light specials down de elevator shaft. He say how dem guinea gray cats go got him a deuce-deuce t'carry....Tell how all he hadda do was sit ina ride out front. He tell me ever damn ting 'bout dat piece a'work."

Now she was on her feet, pacing with the phone.

"You're telling me that Carol Sesnick and the two police officers are at the bottom of the Trenton Towers elevator shaft?"

"Ain't you fuckin' listenin'? Dat's what I be sayin'! I bet you de fat man aginst d'hole in a doughnut dat's where dey be at."

"What's your name?"

"What's my name? Lemme see...for now, I gonna be d'dead cat on de line. Dis here be d'free sample....My Ace Cool, he one dead rag nigga now. Ain't nothin' gonna buy him no more rock. You look down der, you'll see I ain't jaw jackin'. But you want mo', you gotta tighten me up."

"If this is good, I'll pay. How do I get in touch with you?"

"Don' worry, sugga, I gonna be watchin' the T and V. I be come over hit on your wall."

And then she was listening to a dial tone. Victoria grabbed her phone book and dialed Ron Johnson's number. She had written it down yesterday morning. After a few rings she got Ron's wife.

"What is it?" she asked, her voice thick with sleep.

"This is Victoria Hart. I'm sorry to call you so late. Is Ron there?"

There was the sound of the phone being

64

dropped and then passed...then Ron's voice came on, trying to sound wide awake, but he was faking. "Yeah. What's up?"

"I just got an interesting call. He didn't leave a name but he sounded black."

"That's racist shit, Miss Hart. Good thing we get along or I could write you up for that." His voice was a little tight, pissed off at being awakened.

"Come on, Ron, knock it off. You should've heard him. It was all ghettoese. If I didn't spend half my life taking depositions from these guys in jail, I never would've understood. He says Carol, Tony, and Bobby are at the bottom of the elevator shaft at Trenton Towers."

"We looked. Not there."

"What's down there?"

"It's goop. Fifty years of sludge."

"Did you put somebody in there and poke around?"

"No. Like I said, it's just gunk...from years of oil drippings and underground sewage. We looked at the plans and stuck a pole down. There's like a concrete and steel catch basin 'bout five feet deep; you stir it up, it stinks worse than fish house garbage."

"Get somebody over in waders and look again."

"You sure?"

"No, I'm not sure....There was just something about this guy that makes me think it's real."

"This two A.M. bullshit is fun, Vicky, we gotta do this more often," he said, and then was abruptly off the line. She knew he was already on the phone getting a detail together.

♠ ♠ ♠

After making the middle-of-the-night call to Victoria Hart, Beano Bates moved slowly into the kitchen of his motel apartment in Coral Gables. The place was one baby step above a crash pad and depressing enough without the devastating news about Carol. He opened the refrigerator, took out a cold beer, and pressed it to his face, but didn't drink it. He didn't trust his stomach, which was churning. Roger-the-Dodger looked up at him, growled low, and then snapped out a sharp bark. Beano looked down at the dog for a long minute. "Why would she do it, Rog?" he said.

He had seen the report of Carol Sesnick's disappearance that night on the eleven o'clock news. It had hit him like a fist. It was even more devastating than the blows he had taken at the hands of Joseph Rina. As soon as the story was off, he had left the wood-framed, peeling apartment, run to the Escort, and driven to an all-night market that had newspapers from all over the country. He had bought the *Trenton Herald*. With his stomach still rolling, he had looked up the story of her disappearance and had read it carefully. The story recounted his beating under the name of Frank Lemay. It said that after filing his report with the Trenton Police, he had left the hospital....The Trenton Prosecutor, who the writer said was

66

occasionally referred to as "Tricky Vicky" Hart, had refused to drop the charges when she had turned up a witness who had seen the assault. The witness's identity had been kept secret, but the paper said it was generally thought to be a man, until it was learned yesterday that the witness was a pediatric nurse named Carol Sesnick, who specialized in child cancer patients at the Trenton Children's Hospital. He put down the paper and felt tears sting in his eyes. He knew Carol hadn't been anywhere near the Greenborough Country Club when the beating had occurred. She had lied to Victoria Hart because Joe Rina had intended to kill Beano and promised to try again. Carol knew that and had stepped forward. With Joseph Rina in prison, Carol probably thought Beano would be safe. He forced his mind to work for a moment, but only on the facts.

He wasn't sure Carol and the two Jersey cops were in the elevator shaft, but Three Finger Freddy had told Beano the story of how the Rinas used to dispose of their dead bodies. The card shark told him they used to throw them down an elevator shaft. "No, cops," he had explained in the Mercer County Hospital room, "want to go poking around in the sludge under an elevator."

Beano finished the story on Carol's disappearance and then started flipping around in the paper, looking for something plausible he could use. His mind was reeling with the disaster. Tears were in his eyes, but he brushed them away and continued to force himself to concentrate. He found a story on page 20 that stopped him. There was a picture of an Econoline van parked in a Hoboken junkyard. The story said a Rastafarian John Doe had been discovered in the stolen van with three 9mm slugs in him. Ballistics said they were from two different guns. Because the Rasta had heroin in his blood, the police in Trenton suspected it was a drug slaying. It had happened the same night as Carol's disappearance. Beano had heard a rumor that Tommy Rina often used disposable wheel men. That way he didn't have any loose ends or have to pay them the two or three thousand dollars it would normally cost for a getaway driver on a big hit. He wondered if the Rastafarian in the stolen van could have been part of the Rina job. The fact that he had died on the same night Carol had been kidnapped or killed gave the theory some credence.

Beano had gone back to his apartment and had spent an hour recapturing his once near-perfect ghetto dialect. During his one prison stretch, he had learned it from his cellmate, a fractured semi-crazed gang banger named Amp Heywood. Beano had never met Victoria Hart. She'd been put on the case after he'd already left the hospital, but there was a picture of her on the front page of the paper. For a State Prosecutor, she looked uncharacteristically beautiful. She had very short, no-nonsense hair. And she didn't look all that "tricky" to him. She looked earnest.

He folded the paper and sat by the phone. He had to find out if Carol was dead. He had to get the Trenton Police to look in the bottom of the elevator shaft. He picked up the phone and made the two A.M. call to the embattled New Jersey Prosecutor.

After he hung up, he stood in the kitchen, rolling the cold beer on his forehead. His stomach was jumping, threatening to erupt. Then, almost without warning, he turned and vomited into the sink. Roger-the-Dodger never took his eyes off Beano. He cocked his head and watched the grifter solemnly.

"Quit looking at me, Roger. Jesus, you're worse than a Catholic nun down there." He ran some cold water and washed out his mouth; then Beano suddenly had a vision of Carol. It flashed in front of him, playing in his memory and squeezing at his boiling stomach. They'd been in Arizona in the big house that his father, Jacob, had rented at the end of the roofing season. Roofing scams were seasonal. By winter, nobody would risk tearing a roof off, so the family spent two months in Arizona, living in luxury. That had been the first time his cousin Carol had come to visit. She had been six and he'd been nine. They'd hit it off instantly. He loved her shy sense of humor and the little dusting of freckles that spread across her turned-up nose. But most of all, he loved the way she looked at him. It was something close to hero worship, and it brought out the best in Beano.

Not that she was all goodness. Carol possessed an impish sense of the scoundrel that was probably bred in her from generations of family treachery. Beano's mother was a Sesnick and Carol came from that side of the family. The Sesnicks were American Gypsies.... They ran tarot scams and were excellent dips. At six, Carol could pick your pocket without your ever knowing. She taught Beano that Gypsy skill during their first winter together. Beano's mother had worked with them on their academic lessons. They had studied side-by-side in the hot, makeshift schoolroom his mother had set up over the garage. He and Carol had lots of sleep-outs in a tent in the backyard. Once he had tried to scare her; tried to tell her that bears came down out of the hills and pawed through the trash at night. She looked at him, her six-year-old eyes wide with fright. "I'm afraid of bears, Beano," she told him solemnly, then reached out and took hold of his hand. "But if they come, I know you'll protect me." What could you do about someone like that? All Beano could do was love her.

He had never been asked to protect anyone before. There were no bears, but he promised her that he would never let anything happen to her. She held his hand and went to sleep. She was still there in the morning, bundled next to him in her blanket.

Beano had felt so bad about the lie that he never lied to her again. It had been the only completely honest friendship in his life. From that moment on, he had kept his promise to protect her. They had always stayed in touch. He had visited her family three times at Christmas. She had come to see him several times while he was in Raiford Prison in Florida. She was like his little sister. They were first cousins, but more important, they were soulmates. She had been one of the few in her family not to go into the game. She wanted to be a pediatric nurse and lately had been working in the cancer ward at Children's Hospital. When she spoke to him about the children, tears came to her eyes: "Beano, there's such courage in these little ones. They fight so hard, but there's never enough money....If I had any, I'd give it all to them." Beano knew she meant it, but couldn't help wondering if she was trying to compensate for the whole family's engagement in criminal enterprises. Several years ago, Beano had sent her his end of a two-month land swindle to pay for her nursing school. In return, she had lied to try to save him from Joe Dancer. Now he knew Carol was dead. Tears came into his eyes....He couldn't deal with her loss.

He went into the bedroom and flopped down on the single bed. The tears rolled down his cheeks and dampened his pillow. He was crying for Carol, and he was crying for himself. He was crying for the two children holding hands in that pup tent, twenty-five years ago. If she could die for him, then he could die for her. Somehow he would have to get his

71

nerve back. He would take the Rina brothers down. He would bust them so that nobody would be left standing.

Beano Bates, with tears still running down his cheeks, started to think about the layout for his last Big Con.

Part Two
THE LAYOUT

"WE ARE ARRANT KNAVES, ALL; BELIEVE NONE OF US." —William Shakespeare

FIVE

Jeopardy

It was nine A.M. and they were all back in Murray Goldstone's courtroom. Gerry Cohen and the Yale Glee Club were smiling over a long wooden table piled high with juror research. Victoria was alone at the Prosecution table. Joe Rina wasn't there. He was shooting a round of golf.

The prospective juror's name was Gino Delafore and he was turning into a disaster for Victoria. He was only forty-two, but he listed his occupation as *"retired* florist." He had massive shoulders and thick, graying black hair. If Victoria Hart had been looking for somebody to play the Godfather, she would have cast him, but as her second alternate and the last seat to fill on this jury, he was a big mistake. She had a feeling he was a ringer, but with no peremptory challenges left, there was almost nothing she could do about it. As her questioning continued, it became more and more obvious that the Defense had gotten to Gino. After each one of her questions, he would glance surreptitiously at Gerald Cohen for approval. Victoria would have dismissed him in seconds if she had a challenge left. David Frankfurter was on a cellphone out in the corridor, talking to the Trenton PD, trying to get more facts. So far, all they had come up with was that a bookmaking operation had once operated from a magazine stand directly in front of Gino's flower shop. Victoria was trying to establish some contact between Delafore and the Defendant so she could show cause for his dismissal. Judge Goldstone was beginning to fidget, getting set to close her down.

"Did Joe Rina or Tommy Rina ever buy flowers at your shop?" she asked.

"No, ma'am...or if they did, I wasn't aware of it." Another glance at Cohen.

"But it's possible, isn't it? According to the Trenton phone book, there are about twenty florist shops in the city...so there's at least a one-in-twenty chance that he did."

"I think I would'a remembered..." Gino Delafore said. Again he looked over at Gerald Cohen, who was avoiding Gino's gaze by studiously surveying his notes.

Finally Gerry looked up. "Is this going to take much longer, Judge? This juror is acceptable to the Defense. Ms. Hart has run out of challenges. If she's trying to dismiss Mr. Delafore for cause, she needs facts, which are obviously in short supply over there." He waved his arm at the Prosecution table. "Can we get this moving?" His nasal voice whined in the courtroom.

"How 'bout it, Ms. Hart?" the Judge asked.

"Just one or two more questions, Your Honor." She turned back to Gino Delafore. "Do you know somebody named Sam Definio?"

"Yes. He used to have a little magazine stand in front of my shop."

"But you knew he had a long record of

involvement in criminal enterprises, including bookmaking and loan-sharking?"

"No, I didn't know that."

"Come on, everybody tells me he was known as 'Flashpaper' Sam because he kept his books written on dissolvable paper that he could drop into a pan of water when the cops showed up."

"I knew he'd had trouble with the law. I knew he was trying to go straight. I bought a paper from him every morning for five years. Other than that, his business was his, mine was mine."

"But he was reputed to be a member of the Rina Crime Family, wasn't he? And—"

"Objection, Your Honor! What the heck is Ms. Hart talking about? What Rina Crime Family? My client has never even been on trial before!"

"Joe Rina's been arrested ten times," Victoria shot back.

"Sloppy police work and lies by crooked, police-bought informants are not *proof* of crimes, Miss Hart....Show me your convictions."

Judge Goldstone turned to Gino Delafore and threw a judicial slow pitch. "Do you think you can decide this case on the merits, Mr. Delafore?" he asked.

"Of course, Your Honor."

The Judge looked at Victoria. "Unless you have something with teeth, I'm going to seat this juror."

"Could I sidebar, Your Honor?" Victoria asked.

Judge Goldstone motioned Gerry and Victoria forward. They clustered around his desk and talked softly, the Prosecution going first:

"I think it's very relevant that this man ran a flower shop in front of which was a notorious bookmaker, who police believe was involved with Joseph Rina. Gino Delafore had to know that was a betting stand and he allowed it to happen right in front of his business because he also had connections with Joseph Rina. If that's not relevant, then I'm reading the wrong law books."

"You can't inject unsubstantiated allegations into voir dire," Gerry said. "It's all innuendo, Vicky. This man ran a florist shop. He has no criminal record. Period....Can we move on, Your Honor?"

"Victoria, I'm going to seat this juror as your second alternate and attach jeopardy. You have seventy-two hours to prepare your case-in-chief. Day after tomorrow, you will either begin opening arguments or I will have to dismiss. Sleep well, touch gloves, and may the best lawyer win," Judge Goldstone grinned.

Yuck, yuck, yuck, thought Victoria Hart as Murray Goldstone got up from his leather-backed chair and moved out of the ornate courtroom, black robes billowing. It was only ten A.M. The day was starting off disastrously, but before noon, it got much worse.

The Trenton Haz-Mat team had been called in to probe the elevator shaft. They finally dredged up three sludge-covered bodies, which were rushed to the Coroner's office.

Victoria Hart got the call just before lunch and, fearing the worst, trudged across the mini-mall to the Coroner's office, which was in the basement of the Police Lab. She walked down the concrete stairs, her footsteps unsteady, her hand on the metal banister. Her high heels echoed in a tiled corridor crammed with last night's drug and traffic mistakes. It was a depressing parking lot full of metal gurneys and stalled karmas. She went past the reefer room where the bodies were frozen after the M.E. had opened them up and emptied them of their insides, turning them into cadaverous kayaks. She gagged as she passed the decomp room, where decomposing bodies lay under plastic sheets, waiting for autopsies. She found the Coroner's Assistant, Herman Myer. Herman "the German" was six-five and weighed over three hundred pounds.

"I'm here to make a preliminary I.D. on the three bodies you just pulled out of the shaft at Trenton Towers," she said dully.

"Took us a while to get 'em cleaned up. They're a little graphic...."

"I promise, Herman, I'll try not to vomit on your nice, clean autopsy room," she said morosely.

He nodded and took her into a large forensic operating theater where all three bodies were on separate steel-tray autopsy tables. She reluctantly looked down....Bobby Manning's chest cavity had a hole in it the size of a cantaloupe. Pieces of his rib cage poked through, still glistening black from the oily goop that had filled the bottom of the shaft and hidden the bodies for three days.

"That's Bobby Manning," she said sadly. "He liked Nestl;aae's Crunch. I couldn't find the fucking Nestlé's Crunch at the mini-market. They were out." Her voice was shaking.

Herman reached out and put a hand on her arm. She pulled free and went to Tony Corollo. Tony's body was almost unrecognizable. She knew it was him but she couldn't make a positive, legal I.D. There wasn't enough left. His face was gone. She put a hand up to her mouth and fought back a sob. "It's...he's the right size, but I can't tell for sure. You'll have to print him," she said, taking her eyes off the gruesome, faceless mess.

"Already did. We'll get all the prints back in an hour or two. You don't have to do this, Victoria."

She nodded and moved to the table and saw her friend Carol Sesnick. She looked smaller here on the metal table than she had in life. It was as if the wonderful spirit that filled her had somehow made her bigger. She had been shot in the head and the left side of her face was missing. She had bloated badly...but it was her. Victoria reached out and touched the poodle curls, still wet and slimy from the oil. "I'm sorry, girlfriend," she finally managed.

Her phone rang at ten o'clock the following night. The voice on the other end of the line was educated, Eastern, and very precise.

"This is Miss Victoria Hart, yes?" he said slowly. "Your secretary gave me this number."

She had been gathering up the remnants of her case to file in her office. She had armloads of depositions from nurses and doctors, all of whom had witnessed Frank Lemay's injuries, but would never be called upon to testify. The case was over. Jeopardy had attached. After tomorrow, Joe Rina could never be tried on this charge again.

"Who's calling?" she said without interest.

"This is Cedric O'Neal."

"Who?" she asked impatiently.

"I'm Anthony Heywood's criminal attorney."

"Whose criminal attorney?"

"Anthony Heywood's. I believe his street nickname is 'Amp' Heywood, or some such silliness...."

Victoria thought Cedric O'Neal sounded wimpy.

"He told me he called you last night and gave you information about where the bodies of the two police officers and your witness could be found. It's on the evening news that you subsequently found them, yes?" he continued.

Victoria set the folders down, grabbed a yellow legal pad, and wrote down, "Cedric

81

O'Neal." Under that she wrote, "Anthony 'Amp' Heywood."

"Okay, how can I help you, Mr. O'Neal?" she said with interest, and grabbed for her leather-bound copy of the *Martindale-Hubbell Law Directory,* which listed all the attorneys in the United States...where they went to school, what year they graduated, along with other pertinent facts including any landmark cases they had worked on. It also had employment histories.

In his cheap motel apartment in Coral Gables, Beano Bates paced, carrying the phone. A con man working a phone hustle was known in the trade as a yak. Most yaks paced to keep their energy level up when doing phone freaks. He performed Cedric O'Neal with a perfect clenched-jaw, Eastern-old-school accent. "How can you help me?" he repeated her question. "Well, Miss Hart, I was thinking maybe we could help each other, yes? You see, Mr. Heywood has come to me with some legal problems which, frankly, are a mite troublesome. Mr. Heywood is of the opinion that a former accomplice of his is negotiating with the government to get a reduced sentence on a felony charge of grand larceny."

"What accomplice are we talking about? What case? And what does all this have to do with me?"

"I'm not quite ready to tell you that yet....If you don't mind, I'd like to make my presentation, then you can do all of your spiffies once I'm done."

"My what?" she said, confused.

"Give it your own shine, yes?" he clarified.

What a jerk, she thought.

"Mr. Heywood may have some information that would be useful to you in your prosecution of the Rina case...but Mr. Heywood, instead of giving it away free, is finally being pragmatic and is looking to see what kind of assistance you might be prepared to give to him."

"So this case his accomplice is about to pin on him is in my jurisdiction?"

"Conceivably."

"You're very cagey."

"Well, you know how this stage of a plea bargain can be. We're tiptoeing around issues of prior knowledge, yes? If I might continue...? Mr. Heywood might be willing to give you information about the death of the man this morning's paper is identifying as Demo Williams. In return, he'd like your advocacy in any forthcoming criminal action that your office may be contemplating against him."

"Jesus, you're wordy....You can just say it, Mr. O'Neal."

"I'm operating under instructions from my client right now. My client has not been implicated in anything yet, but he fears he's about to be, and I would just as soon handle this negotiation one-on-one. When constructing agreements of this nature, I like to see who I'm talking to."

"Your client seemed to be indicating to me over the phone last night that his 'Ace Cool,' which means best friend, told him that he was part of the killing at Trenton Towers and that some Italian mobsters did the work. At least that's what it sounded like. I don't need to remind you that anything that Demo Williams told your client is hearsay and not worth much, if anything."

"What if Mr. Heywood was in the nightclub, sitting right at the table, when the original offer was made?" Beano said, pinching his voice, giving it some Ivy League timbre.

"That would be very interesting," she said.

"I need three things if we're going to trade, yes? One: your promise that you will gather up a good position against the Rinas for murdering those three before you call Mr. Heywood to testify. He doesn't want to present himself to the court and implicate these Mafia killers only to have you lose the case. He wants them in jail where they can't retaliate. Two: He wants to be absolved of any charges pending against him for crimes currently being considered by your office. And three: He would like to be placed in the Witness Protection Program."

Victoria was still thumbing through her copy of *Martindale-Hubbell* and finally found Cedric O'Neal. The listing said he had graduated top of his Yale class in 1989. *Another Ivy League choirboy. They're coming through the windows.* He was a partner in a law firm in New York, but was also licensed to practice in

84

half-a-dozen other states, including New Jersey. He graduated less than ten years ago. She thought he was very young to be a partner already and it pissed her off. "You still with Lincoln, Forbes, O'Neal, and Ross?" she asked.

"Ahhh. Got your *Martindale-Hubbell* out, do you?" he said in his pinched, clenched-jaw voice. "Yes, I'm afraid I'm still there, despite their best efforts to replace me." And then he laughed; it sounded very close to a cackle.

Lincoln, Forbes, O'Neal, and Ross was actually a non-existent law firm that had miraculously appeared in the 1997 *Martindale-Hubbell,* courtesy of Frank X. Bates. Frank, who did second-story jobs when he wasn't oiling down roofs, had broken into the printing firm in Chicago that put out the directory and added the fictitious law firm to the computer file one day before it went to be typeset. It was very handy for a family of con men to have a registered, but nonexistent, law firm when working a sophisticated mark. It was often necessary to show up in a con claiming to be somebody's lawyer. Beano even had stationery and business cards printed. They were somewhere in his suitcase. The publisher had sent out a letter disavowing the mistake, but the nonexistent law firm was still in the book, long after everyone had thrown the letter away.

Victoria closed the *M-H* directory and pondered what to do with stuffy Cedric O'Neal. She had one or two yellow "Caution" lights flashing on the big emergency panel in her head, but she was still seething with anger about the death of her friend and that energy helped to make up her mind. "Okay, Mr. O'Neal, how 'bout ten o'clock tomorrow morning? My office."

"Ahh, could we perhaps make it someplace where the possibility of recording or eavesdropping is a mite less intense?"

"How 'bout Sam's Deli, down by the river? Nine o'clock?" she said.

"It's a date. I'll be the tall, balding gentleman in the tan suit and the striped school tie."

She hung up the phone and wondered what the hell was going on.

♠ ♠ ♠

Beano hung up the phone, grabbed Roger, and headed to the door. He needed to go dig up the pickle jar he had buried under a rock off Highway 10. The jar contained fifty thousand dollars in cash. The fifty large was his start-up money and all he had left in the world. Then he had to catch the red-eye flight to Jersey, so he could make his nine o'clock meeting with a beautiful prosecutor named "Tricky Vicky" Hart.

SIX

Telling the Tale

Sam's Deli was on the corner of Manchester and O Street. It had large, plate-glass windows and a takeout counter along the east wall. Beano arrived at eight, an hour before the meeting. He was dressed in a blue blazer, tan slacks, and striped tie. His dyed blond hair was falling over his tanned forehead. One of the problems with being on the FBI's Ten Most Wanted List was that Beano's picture had been circulated to police departments all over the country. He picked a table in the rear of the deli. With his back against the wall, he sat scanning the half-full restaurant. Laughter and frying bacon mixed in with the occasional scream of a Waring blender. An aerial circus of black flies competed for a hanging light fixture in the center of the room.

From what he'd been able to find out about Victoria Hart, she was no fool. She might even bring a police investigator to witness the negotiation concerning Anthony Heywood's nonexistent crimes. Beano had selected his old cellmate, Amp, for the co-starring role in this hustle because Beano knew Amp had a sizable record and would be in the N.C.I.C. computer. Beano had also heard from an old ex-con friend that a month after he got out, Amp had stopped a bullet in a street action and had been given the Miami "burial at sea," which consisted of being lugged out to the Everglades and stuffed down a gator hole...an event that made him technically still alive, but forever unavailable for protest. Beano's careful eyes zigzagged the deli and he determined there weren't any cops in the place.

He ordered a tall glass of orange juice from an already tired waitress whose name tag said she was ANGEL. Beano sat watching the door, examining the customers as they arrived, checking them out one at a time as they entered. At exactly nine o'clock, through the door came the woman whose picture he had seen in the *Trenton Herald*. Victoria Hart announced her fastidious personality with her wardrobe and prompt arrival. In person, Beano didn't think she looked very tricky. She looked determined; everything about her suggested intelligence and organization. She was in a tailored, dark green suit with matching shoes and scarf. She was even more strikingly beautiful than the picture in the paper, but she seemed unconcerned with her looks. No makeup or hairstyling. She had a large briefcase and no purse. She seemed impatient as she scanned the restaurant. As her eyes panned across him, he pulled the menu up to cover his face. She was searching for a tall, balding man in a tan suit and school tie, the description he had given her. But nobody in the restaurant matched that description. She glanced at her watch, then moved briskly across the deli and took a table by the window.

He let some more time run off the clock. At nine-ten, Victoria Hart started glancing at her watch. Then she pulled her case files out of her briefcase and started going through them again. Angel poured the New Jersey Prosecutor a second cup of coffee. By nine-twenty she was tapping her fingers on the linoleum table top. Beano watched her carefully with a con man's practiced eye. She was going to be a tough mark. She was definitely Type A, direct, no bullshit...the hardest kind. Type A's were generally fastidious, so Beano decided on a plan. He wanted to wait until she was just about to leave. If this was a trap, and she had somebody else in the restaurant, they would communicate before she got up. She would wave the back-up over and they'd do some whispering...*Whatta you think? Is he gonna show? Did he stand us up?* Beano continued to observe her; she was important to the lay-out of his con. As the Prosecutor on the case, she had spent almost a year trying to convict Joseph Rina. That meant she was the greatest living expert on that Mafia Prince outside of his own family. She would have already deposed all of his friends and business associates. She would know about all of his legal and illegal activities, his known associates, his girlfriends, his enemies. She would have the background information Beano would need. Most attorneys at trial keep a copy of the complete case files with them, so if something comes up, they can have it at their fingertips. He hoped she had the bulk of this information in her oversized briefcase.

Beano had very little knowledge of Joseph Rina beyond the fact that he was an avid card player and was viciously effective with a nine-iron at close range. His brother, Tommy, was reputed to be something of a loose cannon. He was fiercely loyal to his younger brother and had protected him all his life. In fact, at the age of fifteen, Tommy had attacked an Irish thug named Sean Morrisey, who had threatened Joe. Tommy had beaten him to death outside a bar with a ballpeen hammer. Then a miracle occurred: The thug sat up on the Coroner's table just before the autopsy. They rushed Morrisey to the hospital and he had been saved. The way the story went, two months later the resurrected boy had been walking down the street where the beating first happened and was shot in the back from a passing car. Because he'd killed him twice, Tommy Rina had been Tommy "Two Times" ever since. Other than that distressing piece of information, Beano knew next to nothing about Tommy.

Beano waited until the Prosecutor pulled up her huge briefcase and started digging around for her wallet to pay the bill; then he got out of his seat and crossed the restaurant toward her.

"Miss Hart?" he said, slightly out of breath.

She jerked her head up from her wallet and looked at him. "Cedric O'Neal?" Her expression said he wasn't what she expected.

"Actually, no. I work with Ced O'Neal. He got stuck in New York on a pre-trial motion that got expedited at seven this morning. He called me and I got here as quick as I could. I hope you weren't waiting long. I'm Martin Cushbury." He handed her a card that said he was Martin Cushbury, Attorney at Law. The card was embossed in gold with the firm name of Lincoln, Forbes, O'Neal, and Ross. "I'm with our New Jersey office in Newark. I got his call at eight-thirty. I was in the damn shower. He tried to reach you but I guess you'd already left....I got here quick as I could."

"I have a ten o'clock court date, so we don't have much time," Victoria said, looking at her watch again.

"Okay, right. Well, uh...despite our lack of time, would it be all right if maybe I sat down?" he asked, grinning.

She motioned for him to sit and smiled apologetically, but didn't speak. Beano thought her smile was stunning, but he pushed thoughts of her beauty away and went right to work....

"Sorry I kept you waiting," he said.

"Nine o'clock means *nine o'clock,* Mr. Cushbury," Victoria lectured.

Angel came over and Beano ordered another big glass of orange juice. He smiled at her and let his face redden. "Uh...well, let's get started then....I don't quite know what Ced told you, but we represent an African-American male named Anthony Heywood, who has some information which, I guess, Cedric thinks

could be of some use to you on this Carol Sesnick matter. However, Mr. Heywood will
need some protection against future
prosecution. He's afraid he is about to be
implicated in a grand larceny case." He looked
down at some prop notes he had in his hand.
"Scribbled this stuff down pretty hastily this
morning," he alibied lamely. "Didn't quite get
it all."

"After Mr. O'Neal called, I checked with the
police." Victoria interrupted. "Tony Heywood's name hasn't entered into any of our
ongoing investigations. However, I ran him
through N.C.I.C. Your client served time in
Raiford Prison for second-degree murder."

"He did?" Beano stammered, "Oh...well, I
guess...I didn't...But that doesn't really change
anything...or does it?" Beano looked nervously at his notes.

"A convicted murderer isn't usually a cred-
ible witness," Victoria negotiated.

"I suppose it's better than nothing though,
isn't it?" Beano said, sounding confused.
"I'm, ah...If I seem a little lost, it's because
I don't do criminal. I'm in our real-estate
department. Do leases and build-to-suit deals
for corporate customers," he explained. Beano
sensed this news warmed her, as Angel set the
juice down in front of him.

"Why don't you tell me what you think you
can contribute to my case?" Victoria said.
"Then we'll see what kind of deal, if any, we
can make."

Beano consulted his notes. "Let's see....Okay,

Heywood was at a table at the Striped Zebra Club in Trenton. It's a gentlemen's club. I use the term loosely." Beano smiled his boyish rainmaker smile. It brought rain, but only a few drops. She smiled back thinly. "Our client heard somebody named Texaco Phillips offer Demo Williams five hundred dollars to help out with some wet work....'Wet work,' I presume, is like killing," he explained, and she smiled patiently. "Later that night, Demo didn't reappear at his house. He was found the next morning inside that stolen Econoline van in Hoboken." Most of this, including Texaco's name, Beano had gotten out of old newspaper articles about the Rina Crime Family and the killing in Hoboken. The rest was pure imagination. He knew it would intrigue Victoria and it did.

She leaned forward. "So, it wasn't Joe Rina who solicited your client's friend to commit murder...it was Texaco Phillips?" she said, taking out a yellow pad and beginning to make notes. "Exactly when did this conversation take place?" she asked.

Beano gave the story a little more gas. He wanted Victoria to think she could pick his pocket. "To be honest, I'm really ill equipped. I don't have enough background to conduct a negotiation. Maybe you could see Ced sometime later this week."

"Look, Mr. Cushbury, I've got to go into court this morning at ten A.M. and shut down a high-profile case I've been working for a year. Once I do that, I can never try Joe Rina for this crime again. Texaco might turn State's evidence if I could roll him. So if you have anything I can use, I need it *now* or not at all."

"I don't know why Ced called me to do this. It's nuts." Beano could see the tightness around her eyes....He had her going.

"Mr. Cushbury, Tommy and Joe Rina killed my only witness, who was also my friend. They killed two wonderful young police officers as well. I want those murderers in jail. You've got to tell me what you have."

Beano looked again at the prop notes in his hand, as if they might somehow hold the answer to his manufactured dilemma. He saw she was about to pounce, so he helped build her confidence with more manufactured confusion. "This stuff mystifies me...." He looked at his notes for a long time. "Oh boy...here's something I forgot, wait a minute."

"Mr. Cushbury, your client's friend, Demo Williams, apparently was contacted by Joe Rina's bodyguard and solicited to commit a murder. If you have something, then damn it, give it to me."

"Oh dear," Beano said weakly, and looked down at his notes again.

"You won't find the answer on that paper. You tell me now, or when Amp Heywood is eventually indicted for that grand larceny, I'll see to it he gets the full jolt. I'll sharpen his heels and drive him into the ground," she said, leaning in toward Beano.

"You'll what?"

"You heard me. If you have information

94

regarding a triple murder, do you really think you can sit there and plead out your two-bit larceny?...This isn't a real-estate lend-lease deal, it's felony hard-ball."

"You...you can't..." Beano started to sputter. "I...represent this man...."

"Watch me." She took out a cellphone and dialed in a number. Then, before hitting SEND, she looked up at him and scowled. "What's it gonna be?" she bluffed angrily.

Beano thought she was even more beautiful mad. "I...I...okay, but at least let me see the case file. If I'm going to do this, I need to look it over first."

He had placed the almost-full glass of orange juice directly in front of him. He reached his right hand abruptly across the table to grab her folders. She started to grab them back and, in the process, he back-handed his orange juice glass over.

"Jesus, how stupid!" she cried, as the full glass of juice filled the lap of her green business suit and began dripping slowly down her legs. She exploded out of the seat and looked down at the mess he had made of her outfit.

"Oh, my goodness," Beano flustered, "how clumsy...how awful..." He grabbed his napkin and began to spread it around on her suit, making it worse.

"Stop it! Just stop it!" she said, then grabbed two napkins off the next table and looked desperately at Angel, the waitress. "Where's the ladies' room?" Angel pointed to a door in the back of the deli. "Stay here," Victoria ordered Beano, then hurried off to repair the damage, leaving her briefcase behind in the confusion.

When she returned, five minutes later, Beano Bates and the Rina files were gone. "Dammit to hell!" she cursed at herself. Her dress was drenched with cold water and pulp shreds and hung on her like a wet saddle blanket. She felt like a fool as she looked down at the empty table. All that was left was the overturned glass of orange juice. Victoria Hart carefully picked it up and wrapped it in a fresh paper napkin. Then she put it into her briefcase and left the delicatessen. She had five minutes to make it to court.

SEVEN

The Yellow Sheet

After nine months and three murders, Victoria Hart voluntarily withdrew the State's case against Joe "Dancer" Rina. The whole process took less than ten minutes. When Judge Goldstone dismissed the case, the little mobster nodded his head as if it had been God's will and slowly got to his feet.

Gerald Cohen was closing up case folders and filing them in his briefcase as the Princeton Glee Club cleared the battlefield, gathering up pens, pencils, case reports, and unused arguments from the long, wooden table. The handsome mobster timed it so that he and Victoria met in the doorway of the courtroom. He graciously stepped aside to let her pass. When they were in the hall, he turned to her....

"It's gratifying when justice finally prevails, isn't it, counselor?"

"Are you talking to me?" she said, stunned by his arrogance.

"I believe I was." He smiled.

"Then tell your blond flunky who stole my case folders this morning to send them back. There's nothing in there I can use against you. This case is done...but I have to turn over my files for review. I'm sure you want my sorry performance evaluated."

"Of course, I don't know what you're talking about. But let me give you a tip, Vicky...I've been very patient with you. I've endured your subpoenas of my friends and business associates. For almost a year, I've put up with your brash, unsubstantiated allegations. There's a part of me that keeps asking why I've been so charitable. I don't have an adequate answer. Perhaps it's because you're an attractive young woman and I was raised to be courteous to women. However, you've used up all my patience. In the future, you might do well to give me lots and lots of room."

"The room I'm planning to give you is about ten feet square and has a view of the rock quarry. Get used to seeing me around, Joe, 'cause I'm just getting started on you."

She turned and walked away from him,

squaring her shoulders, feeling his glare on her back all the way to the elevators. When she turned to push the DOWN button, she saw him still staring. He hadn't moved, but the look on his face transformed him. He no longer looked like a movie star. In that brief glance, she could see inside him as if some mystic chisel had stripped away his beauty and revealed his inner core. In that second, before he turned and walked away, she saw the deadly glare of pure evil. She wondered if she could deal with such a virulent enemy.

Victoria had given the orange juice glass to David Frankfurter before court and he had run it across the courtyard to the police lab. By the time she got back to her office, she had forgotten all about it, but David came through the door with a police printout in his hand.

"You ain't gonna believe this," he said, holding the crime lab report. "We got three good prints off that glass. Index, middle, and thumb, along with a partial palm. This guy you had breakfast with is quite a catch."

"Works for Joe Rina, right?"

"Not that I can tell." He handed her the yellow sheet.

"Beano Bates?" she said, perplexed. "A confidence man?"

"Not just a con man, *the* con man. This guy is reputed to be the best long grifter operating in America. He actually *has* sold the Brooklyn Bridge."

"Come on, that's a joke."

"No joke...It's a scrap iron scam. The way

he worked it, Beano pretended to be a Brooklyn metal stress tester who was fired by the city. He had metal stress fracture X-rays and a buncha official-looking time line analyses. They convinced the mark, who was the greedy owner of a scrap metal company, that the bridge had serious metal fatigue and had been judged unsafe by the civil engineers and was going to be torn down. They said it was all being hushed up because the public outcry would be enormous. They set up a fake auction and this dummy paid a half-a-million dollars to Beano's phony inside man to rig the bids. The same scam was done once by some French sharpers on the Eiffel Tower. Beano Bates is the only white-collar criminal on the current FBI Ten Most Wanted List."

She started to scan the charges against him. "This guy did a nickel in Raiford. Check and see if he was there the same time as Anthony Heywood, a.k.a. Amp."

"Already did. They were cellmates."

"So what the hell does he want with my case file?" she asked, and then looked at David. Both of them were trying to figure it out, but it didn't add up.

"Nothing here ties him to Joe Rina?" she finally asked.

"Naw. Looks like they run in separate gutters."

There was an empty silence in Victoria's office that was interrupted by her phone buzzer. She picked it up and got her secretary, Marie.

"The Gray Ghost wants to see you, stat,"

Marie's voice said, with concern. "The Gray Ghost" was office code for G.G....Gil Green.

"Okay, I'm on my way." She hung up and looked at David Frankfurter. "Gil wants me. What's the official scuttlebutt on this? Am I headed to Hoboken?" she asked.

"Siberia," he replied sadly.

She nodded, then got to her feet and moved slowly from the office, holding Beano's yellow sheet. She paused in the doorway and handed it back. "Put him through the National Crime Information Center computer. Get me a deep check. I particularly wanna see if he's got any connection to Carol Sesnick." Then she turned and walked out of her office and down the hall to the elevators.

♠ ♠ ♠

"These kinds of things are always hard, Victoria," Gil said. This time he was looking at her and she could tell he'd rehearsed what he was about to say. A bad sign. He had some notecards he was referring to on his desk in front of him. Another bad sign. She assumed he'd been briefed by Labor Relations on how to handle this meeting to avoid a wrongful-termination suit. "The whole Joe Dancer disaster is going to have to be reviewed. I know you may view this as unfair, but as the Prosecuting Attorney, I think you may have made some decisions in this investigation that bear further examination."

"Such as...? Every move in this case was approved by you, Gil."

"Victoria, I don't want to get into this with you now. You are temporarily being reassigned to a lower-profile situation. I want you to work the booking desk for a while."

"You want me to be the booking clerk!" she said, appalled. That was a job usually held by the most junior member of the D.A.'s staff. It involved reviewing arrests the police brought in and deciding if there was enough evidence to warrant a criminal prosecution. Then the clerk turned the preliminary decisions over to a senior prosecutor for approval. Even though the job was always done by an attorney, "clerk" was not an accidental description.

"You can check with Betty on where she wants to put you. It's only temporary, just until the review is complete. You're still on full staff salary. I got that for you, but I think we all need to keep our heads down right now. I'm instructing you to make no statements to the press about this situation." Then his secretary buzzed. He picked up the phone. "Oh, right. Sorry...Yes, right away." He looked at his watch, shook his head, hung up, and got to his feet. It was bad theater. The buzz from his secretary was pre-arranged to bring the meeting to a quick close. "Sorry, Vicky, I'm late for an appointment," he lied, and waited impatiently for her to leave.

She slowly got to her feet. He looked uncomfortable. Gil was non-confrontational, which she always thought was strange behavior for a District Attorney.

"This is chickenshit, Gil. I deserve better than this."

"I'm sure your review will substantiate all of your decisions, but until it comes down, I think this is best. I've already given your background notes and motion files for the Rina case to Mark Switzer. He's doing the prelim. Turn the rest of your Rina stuff over to him ASAP."

She didn't have the nerve to tell him that the rest of her case folders had been stolen from her.

Victoria was popular in the office. She often stayed late and listened while young prosecutors ran their cases by her, hoping Tricky Vicky could find some legal loopholes or creative strategy they could use. She knew there would be a crowd at the elevator wanting to know what happened. She couldn't bear to face them now, so she took the back stairs down to the trial division on the fourth floor, moved quietly past the Xerox room into her private corner office, and closed the door. In Gil's office, she'd been strangely submissive, as if there were some specific protocol for that kind of event that demanded a level attitude. All the meeting lacked was a blindfold and a last cigarette. Now she could feel her anger building. She cursed herself for not having chosen the moment to tell the D.A. what a low, shifty coward he was. She stood behind her desk, chewing a fingernail, looking out her corner window onto State Street Park across from the Criminal Courts Building. Her office was cramped but pin-neat; files and folders arranged by case with tight, usable precision.

The phone rang. She snapped it up.

"Victoria Hart," she said sharply, then her mood seemed to change. "Ted Calendar? From WTRN-TV?" she finally said.

♠ ♠ ♠

The studio at WTRN-TV was small and stuffy, and Ted Calendar looked much older in person than he did on TV. Victoria had let the makeup lady dust her with powder, but there wasn't much she could do with the short hairstyle.

Victoria was miked and sat in a straight-back chair opposite Ted. There was a fake fireplace behind them; a blue oval carpet and bookshelves in the wings completed the economical set. Ted Calendar was reading notes on his lap almost as if she weren't there. They were a few minutes from taping.

"Thanks for this opportunity to tell my side of it," Victoria said.

"Too bad about the Rina trial. Lotta fish got cooked but no dinner served, huh?" he said, still not looking up at her.

She found herself studying his too-blond wig, which was leaking perspiration down the side

103

of his face. Then he looked up suddenly and caught her staring.

"Okay, Vicky..."

"I prefer Victoria."

"I prefer Theodore," he said with a smirk. "Lotta good it does me. What we have here is a live-on-tape interview. It will be broadcast on the evening news in a two-and-a-half-minute segment. We're going to have a hard out. I'll signal you when we're down to five seconds. Wrap it up fast, or you'll get cut off by the booth."

"Okay," she said, not sure exactly what she was going to say, but because of the anger in her, she was fearing the worst.

The stage manager held up five fingers, then ticked them down, one at a time, until he had a fist up and Ted grinned at the camera.

"Welcome to 'New Jersey Talking.' I'm Ted Calendar, and this is our fireside chat with people in the news." He turned to Victoria. "I'm here with Vicky Hart, the Prosecutor just coming off a devastating situation in her trial against alleged mobster Joe Rina. Nice to have you with us, Vicky."

"Thanks. Nice to be here, Teddy," she said, and watched him wince slightly.

"So the trial isn't going to happen. A lot has been made of this prosecution, yet you withdrew your case before opening arguments. Is that it? After all the hoopla, it just goes over the cliff without even a skidmark?"

"The fact that my witness, Carol Sesnick,

and two heroic police officers were brutally murdered and thrown down an elevator shaft is a real tragedy, and it's the reason we're not going to proceed with the attempted murder prosecution. I don't think it takes a rocket scientist to know that these deaths, timed just days before opening arguments, were not coincidental."

"You're accusing Joseph Rina of these murders?" Ted said, sensing a story and leaning forward in his chair.

"You bet."

Ted Calendar looked at her skeptically. "You're saying that you have evidence that Joe Rina killed these three people?"

"I didn't say I had evidence. I said he did it."

"As a prosecuting attorney here in New Jersey, you can't say something like that unless you intend to back it up."

"Says who?"

"I would guess Gil Green. Gil would have both legal and ethical concerns, I think."

"This would be the same Gil Green who encouraged me, at length, to prosecute Joe Rina for attempted murder; who made a TV career out of talking about it for five months to get his political stock up, and now, because my key witness was murdered, is having me reviewed for doing it in the first place? I don't think we need to worry too much about Gil Green's ethical position. Let's worry instead about what happened to Carol Sesnick, Tony Corollo, and Bobby Manning. Those three people were my friends. Those three people were heroes. They gave their lives trying to do the right thing." She turned in her chair and faced the camera. "Joe Rina, if you're out there listening to me, I'm not going to rest until I see you brought to justice. I don't know how I'm going to prove you brutally killed my friends, but I'm going to." Her eyes were pinholes of burning anger as she looked into the camera. "I'm going to see you behind bars. I won't sleep until that day comes."

Ted Calendar looked into the lens as the camera faced him. In his "ear angel," the director told him to go right to commercial. "Powerful stuff..." he said to the camera. "We'll be right back," and they cut to black. He looked at her. "I'd like to do a second segment. Follow this up, if you can stay."

"I think I've done enough damage to myself," she said, and unhooked her mike. She walked off the stage and out of the studio. She got in her car and drove along the Delaware River to the John Fitch Parkway, heading north. Without really planning it, she was heading to her parents' house in Wallingford, Connecticut. She knew the broadcast would end her career in the D.A.'s office. Halfway there, tears started rolling down her cheeks. She wasn't making a sound, but the tears flowed. It was strange, as if sheer force of will prohibited complete emotional collapse, but she couldn't stop the tears. Victoria Hart was hangin' on for dear life and running home to her mother.

EIGHT

The Broadcast

The pictures were more gruesome than he'd imagined: shots of him unconscious in the pre-op theater, his head swollen, his two middle teeth missing. He had blood all over him; his jaw was broken. He was covered with a cold sweat as he studied them.

"Really knocked the shit out of me, didn't he, Rog?" Beano said, and laid the hospital photos aside.

He'd been through the files two times, to no avail. The whole Amp Heywood/Cedric O'Neal/Martin Cushbury scam on Victoria Hart had produced very little...only the horrible pictures, which had knotted his stomach and brought the unreasonable fear bubbling up, filling his senses, like untreated sewage. Beano had read her trial strategy, which didn't help him either. He had her opening statement, which he thought was inventive and dramatic and just ever so tricky: *"More than a man was beaten in the parking lot of the Greenborough Country Club,"* she had intended to say. *"The boundaries of self-restraint and human decency were also viciously and demonically attacked."* Pretty good. She didn't have Beano, so society and human decency were standing in for him. Beano had read it twice and found nothing in it besides some nice imagery and three spelling errors. There were no background facts on Joseph or Tommy. If he was going to run a Big Store confidence game on the Rinas, he would desperately need to know everything about them. But very little of it was here. He had swung for a grand slam and had whiffed completely.

Roger-the-Dodger rolled onto his side, sound asleep. He barked softly and growled, then his feet started running in the air. The terrier was on the foot of the motel bed, involved in some important canine adventure. Beano had the TV on, but was not paying much attention until he caught a glimpse of Victoria Hart. He lunged over Roger, across the room, and turned up the volume. The dog looked up, annoyed. Beano caught the last part of the interview where Victoria Hart stomped on Gil Green's balls, then turned to the camera and promised Joe Rina that she would get him.

Beano waited until the news came back on. Ted Calendar was at his anchor desk in a blue blazer; the red-haired co-anchor, Shelly September, was shaking her vinyl hair in disbelief.

"Quite an interview, Ted," she said.

"Yes, it was. We've asked Gil Green to comment, Shelly, and he said that the District Attorney's office doesn't support Miss Hart's position. In fact, he told me she had been demoted, and perhaps her anger over that produced these remarks. They also said they would have a full statement sometime tomorrow."

"A very strange ending to a very strange saga,"

Shelly said in mock amazement and then turned to other news.

Beano muted the TV and looked down at Roger. "What the fuck is she doing, attacking a monster like that? She's gonna get herself killed."

Roger had no answer, so Beano got up and went into the bathroom and slapped water on his face; then he started to gather up his cosmetics. He took them back into the bedroom, reached under the bed, and pulled out a canvas bag. Inside it was a three-gallon pickle jar with an air-tight metal top. Through the glass jar he could see rolls of hundred-dollar bills. He surveyed his layout money skeptically. "Ain't gonna be enough, Rog. For what I gotta pull, I'm gonna need a lot more." The dog yawned. "The answer is we gotta get Vicky Hart to tell us where Tommy and Joe have their money stashed. We better get to this woman before the Rinas do." He continued packing. He had seen Gil Green on TV three or four times already that afternoon. He turned the volume back up and started flipping around, looking for the District Attorney, who had been getting a lot of news play because of the abrupt dismissal of the high-profile case. He finally found him on Channel Two. It was a taped courthouse interview right after the Prosecution had waved the white flag.

"Of course...this was absolutely expected after the eyewitness was lost. Ms. Hart has made some serious errors in judgment here and we're going to be looking into it."

Beano was listening to the rhythm of Gil Green's speech, the soft low-energy presentation.

He turned to Roger. "Of course...this was absolutely expected after the eyewitness was lost. Ms. Hart has made some serious errors in judgment here and we're going to be looking into it." Beano's mimicking got very close to Gil Green's pinched voice on the first attempt. He thought it needed to be a little higher, a little reedier. He tried it a few more times. Finally, Roger barked at him.

"You think?" Beano asked. "Okay, let's try it."

He moved to the phone book, looked up the D.A.'s office, and dialed. Once he got the switchboard, he asked for Victoria Hart's extension. After several rings, he was forwarded to the Reception Desk just before it shut down for the night.

"Hi, who is this?" he asked in Gil Green's soft, non-confrontational, passive-aggressive voice.

"It's Donna. Is that you, Mr. Green?" the receptionist answered.

"Yes, Donna, this is Gilbert. I'm trying desperately to reach Victoria and I fear I've left my book in the office. Do you have her home telephone and perhaps her address?"

"Yes, Mr. Green," Donna said, eager to please, "but I don't think she's at home just now."

"Do you know where she might be?"

"She's at her parents' house in Wallingford, Connecticut. I don't have the number, but I think it's listed."

"And her father would be...?" He let it hang in the air with arch theatricality, liking the way he was doing the impression. Sometimes, he thought he could even give Dana Carvey a run for it.

"Her father's name is Harry Hart. Harry and Elizabeth Hart."

"How very American," he said condescendingly, and hung up without saying good-bye. Minutes later he had their phone number. He dialed, but got no answer. He tried calling again at seven-ten, then at seven-forty and at eight P.M., but still no answer. *Maybe they're out to dinner*, he thought, *or maybe I'm already too late.*

♠ ♠ ♠

The restaurant was on the ninth fairway of the public links in Wallingford, Connecticut. The windows overlooked the course. Harry and Elizabeth Hart listened earnestly as their daughter finished her tale.

Harry was a retired insurance executive. He had a ruddy complexion and silver-white hair. After he retired, he'd started wearing out-of-style madras coats and white linen pants—clothes Victoria thought he would never have worn ten years ago. Harry was very proud of his daughter. He thought she was the most strikingly wonderful person he had ever known.

Elizabeth Hart had her wheelchair parked

up close to the table. She was holding her daughter's hand under the drape of the table-cloth. Her hands were too slender and heavily veined. The right side of her face sagged and she had lost the ability to walk since her last stroke. Elizabeth Hart's mind was still tracking, even though she slurred her speech in her soft Texas accent. It was hard for Victoria to see her mother this way....She had always been so vital, so beautiful. It had been her mother who had constantly pried Victoria's hand off the achievement throttle as a child, urging her to develop her playful side. It had been a valiant, if unrewarding struggle.

"I suppose it's already aired by now. Thank God you don't get WTRN here in Connecticut," Victoria said, and then they sat in silence until a waiter cleared the plates.

"You did the right thing, Victoria," her father said. "You must do what you feel is right. From everything you've told me about Gil Green, he's not a good manager of his people." He was being the business expert now, falling back on twenty years of management experience at Penn Mutual Insurance.

"But see's been 'ere almos five 'ears, 'arry," her mother slurred, the Texas drawl making it even harder to understand. "Where 'ill see go?" Her mother, as usual, had caught the heart of the problem: Where could she go to practice law after all this?

"So, you stay up here for a while, till it all blows over." Her father raced ahead: "You hang up a shingle. I know some people who will throw work your way. Real estate or business contracts, lotta work like that around here."

"I'm a criminal attorney, Dad." Then she paused before going on. "...And I have another problem...."

They both anxiously waited for her.

"I...maybe..." She stopped and looked down. "Maybe I need to do something about these murders, prove what happened to Carol."

"Let the police do that," Harry said sternly, but Elizabeth squeezed her hand under the table.

"But, Dad, they won't be able to. Joseph Rina is very smart. He doesn't make mistakes. The only mistake I think he ever made was beating this John Doe, whoever he was, with a nine-iron in front of a witness. I need to find a way to get Rina. A police investigation won't do it; there are too many rules, plus evidentiary and procedural roadblocks. He'll never go down that way. I need something else, something..." She hesitated, looking for the right word, then chose the one that had been linked to her by the press. "...something tricky," she finished.

"I won't hear of this," her father said. "If Joe Rina is everything you say, and I'm sure he is, he's not somebody you want to be messing around with. I know I can't tell you what to do anymore, but, sweetheart, I can't bear the thought of you being in danger. It's not your job to go out and try to settle society's debts."

She looked at him and finally nodded.

On the way out of the restaurant, her cell-phone rang. Her father had wheeled her mother over to get their coats when she answered it. It was David Frankfurter.

"You sure knocked the flies out of the garbage," he said.

"Lotta pissed-off people down there, I'll bet," she said softly.

"Yeah, listen, there's something else you oughta know. I got a kickback from the N.C.I.C. deep check on Beano Bates."

"Not that it matters anymore, but let's hear."

"His father was Jacob Bates. The Bates family is sort of well known. There are three thousand of them. Most of the family is on the hustle. There's even an N.C.I.C. information number on them, with arrest records going back six years. If you want, I could order it up, but it's gonna be a phone book."

"Save it. Maybe later. Is that all?"

"That's not the main reason I called." He paused for effect. "Beano Bates's mother's maiden name is Sesnick."

"*What?*" she said; her voice was suddenly too loud in the restaurant entry. Her mother and father turned to look.

"Carol Sesnick was related to him," David finished.

"You think Bates stole the file because he's trying to get even with Joe Rina for killing Carol?"

"Well, he sure didn't steal it because he needed the practice," David answered. "The Sesnick family, by the way, is also in the computer. They're a family of American Gypsies. They work crowds in the Midwest, mostly pickpockets, some tarot card and palm-reading scams."

"Jeez" was about all she could think to say.

"I've got Beano Bates's mug shots and file pictures here. You want, I can fax 'em to your mom and dad's house."

"Yeah." She gave him the number, then stood there, looking out the front door of the restaurant. Her father rolled her mother up to her.

"Ready?" he said.

"Be right there, Dad," she replied, and he pushed the wheelchair out and gave the valet the parking ticket.

"Listen," David continued, "I've had a couple a' calls. It's kinda goofy around here. That Ted Calendar piece was courageous but maybe not too smart."

"I know...I'm sorry. I couldn't just do nothing. It was stupid, but it's done."

"Don't let these assholes run you off, Victoria. They want to sell justice by the pound down here. You're one of the ones who never let that happen."

"Thanks, David. Don't worry, I'm hanging tough," she lied. They both knew that Gil Green would never let her come back.

♠ ♠ ♠

That same evening, Joe Rina had been having a celebration in the plush dining room at

115

the Trenton House. At the table was his fiancée, Stacy DiMantia, and her father, Paul. Tommy and a hooker he had paid five hundred dollars to made up the rest of the party. The French dining room was named La Réserve. Their waiter was named Giraud Le Mousant; Tommy's hooker was named Calliope Love. She laughed loudly and called Tommy "the best little jockey who ever rode her." Joe was getting angry at her vulgarity and was about to say something when the maître d' came over and whispered that Joe had a phone call. He took the call in the lobby. It was from Gerald Cohen.

"Just think you oughta know that you were accused of murdering the witness and two cops on Ted Calendar's TV program tonight."

"Come on, Gerry, they've got no evidence of that....You sure? Who's stupid enough to do that?"

"Tricky Vicky. I've got a copy of the segment. I'll send it over."

"She's not that stupid," Joe said. "What's she think she's doing?"

After dinner, Tommy and Joe watched the tape alone in the Trenton House manager's office. When it was over, Tommy was fuming. "This fucking bitch! Where's she get off? I'm gonna use this cunt up."

"You're going to calm down and watch your language," Joe said, without emotion. He put a tasseled loafer up on the side of the desk and looked at his tan silk socks, which came from Hong Kong and cost sixty dollars.

"We're not going to do anything right now. You got that, Tommy?"

"Joey, accidents happen," Tommy pleaded. "People get hit by falling safes...a car fulla beaners runs a light and whammo, you got avocado salad."

"*You will not do anything*. Calm down, okay? I'll think of something....We'll take care of it at the appropriate time."

Tommy figured the appropriate time was now, but he didn't say anything. They got up; Joe removed the cassette, then turned to his older brother. "One other thing, Tommy. This sperm bank you brought with you...can you possibly get her to shut up?"

Tommy looked at his handsome brother. Sometimes Joe got on Tommy's nerves. With his good looks, manners, and Italian suits, Joe didn't have to work to get a good piece of ass....Since he was thirteen, all Joe had to do was crook a finger. Tommy choked back his anger over the criticism. He knew his little brother was the boss. That had been established when they were barely in their teens. Tommy wasn't about to change things now, but sometimes Joe could really piss him off.

♠ ♠ ♠

It was only nine o'clock, but Victoria was exhausted. She guessed it was from the mental anguish of what had happened in the last two days. She was glad to be back home, in her own bedroom. She put on her old flannel

117

nightgown that she had had since before college. She paused on the way to her bed and looked at her old cheerleading photos from ninth grade. She had been the team captain. She was kneeling in front of the rally squad, her pom-poms beside her, the big white *W* on her sweater. She was the only one in the picture who wasn't smiling. She let her eyes roam the room. Victoria had never allowed herself any leisure time here. She had studied hard, never wanting any seams to show. She had wanted to be perfect. She tried to recapture the countless hours spent in this room, to review them like favorite moments in a scrapbook...but there were none. This was not a room full of fun memories. It was a work space.

Her mother had picked the blue and white wallpaper. It had ballerinas on it; they were twirling, arms outstretched or over their heads, frozen in perfect pliés and pirouettes. She could remember lying in bed as a girl, looking at the dancers on the wall, wondering what it would be like to dance like that, to be free, whirling with abandon, no cares, no fears, no finals. She could not imagine it. Her life was deadlines and due dates. She could never pull her eyes off the finish line. Not then, not now. She wondered where that trait had come from and what it had cost. Her parents had tried to find outside interests for her, but no matter what the activity, Victoria always found the discipline in it. She had pushed her tennis lessons all the way to the Junior Semi-finals;

her cheerleading team won the State Championship. Everything she did was planned out, plotted, and delivered on.

Law had been the perfect career for a beautiful over-achiever. She had been top of her class at Dartmouth and had turned down several prestigious law firms to go into combat training on the D.A.'s staff. She had been called Tricky there, but she knew "tricky" was hardly the word to define her. A better word was "relentless." She refused to give up on a case if she thought the perp was guilty. She would pursue new angles when a confession or evidence had been thrown out. She would research and study and dig till it hurt. She would often come up with unorthodox strategies that worked. Now, at age thirty-five, it had all come crashing down because of a small, wavy-haired mobster who walked on his toes. She couldn't understand how a road so carefully paved, so meticulously chosen, could end in such disaster.

She heard the door of the small elevator close downstairs. Her father had installed the lift two years ago, after her mother had the first stroke. The elevator hummed and Victoria heard it stop upstairs. Then she heard her mother's voice outside her door.

"'ictoria...?"

"Yes, Mom."

"'an I 'ome in?"

"Sure." She got out of bed, turned on the light as her mother came in, and set the brake on the wheelchair.

"Honey, I 'ant you read 'iss," her mother slurred, and handed Victoria a sheet of paper filled with her shaky but legible handwriting.

Victoria read it out loud: "People have to attain their own destinies. Sometimes only you can know what you must do. A long life is nice...and I wish it for you because I love you. But a life full of choices forced on you by others is not worth living."

They sat looking at each other. Her mother had come to her rescue thousands of times in this room, sat patiently helping her with her homework, helping her with her life.

Victoria moved to her mother, bent over, and gave her a hug. "How did I get so lucky to have you guys as parents?" she finally said.

"We lucky ones," her mother answered.

Somewhere in this moment the phone had rung downstairs. Victoria had not paid it any attention. Now her father was calling for her. She moved out of her room and into the hall where the phone sat on a French Provincial table.

"Hello..." she said tentatively.

"Martin Cushbury. I hope that stain came out. Should have. Citrus juice generally isn't too tough."

"Whatta you want?" she said angrily.

"You sure stuck your broom handle into a Sicilian hornets' nest, Vicky."

"I want my case folders back."

"I'm not so sure I would have flipped off Joe Rina on TV, but other than that, it was a pretty good performance. It's about time somebody gave Gil Green a tonsillectomy."

"Just send my case folders back....There's nothing in there you can use. Beyond that, I don't have anything to say to you."

"Don't be so sure. I was wondering if maybe we could get together, have a little talk about the Rina brothers."

"We're not going to get together. You're wanted by the FBI. I don't need to add harboring a fugitive, and aiding and abetting, to my list of this week's fuck-ups."

"FBI?" He said it as if he'd never heard of them.

"For a clever guy, you had one clumsy moment. You left your orange juice glass on the table. I ran the prints. When I pulled your priors out of the computer, the yellow sheet went all the way to the floor."

"I like to stay busy," he said without humor.

"No kidding. I also know that Carol Sesnick was a member of your family. For that reason, I'm going to cut you some slack....I could've agreed to meet you again, then shown up with an FBI escort."

"You can trust me, Vicky. I think, from what I've heard, we both want the same thing."

"Send my files back. The address is on the manila folder. And don't call me again." She hung up the phone and looked over and saw her father standing in the hall. He had a question mark on his face and was holding a fax from David Frankfurter.

"This was in the machine downstairs," he said, handing it to her.

She looked at the N.C.I.C. printout and the fax with Beano's picture. In the photo he had black hair and no mustache. She didn't want to talk about any of this with her parents, so she gave them both a kiss, then went back to her room and climbed into bed, pulling the covers up under her chin. But her mind would not shut down. She was thinking about Beano Bates....Who was he? Had he been close to Carol? How could Carol have been in a family of Gypsies who roamed the Midwest picking pockets? Why had she not told Victoria what was going on? Had Victoria been played for a sucker? All of this went through her mind, and then another thought struck her. She got up and moved to her desk and turned on the lamp. She looked closely at the faxed picture of Beano Bates. She tried to remember the pictures of Frank Lemay that had been taken in the hospital. She wondered if Beano Bates could *be* Frank Lemay. It was hard to tell. The hospital photos had shown a man who had been beaten almost beyond recognition. Still, the age was right, the hair color similar. She moved back to her bed and got under the covers again. She tried to figure out what it could mean. New questions filled her head: *If Beano was Frank, then wasn't it too big a coincidence that his cousin Carol was in that parking lot to witness the beating? Did that mean Carol had been lying? Had her friend played her for a fool? Was Carol going to manufacture testimony, lie in court, because she knew Beano's life was still in danger? Had Victoria so badly misjudged the situation?*

A full moon was low on the horizon and shot cold silver light through the open window. She looked at the ballerinas on the wallpaper, spinning, turning, throwing themselves around with graceful abandon, dancing on her walls in the moonlight. They whirled haphazardly, motionless, in two dimensions. They were whirling without result, just like Victoria's troubled thoughts.

NINE

Information Station

Victoria drove back to Trenton on Sunday night. She had notified the D.A.'s office that she was going to take some vacation time. On Monday morning, she intended to sleep late but woke up at six A.M., just like always. She showered, toweling her short hair, forgoing the dryer. She put on jeans and a T-shirt, grabbed her navy pea-coat, and went out for breakfast.

At ten o'clock, she found herself sitting alone on a bench in Bromley Park, watching birds flutter around, trying to steal an old sandwich crust out of a trash basket. She wasn't sure what she would do. She had decided to set out to prove that the Rina brothers had killed Carol, Tony, and Bobby, but her expertise was litigation, not investigation. She wondered if she could hire Reuben Dickson, a retired homicide detective whom she had befriended. He was good, methodical and not afraid to dig deep, but he was old with arthritis. Last time she'd seen him, he could barely walk. She had several thousand dollars in the bank she could use to hire him. She thought she still had his home phone number from a case they'd worked on together just before he pulled the pin. She was just getting set to leave the park when a small terrier came up and sat in front of her. She looked down at him.

"Hi, honey," she said, and he jumped up on her lap and licked under her chin. She laughed and scratched him behind the ears. Then, without warning, he moved off her lap, snapped up her purse in his mouth, and took off across the park with it. "Stop, come back," she yelled foolishly. Then she jumped up and ran after him. The dog raced into the women's toilet. She chased him in there and slammed the door shut so that he couldn't get out. The terrier came out from the stall and dropped the purse at her feet.

"Bad dog," she said and picked it up and looked inside. "Son-of-a-bitch!" she said, discovering her wallet was gone. "You little thief, what did you do with my wallet?" she asked the dog.

Then Beano Bates stepped out from one of the stalls, holding it in his hand. He had her case folders under his other arm. "He's not the smoothest dip in the world, but in a pinch, it's better then breaking into a house." He was counting her money. "You don't carry much cash, do you?"

"You know something?"

"What?"

"I've never met a bigger asshole."

"Compliment accepted," he said. "I need your help. I think we want the same thing."

"Highly unlikely," she said, thinking he seemed like a completely different person from the one in the restaurant. That man had been unsure and flustered; this one was in charge and self-assured. She could see he was a remarkably good actor. She decided she couldn't trust him for a second.

"Carol was your friend, I could tell. I could see on TV how much you cared for her—"

"Hey," she interrupted, "forget the rub-down."

"You know, for a good lawyer, you aren't much of a listener."

"It's because most everything you say is honeybaked bullshit."

"I'm going to get even with Joe and Tommy Rina for killing Carol. But to do that, I need information. I stole your case files because I thought the depositions you took would be in there. I missed. I need to know where these guys keep their pickle jars buried."

"Their what?"

"Money. I need to know what businesses they're in. How their action works, what peo-

ple they're afraid of, who and where the lever-
age is."

"I hope they're afraid of me." She glowered.

"No offense, Vicky, but they're not afraid
of you. You had your shot, you whiffed it. Now
it's my turn. I'm gonna get these two *gavones*.
All I need from you is an hour or two of careful briefing."

"And just how do you figure to get Tommy
and Joe Rina?" she said, getting mildly interested.

"I was thinking I'd get Tommy to testify
against Joe, get him to turn State's evidence
on the Trenton Tower murders."

"You're a moron."

"I am?" He smiled.

"Yeah, you are. Tommy and Joe are brothers. Tommy thinks his younger brother walks
on water. He's been protecting Joe since the
sixth grade. Tommy's never gonna testify
against Joe. Won't ever happen."

"I don't think their relationship has ever been
adequately tested."

"And *you're* gonna test it?" She was sure he
was wasting her time. This guy had nothing;
she'd be better off taking her chances with an
arthritic homicide dick.

"Hey, you know what a good mark and a mob
boss have in common?"

"What?"

"Greed. Without greed no con works. I'm
gonna throw a few pounds of red meat between
those two Rottweilers and see what happens."

"You're Frank Lemay, aren't you?" she

said, abruptly changing the subject. "You're the one who got beaten at the Greenborough Country Club."

"Yes," he finally said. "Unfortunately, that was me."

"So, if you had come forward instead of running from the hospital, Carol probably wouldn't be dead."

He looked at her for a long moment. "We could do this together, for Carol." And then he said the first thing that touched her: "I loved her, Victoria. She was my only friend in the world."

His eyes were so sad, in that instant she could see how deep his affection for Carol was.

"I'm gonna get Tommy Rina to testify against Joe," he said, with anger in his voice that made her wonder if he just might be able to do it. "All I need from you is a little information."

"Why would I help you?" she said. "You're a fugitive. If I get caught helping you, I could get disbarred, or put in jail."

"It's the price for getting this back," he said, holding up her case folders.

"Tough break there, pal. I don't need that anymore....I've decided to move on."

"Okay, then we share the guilt for Carol. It was because of me she was there in the first place, but you blew the security arrangements. We both need to set things right for that."

She stood silently, her mind a slate of unanswered questions. Now, not just her thoughts, but her emotions were whirling like the ballerinas on her bedroom wall.

"You've read my sheet....I'm not a fuck-up when it comes to this kinda thing. I'll turn these two sharks against one another, but I need information. I can't put a game together unless I know the layout....I need a clear picture of their personal and financial setup to take them down."

They stood in the bathroom with its pungent smell of urine and disinfectant while they evaluated one another. Roger-the-Dodger finally broke the tension, his sharp bark cracking against their eardrums.

"If I help you, what's in it for me?" she asked.

"Satisfaction; knowing you helped pull these two guys under, for Carol's sake."

She suddenly knew what she wanted. She looked at Beano Bates and then down at the dog, who was still sitting at her feet, wagging his tail as if he wanted to be congratulated for stealing her purse.

"Satisfaction isn't enough," she finally said. "If you're going to run a scam on these guys, I want to be part of it."

Beano was caught off-guard. "It's not your style, Victoria. You've got target fixation. That's an okay trait for a D.A., but it's a horrible one for a grifter. Sometimes, in a scam, you have to do everything backward...you have to hold on by letting go, increase by diminishing, multiply by dividing. You'd never be able to do that."

"I'm not interested in your assessment of me. The fact is, I do know about the Rinas; I know where their businesses are, where their hidden gambling interests are, who they associate with, even where their mistresses live...the whole stinking clove of garlic. You want to know what I know, that's my condition."

"I can't," he said slowly.

"Then you don't get anything," she said. "You can drop those file folders in any convenient trash can."

There was a long moment as they stood in the dimly lit toilet. Then she turned to leave.

"Okay," he finally said, "but if I take you along, you stay back. You're just an information station, a resource."

"Go fuck yourself," she said in anger. "You come to me, spill orange juice all over my best suit, steal my case files, pretend to be half-a-dozen people from Amp Heywood to Martin Cushbury...Christ, you have more personalities than Sybil. No, dammit! Carol was my friend too. You take me because you *need* me. We'll negotiate the rest as we go."

"It's not a courtroom, Vicky. There are no rules. No legal equations to stick to, no motions or counter-motions, no judge to referee."

"Yes or no?" she finally said.

Beano could see the fire in her eyes. She was standing before him, defiant and beautiful. He didn't know which of those traits made up his mind, but in that second, he knew the ground had shifted between them.

"Be at the Motel 6 at eight o'clock tomorrow morning. But the first time I need something and you come up dry, I'm gonna leave you on the side of the road."

"You can try," she said.

He moved past her, out of the toilet.

"Hey," she said, and he turned. "Aren't you going to give me my wallet back?"

Irritated, he threw it to her and dropped her case folders in the metal trash container inside the bathroom. She could dig them out if she wanted. Outside he whistled for Roger-the-Dodger, but the terrier didn't come. He went back inside to find the dog looking up at Victoria Hart as if he'd just found the Virgin Mother.

"Come on, Roger. You can drool on her tomorrow," he said.

Reluctantly, the dog followed him out of the restroom.

"What an asshole," Victoria said, then she left the bathroom without even looking at the folders that contained her most humilitating legal defeat.

Part Three
LETTING GO

"HOLD ON BY LETTING GO; INCREASE BY
DIMINISHING; MULTIPLY BY DIVIDING."
—Billie Sol Estes

TEN

"Paper Collar" John

They were standing in the morning sunshine outside Beano's Motel 6 near Trenton. Rusting Pontiacs and primered pickups dripped oil and morning dew.

"We'll take your car," he said, looking at the spotless new white Nissan parked behind her.

"Who's paying for all this?" she asked, as they moved to the car and she got behind the wheel.

Beano put his suitcases and canvas bag in the back seat. He opened the passenger door for Roger. "Atlantic City," he said, without answering her question.

"Why?" she said stoically.

"That's where 'Paper Collar' John is meeting me," he replied, leaving her in just as much confusion.

She snorted her anger, got the car going, and left the seedy motel behind. Roger-the-Dodger found a place right next to Victoria's thigh and curled up there, chin on his paw. He shot Beano a satisfied look.

"I want to know how we're going to fund this operation and why we are going to Atlantic City. I'd like an answer," she said as calmly as she could.

The car was now out on Interstate 295 heading south.

"My uncle John Bates is there," he said. "He's

got my mobile home with all my tricks of the trade aboard."

Beano reached into the back seat and pulled the canvas bag onto his lap. He opened it and pulled out a large glass pickle jar full of cash.

"Here's some of the front money," he said. "Bet you thought I was gonna try and use your maxed-out Visa card."

"You'll never get your hands on it."

"Already did: 596 4376 72 976," he said from memory, then grinned. "The moral of that story is: Never give your purse to a friendly dog."

She looked at him with disgust.

"Don't worry, your balance couldn't buy Roger here a nice dinner." He tapped the pickle jar. "This is everything I have left in the world. Comes to fifty-two thousand dollars and change. When I took the jolt in Raiford, the Feds used their asset seizure law to clean me out, but they missed this. This is seed money, but it's not enough. We need to triple it."

"We need *one hundred and fifty thousand dollars* to run this con?" Victoria was shocked at the size of that figure.

"It's going to be a Big Store. We're gonna set up a trap. I'm gonna run a moose pasture con on Tommy. That means we gotta buy a thousand gallons of paint and set up a phony international conglomerate with secretaries, asset trading, computers, and original art. It's gotta look so legit that Tommy and his accountant won't question it for a minute. That's gonna take some serious seed money."

"Where are we gonna get another hundred thousand?" she asked, letting her confusion about the moose pasture go for a minute.

"I thought it would be nice if Tommy and Joey funded this thing. They're pricks. They killed Carol. Pisses me off. So I think they should put up the money."

"How are we gonna do that?"

"Okay, Vicky, that's where you come in."

"I really prefer 'Victoria.'"

"Of course you do. 'Victoria' suits you. 'Vicky' doesn't have enough cobwebs on it."

She shot him a cold look.

"Okay, smart guy, so how do I come in?" She put on her turn signal and got into the fast lane.

"Tommy and Joe Rina are Atlantic City based. These two goombas make lotsa money on drugs, loan sharking, prostitution, whatever. Their problem is they can't spend it because they can't show the Feds where it came from. That means they gotta have some kinda money laundry nearby to wash their illegitimate funds. I want to get the front money by hitting their laundry, 'cause they can't squeal to the law afterward for fear they'll give up the operation. It'll be some kinda business that runs on cash. A casino is a perfect laundry, but the gambling commissions in Nevada, Jersey, and Louisiana won't license these two clowns because of their alleged criminal backgrounds. That means it'll probably be a chain of video arcades or parking garages...someplace where they can rig up bigger profits than they really have, then pay taxes on the phantom cash and get the money out so they can use it. Otherwise, Uncle Sam will build a tax case against 'em....That's a case where the government proves they spend more than they make."

"I know how upside-down tax prosecutions work, Beano. I'm not from Cowlick, Kansas."

Beano closed his eyes at that, then went on. "Okay, so then you know what I'm looking for. Anything like that in the file?"

"Yeah," she said, and looked over at him, determined to make him ask. She didn't like his loose, breezy manner; he was way too cocky for her taste, and if she was going to have to spend any time with him, she would need to bring him down a few notches.

"So let's go. Let's hear it...or do I gotta get on my knees here?"

"I thought con men were supposed to be charming." she sneered. "You're just rude."

"You *do* want me to beg."

"I want you to stop coming on like you own the show. I'm not going to just blindly follow you around. If I ask you a question, I expect a straight answer. I'm not some table-dancer you picked up in a bar; I'm a prosecutor with a pretty good analytical mind."

"*Ex*-prosecutor. And here's a tip, it's never very effective to do your own commercials. Always get a singer to do them for you...works much better," he said.

She continued on, "If I like what I hear, then I'll cut loose some information."

"Turn around," he said dully.

"Huh?"

"This isn't gonna work. This is nuts. I musta been smoking something. Just take me back to Trenton. I'll find out what I need somewhere else."

"You can't just dump me."

"Turn the car around. This was the worst idea I've had since I tried to cheat Joe Rina at cards."

"You cut me loose, I'll turn you in to the cops. Tell 'em you're getting set to scam the Rinas."

"I thought you cared about Carol. I'm doing this for her."

"I do care about Carol. I just don't trust you." She kept driving and he sat there, sulking like a child. Roger-the-Dodger was looking back and forth at them like a spectator at a tennis match.

It had been close, but Victoria felt she had won that point.

She let him cool down before finally giving him what he'd asked for. "Tommy and Joseph Rina are the silent owners of a chain of retail jewelry stores called Rings 'n' Things." That brought Beano's head around. "Rings 'n' Things is owned by a parent company called Precious Metals, Inc., also owned by the Rinas. Precious Metals is a company that buys silver, gold, and platinum and sells them to jewelry manufacturers. When I found that out, I figured it might be a laundry because Precious Metals sends gold and silver shipments all over the world, and Rings 'n' Things has a store in Geneva, Switzerland, which, as you probably know, is the end of the line for cash in a well-conceived laundry. Rings 'n' Things also has stores in hot-ticket towns like Vegas, Reno, and Atlantic City. All big gambling centers."

"Finally, you give me something other than attitude."

"How are we gonna hit his jewelry stores... buy ski masks and come in waving guns?"

"You think I'm a cowboy, but I'm not. When I hit, if they know it in less than twelve hours, then I've screwed up."

"So whatta you gonna do?" she asked.

"I'll figure something out, Vicky. I just heard about it. Give me a minute or two, will you?" He slumped down into the seat. They rode in silence as Beano was lost in thought. She made the turnoff onto the Atlantic City Expressway and it started to drizzle. The wipers metronomed, slapping the mist off the windshield.

"Okay," he said fifteen minutes later, "got it." Then he put his head back on the seat and closed his eyes.

"So what are we going to do?" she insisted.

"Gonna sell Joe and Tommy a pearl," Beano said without opening his eyes, and that was all he would tell her.

♠ ♠ ♠

The Shady Rest Trailer Park on the outskirts of Atlantic City was about as run-down as the

138

Health Department would allow. There was a pile of garbage rotting by the road out front. Black and green flies performed aerial combat over the reeking mess. The office was under a bare deciduous elm tree. Victoria pulled her Nissan in and Beano found his '95 blue and white Winnebago parked under a dying cherry tree, next to a power and water hookup. There was a canvas tarp lashed over the top of the rig to hold down roofing equipment stored up there. Beano didn't do roofing scams anymore, but there was something about the tradition that was ingrained deep inside him. To him, the Winnebago was home, and that's what had drawn him to the vehicle when he'd seen it marked down for sale last summer. He had loaned it to Paper Collar John to live in because John and his wife, Cora Bates, had come on hard times after John's bust for running a block hustle in the Hamptons last year. In an unfortunate act of piling on, Cora got sick right after John's fifteen-month conviction. She had been diagnosed with pancreatic cancer. It was growing like river moss inside of her. John didn't talk much about it, but there was a deep pain that never left his gray eyes. The cops had John's number and were watching him pretty close. Beano had loaned his aunt and uncle the motor home so they could move around and steer clear of police scrutiny. Two weeks ago, Cora had been hospitalized and had gone into a coma. When Beano had called, John jumped at the chance to get back into action....He needed money to pay Cora's hospital bills. Beano figured if the con went off the way he planned, there'd be plenty to spread around after it was over.

Once they were parked next to the Winnebago, Beano reached over and honked the horn. The door to the motor home opened and Victoria watched as a tall, handsome, gray-haired man, about sixty-five, came down the steps. He had the sincere, confident look of a corporate executive, only he was dressed in blue jeans and a T-shirt. Beano got out of the car and gave John a hug. Once Victoria was out, Beano introduced her.

"John, this is Victoria Hart. She's gonna be a lugger on this hustle." Victoria didn't know what the hell a lugger was, and it sure didn't sound too flattering, but she smiled and nodded anyway.

John shook her hand and looked at her carefully. "You're the Prosecutor in Trenton, aren't you? The one who was gonna put Carol on the stand?" His voice was deep and rich, but there was bitter accusation in it.

"I'm sorry," she said softly. "It went wrong. That's why I'm here."

John looked at her. His hooded eyes gave her nothing. Then he turned to Beano.

"Got a little problem with the motor home hook-up," John said. "The mooch in the front office needs a cool-out. He wants a hundred dollars in advance. He was gonna throw me out when I didn't have it. I told him you'd give it to him, but watch him, he's no laydown."

"I'll go take care of it. Then we're gonna

go over to a jewelry store called Rings 'n' Things. Look it up in the phone book over there," Beano said, pointing to a phone booth by some picnic tables. Then he grabbed a hundred dollars out of the pickle jar and went to the office to pay for their hook-up.

♠ ♠ ♠

The first disagreement came that night at dinner. Beano, John, and Victoria had found the jewelry store, which was under the roof in Bally's Casino. They drove to the hotel, which was a towering monument to bad taste and electricity. The porte cochere glimmered with twinkling lights. The casino was on the Boardwalk and faced the dark blue swells of the Atlantic. The jewelry store was inside, just off the casino. Big interior glass windows looked out on the gaming tables and contained rings and bracelets that were on display there. Victoria thought the jewelry was incredibly ugly...chunky, overdone pieces with too many chipped diamonds. They glittered classlessly and competed for attention with the spinning, ringing slots across from the store. In one window there were men's pinkie rings that looked big enough to anchor a boat. Beano suggested they eat in the casino dining room, and they found a table near the back. The room was dark. Beano explained that casinos all over the world were designed with no clocks and no windows, so the players at the tables wouldn't see any change in time or sunlight.

141

Time stood still in a casino. The management didn't want the losers looking at their watches. They sat in Bally's Bicycle Room, named after the Bicycle cards all casinos used. The best bets on the menu were steak and beer.

"Okay, Victoria," Beano said after the food arrived, "I need to know more about these guys."

"Like what?"

"Any offshore stuff. Do the Rinas have interests in any banks, any savings and loans? Eventually, we gotta get to their big money."

She looked at them for a long moment and then started sawing on her overcooked steak. "I thought we were gonna sell Joe and Tommy a pearl, whatever that means."

"We're gonna sell them a pearl for the front money, but that's not the scam. That only finances the scam. The opening act of this scam has gotta get deep into their pockets. We gotta take these goombas for a million dollars or more, and we gotta set it up so they start accusing each other. We gotta get them going. We need a team of operators working. I need to pull in some more people."

"Tell me about this pearl thing first," she persisted, trying to cover her shock at the million-dollar size of the scam.

"She's not being too cooperative," Paper Collar John said in his soft baritone voice.

"She's a lawyer," Beano said. "Whatta you expect?"

"I forgot that," John deadpanned.

142

"You guys gonna tell me what we're going to do, or are you gonna just sit here wasting time, taking target practice on the legal profession?"

"Okay," Beano said. "The deal is, you and I are gonna be lovers. How do you like it so far?" She showed no reaction. "I'm Bubba Budweiser from Locadocious, Texas. You're Rhonda Roundheels from right here in town. You're gonna dress up in hooker spandex and paste yourself on me like wet clothing. And you're gonna laugh and giggle at everything I say, and I'm gonna be pinching your ass and telling you you're the sweetest little piece of fluff this side of Red Gulch. Then, while you simper and fawn, I'm gonna buy you a twenty-millimeter black pearl."

"Really?" she said deadpan.

"Yep."

"Not on the best day you ever had."

"I thought you wanted to be in on this."

"I do, I just don't have a real strong stomach."

"Listen," Beano said, leaning in and lowering his voice, "if you think I'm interested in copping a free feel, forget it. That's not what I'm looking for." She was really pissing him off. "What I need is your help to pull this off. I can go hire a hooker, but then we got an accomplice who's probably not too smart and will turn us in for money. You said you wanted to be in this....You might as well learn to be a player."

"I'm not gonna dress up like a whore."

"There ain't much you *will* do, is there?"

143

Beano said, slipping back into his native South Carolina accent, which he had all but lost, except when he was truly pissed off. "You wanna have a piece of everything. But you won't tell me nothing 'cept what you think is important. Don't matter you never stole nothing in your life, you're gonna be the expert, gonna approve everything. You wanna tell me and John how to run this game? You wanna dole out information? What the fuck good does that do?" He was almost yelling.

"Calm down, Beano," John said.

Beano leaned back and rubbed his eyes. "You're right. She gets to me, John. Maybe it's just 'cause I feel so shitty about Carol...or maybe it's 'cause she and I are just oil and water, I don't know. All I know is, I wanna do this, and all I get outta Miss Hart here is stupid questions and reasons why what I'm trying ain't right. We won't have any coordination this way. We're gonna crash and burn."

Victoria watched as he bolted out of his chair and went to the bathroom at the far end of the room.

They hadn't planned it in advance, but they'd done so many scams together since Beano was six, John knew Beano was going to throw a fit and leave the table the minute Victoria got stubborn. He left John to be the "singer" and do Beano's commercial for him, the way it was supposed to be done.

"Good goin'. I never saw anyone get to him like that before," John said, laying down a primer coat of guilt.

144

"Hey, Mr. Bates, if you two think I'm going to be a silent partner here, then you're in for a startling disappointment."

"He's good, Miss Hart. Beano could sell Ebenezer Scrooge Christmas trees. There's no grifter on this planet with more natural talent and I seen most of them." His voice turned rich and velvety. "Maybe you should know he grew up with Carol Sesnick. Ever since they were nine or ten years old, they were like brother and sister. He loved her. He ain't gonna show you how much 'cause he's a sharper, and a sharper don't let his feelings show. But his heart's all wrapped up in this thing. I personally think that's real dangerous when you're running a sting. You need to be detached. Him gettin' angry like he just done is a bad sign. If we fail with a mark like Tommy Rina, we're gonna be hanging out with a buncha engine blocks at the bottom of some lake."

Victoria didn't answer, but when Beano finally came back from the men's room, she could see he had water in his hair. She wondered if he had put his head in the sink to cool down. Once he was seated they sat in silence for a while, picking at the overcooked food.

"Okay, look," she finally volunteered. "You mentioned that the Rinas don't have a casino because they couldn't get approved by any gaming commissions in the U.S."

"That's right," Beano mumbled.

"But it's wrong. They do have a casino." Both Beano and John looked up. "They're not on

145

any of the ownership records, but according to my information, the Rinas are majority silent partners in a huge new casino in the Bahamas called the Sabre Bay Club. I couldn't ever prove it 'cause they're not on any of the paperwork, but I suspect they may also have a piece of the SARTOF Merchant Bank of Nassau. SARTOF is an acronym. Stands for Société Anonyme de Refinancement Toutes Opérations Financières."

"Ooh-la-la," Beano said and looked over at Paper Collar John. "That bank could be the dead-drop."

"If it is...that's gonna make it a whole lot easier," John said, and Beano nodded.

"Then we should be able to scam that Bahamian casino for a couple'a million," Beano said, upping the amount. "We need to get ahold of 'Fit-Throwing' Duffy. He's the best tat player in the family."

"What are you talking about? What's a tat?" Victoria said. It was starting again; they were talking in a language she didn't understand.

"A tat is a dice con," Beano explained, then looked back at John. "And I'm gonna need a female mack to steer Tommy."

"The Queen of Hearts."

"No," Beano snapped.

"Just don't fool around with her this time. You want a mack, she's the best. She's also the best looking. You won't have to troll her past Tommy more than once."

"Damn it, stop talking over my head," Victoria said. "I told you about the casino. What's a mack? Who's the Queen of Hearts? I want to know what the hell we're talking about."

John turned to face her. "A mack is a sharper who runs lover cons. Cons of the heart."

"Are we talking about some sleazeball who marries poor dumb pensioners, then takes their money and disappears?" she said.

"Yeah," Beano acknowledged. "That's about it. We're also talking about my cousin-in-law, Dakota Bates. She's a widow now, used to be married to my cousin Calvin Bates. He died in prison. They call her the Queen of Hearts, but she's not going to be part of this hustle."

"Just don't hand your heart to her this time," John advised. "You give a mack your heart, Beano, and she gets confused. She don't know what to do with it, 'cept squeeze it for cash and throw it on the ground. She always loved Carol, she'd wanta do this, and she's the best. Since when did we start usin' seconds on a sting this dangerous?"

"Okay, call her up," Beano finally agreed. "I think she was in California, last I heard."

"She's right here in Atlantic City. She's been bucking the tiger in clubs off the Boardwalk."

"I hesitate to ask," Victoria said.

"Faro player," Beano explained. "She hangs out on the faro tables, looking for full Toledos who pull into town flashing diamonds and driving Cadillacs. She does real good."

There was a long moment and then Beano

147

looked over at Victoria. "Okay, what's it gonna be? You gonna hang on me, laugh at my jokes, and let me buy you a pearl? It's you, or I take a chance on a hooker. Either get in or get out. Last call," he said. Beano felt tired; his vision was beginning to split. And every time he let himself focus on the Rina brothers, he felt a panic attack. He wondered if in a direct confrontation with Joe or Tommy he could hold it together. He yanked these unsettling thoughts away, took a drink of beer, and tried to calm down.

Victoria sawed off another piece of gristly steak and tried in vain to chew it. She finally tucked it back in the corner of her mouth, like a chipmunk with an acorn. "Okay," she said around the ball of gristle, "I'll do what you want...."

"Big fucking deal," Beano muttered.

They stopped at a Western shop across from Bally's, and Beano invested another five hundred dollars in clothes. He bought an expensive Western jacket, a wide-brimmed Stetson, and a big cowboy belt with a real rodeo buckle.

John had the pickle jar in the canvas bag on his lap. He and Victoria were seated on the brass-studded leather bench when Beano came out of the fitting room, wobbling slightly on two-inch cowboy boot heels.

"Howdy, whippersnappers," he said, and bowed slightly.

"Who are you supposed to be now?" Victoria asked, without smiling. She thought he looked stupid.

"Justice R. McQueed, ma'am, an' in case you ain't guessed, I'm just about all hat an' no cattle." The accent was perfect West Texas. "Just in from Locadocious, Texas, with the cutest little piece a'fluff this side of yer mama's apron." He gave her his biggest rainmaker grin, and it brought a few drops. She let a tiny smile play momentarily on her lips.

"You can't be serious," she said. "Isn't that a little over the top?"

"Give 'em what they want. Deep down, all these Yankees think Texans are big, goofy millionaires who couldn't pour piss out of a boot if it had a hole in the toe. So that's what I'm gonna give 'em. A big, dumb, filthy-rich Texas idiot." He looked at Victoria critically, "Now, Sugar Plum, we gotta get you gussied up some yerself."

They found a shop near the casino that looked like it catered to strippers and B-girls. There was an awesome selection of spandex miniskirts and plastic platform heels displayed in the window.

Victoria could not believe the outfit Beano picked. She put it on in the changing room and walked out....Traffic stopped in the small strippers' boutique. The dress fit like a second skin and only barely covered her panties. She kept pulling it down. Beano smiled at her. "Honey-dove," he drawled theatrically, "you

149

look better'n twelve acres a pregnant red hogs. We'll take it," he said to the sales clerk.

♠ ♠ ♠

Ten minutes later, they pulled back up to the overlit entrance of Bally's in Victoria's white Nissan. Beano gave the valet the keys and all three of them walked into the casino. Paper Collar John was carrying the canvas satchel with Beano's pickle jar full of cash. They separated once they were inside. John headed to the hotel cashier. Beano and Victoria walked across the purple carpet, past the flashing entry lights and spinning granny-slots, up the stairs, under the Eye-in-the-Sky where leery casino shift supervisors watched the gaming room for crooked action. They headed straight toward the jewelry store. John was across the room depositing the fifty thousand in a casino bank account under the name of Justice R. McQueed. He waved at Beano as he finished the transaction.

"What do I do?" Victoria was saying, the first degrees of stage fright setting in.

"Have a good time. You're panning for gold and playing me like a widemouth bass. No matter what happens, if ya get tied up and can't think of anything, all you gotta do is giggle. If I ask you anything and you don't know how to answer, just say, 'Whatever you want, Daddy.'"

"I call you Daddy?"

"Yeah...only not like in 'Dad.' It's like in

'Sugar Daddy.' Make it as trampy as you can. Okay?"

"Okay." She took a deep breath. She was teetering slightly on the plastic platform shoes with their five-inch stiletto heels. *What a transition,* she thought. She'd gone from a no-nonsense prosecutor locked in a legal battle with Joe Rina, to a bimbo dressed in a spandex napkin, teetering on hooker heels, nervous about her one dumb bubblehead line. Two days ago, just the thought of pulling a stunt like this would have been enough to cause her massive immobilizing depression....Now her heart was slamming inside her with unbridled excitement. "I feel like I'm the stilt-walking man at the circus on these things," she said.

"Trust me here"—he grinned—"you don't even faintly resemble a man on stilts." He took her by the arm and together they moved into the jewelry store.

"Now, don't y'all say another word. I made up my mind, Sugar-dove." He belched at her loudly without warning as they moved into the shop and over to the glass merchandise case. "Got some mighty fine sparklers here, don't they?" Beano seemed slightly drunk, slurring a word here and there. It was amazing....His drunk was subtle; he never took it too far. "Mighty nice piece'a ice, ain't it?" he said, pointing to a particularly ugly diamond choker.

"Whatever you say, Daddy," she said tentatively.

The store clerk caught a glimpse of Beano's

wide-brimmed Stetson and fixed on him like a heat-locked missile.

"I'm Matthew; may I help you, sir?" he said, rushing up.

"Well, I s'pose we gonna have to go an' get us a little bauble fer Honeybee here. Ain't that right?"

"Whatever you want, Daddy," she simpered.

"'At's right, whatever I want." He grinned at Matthew. "This lady, she already brung me a powerful heap a'luck. Yesterday I got nothin' but losers. Couldn't draw a pistol from a holster. Then I met Sugar Plum, and today I been so lucky, if I was settin' on a fencepost the birds would feed me. Gotta keep the good luck flowin', don't we, Baby?"

"Whatever you want, Daddy." She was beginning to feel like she needed to broaden her responses.

"What did you have in mind?" the young salesman said, as Beano started looking around in the case.

"See, I'm a big un fer lucky charms. How it goes is, I live right smack on the edge of Black Pearl Mesa, in Locadocious, Texas. So fer luck I'm gonna give this little lady the biggest black pearl y'all got in the place."

"Could I suggest instead the diamond choker you were admiring?" he said, pointing to it.

"I ain't about ta go an squat on my spurs here. Y'all don't know much about luck, do ya? Gotta buy somethin' with meaning, son, gotta be a black pearl."

"Oh boy," Matthew said, "that's going to be hard. Excuse me." The young man rushed off and minutes later he returned with a tall, unctuous scavenger in a three-piece black pinstripe. After one look at Beano he started wringing his hands like a praying mantis.

"I'm Donald Stine. I run this store. Matt said you were looking for a black pearl?"

"'At's right, Don. Justice R. McQueed." Beano shot his hand out, and when Don Stine took it, he got his knuckles cracked, Texas style.

"Gonna buy the biggest, largest ol' black pearl y'all got."

"Black pearls are quite rare," Stine said.

"Then we're at the wrong rodeo. Come on, Honeybun." Beano started to lead her out. Victoria now knew why girls in five-inch platform shoes all looked stupid. It was impossible to walk. You had to sort of shuffle moronically. She was teetering along behind Beano when Don Stine stopped them. "We have a few small ones in settings...but matching black pearls of any size or quality are almost impossible to find."

"This here is one pearl we're talkin' 'bout, Bucko. Don't have t'be a match. Only got one girl, only need one pearl...see?" he grinned broadly. "I'm ready t'go to fifty thousand dollars. How's that sound, Sugar?"

"Oh, Daddy, you're so sweet. Whatever you say." Victoria was beginning to get into it.

Donald Stine was distracted. He couldn't take his eyes off her chest. She had to admit

153

the little black stretch dress was providing good energy.

"I could call around, see what's in our other stores. We have reciprocity with the other shops here in Atlantic City. And I'll check the Jewelry Mart."

"Ya got me all spread out like a cold supper here, Donnie. Them tables is a-calling and I'm ready to go....Let's do the deal, that's the Texas way."

"If you would have a seat, I could see what I can get in the next ten or twenty minutes."

"Well, hell, let's give 'er a shake, then."

Stine hurried off and Beano and Victoria moved around the shop, looking at the trashy jewelry in the glass cases while the assistant, Matt, trailed them like a bloodhound. After a few minutes, Stine returned, wearing a greedy smile.

"We're in luck. As you probably know, pearls are measured in millimeters."

"Nope, never bought one before."

"We found a twenty-two-millimeter, perfectly round, opaque black pearl. It's got a beautiful dusky black luster and it's only forty-seven thousand retail, plus tax."

"Well, let's get that little pigeon egg on over an' take us a look-see."

"In the interest of time, could we clear credit now? How will we be handling the transaction? That is, should the pearl meet your specifications," Stine said. Beano wished he'd stop wringing his hands.

154

"Got me a checking account right here in the hotel," Beano said proudly.

While Beano and Donald Stine went to the casino front desk to arrange the transfer, Victoria went to the ladies' room, which was just outside the store off the casino main floor. A frightening thing happened as she was leaving the restroom. She ran smack into Tommy Rina. They actually collided.

"Watch where the fuck you goin'," Tommy growled.

"'Scuse me," she said and hurried off....She could feel his eyes on her, as she moved off across the casino....She didn't dare turn to see if he had recognized her. She walked across the casino toward the front door, her unbridled excitement suddenly transformed into bile-soaked fear. When she was sure he couldn't see her, she finally doubled back to the store. She prayed Tommy wouldn't come in. Beano was already back there with Donald Stine, so she had no chance to warn him.

The pearl showed up a quarter hour later, and Beano looked it over carefully. He had more than passing experience evaluating jewelry, having spent two years as a jewel thief in Nevada in the late eighties. He gave it up when he almost got shot by a night watchman. He knew natural pearls were never perfectly round. Value was determined by size, shape, color, and opaque luster. He knew a pearl this size would be one of a kind. He guessed that the pearl they were showing him was worth about thirty-five

155

to forty thousand. He was being gouged slightly, but it didn't matter.

"Mighty pretty," he said, looking down through the jeweler's loupe, "this thing's black as truck stop coffee." Then he handed it to Victoria. "Whatta ya think, June Bug?"

"Oh, Daddy, it's so pretty. I simply adore it," she said, her eyes darting out the front windows searching for Tommy Rina.

"Can we make it up into a necklace?" Stine asked, trying to improve on his good fortune. "Perhaps a nice platinum chain with a three-prong setting?"

"Let's see how lucky ol' Justice is gonna get 'fore we get ta buyin' a mess a platinum rope. We got more'n one category we're workin' on, don't we, Sugar?"

"Whatever you say, Daddy." She almost lost her balance and hugged his arm.

The deal was closed quickly. The fifty thousand dollars was immediately transferred to Rings 'n' Things.

Beano and Victoria walked out of the jewelry store, through the casino, and into the sunlight, with the black pearl in an ugly purple box with green felt. She didn't see Tommy Rina anywhere. The Atlantic Ocean was sparkling just beyond the Boardwalk. As they moved out into the late-afternoon chill she started shivering and Beano took off his Western jacket and draped it over her. "That guy gouged us a little; it's only worth forty grand, at most," Beano said, as he spotted John across the street, behind the wheel of her car.

"Then why'd we pay fifty?" she said, confused, as she hugged the coat around her.

"We're increasing by diminishing, holding on by letting go. Didn't I tell you?" Seeing her look, he smiled. "Don't worry. Trust me. This is our lucky day," and then he proved it as they walked across the street and were just missed by a speeding cab. Once they were in the car and pulling away, she told him about running into Tommy.

"Did he recognize you?" Beano asked.

"I don't know. In this outfit, probably not."

Beano was quiet for a long time, then he turned to her and smiled. "Then we'll play it like it never happened. Kinda ups the ante, and puts a little kerosene in the deal," he finally said, and hoped they stayed lucky.

♠ ♠ ♠

They had dinner at a crab house on the garden pier. It jutted two hundred yards out into the Atlantic. The seven-thirty sunset tinged the slate-gray sky and the ocean whitecaps with a subtle but beautiful flamingo-pink. Beano stopped his conversation for a minute to watch it, something that surprised Victoria. She never stopped to look at a field of flowers or a pink and orange sunset. Her mother had once criticized her for this, saying that these were God's gifts and should not be ignored. Victoria saw beauty in other places: in a carefully prepared brief, in a goal attained, in a job well done. She saw beauty

157

in the precise organization of her own thoughts. She now looked at Beano, who had fallen silent, watching the changing colors of the sunset. He was like a child fascinated by a wonderful new gift. She wondered if her mother would approve of him or be appalled. She couldn't decide.

♠ ♠ ♠

They had a table by the window and the salt air blew through the open front door. Victoria had changed out of her "fuck me" outfit and was back into her jeans and pea-coat, something her personality could fit into more easily. The pearl was locked in the safe under the sofa in the motor home, and Roger-the-Dodger had been assigned to stand guard while they went out and ordered New England clams. Beano had also ordered a steak and a Bud Light to go for the dog.

Victoria could tell that John and Beano were still holding back with her. But that night she was strangely elated. She would never have imagined that playing a dumb hooker would be so much fun. It was actually liberating, and her encounter with Tommy really did "put a little kerosene in the deal." She remembered the hours her mother had spent trying to get her to loosen up. Yet this con man with the dazzling smile had somehow accomplished it in one afternoon. For the first time she understood the exhilarating thrill of the unreasonable risk.

"This thing with the pearl," she said, "I still don't know how it works. How are we gonna get a hundred and fifty thousand dollars? We paid fifty; you said the pearl we bought is only worth forty. I know we're increasing by diminishing, but I don't get it. So far we're losing money, not making it."

"We're multiplying by dividing, so it doesn't matter what it's really worth," Beano said. "Tomorrow, first thing, I'm gonna go into that same store and try and buy another one just like it. We're gonna offer to pay as much as it takes."

"But we don't have any seed money left," she reminded him.

"Ouch...there's a showstopper"—he grinned—"I never thought of that."

"Stop fucking around with me, Beano," she said. "I'm not used to being played like a mark. If I'm in on this, I wanna know what I'm doing. I'm sure we're breaking half-a-dozen laws here."

"We might have to break a few before this con is over, but not on this pearl gag. We're not doing anything illegal. Least not yet," Beano said.

"Don't forget, I've read your yellow sheet. You're no choirboy."

"That's true," Paper Collar John said, straightfaced. "Once, when he was ten, in Bend River, Arkansas, I was doing a faith healer con. I was the Reverend Yancy L. Anthony of the Church of Christ Manors. I let Beano sing in the choir. He's got a terrible voice…chased most of the faithful right out of the tent. Hadda make him into 'Little Lord Angel'…youngest faith healer in the Southwest…Even at ten, you was damn good, Beano. You shoulda heard him preach. He could talk the money right out of a banker's pocket." Beano reddened slightly at the compliment. Finally, in a courtly gesture, he bowed his head to acknowledge his talent.

"Come on," Victoria pushed, "I want to hear it. Just start with the pearl. How are we going to turn a ten-thousand-dollar loss into a hundred-thousand-dollar profit?"

So Beano filled her in. When he was finished, she looked at him, her mouth slightly open. It was close to brilliant, and he was right…she couldn't find one single law that they would be breaking.

"Increase by diminishing," she said, slowly. "Hold on by letting go, multiply by dividing. It's really true, isn't it?"

"If you do it right," Paper Collar John said.

Then they started talking about members of the Bates family, evaluating traits and skills, eliminating and accepting candidates. It was, in her opinion, a very colorful voir dire. Besides Fit-Throwing Duffy Bates and Dakota Bates, there were the Hog Creek Bateses, whom they didn't talk about much, but who seemed to be important if there was ever any trouble. There were also "singers" to give background information to Tommy Rina when he was checking Beano out, and inside men who, she learned, were the stars of the con. Beano and John were inside men. There were outside men who roped the mark then steered or stalled him. They were assigned to control his movement. There were "shills" and "luggers," who she found out, to her dismay, were basically extras. She was determined to somehow upgrade her category. John and Beano discussed each candidate thoroughly before putting his or her name on the list. They divided up half-a-dozen names and agreed to start calling them first thing in the morning.

Victoria Hart sat there, eating cooked crab and wondering if this was going to be the worst situation she'd gotten into in her life...or the best.

♠ ♠ ♠

The next morning Beano was in his cowboy getup: fringed jacket, boots, and Stetson. All alone, he opened the front door of Rings 'n' Things at a little past nine and stuck his head in.

"Howdy do," he shouted into the empty store. Nobody bought jewelry at nine A.M., so the staff was having coffee in the back. After a moment, Donald Stine came out with a cup in his hand.

"Good morning...Mr. McQueed, wasn't it?"

"Justice McQueed...sure 'nuf. Good goin' on that. Y'all got a minute? I got a little bit of a problem here...."

"Uh...well, what kind of a problem? The pearl

161

was okay...?" Donald looked worried, even slightly frightened.

"That pearl set me up fat as a Persian prince. Little Honey-dove an' me, we been talkin' 'bout her goin' on home t'Black Pearl Mesa with me to stay a spell."

The store manager exhaled with relief. "That's wonderful. I'm glad everything worked out."

"'Cept she changed her mind...ain't it just like a woman...?" Beano let this moment ripen until a look of full panic formed on Donald Stine's face. Donald didn't want to have to take the pearl back in trade. He had purchased it from the Jewelry Mart and sold it to the Texan. He knew a 22mm one-of-a-kind black pearl was a white elephant. He would never get rid of it. It would become perennial inventory.

"Changed her mind?" Don breathed in as he said it, ending with a slight hiccup.

"Well, not exactly changed it....I mean, what she wants is, she wants another one just like it. She wants earrings. She says she wants me t'buy her a duplicate. So I guess she's got me running with the big dogs now." He reached for his wallet. "I'm gonna let you make 'em up into a set of earrings, maybe get us platinum settings, like you was sayin'."

"Oh. Oh...well, look, a pearl of that size and color is very, very rare. You see, they're made by oysters."

Then came the nature lesson. Beano put his empty wallet away and listened patiently.

"As you probably know, a little grain of sand gets inside the oyster shell and the oyster makes the pearl to protect itself from the sand. It's a very slow and very individual process. Size and color are all variables. To find a matching pearl of that size would be almost impossible. We'd have to get very lucky."

"Rich beats luck ever damn time." Beano grinned.

"Beg your pardon?"

"I want her t'come home t'Black Pearl Mesa with me, Mr. Stine, and them earrings is gonna do the deal. So, we gotta get her that matchin' pearl at any cost. Comprende?"

"Well, that's all very easily said, but I'm afraid nature didn't make two pearls in that exact shade and color."

"Bet nature made one pretty gol-dern close, though. I'll pay you one hundred and sixty thousand dollars for a pearl that's close enough t'be the mate."

"One sixty?" Don said, greed overtaking good sense. "Lemme get this straight....It doesn't have to be exact? Just close?"

"Hell, son, they're earrings. We ain't mintin' money here. Close is all we need. She's gonna wear the dad gum things on opposite sides of her head."

"It will take some time. That was a huge pearl. I'll have to put out a fax bulletin and a notice on the International Jewelry Exchange."

"How long is that gonna take?" Beano asked, sweeping his hat off and dropping it on the glass counter between them.

"I don't know, Mr. McQueed...maybe never."

Beano looked at him sadly. "But you'll try?"

"For a hundred and sixty thousand dollars I'd swallow a grain of sand and start making one myself," Donald grinned.

Not a bad joke, Beano thought. But on this hollow-chested man who kept rubbing his hands together like an insect, it only managed to be annoying.

Beano promised to check back later in the day. After he left, Donald Stine went to the back of Tommy Rina's store and put out a call for a 20-to-24mm black pearl with opaque luster, almost perfectly round. He faxed it to the International Jewelry Exchange. He also put it on the New York–New Jersey jewelry fax. He offered to buy the jewel for sixty thousand dollars, giving himself a hundred-thousand-dollar profit on the deal if he could find a pearl close enough to match.

Two hours later, a Mr. Robert Hambelton of Hambelton, Deets, and Banbray, a wholesale jewelry company, answered with a fax responding to the recent inquiry. The letterhead said his firm was across the river in New York. The fax pictured a black pearl, opaque, almost perfect. His memo said the pearl he had in stock was 22.5mm in size, but was in a diamond-encrusted setting and that he would have to break up the necklace. He was asking a hundred and fifty thousand, no negotiation. There was a number in New York to call.

164

Donald Stine figured a ten-thousand-dollar profit was better than nothing, so he rushed to his phone and dialed.

"Hambelton, Deets, and Banbray," a woman's voice said.

"I'd like to speak to Mr. Robert Hambelton about the twenty-two-millimeter pearl he faxed me a picture of.

"One moment, please, I'll see if Mr. Hambelton is in." In a moment, Bob Hambelton came on the line.

"Bob Hambelton here," a thin voice said. "How can I help, please?"

Donald explained about his customer and about the pearl and the need to make earrings, and that was why his client would vastly overpay for the jewel. Robert Hambelton said he would send the pearl down to Atlantic City that afternoon and Mr. Stine could buy it from their representative, a Mr. Carl Forbes.

At five o'clock, just before closing, a distinguished-looking man with gray hair and an expensive suit came through the door of Rings 'n' Things. He asked for Donald Stine. His Jewelry Mart I.D. indicated that he was Carl Forbes. He opened his metal suitcase and produced a pearl that Donald Stine would have sworn was almost a perfect duplicate of the one he'd sold the Texan. Donald appraised it and signed for it, then gave a cashier's check for one hundred and fifty thousand, made out for cash, to Mr. Forbes, who then handed Donald the pearl. Then Mr. Forbes put the cashier's check in his briefcase and left.

Of course, the whole thing had been set up by Beano, using a call-forwarding system he already had in New York. The system routed the call from the number on the fax back from New York to the pay phone at the Shady Rest Trailer Park. Victoria played the secretary; Beano was the thin-voiced Robert Hambelton. Paper Collar John performed the distinguished Mr. Forbes.

Beano had just sold Don Stine his own pearl back, but better yet, Joe and Tommy Rina had just put up one hundred thousand dollars to finance their own destruction.

ELEVEN

Dakota, Nassau, and Tennessee

"Unbelievable," Victoria said, her voice triumphant. "I never saw this much cash outside of a police property room."

"To Carol," Beano toasted, and they all raised a glass of champagne, including John, who was on the cellphone to Fit-Throwing Duffy in Cleveland. Beano had turned the cashier's check into fifteen hundred crisp $100 bills. They were stacked on the Winnebago's dining table. A celebratory bottle of Dom Pérignon was being passed around.

John closed Victoria's flip-phone and raised his glass in a second toast. "Duffy's aboard. He's gonna catch the next flight to the Bahamas.

I told him to find us a place to work out of, somewhere down the road from the Sabre Bay Club. Said he'd bring the drills, the cellophane gas, and the '97 *McGuire Financial Listings,* but he needs us to bring your wheelchair."

"Cellophane gas?" Victoria said. She was feeling a little giddy. She didn't usually drink, and just two glasses of the imported champagne had her off balance.

"For the tat," Beano said. "We drill the dice and load 'em with cellophane gas, which is the only substance on the planet that turns from a gas to a solid when you heat it. Every other substance goes from a solid, to a liquid, to a gas. Cellophane gas dice are much better than regular loadies."

"How so?"

"Duffy found out about this cellophane gas stuff in an article in *Scientific American.* He figured out how to use it in the tat. It's his discovery. No one else even knows about it, so don't spread it around. It's a family secret." She nodded. "Duffy is the best dice mechanic in the game. He'll switch out the table dice at Sabre Bay with close counterfeits he'll bring with him. This is important because all casinos change the dice at odd intervals and the official dice all have minor imperfections. The Pit Boss can quickly check a pair of dice to make sure they're casino issue. When we hit them big, they're gonna be checking the dice hard, and we need to be using their cubes. Once Duffy's got us ten or twelve sets of casino cubes off the tables, we'll go to our room and drill 'em and put the cellophane in. The way it works is, when the cellophane gas is heated by your hand, it turns solid. That loads 'em so when you roll the dice, they come up on whatever number they're weighted to make."

"Why do you need cellophane gas?" she asked. "Why not just use regular weights?"

"Because, once you start to hit these casinos, they get very nervous and, besides checking the dice, they send over a pit boss who's gonna stand at the table, watching the action. If you're winning too much, he'll also float the dice." Seeing her confused look, he explained: "That means he'll drop 'em in a glass of water. If they roll over, he knows they're weighted on one side and you're busted. Thing about cellophane gas is, it heats fast, but it also cools very fast. By the time he gets it into the water, it's already back to being a gas and therefore equally distributed, so the dice don't roll."

"Pretty clever."

"In order to get Tommy's attention, we're gonna have t'hit his casino for a pile of dough. Between the table and the 'fill cage,' I'd like to get as close to two million as I can. To do that, we're gonna have to be at that table for a while. They won't shut us down if they can't catch us cheating. These dice should have 'em stumped."

"Okay, so what's the deal with the wheelchair?"

"I'll show you." Beano got up and went

out of the motor home. Victoria and John followed, watching as he climbed up the back ladder and untied the tarp on the roof. Then he handed down a Quickie Grand Prix Victory folding wheelchair with no seat. Victoria watched as Beano dug around on the roof for a minute. He climbed down with what looked like a portable toilet with a plastic catch basin attached.

"That's a Porta-Toilet seat," she said, grinning foolishly, still feeling giddy from the champagne.

Beano opened the chair, John handed him a rag, and Beano wiped the dust off. He then attached the Porta-Toilet to the seat on the wheelchair and looked up at her. "This is gonna be Fit-Throwing Duffy's work station. He's gonna be a gimp at the table. I wheel him in, park him, and create the distractions. Once he pulls the dice off the crap table, he drops 'em between his legs into the Porta-Toilet. At the same time, he makes a palm switch putting counterfeit dice in the game. Since we're going to be losing big at this point, the Stick-man on the table won't bother to check the dice. They never worry about dice being used by a loser. It won't be until the new Shift Manager comes on and they do a dice count that they'll find our dice, but since they're not loaded, they'll probably just fill out an incident report and do nothing. Neither the Pit Boss or the Shift Manager watching through the Eye-in-the-Sky camera will spot Duffy's switch. He can palm stuff like a close-hand magician. In an hour he'll get us twelve pairs of their trademark dice to drill." Beano turned the wheelchair upside down and showed her a specially designed cartridge clip under each arm where the drilled dice could be snap-loaded. "The doctored dice fit in here. If Duffy wants a seven, he pulls the ace from this side, the six from the other, and holds 'em for a minute, doing some player hooey to stall long enough for the gas to warm up and turn solid. At the same time, he ditches the table dice into the Porta-Toilet. He blows on the loadies, starts sayin' stuff like 'Come on, come on seven. Baby needs a new pair a'shoes,' some bullshit like that. Once the cellophane is solid, he rolls the number and wins."

"You guys have this down to a science."

"It's not a science," Beano grinned, "it's an art."

As they were talking, a brand-new red Corvette with the top down pulled through the arch at Shady Rest and parked next to the motor home. Behind the wheel was one of the most extraordinary creatures that Victoria Hart had ever seen. She had long, luxuriant jet-black hair and ivory-white skin. Her green eyes sparkled when she got out of the car. She was not saving anything. Her luscious frame was poured into skin-tight, ripped jeans. She was wearing a tank-top, her chest jutted, and when she moved it didn't look to Victoria like a silicone job. Beyond all of those breath-taking physical attributes there was some-thing else, something intangible: a smoldering, musky sexuality that was palpable and sucked all the available oxygen from the spot where they were standing. Victoria was no wall-flower, but she instantly knew she was no sexual competition for the Queen of Hearts.

"I understand you guys are looking for a capper to rope a mark," she said as she hugged John, but only looked over at Beano. They kept their distance. There was negative tension between them. "How you doing?" she said to him.

"I'm okay. I see you're having a good year," he said, eyeing the Vette. There was a coldness in the remark that startled Victoria.

"If you're still pissed, Beano, I'm sorry. I thought we were just screwing around."

"Yeah," he said, "I guess that's what we were doing."

"I wanna help. Don't freeze me out," she said, looking at him, holding his gaze until he spoke.

"You know we're talking about Tommy Rina?"

"So, I'll thumb some Vaseline up my nose to help with the smell. I can rope that little shit. I'll steer him for you, and if he comes off hot, I'll play the little monkey against the wall." Then, without warning, she turned to Victoria and threw out her hand. "Hi, I'm Dakota Bates."

Victoria shook hands and introduced herself. Victoria was five-nine but Dakota must have been close to six feet tall. She had show-girl dimensions.

171

"Come on inside," Beano finally said, and they moved into the motor home.

The cash was still on the table. Dakota looked at it. "John said you're running a moose pasture in Modesto with a Big Store in San Francisco." Beano nodded. "You think that's gonna be enough cash?" she asked.

"If we're careful. We need that to set up the field and rent offices. Victoria, John, and I are gonna fly to San Francisco tomorrow. We'll take around a hundred thousand, you take the other fifty and catch a flight to the Bahamas and meet Fit-Throwing Duffy there. We'll see you in two days. One of us will have to deliver the new *McGuire Financial Listings* to the casino credit department."

"How you gonna get Tommy to the Bahamas?" Dakota asked.

"I checked around. His latest roommate is a redheaded hooker named Calliope Love," Beano said. "Boardwalk Radio is about to call her up and give her two free tickets to paradise."

"I thought you 'never pitch a bitch,'" Dakota said, turning to Victoria. "Beano thinks girls tantalize but analyze, while guys just jump at the con feet first."

"Sometimes you gotta break the rules," he said.

Dakota nodded and put her overnight case on the table.

"By the way, you don't have to sleep with Tommy," Beano said awkwardly, "just steer him."

"Hey, sweetheart, let me handle my end of it. How I get this mooch to cooperate is my business."

"I'm just saying—"

"Don't," she interrupted firmly; then she saw Roger. "Hey, Rogie. Good to see you, honey." Roger-the-Dodger ran across the motor home and jumped up into her lap, putting his paws upon her magnificent chest.

"How you doing, Roge?" Dakota said to the terrier as she nuzzled him.

"A hell of a lot better than you," Victoria whispered to Beano softly.

♠ ♠ ♠

Tommy Rina heard about the pearl at noon. When the rich Texan didn't show up to purchase the "matching" pearl, it took poor Donald Stine half a day to figure out what had happened to him. When he realized that he had just bought back the same pearl for a hundred and fifty thousand that he had sold the day before for fifty, he knew he was in big trouble. He couldn't figure out a way to hide the mistake, so he finally called Tommy, who was his boss, and told him what had happened.

Tommy was standing in the jewelry store in less than twenty minutes. "You fucking let this Texas goof sell you back the same fucking pearl?" he said, amazed. "Did you fucking check your brains at the Automat?"

"I didn't know it was the same pearl at

173

first. The more I looked at it, the more I wondered. I had the guy from the Jewelry Mart who I originally bought it from come over. He told me...." Donald Stine was scared to death. He was sure that Tommy would take him out back and beat him to death with his trademark ballpeen hammer, but that wasn't what happened.

"Okay," Tommy said, a strange, deadly calm coming over him. His close-set, prehistoric eyes blinked lazily. "I'm gonna get these sorry fucks and put 'em in a new category."

"Yes, sir," Donald said, figuring the new category was *deceased*.

"Happens again, you're gonna be more than sorry, you're gonna get some flashlight therapy. Gonna be a fucking Jersey River whitefish. Smarten up, asshole; this is your only mistake, don't make another." And the little mobster turned and walked out of the jewelry store without another word.

Tommy moved across the purple and red carpet of Bally's past the faro tables, past the banks of dollar slots, then across the lobby where the chemin de fer tables were located in a plush pit. He moved up to Gus Taggert, the Floor Boss, who was sitting on a regal velvet chair next to a mahogany elevator door that led to the High-roller tables on the second floor.

"I wanna see S.B.," he said.

"Come on, Tommy, I can't let you up there. You know you're not carded; I got gaming commission rules to follow." Gus had been given this job because he was harder to get around than a free safety.

"Hey, fuck you, Gus, and fuck your fucking rules. You want me for a fucking enemy, I'll turn your fucking world shit-black." Tommy was smoking mad. His prehistoric eyes now shone with carnivorous intent. There was something about Tommy when he was mad that melted all resistance.

"Okay, okay. Calm the fuck down, will ya?" Gus said, backing up, losing all his field position.

"You calm fucking down!" Tommy shouted back. "Some cowboy hit my jewelry store for a hundred K. I wanta see S. Bartly's cameras. You fucking better get on my team, Gus...or you're gonna have a fucking scar down where your snake used to play."

"Take it easy....You can go up, just don't say it was me that let ya, okay?" he said, folding under Tommy's withering glare.

Gus pushed the button on the mahogany elevator, the door opened, and Tommy went inside the brass-railed, carpeted box. Gus leaned in and put the key in a lock on the elevator panel, turned it, and stepped back as the door closed and Tommy rode up past the lush High-roller area to the third floor, where he got off.

The floor was sterile. It was a painted concrete utility area where shift supervisors and casino muscle hung out on folding metal chairs. The central security room was up here. Tommy knocked on the door and S. Bartly Kneeland opened it and looked out at Tommy, staring at the simian thug through Coke bottle glasses. S.B. was a thin, crater-skinned, tubercular-looking geek. He had designed all of the security video in the hotel, including the Eye-in-the-Sky that monitored everything. All of the surveillance feeds were wired to this room.

"Tommy, you can't be up here. You're not rated," S.B. squeaked.

"Fuck that," Tommy said and pushed the little man with the palm of his hand. S.B. stumbled backwards and was now standing in the center of a twelve-foot-square room full of TV monitors, each equipped with a VCR machine. Tommy moved into the room and looked at the equipment. He had never been up here before because, as everybody kept reminding him, he'd been denied a license by the gaming board and this whole floor was off limits to anybody without a gaming com-mission card. He'd heard about it, though, and it lived up to his expectations. There were more than thirty TV monitors, each covering a dif-ferent part of the hotel. They kept a lookout for known casino cheats and card counters, along with the growing legions of slot bandits using wire triggers. These were tools bent in the shape of a 7 that could be slipped up inside slots to trigger payoffs. These cheaters were known in the casino security business as "7UPs."

There were monitors watching the High-roller

rooms, along with monitors covering the entire casino, including the drive-up at the entrance out front. Since all of the surveillance was from ceiling cameras, the room was called the Eye-in-the-Sky. There were other technicians in the room who walked around constantly looking at the various monitors. On one wall hung ten or twelve large leather-bound photo albums that had pictures of card sharps. Each leather-bound volume had a spine slip indicating what kind of cheats were pictured inside. Besides dice tats and 7UPs, there were volumes for nail nickers and crimpers (card markers), hand muckers and mit men (card switchers), as well as card counters and shiner players.

"I need to look at the lobby tapes for two o'clock yesterday and nine o'clock this morning," Tommy growled. "I also wanna see the tapes on the pull-ups out front for both those times."

"You can't be in here," S.B. said. He was sweating and he straightened his glasses, which had been knocked askew on his beak nose when Tommy had pushed him.

"Hey, dickhead. I didn't hear you right. I think it sounded like you just said I couldn't be in here. I hope, for your sake, that ain't what you said." Tommy's balls were clanging.

"Tommy I—" But S.B. said no more as Tommy interrupted him.

"I pay rent to this fucking joint for my jewelry store. For what? My store just got clouted. I wanna look at the security tapes now." He moved toward the little man, who took a quick step back and finally nodded his head, which bobbed up and down on his pencil neck like a dashboard doll. S. Bartly Kneeland's balls didn't clang; they chimed like Baccarat.

"Okay, okay. I'll get 'em, Tommy." He turned and moved to the rack of tapes. He pulled the four tapes Tommy had asked for, then slammed the lobby tape for yesterday afternoon into a separate viewing monitor on the far side of the room. Tommy elbowed him out of the way, grabbed the remote, and scanned the tapes, looking for anybody in a cowboy hat. Finally he saw him: A big guy in a fringed jacket and cowboy hat was walking across the lobby with a hooker. The time code read: 2:35 P.M. He hit regular speed and watched. He didn't recognize the cowboy and it was hard to see him under the hat, but there was something familiar about the hooker. He didn't think he'd ever fucked her. He would have remembered, 'cause she was a beauty. Still, he thought he knew her.

"I think I know this cunt with him," Tommy said. "I know this fucking bitch from somewhere." His simian brain struggled to make the connection, and then the cowboy and the hooker walked off frame. Tommy ejected the tape, then slammed in the front entrance tape for yesterday. He rolled it down to a few minutes earlier, and started to fast-forward again until he saw a white Nissan pull up in front of the hotel. The time code read: 2:15 P.M. He saw three people getting out. He couldn't

178

make out the older man because he moved immediately into the hotel. The hat still blocked a good look at the cowboy's face, but now he got a full-face shot of the girl in the miniskirt. He froze the tape; it was the hooker he'd run into coming out of the can yesterday. Then realization dawned....

"Fuck me!" he cried out in amazement.

"You know her?" S.B. said, wishing Tommy would get the hell out of his room.

"It's 'Tricky Vicky' Hart, all dressed up like a hooker. It's the fucking bitch who prosecuted Joey." Tommy took the tape out, grabbed the other ones, and started to leave the room.

"You can't take those," S.B. said. "The shift boss has to sign for all of them every twenty-four hours...."

But Tommy Rina was already gone.

He called his brother Joe from the lobby and told him about the pearl and the tapes and Vicky Hart and the cowboy. His brother greeted this information with dead silence.

"Joe, you hear what I'm fucking saying? This cunt hit us for a hundred large."

"Something else is going on, Tommy," Joe said calmly. He never let his voice reveal his emotions.

"Fuckin' A, this split-tailed D.A. stole a hundred K from us. I told ya this bitch needs to get hit by a speedin' car."

"Tommy, when the facts in evidence don't fit the parameters of common sense, there is usually a piece of the equation missing. It makes no sense for Victoria Hart, a prosecuting attorney, to commit a jewelry hustle at our store. So that means there's something else going on. Unless you misidentified her?"

"Joe, this is her. I been watchin' her on the news since you got busted. Lemme go get this twat and finish her off. This is nuts. We can't let these people piss on us."

"I'm gonna send Texaco down to work with you. In the meantime, check the airplane arrivals and departures for her name. Peter can do that for you. Let's see who Miss Hart is traveling with. Let's find out who this cowboy is before we make a move."

Tommy was frustrated. "What we gotta do, Joe, is get this caravan of camels outta our asshole."

"Don't do anything till I tell you," and Joe hung up.

♠ ♠ ♠

When Tommy got to his penthouse on the top of the Ignatious Hotel, Calliope was standing there, holding two airline tickets for the Bahamas that had just come special delivery.

"Look what I won!" she trumpeted proudly as he came through the door, scowling. "I wasn't even listening to the dumb station. It was rock 'n' roll and I only listen to country, but I guessed 'Long-stemmed Roses' by Tanya Tucker, and guess what...? They were having a weekend country countdown and I won anyway. Is that lucky?"

Tommy wasn't listening. He was starting to call friends at other hotels in Atlantic City to see if Victoria Hart was registered.

"I won two round-trip tickets to Nassau!" she squealed, hoping he'd get interested by her excitement.

"I can't go down there right now."

"Well, I wanna go," she said petulantly. "They're my tickets and they're only good for two days."

"Look, I'll buy you tickets later, or we'll fly down to Sabre Bay on Joey's jet. Who da fuck cares about free airline tickets? I gotta deal with this thing. My jewelry store got hit. Ya know how that looks? Everybody knows that's my joint. Somebody hits my joint, they gotta catch a bus or I look like a piece a'shit."

"I'm going, with or without you," Calliope said, holding her ground, figuring that she had the advantage because she was a magnificent bed partner. She knew Tommy had never had better tube cleaning in his whole life, and Calliope wanted to go to the Bahamas on these tickets. There was principle involved.... She had won them herself and she intended to use them.

The argument lasted an hour. "They *do* have phones in the Bahamas, y'know," Calliope reasoned savagely.

He finally agreed to go the day after tomorrow, just to shut her up. If he made that flight, it would put him at the Sabre Bay Club on the same day Victoria Hart and Beano Bates had planned to arrive in Nassau.

TWELVE

The Moose Pasture

Beano finally told Victoria how the main con was supposed to work. They were all on the Delta flight to San Francisco. Roger-the-Dodger had his nose pressed against the screen of a large carrying case that had a sign across it that read CANINE DRUG ENFORCEMENT, U.S. CUSTOMS in large red letters. Beano had told the stewardess he was a government dog trainer and that Roger was being delivered to the Customs Drug Enforcement Team at SFO. This allowed the terrier a privileged position on the floor between their seats, in first class, instead of a freezing ride in the nut-puckering environs of the luggage compartment. As the engines hummed softly and flight attendants took drink orders, Beano explained to a partially awestruck Victoria how a moose pasture con worked. He told her about preparing the field, which included the government painting scam, and about the Fentress County Petroleum and Gas Company, which was a Bates family–owned business. He explained how the oil company was nothing but a watered-down corporate shell that Paper Collar John had bought for a hundred dollars five years ago for possible future use in a moose pasture. FCP&G's most attractive feature was that it ostensibly owned thousands of acres of prime land in north Fentress County, Tennessee. He explained that these deeds of ownership were basically worthless, because they came from old land grants issued a hundred fifty years ago at about the time of Andrew Jackson.

"A lot has happened since then," he grinned at her from seat 5B of the westbound flight. "The land has all been settled on by squatters who now have clear title. Technically, the land grant is still valid but not enforceable. The neat thing about Fentress County is that the County Clerk still has the land grant and deeded plot numbers on record, and if anybody calls to verify our deed's historical existence, she'll look it up and tell you that good ol' FCP&G owns the parcels in question, even though these lots are legally owned by the people living on them. This wonderful act of confusion is being supplied by the State of Tennessee because they haven't bothered to take the old land grants off their books. We can value that property at whatever we want. When Tommy's accountant checks, it's gonna look damn good on our balance sheet. Another plus is that this old dead company actually still has real live stockholders. They invested in the company when it was active ten years ago. It went broke, so they wrote it off on their taxes and forgot it, but legally these stockholders still own thirty percent of the Class-B stock. It's still registered, giving it the look of an operating public company. The stock is listed on the Vancouver Stock Exchange, where the listing requirements for companies are very lax. Up till a week ago it was a penny a share; the total value of the outstanding stock was less than twenty-five thousand dollars. Since then, my uncle John and I have been trading a block of hundred thousand shares back and forth to create an artificial market. We've already got the price up to almost a dollar. The float on this stock is so thin, it goes up fast. In a week, if we keep making two trades a day, we should have it up over ten. We're going to sell it in San Francisco because the *Chronicle* lists the stocks traded on the Vancouver Exchange. When Tommy's people try and get a value, that Tennessee land is going to make the ten-dollar price seem legit."

She was writing all this down on a yellow legal pad. Beano had considered telling her to stop because it was spooking him. He was more paranoid than a corrupt S&L president, and he hated leaving a paper trail, but it was part of Victoria's anal compulsion, so he let it go without comment.

An hour later, when he had finally finished describing the whole hustle to her, she closed the yellow pad and looked straight ahead, saying nothing. He finally leaned his seat back and tried to go to sleep, but he could feel her gaze on him. Occasionally, he would open his eyes and catch her staring. He wasn't sure if he had impressed her or frightened her to death.

They landed in San Francisco and carried their overnight bags and the oversized empty kennel coop, along with the canvas satchel containing a little over a hundred thousand dollars, down the long terminal to the rental car area. Roger-the-Dodger trotted along beside them on a red leash that Beano had bought for him last Christmas.

Beano was very specific with the Hertz girl about the make and color of the rental car he wanted. He demanded a mid-sized light green two-door. He turned down a blue Mustang and finally accepted a light green Ford Escort with a tan interior.

They drove to the Stanford Court, which was an upscale executive hotel on Nob Hill, where John registered under his own name and was shown to his room. Then they all met ten minutes later in a booth in the darkened executive bar. Roger curled up on the seat and put his chin on Victoria's lap. He watched carefully as Beano counted out ten thousand dollars on the seat beside him.

"Take the rest of this and set up a bank account for FCP&G with B *of* A," Beano instructed, handing John the canvas bag with ninety thousand dollars in it. "Take Victoria with you. I'll take Roge and go pick out the moose pasture."

"Not so fast, Bubba. I'm with you," Victoria said.

"Why? It's just a trip to go look at farms.

You're a lawyer; you can help negotiate the building real-estate contract," he said, using some "Ditch Vicky" logic.

"The way you explained it on the plane, it's a lot more than looking at farms, and I want to see some of these Bates family members everybody's been telling me about."

She was like gum he couldn't get off his shoe, but Beano decided since she knew the whole scam anyway, it was better to get her aboard psychologically than to isolate her. "Okay, we'll drive to Modesto." He turned to John. "We should be back here tomorrow night. Start trying to find two floors in a high-rise office building we can rent. It would be great if it was downtown near the other big oil companies. Be nice to look out our corporate windows at the Texaco or Shell Building across the street."

"I'll find us a couple'a top floors down on Market, near the Exxon Tower, where we can get signage rights," John said. "How 'bout a lighted sign on the roof with the FCP&G logo on it?"

"What's the FCP&G logo?" she asked.

"It's a moose with an oil derrick up his ass." Beano grinned. John got up, said good-bye, picked up the canvas satchel, and headed out of the bar.

"Why Modesto?" she asked.

"The San Joaquin River valley is one of the last potentially huge oil basins in the Northern Hemisphere. Only a few meager natural gas wells have come in so far, but there's still a lot of speculation. That valley has what

186

geologists call a huge sandstone stratigraphic trap. That gives it the makings of a major discovery. It also makes it a perfect place to run a moose pasture, because if any mooch we're targeting decides to check it out, our story is gonna make sense geologically."

They drove the light green Ford Escort out of San Francisco and headed east on State Highway 9. Soon the cityscape turned to rolling farmlands. Roger had found a place in the back seat and was back there having doggie dreams, yipping and licking his lips. They drove in silence for almost an hour. Beano was still wondering about Victoria. She was an ex-prosecutor....It was a little disconcerting to him to think she had been able to infiltrate him this deeply. He wondered if it was her guile and beauty that had softened him, or perhaps their common interest in revenge. Or maybe it was just another by-product of the beating with the nine-iron that he suspected had turned him soft. He had caught himself several times trying to make her smile, using his number-ten rainmaker and being crushed when it failed to get results. Now her silence was beginning to bother him more than his failed smile.

"You okay?" he finally asked.

"Yeah, I think." Victoria had a strange expression on her face.

"Say it," he encouraged. "What's on your

mind? You've been too quiet. It's beginning to spook me."

What she said was not the condemnation he expected, but unrestrained excitement.

"I didn't know it was so easy to do stuff like this. I mean, that gag with the pearl was brilliant. We didn't even break any laws. We just sold a pearl for an inflated value...now we got this phony oil company complete with stock-holders and registered land."

"Didn't you ever work bunco?" he said, surprised. "Didn't you ever catch a big securities-fraud case?"

"I prosecuted a few bunco cases, but they were just block hustles, street scams. Two years ago I plea-bargained a case where this street hustler, I can't remember his name, was selling mechanical dogs that were supposed to bark and walk around, only they were defective. They would walk but not bark. The con man got 'em from the factory for two-thirds off, and when the mark would bend down to look at the toy dog, this faker would actually throw his voice and make the barking sounds himself. He sold hundreds at Christmas. It was so cheesy it made me laugh. He got seven months, but it was nothing like this. This is a big-time criminal enterprise."

Coincidentally, Beano knew the block hustle she was talking about. It was a Bates family specialty. They bought the defective toys from a manufacturer called The Talking Animal Farm. They also bought ducks that didn't quack, which were Easter favorites, and Santa's

188

elves that refused to say "Ho-ho-ho." He also thought he might know the arrestee in Victoria's story. It was most likely a second cousin of his, named "Sidewalk Sonny" Bates. Sonny had taken a fall in Trenton about two years ago for running that grift, but Beano decided not to mention it.

"Victoria, if you want justice for Carol, I promise I'll get it for you. I'll get Tommy and Joe to rat each other out, but you gotta stick with me."

"I know. Hold on by letting go, multiply by dividing. It's just that I've always held on by holding on, multiplied by multiplying. This is a big change for me." She was silent for a minute. "My whole life I've tried to stand for something, something I could be proud of."

"And that thing you were standing for...did I miss a beat or didn't it just chew you up and spit you out?"

"That doesn't mean it wasn't worth believing in."

There was a deep silence in the car, and then Victoria smiled. "Well, that's over with now. We're near Modesto. Let's go find our moose pasture."

"Gotta pick a company color first. There's a hardware store up ahead."

They pulled up in front of a turn-of-the-century wood-frame building called Hobbs Ranch and Farm Supplies, got out, and went inside. The store had metal racks, neon ceiling lights, and a linoleum floor. Beano moved past the farming displays to the back of the large, brightly lit store. The entire back wall was devoted to outdoor paint products. He stood with Victoria, looking at a paint-chip sampler that was on the wall.

She reached out and took an emerald-green chip and showed it to him. "This is pretty. Tennessee is a green state, looks kinda like what I think a Fentress County, Tennessee, company should look like."

"When I say the words 'ferrous oxide,' what color comes to mind?"

"Some kinda rust, I guess...."

"We need something that looks like it could contain ferrous oxide. This hustle has to work in two directions."

"Of course you're right." She turned and picked out a bright orange chip and handed it to him.

"Yuck." He winced.

"It's not such a bad choice when you remember everything our government does is intentionally ugly," she said. "It's part of the government's design-cost-use equation. It promotes function over style, and cost over function. It's why everything looks like hell and doesn't work."

"Okay." He smiled. "But this orange is just a little bright for a corporate folder. What if we dulled it down by adding one-third of this?" He picked out a deep ox-blood red and held them side-by-side. "Kinda rusty copper, just like you said," he reasoned. "Then we could use the rust-copper paint for the moose pasture and on our annual reports."

He turned and, for the first time, saw her give him a full smile. It lit her face, softening it. She was truly beautiful. In that second, he saw what she must have been like as a little girl, before the self-driving compulsions took over.

"Copper it is," she said.

Beano went up to the front of the store and held out two chips to an old man behind the counter wearing a name tag identifying him as GARY HOBBS, OWNER AND COMPLAINT DEPARTMENT. "I may need as much as four hundred gallons of this"—Beano held up the orange chip, then the red—"and two hundred of this. And I need spray-painting equipment and compressors. Just bought a farm up in Marysville, and I need to paint all my outdoor metal."

"That'll make a nice little order," Hobbs smiled. He picked up a catalogue and started thumbing through it.

"I'd like to know your discount for volume," Beano said, and Hobbs nodded. "I'd also like to get this in a day or so. I'll pay the shipping. I may need to cut the order slightly, or add to it, depending what my painter thinks. I just want to be sure the paint is readily available. I'll give you a down payment to hold the order."

"Lemme check the inventory in Bakersfield." Hobbs picked up the phone and dialed the number.

"Can I borrow your phone book?" Beano said, and Gary Hobbs pushed it across the table at him while he checked with the warehouse

191

in Bakersfield. Beano took the phone book over to where Victoria was standing. "You still got that note pad?" he asked. She nodded and pulled it out of her purse.

Beano looked up "Bates" in the Central California Directory. When he found "Steven X.," he wrote down the number.

They cut a deal with Hobbs for the paint, which he said could be delivered anywhere in the San Joaquin Valley within a day. Beano paid him a thousand dollars cash in advance, to hold the available stock. Inside the little chain-linked stock yard at the back of Hobbs Ranch and Farm Supplies, they picked out a compressor and some spray equipment with three tanks. They took two cans of orange and one of red with them. Before they left, Beano bought three sheets of yellow decal letters, two inches high, and three sheets of half-inch white letters. He also bought two green jump-suits.

With Gary Hobbs's card in his pocket, Beano went out to a pay phone in the parking lot and dialed up Steven Bates.

"Bates Roofing," a young boy answered the phone.

Victoria couldn't hear what was being said on the other end of the line, but looked up sharply as Beano whistled three notes into the receiver and waited. Beano took the phone away from his ear; then she could hear the faint sound of three other notes being whistled back. It was some kind of secret identification code.

"This is Beano Bates," he said, pressing the phone back to his ear. "Who am I talking to?"

"I'm Lawrence Bates," the young boy said proudly over the receiver...."Come on, really, who is this?"

"It's your Uncle Beano."

"This is King Con?" the boy said, awe in his voice.

"Yeah, but I hate that name 'cause it brings too much heat."

"Just a minute, sir," and the phone was dropped. Beano could hear the boy yelling for his father at the top of his lungs. After a moment a man came on the line.

"This here's Steven Bates," the man said. "Who is this again?"

"This is Beano Bates, Steve."

"Can I hear them notes again?"

Beano whistled them again.

"Son-of-a-bitch! I seen you 'bout three, four weeks ago on *America's Most Wanted*."

"In our game, celebrity ain't always a blessing."

"Imagine so."

"Listen, Steve, I'm running a moose pasture up here in Modesto. I could use a little help."

"Modesto ain't bad for it, but you seen them farms around Oak Crest? Real good, and pretty too. Lotta pipe above ground."

"I haven't been over there, but I'll check it out," Beano said. "Can I buy you and your family dinner tonight?"

"You bet," Steven answered. "We'd be honored."

"Where do you like to go?"

"There's a place called the Red Barn up near Keats. It's on Highway Seventeen. How 'bout there?"

"Around seven-thirty, and Steve, I'm looking for somebody to be the painting contractor. You think you could pull some family together for that?"

"I figured that was what you wanted. There's a bunch of us up here for the summer. You think ten would do it?"

"Oughta do. We'll cut the deal tonight."

"Be a pleasure, sir."

Beano hung up. Victoria whistled the three notes at him. They sounded slightly familiar. She shot him a puzzled look.

"The first three notes of Brahms's 'Lullaby,'" he answered, before she could ask. "He whistles back the last three."

"So now I know a family secret."

He moved to the car. "Only it changes every month, and you've gotta know what music publication to look in, what list of songs, and what number on the list. It's a variation of the key book code used by spies during World War I. It's basically an unbreakable code unless you know the keys."

"And everybody in the family goes out and buys the music publication and memorizes the melody each month?" she said, cocking an eyebrow, thinking that was a hell of a lot of trouble to go through.

"It beats doing prison time because you trusted the wrong person."

"What if you're tone-deaf?"

"We take all our tone-deaf children out in a field and shoot 'em," he said, a smile playing on his expressive features.

"Perfect solution. Why didn't I think of it?" she smiled back.

They got into the car and he looked up the town of Oak Crest on the California map, then swung out of the parking lot and headed east.

♠ ♠ ♠

Oak Crest was beautiful, the acres growing green with alfalfa. The clear California sun beat down on this lush valley. Beano filled his lungs.

"Whatta you smell?" he said expansively.

She took a deep breath. "Alfalfa," she replied.

"No, down under the alfalfa, under the subsoil and the cap rock...down where the arenaceous shale butts up against the anticline, down there in that great stratigraphic trap."

"Oil," she said, grinning.

"Me too," he smiled.

They drove around looking for the right farm. Beano thought Steve Bates was right. This place was perfect. To begin with, it was beautiful. "It's always better to take a mark to a beautiful setting," Beano explained as they drove around looking at the farms. "It makes them feel good. It's always hard to sell lake-front property in a desert." There was lots of greenery in Oak Crest, California. Old oak trees hung shade over the two-lane highways like gnarled visitors from another world. The architecture was rustic, with old wood-frame, brightly painted houses. Where the lush green alfalfa didn't grow, cattle or horses grazed in picturesque herds.

Beano was looking for a particular setup, and he found it at Cal Oaks Farm. The farm, like most in Oak Crest, grew alfalfa. The irrigation pipes were large, but needed painting. They ran for miles next to the road aboveground. There were huge water cisterns to help the farm through California's frequent dry periods. The cisterns dotted the landscape like big, two-story pillboxes. Horses grazed lazily in the lowland down by the river. It was truly beautiful, but what made it perfect was that directly across the street from the farm was a large construction company that had gone out of business. A weathered sign banged in the afternoon breeze, hanging from two chains on a post arm. The office building was three stories high and had plate-glass windows that looked out at the picture-postcard farm on the other side of the road.

Beano parked the Escort and climbed over the gate. He walked all around the empty building. Before he climbed back over, he got the name of the real-estate agent off the sign in the window and called her from Victoria's flip-phone. He was told he could lease the property on a month-to-month basis for a very reasonable rate. Beano told the agent he would call her back. He explained to Victoria that he wanted to make sure he could cut a deal with the farm before he tied up the construction company property.

Beano got out of the car and looked at the pillbox cisterns and miles of exposed metal pipes punctuating the expansive landscape. "Think we mighta found our moose pasture," he finally said.

THIRTEEN

Posse

Fucking Texaco Phillips, Tommy thought as they sat in his apartment overlooking the Boardwalk. Calliope was shopping her brains out, looking for "darling outfits" to take to the Bahamas. Texaco sat across from Tommy, looking red-faced and stretching the seams of a maroon, thousand-dollar sport jacket, like a corn-fed ham in Saran Wrap. For the life of him, Tommy couldn't understand why his brother kept this foul-smelling, ignorant piece of shit around.

"Look, Tex," Tommy said slowly, "all I want you to do is find 'em. My cousin Peter works for a travel agent and he punched up the flight manifest for Delta. She flew to San Francisco with two guys named B. Bates and

J. Bates. I don't know who the hell these two fucks are, but don't you try and find out. Don't fucking try and solve this, you'll fuck it up. You just find 'em. They got phones in San Francisco, pick up a fucking phone and call me. Got it?"

Texaco both nodded and shrugged at the same time. It was a gesture of acknowledgment and indifference and it pissed Tommy off, so he back-handed the big, ugly ex-linebacker on the shoulder.

"Hey, dipshit, I don't hear no answer here."

"I'll call ya, Tommy," Texaco said softly.

"My cousin Peter will be checking to see if they book seats outta there. His number's written on this card." He stuffed it in Texaco's tailored breast pocket. "His name's Peter Rina. The kid's just outta college, so don't tell him nothin' he don't need ta know. He's in Jersey, but he can check this shit anywhere in the country."

♠ ♠ ♠

So Texaco became a posse of one. He flew to San Francisco, and was now wandering around in the City by the Bay looking at brightly clothed tourists and wondering how the fuck he was supposed to find Victoria Hart and these two guys named Bates. What he did find was a great gym near his hotel where he could get illegal steroid shots in the ass for fifty bucks a jolt. He also found a great Italian restaurant half a block from there, where the

198

osso buco and the mozzarella marinara were world class. He alternated between four-hundred-pound dead-lifts, shots of jump-juice, and the great Italian cuisine. He was power lifting and eating his way through the first day, when he decided to finally call Peter Rina and have him scan the airline reservations for Victoria Hart and the two Bateses on all flights out of SFO. The kid told him he'd found nothing so far. Texaco figured eventually they would either leave and go someplace else or Tommy would tell him to come home. His heart wasn't in the hunt. Beyond that simple truth, his walnut-sized brain had not wandered. When he got back to the hotel, he had a message to call Tommy.

"The fuck you doin' stayin' in that hotel in town?" was Tommy's first question, passing right over "Hi" and "How are you?"

"You said—"

"Hey, musclehead," Tommy charged on, "you gotta wait at the airport. If they show up and buy tickets at the counter, you gotta be there. What the fuck's wrong with you? I give you Peter's number and he tells me you only call him once."

"Jeez, Tommy," Texaco whined, "what'm I supposed t'do, call him every hour?"

"Fuckin' A right. He's checking every hour, you call him every hour. What're you doin' out there? Gettin' a Chevy parked up your asshole or something?"

"Come on, Tommy." Texaco Phillips was beginning to truly hate Tommy Rina, but the more he hated him, the more he was afraid of him. It was a strange formula. He promised he would call Peter Rina every hour on the hour and move to a hotel at the airport. When he hung up, he had completely lost his appetite.'

There was a small Western combo and some pretty slick line dancing going on in the night-club at the Red Barn in Keats. Steven Bates and his wife, Ellen, were dressed up, starched, and pleated. Twelve-year-old Lawrence had on a wide, frayed, striped tie that looked like it had been handed down through three gen-erations. The music flowed through the open door of the nightclub into the dining room while they all ate delicious barbecued ribs and but-tered corn.

"…'course, since we settled down here in Keats, we ain't been doin' no roofing or driveway hustles. We go out on the road once, twice a year, fleece some mooches, come back, and use the money to build our legit contracting business," Steve said. He was talking as he ate, wiping barbecue sauce off his chin. They were a lean, raw-boned couple, weathered by exposure to the outdoors. Steve had a con man's kind blue eyes and a receding hairline. Ellen was a fading beauty with a short, no-nonsense hairstyle and intense black eyes that examined you with a laser focus. Victoria thought that little Lawrence was going to be quite a charmer. He was just twelve years old, and his voice had not changed yet, but he had the same dazzling con man's smile that seemed to run in this family, and he was not afraid to use it.

"How you gonna play the bubble?" Steven asked, leaning in closer.

"Gonna rope the mooch with a tat, steer him with a mack, probably put him on the country-send to his drop, and play him off against the wall."

Victoria wondered what the hell they were saying as Steve continued....

"A cold playoff is kinda dangerous."

"If I have to, I'm gonna bring in the Hog Creek families," Beano added.

"You ever worked with them before?" Steve asked.

"Nope."

"Watch out. Them Bateses been living up in that Arkansas valley for a hundred years, inbreedin' an' drinking sour mash. They come rollin' outta them hills in wide-tire trucks, kickin' ass and eatin' their victims. They ain't too delicate."

"I'll bear that in mind." Beano put down his fork. "Probably set up the farm tomorrow. I think I found one that looks good for the play. I want you t'run the paintin' crew and I'll pay you ten thousand dollars, plus one tenth of anything we can skim."

Steven Bates closed his eyes. He didn't say anything for a long time. Victoria almost thought he'd gone to sleep until he opened them and looked at his wife, Ellen, who seemed to read his mind, and nodded. He turned back to Beano.

"You mentioned you was doin' this on account'a your cousin Carol," Steven finally said.

"Yeah. She got killed by the two mooches we're gonna play this game on."

"Kinda pisses me off when one of our extended family gets screwed up. I don't take that kindly. Seems wrong fer us t'be makin' money off Carol's death."

"Look, I appreciate that, Steven, but she was very close to me—you don't have to work for nothing."

"Thing is, I never run a Big Store. You let me in on this...lemme play on the inside. That'd be enough payment for me."

"You sure?"

"You're somethin' of a legend; be an honor," Steve said, and Ellen nodded in agreement.

"We seen you on *America's Most Wanted*," Lawrence chipped in. "Only you had black hair an' no mustache."

"Okay," Beano smiled at the couple, "but if we end up with surplus cash, I'll cut you in for a tenth."

"Fair 'nuff."

The business having been completed, they switched to other subjects. Victoria said very little. There was one family detail that amazed her....All of them had a tattoo under their watches, including Beano. The tattoo was a script B with the date of each family member's first scam. Lawrence Bates had gotten his just last summer.

202

"Yep," Steven said, as his son removed his watch. "Dropped some leather over in Portsmouth at the fair. Worked the drag with his fifteen-year-old cousin Betsy." Lawrence showed his tattoo proudly. Under the capital B it said: 7/3/96.

Later that night, after they rented rooms in the motel in Keats, Beano invited Victoria to his room for a nightcap of vodka and Coke that he had picked up at the liquor store. Victoria was determined not to get giddy this time and sipped her drink cautiously as Beano pulled a small, electrically heated press-on steamer out of his bag.

"This is the same kind of thing they use to steam pictures and logos onto T-shirts," he said, as he filled it with water and plugged it into the wall socket to let it warm up. He pulled out the two jump-suits they had bought at Hobbs Ranch and Farm Supplies. He laid them out on the faded green motel bedspread. Beano took the small white decals, which were only a half-inch high, and placed them over the breast pocket so that they said U.S. AGR. DEPT. He looked at them critically.

"Whatta you think?" he said. "Would you buy into that?"

She looked for a minute, then rearranged them in a semi-circle above the pocket. "Better?" she asked.

"Much," he acknowledged. He tested his steam heat iron and, using the hard desk top for a base plate, he imprinted the decals onto the jump-suits.

After fixing both jump-suits they moved out into the motel parking lot and began to affix the same letters to both front doors of the Ford Escort, this time using the larger two-inch yellow decals. As they worked, she asked him what "dropping some leather" meant.

"It's the old pigeon drop," he explained. "Actually the con is almost a thousand years old. It was first played in China. It's been called a bunch a'different things over the years: 'Doping the Poke,' 'The Drag,' 'The Spanish Handkerchief Switch.' Had a lotta names, but it's always the same game."

"How's it work?" she asked, fascinated.

"Two con men work together. They pretend to find a wallet stuffed with real money in the near vicinity of the mark. The mark needs to be chosen carefully. Usually a wealthy person, a matron or a business executive, well dressed, good shoes. Always check for quality shoes and purses. It's a dead giveaway on a wealthy mark. You position the wallet so that he also can be considered a legitimate finder. Next comes the big argument. What to do, should we turn it over to the cops? No way. Cops'll just keep it. Then the two grifters agree that the wealthy mark should hold the wallet with all the money for a week to see if anybody comes forward."

"Hold on by letting go," she said.

"Exactly. But at the last minute the grifters decide that the mark should give each of them a fraction of the amount out of his own pocket as good faith money, maybe only ten percent. The mark doesn't mind 'cause he's gonna be holding the poke worth five times that much. He gives 'em the money. The grifters take off....Then the mark opens the wallet to find out that they switched the poke on him and he has a wallet full of cut paper."

"People fall for that?" she said, amazed.

"Every day, Victoria, in every city in the world. It's one of the most common hustles around."

He straightened up and looked at his work on the door of the light green Escort. Now she understood why he had insisted on that color and size car....The mid-sized light green Ford Escort with yellow letters on the door now looked exactly like a government vehicle.

"Now all we need is yellow hard hats and clipboards. People always believe you when you've got a clipboard," he grinned. "Don't ask me why."

That night Victoria lay in bed and listened to the crickets sing. Yesterday it had been a spandex dress and hooker heels. Tomorrow, the silly green jump-suit and a yellow hard hat. They would walk up to an unsuspecting farmer carrying clipboards and pretend to be from the Department of Agriculture. No big deal! So what? She tried to go to sleep, but for some reason her heart wouldn't slow down; her adrenaline wouldn't stop pumping. It was strange....Why was this even more exhilarating than the pre-game jitters she got before a big court case? She didn't want to admit it, but she finally had to face the truth: *It's more exciting,* she thought, as she adjusted her pillow in the darkened room. *Because it's against all of my rules.* But that wasn't all there was to it. All her life her mother had tried to get her to loosen up, but Victoria had kept strictly inside the white lines, never straying, always staying on course. Now, because of the horrible guilt over Carol's death, she had put herself in the hands of this charming con man. She was lying and cheating and, strangely enough, loving every minute of it. In some deep part of her, a dormant ember, long dead, had started glowing again....She had almost forgotten this feeling, but it had happened before, when she was a small child and her mother had taken her to the market. She had stolen candy from the big open bin, her little six-year-old heart beating wildly on the way out. She had gotten away with the theft, but later her mother had caught her eating the candy and had loaded her into the car along with the candy and driven her back to the market. All the way, Victoria had pleaded not to make her go. Her mother marched her inside the market and got the manager. She had to give back all the candy, apologize, and promise to pay for whatever she had eaten. She was so humiliated, she cried all the way home. She promised herself she would never ever steal again. It was a promise she had kept for almost thirty years, but now was about to break. And she had never felt more alive.

♠ ♠ ♠

The next morning they set up the moose pasture. It was so easy, it was almost ridiculous. They drove down the entrance road of Cal Oaks Farm in their green Escort with the Agriculture Department decals on the door, decked out in their doctored jump-suits. The clipboards held prop pages torn from the phone book. Yellow hard-hats rode officially on their heads. They pulled up next to the barn where a startled, heavy-set blond man in coveralls looked up. Beano already knew that his name was Carl Harper from some letters he'd looked at in the mailbox out by the road. Beano glanced down at his clipboard as he got out of the car.

"Jill, this is the Harper place, am I right?" he said, loud enough to be heard.

"Believe so, Danny," she said, her heart beating frantically as Carl Harper walked up.

"I help you folks?" he said; his pale eyes zigzagged suspiciously around, from their faces down to the door of the car and back up to their uniform pocket decals.

"Well, I'm hoping," Beano said and gave him the rainmaker. "I'm Danny Duncan with the U.S. Department of Agriculture, and we're out here trying to help the space engineers at NASA this morning," he grinned.

"How's that?"

"Well, NASA and the U.S. Army coordinated on developing a brand-new kind a'paint." He turned to Victoria. "You wanna show him, Jill?"

From the back seat she pulled a can of paint that they had mixed that morning with their two-to-one formula. The paint was now a rusty, coppery-reddish color.

"This here is called Ferrous Oxide Paint," Beano began, "and what it's supposed to do is protect exposed metal, for in the neighborhood of fifty years. The deal here is once it's on, you don't have to repaint for half a century, if you can imagine that. NASA and the Army came to us over at D.O.A. and said maybe we could get some farmers around here to allow us to put it on their pipes and water cisterns, sorta give it a test."

Harper wiped his nose with a big red handkerchief, then stuffed it back into his back pocket. "Kinda bright," he said, looking at the paint, already trying to imagine it on all his exposed metal. "What you say's in it, again?"

"Well, I admit I ain't a chemist," Beano said, "and I ain't quite sure. Jill, what's in this stuff? You got them specs?"

Victoria looked on her prop clipboard. "It's basically an aluminum-phosphate-based paint with sulfur and cilineum nitrate," she said, cursing herself because her voice was shaking.

"There ya go," Beano said, smiling. "I think the cilineum nitrate is yer magic ingredient."

"What's the deal again?" Harper said, looking at them closer.

"Well, sir, I've been driving around all morning looking for a farm that looks like the pipes and cisterns're about due for a paint job. What we'd like to do is paint your exposed

208

metal out there with this stuff and see if NASA and the Army are right. You probably won't have to paint again for fifty years. Cost to you is not one red cent. We'll wanna put some white letters, FCP&G, on the cisterns to identify your farm from the air," he said, reading off the Fentress County Petroleum and Gas initials.

"FCP&G? What's that stand for?" Harper asked.

"It's the paint. Ferrous-oxide Cilineum Phosphate. *G* stands for government," he smiled. "Also, they wanna see if the normal letter paint affects the base coat. If ya say yes, you're gonna be helping your government. Can you imagine the tax savings if all the tanks and jeeps and such don't have to be painted but once every half-century?"

"I don't gotta pay nothin'? And you all're gonna paint all my pipes and cisterns for me and this stuff is gonna last fifty years? What's the catch?" he grinned.

"Kinda strange, ain't it?" Beano grinned. "Your government's finally givin' ya something back."

"Son of a gun," Carl Harper said, figuring this was indeed his lucky day. "When y'all need to start?"

"First thing tomorrow," Beano said. "Just need you t'sign this official release...." He had typed up a release on the motel office typewriter that morning. It didn't look very official, but Beano said once they got that far in the scam, it wouldn't matter. The farmer would already be a laydown. And since they were really going to paint his pipes for him, he was the only mark in this scam who would actually be coming out ahead.

Mr. Harper signed the paper without a second glance, then shook hands with both of them, grinning the whole time.

As they drove away, Victoria couldn't stop smiling.

"We're gonna have to get you a tattoo under your watch," Beano said, and suddenly they were both laughing.

FOURTEEN

The Big Store

Paper Collar John walked them through the Big Store, which was on the top two floors of the Penn Mutual Building on Market Street. The offices had once belonged to State Mutual Insurance, and had housed the Account Supervisors, Vice-Presidents, and the company's Regional Director. The spare-no-expense, taste-conscious executives had put in matched blond cypresswood paneling and white plush-pile carpet. When S.M.I. had closed this office two months ago, they had removed everything of interest except for some built-in lighting and one brass chandelier in the main conference room. The two floors were now empty, but very promising. Beano, Victoria, and Roger followed Paper Collar John around the floor, over parqueted wood where Roger's toenails tapped musically, then across plush white carpets where everybody's shoe leather squeaked. They walked in and out of sumptuous office suites and secretarial areas with their matching wood walls and paneled filing cabinets. Beano had already filled John in on the moose pasture at Cal Oaks Farm, and had given him Steven Bates's name and number, and the number of the real-estate agent who handled the deserted construction company across from the farm. Now, John was giving Beano the terms of the lease deal:

"I got both floors on a short lease, first and last month in advance. It was more than I planned to spend, ate up half the front money, but it's as good a setup as I ever saw, so I went five grand over budget." John stopped in front of a picture window that looked out over the city. Cable cars climbed the steep hills like brightly painted Chinese beetles. "I called the museum and told them I was the President of Fentress County Petroleum and Gas. By the way, I'm calling myself Linwood 'Chip' Lacy. I said I was a big art lover and that I'd like to sponsor some young local artists...but that I need to live with the art for a month before buying. I said we'd be interested in donating some of our wall and pedestal space to promising San Francisco artists and sculptors to be reviewed by major art critics at our grand opening in January. They're ecstatic. It should get some pricey stuff in here for no money," he said, surveying the acre of paneling.

"Good going," Beano said as they wandered in and out of the offices.

The west windows looked out at Exxon Plaza and the Golden Gate Bridge. The huge Exxon sign with the double locking *x*'s glittered in red from the roof across the street.

"Damn, that's sweet," Beano said, as he admired the view. "Nice to be able to keep an eye on our competitors," he grinned.

"I'll rent furniture and do the decorating myself," John said. "Fax machines, phones, all that stuff will be mostly rentals. We'll put extra office noise and pages through this speaker system from a background tape," he said, pointing to recessed speakers in the ceilings. "Still, I'm gonna need five to ten thousand more to do it right," he said.

"Looks great. How long will it take?"

"Two, three days, if I hurry and don't get messed up. Also, I need to staff this place. I need at least forty-five people, so I'll have to see how many Bateses are in the area. I checked the book, it looks pretty thin."

"That's because they aren't all in there," Beano said. "The sharpers doing local cons aren't listed 'cause the cops are getting hip to the X. You'll have to get one of our cousins from around here to help you make contact. We need to put the mark in play by Sunday. Once we run the tat, we don't want to give him any time to think."

They moved to the ornate elevator and went down to inspect the floor below.

"I'm gonna put the big conference room down here for when we run the fire sale," Paper Collar John said grinning, and Beano nodded.

John handed him some airline tickets. "I had these messengered over from the hotel. You and Victoria are booked to Miami at six tonight. You gotta buy your tickets to the Bahamas from there. The Customs Shed at Sabre Bay closes at five and the last flight gets in at four-thirty, so you'll have to go over to the island tomorrow afternoon. Duffy's already there with Dakota. They took a peek at the casino, and they think the tat's gonna work fine in the main room, ground level. There's a High-roller room on ten, but they didn't want to run the risk of staying in there too long, so they didn't try to case it."

"Okay, good," Beano said, as they moved out of the twenty-fourth floor, got in the elevator, and descended to street level.

"I'll be staying at the Stanford Court, so you can reach me there," John continued as they rode down. "I'll keep you up on how I'm doing. Don't worry; even though it's short notice, one way or another, I'll be dressed and ready when the ball drops."

Because Beano always liked to have a second way out of any location, he checked the ground-level fire door on the east side of the building as a possible "blow-off" escape route. He disarmed the alarm with his pocket knife before he opened the door. Then he swung it wide...and found himself looking straight at Texaco Phillips! The big ex-linebacker was leaning against a pole, holding a newspaper, pretending to be reading while he watched the front entrance. He looked directly over at Beano, but no recognition registered on his huge, flat face.

"Hi," Beano said, smiling.

"Hi," Texaco said back.

"Just checking the fire doors." Beano made a big show of carefully checking the latch. He worked the mechanism once. "That's a big okey-dokey," he said to the mechanism happily, then closed the door. He turned with panic on his face and looked at John and Victoria. "We're fucked," he said.

"We're what?" Victoria said.

"That steroid jockey that Joe Rina keeps for a pet. He's right out there."

"Texaco Phillips?" Victoria asked, amazed.

Beano nodded. "He's out there, watching the front entrance. This jerk-off is actually hiding behind a newspaper like some character from a Bogart movie."

"Whatta we gonna do?" John asked, worried.

"Upstairs," Beano said.

They moved quickly back to the elevators and punched the button. Victoria was holding Roger. Sweat was forming on Beano's face and neck, as he waited for the elevator. The panic he often felt about Joseph Rina now enveloped him. When he'd seen Texaco Phillips, adrenaline hit his heart like a shot of cold piss. He could barely catch his breath. When the elevator arrived, he pushed twenty-five and they rode up in the plush antique-mirrored car. Nobody said anything. Beano tried to get his unreasonable panic under control. How could he possibly run a complex game against Joe Rina if the mere sight of his dumb, ugly bodyguard threw him into such distress?

When the elevator door opened on twenty-five they got out and moved into the office and locked the lobby door. Beano was badly shaken.

"Are you okay?" John finally asked, noticing the trembling.

"I'm fine," Beano lied.

"How could he be here?" Victoria asked. "We didn't tell anybody but Dakota we were coming out here."

"Dakota didn't finger us," Beano said immediately.

"How do you know? Just because you've still got a thing for her? Maybe she's mad at you."

"It's not Dakota," he said again, and this time his voice was angry, exacerbated by the adrenaline coursing through his body. His tone said that the subject was closed. "It's something else."

"You don't know that," Victoria pressed. "Somebody had to tell him. That moron isn't telepathic; I deposed him. He needs instructions to get his pants on."

"Dakota and Duffy don't even know about this building," John said softly. "I didn't tell them about it yet, so Texaco didn't get it from them." It was unassailable logic and Beano was grateful that it shut her up.

He turned to John. "Maybe he just spotted you. Have you been out of here, walking around on the streets?"

"No, never left since the real-estate deal was closed. I even had a guy from the hotel bring the airline tickets over. I booked them through the Concierge Desk."

"The fucking tickets!" Beano said and he yanked them out of his back pocket and stared at them like disloyal culprits. "Joe could have scammed an airline computer. They have cross-checks on reservations now from the city of origin. You bought them at the Stanford Court Concierge Desk; he could find that out and send Texaco over. You're registered under Bates; he followed you here."

"But how did they even know we were in Atlantic City?" she asked.

"I don't know." Beano studied the tickets some more. "Maybe Tommy finally figured out who he ran into coming out of the can in the casino. Or maybe somebody recognized me....I've been the star of that fucking *Most Wanted* program."

"We gotta find a way to lose this guy," John said. "He'll come back here. I haven't got time to screw with him. I got a lot to do, and no time to do it. We gotta lose him so he stays lost."

"I could call the Hog Creek Bateses, and they could sit on his chest till this is over," Beano suggested.

"Those hillbillies won't fly. They're strictly a Ram truck posse. 'Sides, they couldn't get out here till day after tomorrow."

"We gotta call 'em and then find a way to get Texaco off the road till they get here."

They were pacing around in the office. Beano was chewing on the side of the tickets, running the catalogue of usable scams in his mind. No hustle seemed quite right, except for one. Then he turned and looked at Roger.

"I gotta pick this guy's pocket, Roger. We need to kick him to the curb. I gotta sell you again, buddy. I know you hate it, but we've got no other choice."

Roger, being the good sport and team player that he was, just barked at Beano and wagged his tail.

♠ ♠ ♠

Beano thought that Victoria was the only one that Texaco would definitely recognize. But Beano had looked the big steroid jockey directly in the eye and, dumb as he was, Texaco might still remember him, so Beano decided to go to a drugstore and buy a new hair color.

He found another side door in the building and slipped out, located a drugstore, and bought a bottle of Lady Clairol Summer Sunset and a razor, 'cause he needed to sacrifice the mustache.

He arrived back at the building ten minutes later. Before he entered by the side door, he crept around and found Texaco sitting on a bus bench across the street from the entrance. He was still hiding behind the paper like fucking Sydney Greenstreet. Beano ducked back inside, went into the ground-floor bathroom, and did the dye job. He shaved off his mustache and rinsed the excess color out of his hair. He surveyed his work in the mirror. He hated Summer Sunset 'cause it turned him into a redhead, but he was running out of Lady Clairol shades. He had added just enough red to kill the blond surfer look. He combed it quickly with his fingers and moved out of the bathroom and back up to the twenty-fifth floor.

When she saw him, Victoria thought she liked Beano much better without the mustache. Even the reddish-blond hair looked good on him. He was, she thought, one of the most handsome men she had ever known, or perhaps Beano was somehow growing on her...?

They talked through the scam until Beano was sure they all had it down. He said he was pretty sure Texaco would have a gun, probably a plastic Glock automatic, which was in style because it didn't set off airport metal detectors. Beano assigned them all roles. The game was called "The Most Valuable Dog in the World." Victoria was the shill who would also rope the mark. Paper Collar John was the singer and would tell the tale. Beano was the capper and would lure the mark and do the sting. Roger-the-Dodger was the inside man. They gave Victoria the keys to the green Escort, which was in the parking lot with the decals now peeled off the doors. Beano and John would follow in a cab.

Victoria had the plane tickets in her hand as she walked out of the building to the car. She got in and drove toward the airport. Her heart was beating wildly.

"This is crazy," she said under her breath, as she got on the Bayshore Freeway heading to San Francisco Airport. Texaco Phillips was following her two cars behind.

FIFTEEN

The Most Valuable Dog in the World

Victoria could see Texaco Phillips in his rental car two lanes over, one car back, as she made the turnoff to the airport. She watched him out of the corner of her eye as she returned the car to Hertz and walked into the large glass-front terminal. With his muscle shirt and huge size, he was easy to spot in the crowded airport. Her pulse was racing, but it calmed her slightly that he seemed to be trying to tail her and not be seen. That probably meant that he wasn't going to grab her and drag her, kicking and screaming, into the parking lot.

She went to the American Airlines counter and stepped up when it was her turn. She told the lady that she wanted to buy three tickets to Cleveland. Beano had said if the Rinas were tracking them through airline computers, this Cleveland buy would throw them off. She could see across the airport lobby, where Texaco Phillips had moved to a telephone and was dialing a number from a card he had in his hand.

"She's at the fucking American Airlines counter right now," Texaco said to Peter Rina, who was at his computer in the New Jersey travel office. Peter hit the AMA symbol for American Airlines on his keyboard and then SFO, and up on the screen came the current reservations table. He began to scroll it, looking for their names.

"You find it yet?" Texaco brayed. "Where the fuck's she going?"

"Wait a minute. I gotta go through thirty flights," Peter said, thinking Texaco sounded as intelligent as prime-cut beef. Then he saw their names being added to the computer listing on a flight to Cleveland.

"Three tickets on Flight Three-seventeen. It's for the nine P.M. flight to Cleveland."

"Shit, that's five hours from now," Texaco said, looking at his watch, thinking that at least he wouldn't have to haunt the gate all night. He could buy a ticket and wait to see who her two traveling companions were. Better still, he could get a drink and some dinner and relax for a while. He hung up on Peter without saying another word.

Texaco was sitting in the flight lounge across from the American lobby, nursing a beer and watching Victoria Hart, who was in a leather chair in the waiting area, reading a paperback. He thought she was beautiful. Texaco decided to make a date to give Miss Hart some flute lessons. All he needed was ten minutes and a quiet spot. He'd screw a gun in her ear and have her buff his pink helmet. She needed to have some of the starch taken out of her the hard way. And then he heard a commotion outside the bar....A red-haired man was arguing with a cop:

"Whatta you mean, I can't? But she's coming in right now! Okay, okay, you don't have to be an asshole."

The red-haired man turned and moved into the bar with a little terrier on a leash. He walked directly up to the bartender, reached into his pocket, and pulled out a hundred-dollar bill.

"Listen, pal, I hate to be a problem, but would you keep an eye on my dog?"

"This ain't a kennel," the bartender said.

"He's a very rare Baunchatrain Terrier," Beano said, earnestly handing the bill to the bartender, who took it and looked at it critically. "They won't let me take him down to meet the Hawaiian flight because they got some quarantine regulation, or some damn thing. I gotta go meet my daughter. She's on that flight, sick in a wheelchair, but she's coming home. Don't let him out of your sight. Like I said, he's very rare."

"Okay," the bartender said, and he put the crisp new hundred in his pocket. Beano hurried out of the bar, right past Texaco, who still didn't recognize him.

Texaco looked at the dog for a long moment, then went back to his drink. "Don't look too fuckin' rare to me," he mumbled under his breath, making his first and only shrewd observation of the day.

Ten minutes later, a very distinguished looking man with gray hair came into the bar carrying a briefcase and sat at one of the tables. After a minute he got up, crossed the bar, and looked carefully at the dog...."Son-of-a-gun," he said softly, in an English accent. Then he lifted Roger-the-Dodger expertly and checked his privates.

"Don't touch the dog," the bartender said.

"I'll be snookered," Paper Collar John muttered softly, admiring the dog. "That's the damnedest thing I ever saw."

"What?" Texaco said, his interest vaguely piqued.

John ignored him and turned to the bartender. "Y'know what this little bloke here is?" he said.

"No, sir," the bartender answered. "Guy said he was valuable, is all."

"Valuable?" Paper Collar John started to laugh. When he finally got himself under control, he shook his head in lingering amusement. "Valuable, I daresay, barely captures it. Try *priceless*."

"Really?" the bartender said.

Texaco had all of his attention on this conversation now, his pea brain cranked up to its full cerebral volume.

"I'll give you nine thousand dollars for this animal, right now." John put his briefcase up on the bar, snapped it open and started to drop crisp new hundred-dollar bills on the bar. "I just sold one of my racehorses for cash," he said to Texaco, who nodded dumbly, eyeing the money like a timberwolf scoping a jackrabbit.

"Whatta you doing?" The bartender tried to stop John, who now had hundred-dollar bills all over the bar. It was some of the pearl money stolen yesterday from Texaco's psychopathic boss.

"Look, put your money away, mister. The dog isn't mine," the bartender said. "Some guy just left him here for me to watch 'cause the ramp guards wouldn't let him go to the gate."

Having shown the poke, Paper Collar John scooped up the bills and put them back into his briefcase, snapped it shut, and looked at the bartender. "That dog is a bloody rare Baunchatrain Scottish Terrier. I venture there are only a hundred of these animals in the world. Not only that, he's a stud. Most of that breed has been neutered. They were originally for Turkish kings who had them bred in South Scotland. The Turkish prelates killed all of the males except for a few to protect their ownership of the line. Besides breeding racehorses, I sometimes write articles for the English Kennel Club," he explained. "There are less than ten or twelve ungelded males in the world...and you've got one of the little buggers sitting right here in front of you. This little fellow is worth a fortune in stud fees."

Roger was panting; he seemed happy to be ungelded and worth so much money.

223

"If the lucky gent who owns him wants t'sell the dog, my offer still goes. I'll be over at Gate Sixteen. My flight to Dallas leaves in an hour." He finished his drink, threw a huge tip on the bar, and left.

Texaco watched him go, then slid off the stool and found Beano on a phone down the corridor.

"...I don't know," Beano was saying into the receiver. "We don't have enough money for that. When did he say she had to have it done?" He listened for a moment and frowned. "I thought you said she'd be on this flight."

Texaco tapped him on the shoulder. "Hey, bud, I wanna talk to you about your dog," he said.

Beano turned and looked at him for a long moment, listening intently to the receiver.

"I can't talk to you," Beano whispered and turned away from him. "But look," he said into the receiver, "how the hell much could that possibly cost? I was just getting set to pick her up. I thought you said the tests came back negative." There was a long pause while he pretended to listen. ..."Is she gonna stay in the hospital over there?" And then he pulled a handkerchief out of his pocket and wiped his eyes. "Okay. But where the hell am I gonna get ten thousand dollars for a bone marrow transplant? You sure the insurance won't handle it?" And then he nodded. "Okay, I'll find a way. Okay...okay, kiss her for me. Tell her I love her and I'll get the money somehow," and he started to sob again, softly. When he

224

hung up he had tears on his face. Beano turned and started to walk back toward the front of the airport. Texaco grabbed him by the arm.

"Hey, bud...maybe I can help ya," he said.

"Huh?" Beano looked at him as if seeing him for the first time. "Who are you?" he said, distracted, looking down at his watch.

"I was in the bar back there where you left yer dog. My kid was with me and he was, well, he kinda fell in love with that little mutt, and I promised him I'd look for you and see if you'd sell him."

"I can't sell him. He's too valuable." Beano started away.

"I couldn't help but overhear you on the phone there....You got problems, from what I heard. That's rough. I could go maybe two thousand for the mutt, just 'cause I never saw my kid go so goofy for a dog like that before."

Beano thought Texaco was a terrible liar; the deceit was all over his face. "That dog is priceless. I wouldn't sell him for twice that."

"Okay. Twice that, then. Four thousand." Now avarice and a low IQ were cooking the deal. Texaco's eyes were lit with greed.

Beano let himself look torn for a moment.

"My little girl has leukemia. They need to do a bone marrow transplant." He started to cry again and pulled out his handkerchief. He struggled to control himself. "I'm sorry, I gotta go," he said. "My car's double parked."

"Okay, I'll go forty-five. Top offer. That's half what you said you need. Okay? You go sell

225

your car or something, then you got the whole bone."

Beano looked at him for a long moment. "How would you pay?" he said, readying Texaco for the sting.

"We take my Visa card over to that machine there and run it through, then I give you cash," he said.

Texaco knew he could make a clean forty-five hundred when he sold the dog to the gray-haired asshole who wrote articles for a fucking kennel magazine. "If it was my kid dyin'," he pressed, "I wouldn't put no dog in line ahead a'her."

"You're right," Beano sniffed. "You're absolutely right."

They went to the cash machine and got the money. Texaco counted it out for Beano, but wouldn't let him have it yet. As they went back into the bar to get Roger-the-Dodger, they could see Victoria still reading, and Paper Collar John sitting by Gate 16, waiting for the flight to Dallas. In the bar, Roger-the-Dodger had drawn quite a crowd. Three flight attendants were petting and scratching him under the ears. Beano opened his wallet and took one of his American Kennel Club certificates out. "This verifies his pedigree," he said, handing the worthless Xerox over to Texaco, who now released the money. Beano handed the leash to Texaco, then he kissed Roger good-bye. "So long, old friend. I'm sorry, but you're probably saving Cindy's life." Roger licked his face. "His name is Sir Anthony of Aquitaine,"

Beano said sadly. "He likes Pedigree Dog Chow, the beef with liver and chicken. I get him the Doggie Cookie Treats from Alpo if he's been good."

"Whatever," Texaco said and, in a hurry to complete the transaction, walked out of the bar holding the leash.

Roger-the-Dodger bounced right after him. The dog was well trained. Each time Texaco thought he would have to tug on the leash, he found Sir Anthony of Aquitaine right on his heels.

He went to find the man with the gray hair who had the crisp hundred-dollar bills in his briefcase. He went directly to Gate 16, the flight to Dallas. But the man wasn't there, and Texaco started to panic. *The man had been there just seconds ago.* And then the flight to Miami was called. Victoria got up and walked to the gate, showed her original ticket, and put her purse through the Security check. Then she walked through and down the ramp. Beano followed her. Texaco turned and, with panic in his eyes, watched them go. Then, once they were through Security, Beano turned, stuck two fingers in his mouth, and whistled for Roger-the-Dodger. The dog took off running.

"No, you don't," Texaco said and yanked back on the leash, now discovering why Roger had heeled so precisely...the dog was wearing a tear-away Velcro collar. Roger zipped out and away, leaving Texaco dumbfounded, holding a leash and an empty collar.

Roger ran right through the Security check area and jumped up into Beano's arms. Beano and Victoria took off running down the ramp. Texaco Phillips went after them. He tried to crash the gate at Security, but two airport cops grabbed him and tried to hold him down. What happened next was not pretty. The ex-Patriot linebacker threw a meaty left hook and knocked one of the cops out.... He hit the ground unconscious. All that was missing was the Tweety Birds over his head. Texaco Phillips was now loping down the corridor, a team of angry airport cops trailing behind him like determined wake sewage. Finally he was tackled by four at once, then wrestled to the floor. He put up a horrendous struggle.

"My dog," he yelled, "my dog! He stole my fucking dog!"

But the cops were not about to listen. They were too busy playing catch-up. They hammered his already flat face with metal billy clubs, and took fungo shots at his puckered balls. They Maced him until their cans spit air. When they were done he was on the floor, doing a reasonable imitation of a beached flounder.

Beano and Victoria stopped before boarding, and opened the folding kennel case that read CANINE DRUG ENFORCEMENT, U.S. CUSTOMS. They put Roger inside and then went aboard and settled into their first-class seats to Miami.

Beano counted the forty-five hundred dollars he had just gotten from prison-bound Texaco Phillips. He put it into an envelope,

228

licked it closed, wrote *John Bates* on the outside, and called a flight attendant. "Could you page this gentleman and ask him to pick this up at the ticket counter?" he said, handing it to her. "Tell him I couldn't get the whole ten, so he'll have to make do with forty-five."

"Of course, sir," she said and left. When she came back, she said that Mr. Bates had been waiting out front and had been given the envelope and the message.

"What was all that commotion out there?" Beano said pleasantly. "That man the police were chasing, what did he do?"

"He tried to break through Security. That's a Federal crime. Apparently he had a gun; that carries a mandatory sentence of ten years. I don't think we'll be seeing him for a long time," she said.

"Really?" Beano said with mock surprise.

"The Feds take that very seriously," she answered, and moved off.

Victoria smiled. "I am very impressed, two birds with one dog," she grinned.

Roger-the-Dodger was wagging his tail inside the case; it banged happily against the side of the carry-kennel, giving the effect of well-deserved applause.

The plane rolled down the runway ten minutes later.

They were off to Miami and then to the Bahamas. They had eliminated Texaco Phillips.

It was time to put Tommy Rina in play.

Part Four

PUTTING THE MARK IN PLAY

"SOME LIES ARE MORE BELIEVABLE THAN TRUTH."
—Anonymous Gypsy Proverb

SIXTEEN

Sabre Bay

Bahamian law insisted they get Roger-the-Dodger a rabies shot and a veterinary certificate at the Freeport International Airport. Now, as they pulled out of the palm-lined airport drive, he sat on the front seat of their rented, air-conditioned English Ford, very unhappy about the shot he had just received. Roger had a new green plastic tag on his collar that said he had been inspected by the Grand Bahamian Ministry of Agriculture and Trade.

Once out of the airport, they turned right and took the Grand Bahama Highway east toward the Sabre Bay Club, which was located on the easternmost tip of the island. The road led them past Pelican Point and through a dusty village named McLean's Town, which was dotted with remnants of fifteenth-century architecture from the time of Columbus. Brightly painted wood-frame buildings from the intervening years were shaded by huge cypress trees. There were narrow tin shacks with wood-supported awnings that seemed to lean like old men on canes in the withering tropical sunlight.

Whoever had designed the Sabre Bay Club knew a lot about tropical luxury. It was situated on the tip of the island so it could take advantage of the Atlantic winds, as well as the

Channel Trades that blew down the inland Providence Cut.

Beano turned into the resort under a huge European arch guarded by statues of both Columbus and Magellan. The white ground-shell road wound past a magnificent Arnold Palmer–designed golf course and finally brought the club building into view. It was a mixture of architectural styles that somehow miraculously blended together. The brochure Victoria had bought at the airport said that the entrance and porte cochere were constructed from the remnants of a fourteenth-century Gothic monastery. The pamphlet said William Randolph Hearst had discovered the already dismantled structure at a warehouse in Lourdes, France. Still stored in crates, it had been sold to Huntington Hartford, who then shipped the remnants to Grand Bahama Island. The artifacts had somehow found their way to the drive-up entry of the Sabre Bay Club. The effect was startling. A piece of old-world feudal grandeur mixed with the windy indifference of the Bahamas. Completing the display of colorful ambiance were a flock of pink flamingos that wandered freely on the grounds. Moving in graceful awkwardness, they thrust their long necks forward as they walked on stilted legs.

The porte cochere was open, and from the drive-up, they could see all the way through the lobby to the emerald-green Atlantic beyond.

"They sure didn't spare any expense, did they?" Vicky said, breaking the silence.

"Drug money. This whole thing came out of the end of a needle," he said.

She looked over at him. There was a bubbling anger in his voice she'd never heard before.

There was a sign near the entrance that said that the Hemingway Bar was at the east end of the hotel and that the Billfishing Club was down by the dock. The golf clubhouse was standing elegantly under a crop of wind-bent palm trees that swayed constantly in the sea breeze. From somewhere nearby they could hear the *whomp* of tennis balls.

"Let's get outta here before I decide to drive this little Ford through the lobby and park it in the pool," he said.

Victoria looked over and, without asking, she knew he was thinking of Carol.

Beano drove out past the flamingos, past the two famous stone explorers, and back out onto the highway.

♠ ♠ ♠

They had booked rooms in the Xanadu Beach Hotel and Marina in Freeport. It was on a wide ocean strand of beach that was backed up by a small inland harbor. One side of the hotel faced the white sandy beach and rolling Atlantic; the other looked back at the quaint marina. Once they had registered, Beano helped get their bags in their rooms, then said he would hunt up Dakota and Duffy and they'd all meet in the Wicker bar in an hour. He took Roger with him as he headed off to look for his "cousins."

Victoria went to her room and unpacked. Then she stepped out on her narrow balcony and took in the beautiful aqua-green sea. The brisk ocean wind snapped her short hair. She closed her eyes and felt a little dizzy....She knew she was desperately out of her depth in a game that had at worst no rules, or at best ones she didn't understand. She wondered how it would end, or if she would even survive to witness its conclusion. She found it both troubling and exhilarating that she was embarking on an adventure with people that, just two weeks ago, she would have had an urge to indict and prosecute. She changed her clothes and an hour later went downstairs to the appropriately named Wicker Room.

The bar was small but faced the ocean. A cooling, tropical wind blew across the rattan furniture and slow-turning ceiling fans. When Victoria entered, she looked toward the window and saw Beano and Dakota sitting at a table with an old man who looked like he had recently died, then had abruptly decided to get out of his coffin and come back for one last drink. His wiry white hair hung off his head in Einstein unruliness, and his blue veins shone through white, papery skin, like winding highways on a road map. Like Beano, he had that charming Bates smile, and the old man flashed it as she sat down.

"Hi," she said, looking over at Dakota, who had gotten some sun since Victoria last saw her. It only served to make her more radiantly beautiful.

Dakota had on a white shirt, tied at the midriff, and pink shorts. Her black hair hung in glossy luxury around her shoulders. She was sipping some sort of island drink through a long straw. She didn't nod or acknowledge the greeting. It was obvious from her manner that Dakota thought Victoria was a loose wheel threatening to come off and spill the load.

"Victoria, I'd like you to meet my uncle, Duffy Bates," Beano said, somewhat formally.

"Fit-Throwing Duffy?" she said, remembering what Beano had called him.

"A moniker I can do without," Duffy said, exposing his beautiful smile again.

"They checked the casino out last night," Beano went on. "Duffy stole a pair of table dice and sent them to Miami to his brother. The Sabre Bay Club is using expensive 'true cubes' called 'casino perfects.' They roll true because they're milled to a tolerance of one five-thousandth of an inch. Duffy's brother is going to get two dozen sets of counterfeits made that are close enough to fool the Pit Boss at first glance. They won't check too close because, to begin with, we'll be losing and they never check the dice on a loser. We've got to get at least twelve sets of real casino dice off the table to drill and load. Besides various letter 'imperfections,' the Sabre Bay casino perfects probably also have black-light marks or some other identifying device."

"Black light?" Victoria asked.

"There's a dye you can put in the plastic that shows up when you put the dice under an ultraviolet light. According to what Duffy can tell, they change dice once a day, starting at nine P.M. Each new set probably has different identifying markers. We've gotta get the dice off the table, drill and load 'em, then go back and hit the place during the same twenty-four-hour period, before they change dice and put in ones with different identifiers. Duffy estimates the A.M. shift will have over two million in the Cage Room. As soon as we get in the casino, Dakota has to split off and pick up Tommy. She's gotta rope and steer him. He's at the Sabre Bay Club now, staying in his brother's private villa on the beach. The tickets we sent Calliope worked. If everything goes right, Duffy and I are gonna run the tat tonight at around three A.M. We score the two mil and then we run like hell, 'cause this is planned for Tommy to come off hot. Dakota has to remain behind after we run so she can tell the tale to Tommy and control the 'come-through.'"

"The come-through is when the mark gets wise and comes after you once you've fleeced him," Duffy explained.

"We got a cousin from Miami scheduled to fly down and pick us up at six A.M. tomorrow at the private air field near Deep Water, just ten miles west of Sabre Bay," Beano said.

"What do I do?" Victoria asked.

"Didn't you bring your knitting, dear?" Dakota said in her husky, sensual voice, with just the hint of a smile on her lips.

"Am I somehow pissing you off, Miss Bates?" Victoria asked, doing what she always did with a problem...turn directly into it.

"You're not pissing me off, it's just that you've got no function. All you are is a potential problem. If Tommy trips to this, I'm gonna be the one he's closest to....I'm the one who's gonna get grabbed and beat senseless."

"I found this place. If it weren't for me, we wouldn't even be here. I'm the one who told Beano about the SARTOF Merchant Bank of Nassau where they store all their drug assets."

"So, whatta you want, a parade?"

"I'd like you to lose the attitude," Victoria snarled.

Beano and Duffy had been watching this without comment. Finally, Dakota nodded and sucked the last of her drink into her straw with a huge slurping sound that made them all stare. Then she pushed the tall glass away and smiled.

"Sucking is my best event," she said dryly. "What's yours, Vicky?"

"Putting up with bullshit." The exchange was cold enough to freeze mercury.

"Got to go get ready to speargun Tommy. Somebody named Calliope Love is my competition." Dakota walked out of the bar, turning everybody's head in the place as she went.

"What does she do to loosen up?" Victoria said coldly.

"Don't start a cat fight with Dakota," Beano warned. "She has the most dangerous part of this scam. She's gotta rope that psychopath and steer him till this is over."

"Does she have to sleep with him?" Victoria asked, the distaste heavy in her voice. Tommy was slimy as boiled garbage. She couldn't imagine climbing into bed with him.

Beano didn't answer. He looked out at the sailboards in the cresting surfline.

"She does what she has to do to get him to believe what we want him to believe," Duffy said. "If that means she's gotta do some plumbing, then that's what she'll do."

"Yuck," Victoria said.

Beano's blue eyes were fixed on the sea, and his mind seemed far away.

"Maybe Victoria could do the bank-clearing scam," Duffy said, causing Beano to look back at them.

"I'll do it, whatever it is," Victoria said.

"We sent the casino credit department a new set of *McGuire Financial Listings* yesterday," Duffy explained. "The listings include every financial or banking institution in America. Casinos all use them to check the credit on players. We reprinted a page and added a bank in Fresno called the Central California Cattlemen's Bank. When they call the number in Fresno, a rollover line will call forward it to

240

the pay phone outside the Sabre Bay Club. How'd you like to take the call and do some singing for us?"

"I'd like that," Victoria said.

The dice arrived back from Miami by special courier at three in the afternoon. Beano and Duffy loaded them into the arms of Duffy's wheelchair and snapped the Porta-Toilet into place. Then they got into Duffy's rented, mid-sized blue Chevy van. Beano loaded the wheelchair into the back. Roger hopped up into the front seat beside Victoria, who was behind the wheel.

Victoria had also been assigned the task of getaway driver and "lay chickie," which she found out, to her relief, was a lookout. Her job was to wait in the van with Roger near the Sabre Bay Golf Shop pay phone and watch the front entrance. They told her she had to be ready in case they needed a fast "out." She resented her minor role in the tat, but was looking forward to being the singer. In her purse she had all the information that she would give to the Credit Manager of the casino when he called. She couldn't defeat their logic. Tommy would spot her immediately. He knew her from his brother's trial. If she got close enough to be seen, his guard would come up and it would probably end the whole thing. But Victoria knew she couldn't stand on the sidelines. She'd been thinking about the problem and had been trying to come up with a possible solution.

They were ready to go and were all sitting out in front of the Xanadu Hotel in the late-afternoon heat, waiting for Dakota, who had not come down yet. When she finally walked out of the entrance and across to the van, Victoria was startled. Dakota was dressed in a sexy, yellow evening gown that was slit up the sides and was low in front. You could see everything she had right through the thin, silky material. Her nipples and hips poked against the fabric with arresting results. It was sleazy and classy at the same time.

Dakota got into the van, picking up Vicky's expression. "It's a little slutty, but I'm only allowed to bait my hook once."

They took off with Victoria driving and Roger-the-Dodger nestled in beside her, his chin on her thigh. The little terrier had definitely adopted her. They were headed back along the Grand Bahama Highway toward the Sabre Bay Club. It was almost eight-thirty when they got to the eastern tip of the island. The sun had just begun to set: a fiery orange sphere on the tropical green vanishing point. Then, like a slow-motion shot of a cue ball dropping into the pocket, it slid below the horizon.

Beano looked at his watch. "Almost nine. Where the hell is the night shift?"

Finally, several hotel vans pulled up in the employee parking lot.... Ten men and women in black tie got out and headed into the side door of the casino.

"The night team," Beano said. "Table bosses, pit and stick men. Okay, you ready, Duffy?"

The old man nodded. "I'm gonna start with a 'splash move,'" indicating he was going to rehearse the switch of the dice first without actually playing them, to see if the Pit Boss would spot it.

Beano nodded. "Dak, you ready?" he asked.

She nodded, took a deep breath, and checked herself in the visor mirror.

Beano retrieved the wheelchair, bringing it around to the side where Duffy sat by the sliding door. He helped Duffy down onto the potty seat. Victoria could see that there was a hotel towel placed inside the plastic catch basin of the Porta-Toilet to muffle the sound of the dice once they were dropped between his legs. Duffy lowered himself into the chair and took out some eye drops that he had mixed. He put several in each eye....They would make his eyes turn red and watery, making him look sick. Then he began to shake with a practiced but very realistic palsy.

"You set, Uncle Harry?" Beano said, using the alias they'd agreed on. They both had phony I.D.'s saying they were Harry S. Price and his nephew, Douglas.

"Time to go south," Duffy said. "Going south" was a grifter's term for any play where you illegally removed dice or money from a casino table.

"There's a good easy-listening station on 107.6," Dakota said to Victoria as she climbed out of the van.

"Hey, Dakota..." Victoria responded, and when the beautiful mack turned around, Victoria gave her a thumbs-up. "Break a leg, kid."

Dakota nodded solemnly and then followed Beano, who was already pushing Duffy's wheelchair into the casino.

Victoria watched them until they were deep inside the Sabre Bay Club, then she drove the van around to the golf shop. She got out and moved over to the pay phone where she had an unobstructed view of the front entrance. She stood there patiently and waited for her part in the tat.

SEVENTEEN

Deadwood Players

Dakota followed as Beano pushed Duffy into the windswept ocean-view hotel lobby. Then he turned right and rolled Duffy through a massive threshold, across an open courtyard, and into the dark, air-conditioned, windowless casino. The sound of trade winds and vibrating palm fronds was quickly replaced by ringing slots and the drone of a dozen Stick-men calling the games at their tables. Beano wheeled the chair across the rich, two-toned purple and red carpet and up to the Cashier's cage.

"Like to deposit some cash an' shoot some craps," Duffy said, his voice shaking now, his palsied hand waving uncertainly in the air as he raised it to get the cage clerk's attention. She looked down and saw him in the wheelchair, then smiled at Beano, who now seemed both bored and angry. Dakota had already split off, heading to the bar.

"Come on, Uncle Harry, you're just gonna lose it like yesterday at the Freeport Princess Casino."

"Don't you start in on me again, Douglas. All you been doin' is carpin' an' complainin'. What'm I supposed t'do, put on one a'them jock strap bathing suits a'yours an' jump in the pool?" He looked up at the clerk, whose name tag said she was CINDY. "Gonna buy fifty thousand in chips, then maybe we could arrange some credit if that runs out." He pushed an envelope full of cash through the cage and watched with red-rimmed eyes while Cindy's nimble fingers counted the bills.

"That's fifty thousand dollars U.S.," she said. "Do you want that all in chips?"

"Yes siree," Duffy trumpeted. "You can deliver it to the nearest table over there and then stand back and watch a master at work."

"Jesus Christ," Beano groaned. "Some master. You been losing worse than the New York Jets."

Cindy shot Beano a look hoping to shut

245

him up, then said, "I could get that credit-ap started if you want. It'll only take a minute."

"Let 'er rip," Duffy honked loudly, which triggered a coughing spasm that doubled him over in the chair.

Cindy got a credit application out of a drawer under the counter. "Could I have your full name?" she politely asked the now-sputtering old man.

"Harry Stanton Price," he said, getting the coughing spasm under control and regaining his composure.

"Place of business?"

"Price Is Right Automotive Center, Fresno, California. I own the sucker," he smiled, but his voice was shaking slightly, his head nodding forward as if it were a constant struggle to keep it up on his wobbly pencil neck.

"Banking affiliation?" she said.

"The Central California Cattlemen's Bank, Fresno," he wheezed at her.

She carefully wrote that down. "Do you have any objections if we contact your bank, Mr. Price?"

"Hell, no! You gotta find out how much I got in there, don'cha? Just tell 'em I'm down here, my luck's finally changed, and I'm about ta kick some serious ass," he said, grinning and letting his head loll slightly over to one side.

"This should only take a short while, sir...if you want to check back in half an hour. In the meantime, I'll send your rack of chips to table three." She smiled at him and pointed to the nearest crap table.

He waved his hand at her, letting it make small, palsied circles in the air.

"Jesus," Beano moaned, "can't we at least get something to eat, Uncle Harry? You need to take your medicine."

"Y'just don't know how t'have fun," Duffy said weakly, stifling another war with his own lungs. Then he straightened slightly and in a high, reedy voice barked at Beano, "Let's go. Take me, take me...gotta go," he wheezed.

Beano turned and wheeled the chair across the carpet to crap table three.

Cindy watched them go, then picked up the phone in her cash cage and called the Box-man in the pit. "Zig, I'm sending two deadwood players to table three. They bought fifty thousand in chips. They sound like they already dropped a bundle at the Princess in Freeport. I'll send a tray over and get them photographed by Security. You might wanna comp 'em."

The casino Box-man was the individual who was in charge of the crap tables. Luke Zigman was sitting on a metal-backed folding chair with the phone up to his ear. He looked over and saw Beano pushing Duffy up to table three. "The old duck in the rolling seat and the good-looking, red-haired guy?" he asked Cindy.

"That's them. Couple of laydowns if you ask me; keep 'em happy."

"On it." He hung up and watched as a casino employee in a uniform brought over a large tray of colorful chips on a rolling cart and parked it near Duffy's wheelchair.

"Okay, okay, time t'roll, time t'roll," Duffy said, smacking his lips and grabbing some hundred-dollar chips off the tray beside him and throwing them over the rail onto the table, where they bounced on the green felt. "What's the table limit?" he bellowed.

"Two thousand dollars, sir," Zigman said.

"Gimme the big six-eight for two thousand and insurance. Cover the six and ten for five hundred each, the hard way."

Zigman smiled slightly. The big six-eight, hard way, and insurance bets were all sucker plays. He stepped up and watched as the dice were passed to an elderly woman in pink pastel shorts and beach thongs.

"New shooter coming out," the Stick-man said, beginning his unending line of patter known as table barking.

The woman threw the dice and they came up three and five.

"Eighter from Decatur," Duffy shouted. "A winner."

The Stick-man, who was dressed in white shirt, red vest, and tie, corralled the dice with the curved stick and pushed them back to the lady. Then he paid Duffy's big six-eight, which was a winner. Duffy was determined to lose, so he left his winnings on the table, pushing it all on the line. The lady grabbed the dice and immediately rolled a seven.

"Seven, a loser," the Stick-man droned. "The line loses. Pay the don't come." And he scraped Duffy's lost bet off the table. When the dice were passed to Duffy, he looked at them with a practiced eye.

"Be good t'Harry Price, good t'Harry Price," he mumbled at the red translucent cubes. "These are the dice t'pay the price," he chanted maniacally. While Beano looked at the other players apologetically, nobody noticed as Duffy palmed the dice, expertly dropping them between his legs into the Porta-Toilet, at the same time switching them with a set of his brother's Miami-made counterfeits. Then he put the switched dice down on the table. From his wheelchair seat, his head just barely appeared above the rim of the table. He reached over the rail and arranged the dice in a five-two combination of seven. He was giving the Stick-man a good look at his ringer dice to see if they would pass muster at that distance. Nothing happened so, with his "splash move" completed, he picked up the dice and shook them next to his ear.

"Okay, okay. Talk to me. Be nice to Harry Price," he said to the dice in his fist. Then he turned and snapped at Beano, "Get me down on the come line, Douglas. Wanna raise the limit...five thousand."

"I'll approve the bet," Zigman said to the Stick-man, raising the table limit.

There was a gasp from the table and, once his bet was down, Duffy rolled the bones. They came up six and four.

"Point is ten," the Stick-man said.

"Get me down for two thousand, the hard

way," Duffy said. And Beano handed the Stick-man two thousand in chips to buy the longshot sucker bet that the ten would eventually get made as double fives, before he sevened out.

Zigman smiled from his place behind the Stick-man. If the old crippled guy kept betting like that, they'd take his whole poke in half an hour.

For the next thirty minutes Duffy threw his money away like a street sucker betting Three-Card Monty. The Box-man grinned as Duffy's chips were repeatedly scraped off the table. Luke Zigman had quickly figured out that the old man was using a Martingale System, which was a complicated betting scheme often employed by losers. It basically consisted of doubling and quadrupling bets after every other loss. Twice Duffy had to ask that the table limit be waived so he could quadruple his bet. Both times this happened he lost, and the Stick-man would rake over ten thousand of the old man's dollars off the table. Duffy ended up being the only player shooting at table three because he was so cold he had become a plague on everybody's luck.

"Jeezus, Uncle Harry...whatta you doing? Don't bet all the hard-ways; it's a jerk-off bet," Beano whined with no effect, as Duffy hissed at him to shut up and did it over and over again. What nobody noticed was that, with each loss, while the Stick-man and Box-man were trying to contain their grins, another pair of casino dice rained down into the Porta-

Toilet catch basin under Duffy's bony ass. After he lost a big roll he would yell, "New dice! New dice!" in his wheezy rasp and the casino would only too gladly oblige this loser, pulling his counterfeit dice off the table and supplying him with a new set of casino perfects, which would hit the plastic catch basin under him a few moments later.

"Jeezus, Harry, can't we get outta here?" Beano whined. "You need to take your medicine." But the old man waved him away.

Zigman moved up and whispered to the Floor Manager, "We're gonna Schneider this jerk in less than an hour."

Every employee in the casino knew in minutes there was a major slab of deadwood on table three.

In the Credit Office, the Shift Manager, Arnold Buzini, was waiting for his Credit Manager to confirm the sucker's net worth. Buzini was known around the Sabre Bay Club as the Buzzard, and was leaning over her desk, impatiently tapping his fingers.

"Try and verify him as high as you can," Buzini said; his close-cut hair was steel-gray and he had gray-white skin. He lived indoors and loved to see "leakers" like Harry Stanton Price show up. He lived for dumb bettors with systems.

The Credit Manager was named Angela Hopkins and she had just dialed the Cattlemen's Bank of Fresno, using her new set of *McGuire Financial Listings* that had been unexpectedly delivered yesterday. After a series of clicks, which she assumed was the island telephone system but was really the rollover call-forwarding mechanism in Fresno, the pay phone at the golf shop, not two hundred yards away, rang.

"Cattlemen's Bank of Fresno, one moment, please," Victoria said in a high sing-songy voice; then she hit one of the numbers on the punch-dial to make a tone sound and held the receiver to her stomach until an island workman's car with a loud muffler passed by. "Yes, how can I help you?" she said, coming back on the line.

"This is the Sabre Bay Club on Grand Bahama and we'd like to get a credit verification," Angela said, while the Buzzard leaned closer to try and overhear.

"That would be Miss Prentiss. One moment, I'll transfer you." And she hit a number on the keypad for a sound effect, then put the phone back up to her ear.

"Louise Prentiss, Personal Accounts Manager," she said, now using her normal voice. She was holding the sheet of paper in front of her with all of the information Beano wanted to impart.

"This is the Sabre Bay Club on Grand Bahama. We're doing a credit check on Mr. Harry Stanton Price. He told us he banks with you."

"That's correct. Let me get his account on screen. Do you have an International Verification Number?" Victoria asked.

"Two-four-five-nine-eight double-zero." Angela gave the number from memory.

"Thank you. How can I help?"

"He's requested a loan from us of two hundred thousand dollars. We need verification up to that amount."

"Is this a casino hotel?" Victoria asked.

"Yes, it is," Angela responded.

"Both Mr. Price's personal account and his Price Is Right Automotive Center bank with us. Mr. Stanton has a net worth in excess of ten million dollars. His cash-on-hand balance is well in excess of the required two hundred thousand. We can reserve it here, but would rather not wire it unless it becomes necessary."

"That's fine. Reserve it and we'll issue the credit and settle with you if need be when he checks out."

Buzini was out of the office before Angela hung up. He made his way across the carpeted casino to where a small crowd had gathered to ooh and aah as Duffy threw his money away with stupid bets on table three.

"New dice," Duffy yelled after each miserable roll. When Buzini got to him, he was down to less than five thousand dollars, and half of that was scraped away two rolls of the dice later.

"Sons-of-bitches," Duffy scowled at the dice. "Losing's worse than a Communist dictator." He looked up at the casino Shift Manager through bloodshot eyes; his head lolling badly to the right side, he had let a fine line of spit drool down his chin.

"It's a pleasure to have you at the Sabre Bay Club," Buzini said, smiling at the horrible-looking cripple, praising his good fortune and thinking the old man would be better off in some vegetable ward at a mainland hospital.

"Goddamn dice, can't *buy* a fucking winning number," Duffy complained.

"Sir, I'm sorry you're experiencing a run of bad luck," Buzini purred, "but Sabre Bay would like to extend you the courtesy of one of our priority suites. Everything that's here, dinner, the shows, all of the resort amenities, will be complimentary."

"How's my credit check coming? Need more cash," Duffy wheezed.

"I've checked that, sir, and your credit has been approved to two hundred thousand dollars." He smiled, hoping the old leaker didn't croak before he had a chance to lose it all.

"Harry, can we get out of this casino for a while? You've lost enough for one sitting," Beano moaned. "Let's go before you lose the whole car business."

"Goddamned whining and complaining. All you do is groan an' moan an' ruin everybody else's fun."

"Sir, would both you gentlemen honor us by being our complimentary guests for as long as you'd like to stay?" the Buzzard said, exposing his carrion smile.

"Damn right I'll stay, bet yer ass I'll stay. I gotta get even here. Luck's bound ta' change. Bound ta' change."

"Can we at least get something to eat?" Beano whined.

"Our Pelican Room is excellent; the dinner menu is exquisite. I'll bring your room key over to your table. Allow me to make the reservation," Buzini said, wringing his hands and reminding Beano of the manager who ran Rings 'n' Things in Atlantic City.

♠ ♠ ♠

Tommy finally agreed with his brother, Joe, that Calliope Love was a head-splitting pain in the ass. They were sitting in the bar at the Sabre Bay Club. Tommy had the gunfighter seat, with his back to the wall so he could scope out the hot-looking talent coming up from the pool. His eye had locked onto a brunette in a yellow silk dress the minute she arrived....He could barely pull his gaze away. The dress was little more than a nightgown and his sexual imagination was filling his loins with lust while Calliope's flat Boston vowels were filling his ears with complaints.

"All them little kids down by the pool, screamin', throwin' their Frisbees," she complained, while Tommy was studying the beauty sitting alone at the bar. Several men offered to buy her drinks or to dance to the music of the small calypso band that was set up next to the dance floor. The brunette spurned them all. "You should make it an adults-only hotel, Tommy, I swear," Calliope contin-

255

ued. "It's a casino. Them little brats can't gamble. Why they gotta be here? You just know them little shits is pissing in the pool."

"This was your idea, comin' down here," Tommy growled. "Why don't ya shut yer yap for a while? All you fuckin' do is gimme a fuckin' list a'things that piss you off; I ain't the fuckin' complaint department, okay?" His gaze was focused past Calliope as the brunette at the bar crossed her legs and the slit dress fell away, almost exposing her. Tommy's expert eye had already determined she wasn't wearing anything under the silk dress...no outline of underwear, nothing. She was naked as an egg under there. The only thing keeping his pecker down was Calliope's constant braying.

"The hamburger was absolutely ruined," she observed. "You should talk to the guys that cook at the grill. Tell 'em we don't need our meat burned to charcoal, for Christ sake."

"Why don't you give it a rest?" Tommy sighed, hoping to shut her up.

"I'm only trying to help improve this joint. They overcook everything," she said, pouting slightly, "but maybe the only meat you give a shit about is that tube steak between your legs."

"Stop talkin' like a whore. Joe says you talk like a street hooker and he's right." Tommy moved slightly to his right, so he could see better over Calliope's shoulder. A red-haired man came into the bar, walked up, and started talking to Tommy's almost-naked fantasy Goddess. She made no move to pull her dress back over her legs or to cover her exposed thighs. She also didn't wave the guy off like she had the others. He was too handsome and too tall and Tommy hated him on sight. Then the redheaded man committed the ultimate sin: He put his hand on the Goddess's shoulder and leaned down and whispered in her ear. Tommy dug into his pocket and put five hundred dollars on the table.

"Why don't you go play this?" he said, and Calliope snapped up the money like a hungry tree lizard, tongue-zapping an insect.

She got up and faced him. "Y'know, Tommy, you don't always have to treat me like I'm some kinda rental. I have feelings."

"Right, but ya don't give a shit about mine. You're in my ear all day long.... 'Do this, change that.' This ain't my hotel."

"You said it was...."

"Joe makes all the decisions."

"You let him boss you around. He's your little brother, you should stand up to him. He's not so smart."

"Just go blow the five benjies and stop chewing on me."

She turned and walked away, swaying her ass, trying to cool him down by giving him a show, but Tommy missed it. His eyes never left the girl at the bar. When the tall, redheaded guy turned and left her, she immediately motioned for the bartender to get her check. Tommy waved to the bartender, shook his head, then pointed to himself. The bartender nodded, then leaned down and spoke to the girl, who glanced at Tommy. Then she deliberately opened her purse and paid her bill anyway. She got up from the bar stool, started to leave, then abruptly turned and moved toward him. He could see the sway of her hips, see the outline of her nipples through the translucent fabric of her gown. She moved to him, stopped, then put one hand on her hip and smiled.

"I can afford my own drinks. But thanks," she said; her seductive voice whistled like a cold wind blowing across smooth marble.

"They're complimentary," Tommy said. "Compliments of the casino. I'll have the money returned to your room if you give me the number."

"You work for the casino...?"

"I own the casino....From now on your money is no good in this place," he said softly. Then he followed that with his best smile, which would qualify at most hangings as ghoulishly speculative. "Thomas Rina," he said and stood, putting out his hand. She was almost four inches taller and he had to look up at her, but for once he didn't mind being shorter because he was too busy admiring her. She was the best piece of free-floating pussy he had seen in his entire life.

"I noticed a lotta guys asked you to dance....What's wrong, you don't like to dance?"

"Wrong verb," she said coolly, and Tommy's grin widened.

"How'd you like to join me for dinner on the

High-roller floor?" he said, thinking he could get her out of here and take her to the private dining room on the key-locked High-roller floor on ten, and avoid running into Calliope. He hadn't given Calliope a key to the High-roller floor because she would probably spew out her complaints and upset the thousand-dollar bettors. He also didn't need her up there dressed in short-shorts and heels, pissing on him in public. This Goddess was different. She was sexy and classy at the same time. "How 'bout you join me for dinner?" Tommy pressed.

"I'm with some people," Dakota smiled.

"Friends?"

"Not exactly...I met 'em in Vegas, flew down here with 'em on their private plane. Now I'm kinda stuck."

"What's your name?"

"Dakota Smith," she said softly, her husky voice sensual and full of promise.

"And that guy you were with over there...he's not your boyfriend?"

"I don't know what he is right now...a mistake, probably."

"Well, things're definitely looking up," Tommy said, again smiling unattractively.

"You own this place? Really?" she said, and he nodded. Then a thought seemed to hit her. "Douglas and his Uncle Harry have a table in the Pelican Room for dinner. They paid my way so I better join them, but I've never been to the High-roller floor. Maybe I could ditch them and meet you for a drink later."

"How 'bout right here, ten-thirty?"

"Make it eleven," she said, smiling at him. "Am I dressed okay for the High-roller floor?" she asked.

"Baby, if you were dressed any better you'd set off the fire alarm."

She smiled and walked out of the bar, turning every head. Tommy didn't usually connect so easily....He had sometimes dated beautiful women, but they were pros and Tommy always had to pay, but luckily, this Goddess was different.

♠ ♠ ♠

The Pelican Room overlooked the ocean on the mezzanine level. It was elegant, with off-white carpet and dark wood antique tables and chairs. The silver was authentic. Buzini gave Beano and Duffy a key to Suite 10-B. He told them it was one of their best High-roller suites and was on the key-locked tenth level. After he left, Dakota joined them at the table in the magnificent dining room, but was strangely silent.

"You hook up with Tommy?" Beano finally asked.

She nodded. "We're meeting later. He looks worse than I remembered. A housefly in loafers."

Beano nodded and started to say something....

"Don't, Beano. Okay? I'll do my end, you do yours. It's about Carol, not about you and me." She looked at Duffy. "You get the perfects?" she asked, referring to the casino dice.

"Twelve sets. I'm blowin' farts on 'em right now t'keep 'em warm," he grinned.

They ordered dinner but said very little. There was a strange tension between Beano and Dakota that cut through the air like words screamed in silence. Finally, after they finished their coffee, the beautiful mack put down her napkin. "If you're looking for company, you should take Victoria out. Show her your multi-terrain personality. Might stir up some of her bottom sediments."

"Maybe I'll do that," Beano said.

Then Dakota turned and walked out of the restaurant.... Neck cartilage snapped all around her.

"You two should lay off," Duffy said.

"I fell in love with her once. She spit me out like fish bones."

"So it's over."

"I know." He tapped his head. "At least in here, I know." Then he got up, pulled Duffy away from the table, and pushed him out of the room.

EIGHTEEN

Loading the Dice

Victoria was still down by the golf shop, waiting with Roger, when Beano finally called and told her to get Duffy's overnight case from the car and come to the fire door on the east side of the hotel. The little terrier followed her as she got the small blue canvas bag out of the van and went off in search of the door. She found Beano standing outside, looking out at the moonlit ocean.

"How'd it go?" she asked, handing him the bag.

"We got the casino perfects. We're comped into a High-roller suite on ten. It's a key-locked floor. How you doing, Rog?" he said, and the little dog looked at him and cocked his head as if he wasn't certain. "Come on," Beano said.

He opened the door, which he had propped open by leaving his shoe in the threshold. He removed the loafer, slipped it on, and they climbed the stairs to the third floor. He opened the door there and checked the hall before leading Victoria and Roger-the-Dodger out to the elevator. They got in and he used his key to activate the button to the tenth floor. They rode up without speaking as calypso music from the recessed speaker washed over them.

Victoria followed him out on the tenth floor and over to Suite 10-B. Beano knocked on the double doors and Duffy opened one a crack and peaked through before opening it wide. Victoria walked into a magnificent beige and white suite with a twelve-foot exposed-beamed ceiling, a wide balcony, and louvered windows to deflect sunlight. The furnishings were tasteful, but slightly bland, the major exception being several pieces of Bahamian metal sculptures of native spear fisherman that she thought were truly stunning. Beano and Duffy had ordered caviar and champagne which they had barely touched and, since she was starved, she took several toast squares and loaded them with the tiny black fish eggs, wolfing it down. She fixed one for Roger, who sniffed it before looking up at her with wise eyes that seemed to say, "What, are you kidding me?"

"It's an acquired taste," she said to the dog, while Beano handed Duffy the blue canvas bag. Duffy opened it and started laying the contents out on the blond-ash dining room table. The plug-in drill and bit were very small.

"Dentist drill," Duffy explained as Victoria wandered over, holding the last toast square with caviar. He laid the drill carefully on the table. Then he unpacked an assortment of blades, several dark glass vials that Victoria assumed contained the cellophane gas, and a jar of epoxy, plus a bottle of white paint. The last thing he removed was a small case that contained several tiny single-hair paint brushes.

"This is gonna take a while," he said as he attached a small vise to the edge of the table. Victoria moved over and looked at the twelve pairs of casino dice that were lined up on the far end of the table.

"These the perfects?" she said, picking one up and examining it. "Aside from being perfect cubes, I don't see any difference between these and the counterfeits your brother made," she added.

"Look at the *S* in Sabre," Duffy said.

She held it close and squinted at it. "The *S* is closed at the bottom, like an eight," she said.

"Right. That's the intentional flaw. There's also some dye in the dice. Look't this..." He picked up a small black light and plugged it in.

"Hit the light switch, Beano," and Beano turned off the dining room lights. Duffy put the dice Victoria had in her hand into the table vise and then shined the ultraviolet light through them. There was a purple glow that ran diagonally through the cube.

"Very cool," she said softly.

"Okay, Beano," Duffy said and Beano switched the overhead lights back on.

"We gotta drill this so we don't interfere with that purple stripe. What I do is, I go right through the white spot on the face of the die, create a little hollow tube with the dentist drill. We put the cellophane gas next to the open oven to warm it, which makes it heavy and thick so we can pour it in, then fill the drilled hole halfway up, leaving room so it can expand when it cools and turns to gas. Then we fill the top of the hole with epoxy, closing it, hollow it out slightly to match the others...and paint the dot white again with these single-hair paint brushes."

"How long is all that gonna take?" she asked.

"'Bout four hours if I hurry." He looked at his watch. "We should be ready to run the tat by three A.M. Dakota is gonna get Tommy hammered and get him to her room around one."

Beano turned and moved unexpectedly out of the dining room and into the living room. She could hear him slide open the balcony door and go out, then a patio chair scraped against the concrete deck as he moved it.

"Can I help?" she asked Duffy.

"Nope. This is an art form. Very delicate work. One little slip and the pair are ruined. We might need all twelve." He took the vials of cellophane gas and put them on a chair in the kitchen, next to the open oven. Then he turned the flame on and came back. He picked up the first of the translucent red dice and put it into the vise. "Gonna make my set of weighted sevens first. That means I drill the one and the three, which then brings up the light side, which is two and five." He then picked up the dentist drill, affixed a tiny round drill bit, and turned the instrument on. It made a light whirring sound. Then he poised over the single die in the vise and slowly began to drill out the center spot in the three. Occasionally he would shine the U.V. light to make sure he hadn't hit the purple strip. "In the old days I used ta *skip roll* the dice," he said, as he worked. "Perfected my Greek shot...That's a controlled roll, where the dice hit the rail one on top of the other so the bottom cube doesn't roll over. Only an expert could do it, but it's easy for a Box-man to spot.

265

Then I started using flat passers; they're basically shaved dice so the four, five, nine, and ten turn up more frequently. Then I invented electric dice," he grinned.

"What're they?"

"Drilled dice loaded on one side with tiny steel slugs. Hadda get in the casino storage room where they worked on the tables and install an electromagnet under the felt. Tough to install, but worth the risk. 'Course that was back when the Pit Bosses were called Laddermen 'cause they sat up on ladders and watched the tables. That was before TV surveillance, before the Eye-in-the-Sky. I used ta' only work carpet joints 'cause the ritzy casinos didn't float the dice. Them metal slugs would take my loadies straight to the bottom of the glass." Victoria watched in fascination as he talked and finished the work on the first one. "I done 'em all. Worked every tat there is, from Dead Aces to beveled dice with rounded edges, but I ain't never come up with nothin' as good as this." He grinned as he placed the second cube in the table vise. "While I finish this, go out there and calm Beano down. Something's wrong, he ain't been actin' right."

"Maybe because he's still in love with Dakota, who's about to sleep with a hood who could qualify as a hemorrhoid substitute. Some life you people lead."

"It's a living," Duffy said, and he went back to work.

Victoria moved out of the dining room into the living room, got a Coke out of the mini-bar, and slipped out onto the deck, passing Roger, who had curled up on the silk-covered sofa and was snoring. She sat next to Beano in one of the patio chairs and looked out at the moonlit ocean. A searchlight on the hotel roof was aimed out at the jagged rock outcroppings and lit the sharp foam-wet ridges. They glistened in spotlit beauty.

"Duffy's credit is approved," she finally said. "You didn't ask, but that went off just the way we planned...two hundred thousand."

"The casino manager told us," he said and he fell silent again.

"You didn't want Dakota to be the roper? Was it because you didn't want her with Tommy?" she said.

"It's not about Dakota. I was stupid. I knew she was a mack when I took up with her. I was just so damned lonely I made a mistake. It's over."

She wasn't sure what else to say to him. He was so unlike the Beano Bates of two days ago. The one who'd conned her in the Jersey restaurant and sold the pearl; the one she'd helped set up the moose pasture. This Beano Bates was sad and vulnerable, and she found herself drawn to him.

"Are you afraid of Tommy?" she finally asked.

There was a long moment while he sat absolutely still, not moving a muscle. Then he started to talk. His voice was very soft, almost blown away by the tropical wind.

"I don't know why," he started, "but something happened to me the night Joe beat me with that club. I lost my edge, my mental toughness. I walk around and I think I'm the same, but I'm not. At first, I thought I *was* afraid of Joe and Tommy, but now I think that's not it. I'm not afraid Tommy will hurt me...but that, somehow, I won't be able to square things for Carol." He never looked at her. His handsome profile was lit by the distant moon and the kick from the hotel lighting.

"All she would ask is that we try," Victoria said.

"No, she wouldn't ask that, not Carol, not the nurse. She'd say, 'Go home, Beano. Don't do this. It's not worth it.'" He hesitated, then went on, "All my life I've been alone. Even with my parents I was alone because we never talked about what we were feeling. For a sharper, that can never be part of it. You're taught to act a role and never reveal anything. You suck it up, play the game, never show weakness. Only suckers show weakness. But I am weak. I'm weak in my center and I've done it to myself. There's an old Gypsy saying: 'If you don't believe in your con, the mark won't believe it either.' I've believed in too many cons. I've passed myself off as so many people, I don't know who I am anymore. I've traded myself away, with tiny pieces of bullshit. The only one I could ever talk to about it was Carol. Carol knew. She was raised by her parents with the same values I was raised with, but she rejected them. We talked about it when we were chil-

268

dren. Later, when I was in prison, she told me, 'What you steal won't nourish you. In order to be nourished you need to care about what you're doing.' I used to think I could take pride in running a great hustle...but there was never anything left behind. I had no legacy, nothing to pass on to my children. No children to pass it on to, anyway. Everything was bullshit. So, she was right. Now I'm only left with revenge. Revenge is a pitiful emotion, and it's leaking out of me faster than I can pour the hate back in. So I'm here wondering whether I can even pull this off. I keep thinking, 'What the hell am I doing? How is this going to help her? Am I just trading another piece of myself away, devaluing what's left?' I think that's what's been scaring me."

When he finally fell silent, she didn't know what to say. They were so different, and yet exactly the same. "Carol lied to me to save your life...."

He turned and looked at her.

"...She never witnessed that beating. She was trying to get Joe Rina convicted. She loved you, Beano...so much she risked and gave her life to save you. She used me, but you know something, that's all right because it's brought me to this place. You know what I think...?"

"No."

"Carol has brought us here. She put us together and she expects something from us. Maybe not revenge for her death...maybe it's not that at all. Maybe she's trying to teach us something. But I know this much, she's watching.

"I've spent five years in courtrooms prosecuting scum like Joe and Tommy Rina. For them, people have no value except as criminal end users. They can kill us, but Joe and Tommy Rina can't control us anymore, because they have nothing we want except them. Their usual tools of money, bribery, and intimidation won't work against us, and that's what gives us power. Carol wanted to protect you. She gave up her life trying. It's a legacy, Beano. You can't spend it or trade it, but it might nourish you with its memory."

There was a moment of silence, and then he reached out and took her hand and held it for a moment, before he got up and walked inside. It was far from her best closing argument, but she hoped she had reached him.

Tommy had taken a shower and had changed into a silk shirt that his brother Joe had brought back for him from China. Joe said the silk worms were specially cultivated and that the shirt had cost a fortune. He'd spent another thousand in "ditch Calliope" money, telling her he had business in the casino office. He had left her standing at the roulette table with a handful of hundreds, chewing on a nail, wondering whether to bet red or black...a decision that promised to consume all of her thoughts for hours.

When Dakota walked into the Flamingo Bar again, Tommy couldn't believe his good fortune. She moved right to him and smiled. "You changed," she said, looking at his green silk shirt and taking his hand.

"No, I haven't," he said, missing the point badly. "I'm the same guy I was this afternoon."

"I can hardly wait to see what a High-roller floor looks like," she said, still holding his hand.

Tommy led her to the elevator and put in his key. They went up to the tenth floor, exited the elevator, and went past Suite 10-B, where Duffy was at that moment doctoring the dice, then moved on to the end of the hall to a very small but beautiful gambling area. The Stick-men and Croupiers were all in tuxedos; the crap tables were hand carved and imported from European casinos. There were only half-a-dozen players, mostly Arabs and Asians. Crystal chandeliers hung low over the tables. The effect was startling.

"You really own this place?" she said, still holding his hand.

"Ask anybody. Ask him," Tommy said, pointing to the Host of the room, and Tommy led Dakota to the tuxedoed man. "Go on, ask him."

"He says he owns this hotel," she said.

"If Mr. Rina says it, then you better believe it," the Host replied.

"That makes me the luckiest girl on the island." She sat on the bar chair, letting the slit on her dress fall open. Her long legs flashed in the incandescent chandelier light.

"Buy ya a drink?" Tommy said, hoping to get her blitzed.

"Only if you'll join me. Scotch straight," she said, smiling.

The challenge was drawn, and Tommy ordered two double Scotch shooters, falling into her trap. One thing Dakota Bates could do was drink. In fact, she could out-drink every man she'd ever met. It came in very handy in her profession. She would drink them under the table, romp them, roll them, and be gone with their money and credit cards before sun-up.

When the double Scotch shooters arrived, she teased…"I hope you wouldn't take advantage of a poor girl?" She smiled as they clicked glasses.

Tommy grinned back. He intended to take advantage, all right. First, he was going to get this luscious creature to smoke his pink cigar. Then he was gonna screw her blind.

Trouble was, she matched him drink for drink, and by one-thirty he could barely stand. "Enough drinking," Tommy slurred, "let's fuck." He spewed a spit-spray of Scotch mist and bad breath into her ear, then pulled back and leered at her through alcohol-dimmed eyes.

"My place or yours?" she cooed.

"Wishever closer."

"I've got oils and lotions in my room. I'll rub them all over you. I'll massage you and lick you clean," she promised.

"Fuckin' A…" Tommy said.

She helped him up and led the teetering mobster out of the High-roller casino. She guided him to the elevator and down to her room on eight. She got the door open and he stumbled in, falling and dragging her down to the floor with him.

"Jeezus, I'm loaded," he said, shaking his head.

"Let's get on the bed," she said. "This is gonna be a great party." She led him to the double bed. He turned and flopped down on it, lying back. He closed his eyes dreamily and she thought for a moment she was home free. But then he opened them again and focused on her. He wasn't going to give up yet. She hoped she wouldn't have to fuck him. Then he stood and stumbled into the bathroom and poured col̇ ẇater onto a wash cloth and mopped his faċ with it. Water ran down his neck and ruineḋ the two-thousand-dollar Chinese silk shiṙ. He dropped the cloth in the sink, turneḋ ȧnd leered at her. "Let's go, baby, get fuckin' naked. Gotta see the wet spot."

Dakota silently cursed her luck, but dropped the straps of her silk gown and let it fall down her perfectly tapered body. She was now standing naked in front of him, still wearing her high heels. Tommy gulped several times, like a trout in the bottom of a boat, then moved awkwardly toward her. He grabbed between her legs and groped her roughly.

"Easy, baby, take it easy...we've got all night," she cooed, pulling away so he wouldn't claw her down there. She decided it was better to just get the job done and be over with it. He'd fall asleep right after he scored. They all did. It was her one universal observation about men. She unbuttoned his ruined green silk shirt and took it off him. He was surprisingly strong. Ridges of power were stacked in useful slabs of hard muscle on his shoulders and short arms. He stumbled out of his pants, sitting awkwardly on the bed. He ripped off his underwear and stood up to face her. He was huge and, for a moment, it startled her. Then she took him into her arms and pressed her body against his. Tommy moaned with pleasure. She led him to the bed and lowered him down. He grabbed for her and she let him pull her down on top of him. Then, with no preamble, she mounted him. Tommy thrust his hips at her savagely. It was a carnal, desperate act of possession. Within minutes he was finished. She rolled off of him and looked down at the despicable little slime who had killed her cousin Carol.

"You're a wonderful lover," she said softly. "You have such stamina, such magnificent equipment."

"Ahhh," Tommy said as he closed his eyes. "Fuckin' room is spinning. Fuckin', goddamn room is fuckin' spinning all over the fuckin'..." And then he rolled over and vomited almost a quart of blended Scotch onto the plush carpet next to the bed. He lay face down on the bedspread, gasping for air, spit draining out of his open mouth. *He is truly a ghastly creature*, she thought. It would be so easy to go over to the desk, get the scissors, and end his life right there, but Beano had told her it was his brother, Joe Rina, who had ordered the hit on Carol....Tommy was just the instrument of the act. They needed Tommy to get to Joe. Besides, she mused as he began to snore face down before her, she wasn't a killer. She was a Bates. A high-stakes player and the best mack on the planet. She always won in the bedroom. The bedroom was her field of combat. She looked down in victory on the snoring killer, then moved to the phone and dialed Beano's room.

"Yeah," Beano said, getting it on the second ring.

"He's out of the play. You're up."

♠ ♠ ♠

Beano looked at his watch; it was almost three A.M. "Tommy's on ice. You ready?" he said to Duffy, who had the loaded dice all finished and lined up on the table. Duffy picked up the last one and checked to see if the white paint was dry. "Ready," Duffy said.

"Okay," Beano said to Victoria, who was sitting on the bed, "the plane should be at the private air strip at dawn. We gotta be there when it arrives."

They turned the wheelchair upside down and snapped the dice by pairs into the cartridge under the wheelchair arms, so that Duffy could pull out the loaded number he wanted. Then they put the wheelchair right side up, and Duffy got in the seat, back on top of the Porta-Toilet.

"Take Roger, get the van, and wait for us

275

in the parking lot. If anything happens that's not part of the plan, I want you nearby. If the whole deal blows, get on the plane and leave without us," he instructed.

"What about Dakota?" she asked.

"Dakota stays with Tommy either way. She's gotta steer him once we're gone. If the deal jackknifes on us, she's damage control."

Victoria opened the door for them, and then Beano paused for a moment. His blue, sensitive eyes found hers. "Thanks," he said, "for everything."

She nodded, then stepped aside as Beano pushed Duffy out into the hall, over to the elevator, and they took a long, quiet ride down to the casino on the main floor.

NINETEEN

The Tat

Luke Zigman was surprised to see the old deadwood player being rolled back into the casino by his nephew at three in the morning. The old duck's head was lolling and he looked half dead. He now knew the man in the wheelchair was named Harry Price. They'd taken hidden-camera pictures of him and his nephew and put the pictures on the big "losers board" in the employee lounge, so that all the casino workers would know them and treat them special. The casino didn't want them getting out of Sabre Bay before all of their money was gone. Harry's chair was parked opposite the Stick-man by his whining nephew, who Luke Zigman now knew was named Douglas Price.

"Jeezus, Uncle Harry, can't we go to bed? It's the middle of the fucking night."

"Got the credit, yessiree, grooved and approved," he rasped. "Yessiree, two hundred big ones, the whole stack. Get the chip girl, Harry wants t'roll the bones, roll the bones."

The Night Shift Manager, Arnold Buzini, was in his office, so Luke picked up the phone and notified him that Mr. Price wanted his whole two hundred thousand in credit delivered in chips to table three.

"Go ahead and give him the ride. He's approved," Buzini said, glad the old leaker was back at the shooter's rail.

Within minutes the tray arrived with two hundred thousand in pre-counted plastic chips aboard. They were piled high on the racks in hundred-dollar blues, five-hundred-dollar reds, and thousand-dollar golds. Beano took them down and stacked them on the table while Duffy watched, wheezing badly.

"What's the limit?" Duffy croaked.

"For you, sir, it's five thousand," Luke said.

"Jesus H. Keee-rist on a bright blue bicycle," Duffy wheezed. "Can't you boys do better than that?"

Luke picked up the phone and redialed Buzini, who gave him permission to "no limit" the table. The main casino room was almost empty at three. In Las Vegas casinos, people played all night, but Caribbean hotels had more daytime than nighttime bettors, so Buzini didn't mind removing the limit.

"Ten thousand on the come line," Duffy said, and he pushed his bet out, reaching over the rail, pressing his skinny, hollow chest against the table and coughing badly.

"Aren't you gonna buy some insurance, like this afternoon?" Luke prodded.

"Nope, nope. Not now, not now. Let's go, gotta roll, gotta roll." And he got the table dice and tossed them down to the end of the table. They bounced off the rail and onto the green felt. His point was ten.

Luke smiled because ten was a hard point for the shooter. There were only three ways to make ten...the six-four, the four-six, and the double five. There were six ways to make seven, which made the odds two-to-one against the shooter on the point, but if he won, the bet only paid off at even money. That was the edge for the house. Luke didn't see Duffy's hand go to his wheelchair arm, extract the doctored dice, then palm the house dice in his other hand. He held the two fives in his palm for twenty seconds, shaking them by his ear, stalling so he could warm the cellophane gas, turning it solid.

"Want the hard five," Duffy shouted. "Gimme five thousand on the hard five."

Beano threw the chips out and Duffy threw the loaded dice. They hit and rolled and came up ten, the hard way.

"Eeeeaaahhh," Duffy shouted and then began to gag and choke.

"Pay the line. Pay the hard ten," the Stick-man droned.

Luke watched as thirty thousand dollars was pushed up against the rail where Duffy was sitting. Duffy quickly retrieved his doctored dice and palmed the casino's original dice back into the game. He bet another twenty thousand on the come line and rolled the casino dice again.

"Point is four. Four is the point," the Stick-man droned. Four is also a two-to-one bet against the shooter.

"Double odds on the four," Duffy wheezed, making his first really shrewd bet. In craps it is possible, after rolling a point, to bet twice your original bet as an odds bet. That meant if he made the four he would get paid on the original bet at even money, but the odds bet, which was twice as large as his original bet, would pay off at two to one, or at the correct odds. Luke Zigman didn't like the fact that this deadwood player had stopped making sucker bets and was now playing smart.

"Be good to Daddy, be good, be good," Harry said as he pulled the casino dice out of the game and switched them for a loaded pair of hard fours he secretly snapped out of the wheelchair arm. He rolled the loadies.

"Hard four, a winner. Pay the line, pay the odds bet," the Stick-man said, and looked over at Luke. The old duck had won back all of the money he'd lost that afternoon in two rolls.

279

Luke picked up the phone, turned his back to the table, and dialed the office again. "Mr. Buzini, this guy just hit us twice for over fifty grand. You wanna leave this no-limit on?"

"Is he still betting stupid?"

"No. All of a sudden he's turned into a player."

"Float the dice. If they're okay, leave it on, but keep me posted."

Luke hung up and turned around as the Stick-man was about to push Duffy's dice back to him with the curved stick. Luke scooped them up off the table, looked for the imperfect *S*, then dropped them into a glass. They all watched as the dice floated but didn't roll. The cellophane had already returned to its natural, gaseous state.

"Want my lucky dice," Duffy wheezed angrily.

"Okay, let's play," Luke said and the doctored dice were dried with a napkin and pushed back to Duffy, who palmed them immediately off the table and replaced them with the casino's original dice.

Now Duffy pushed out the whole fifty thousand dollars he'd just won. "Let 'er go," he said. And then he began to wheeze and cough and cause a huge distraction to take everybody's mind off his bet. His body started to convulse. The few people who were in the casino had found their way to the crap table.

The Stick-man counted the fifty-thousand-dollar bet and became nervous about letting it stand.

"We'll allow twenty," he said, finally making his decision. "That's the new table limit."

Duffy was shaking his withered body. He was beginning to convulse slightly.

"Uncle Harry, you've got to take your medicine. You'll have one of your seizures if you don't take it now."

"Fuck it. Fuck the medicine," Duffy wheezed. "These ass wipes was perfectly willing to take my money when I was losing with no limit. Now...I'm winning, all of a sudden we gotta new set of rules." The people standing around murmured their assent. They agreed it didn't seem fair. Duffy was shaking badly now, his chest heaving torturously.

Luke called for Arnold Buzini, who now hurried out onto the floor and was witnessing the disturbance. Some of the other players were now siding loudly with Duffy.

Luke looked up at Buzini questioningly, and the Shift Manager nodded his approval.

"Okay, we'll accept the bet," Luke said.

Duffy grinned and shook and drooled slightly as he picked up the casino dice and rolled them.

"Seven, a winner," the Stick-man said, and Duffy's bet was matched. A hundred thousand dollars was now out on the green felt.

"Let the fucker ride," Duffy wheezed. "Let 'er ride."

"Take the medicine, Uncle Harry," Beano said. "You'll have a convulsion."

"Shut the fuck up," Duffy croaked, his arm now started convulsing as he reached for the dice. He dropped them once, had trouble regaining them, and finally rolled them feebly. They barely hit the rail at the end of the table.

"Point is eight."

"Eighter from Decatur." Duffy shook and wheezed.

"What the hell's wrong with him?" Buzini said.

"He's epileptic. He won't take his medicine. Says it jinxes him."

"Sir, you should take your medicine," Buzini said.

"Go fuck a duck," Duffy replied. "Eighter from Decatur. Come to Papa," he drooled and switched the dice again. Now, with the doctored eights in his hand, he warmed them...holding them in his palm while Beano shoved the bet out. Duffy rolled the loaded dice and won.

"Winner. Pay the line," the Stick-man said.

There was now over half-a-million dollars in chips on the table.

"Float 'em," Buzini demanded again, and Luke grabbed the dice off the table, first checking them under an ultraviolet light for the stripe of color, and then dropped them in a glass of water. Buzini leaned in and watched closely. They didn't roll.

"The Price Is Right," Duffy trumpeted. "My lucky dice. Harry wants them bones." Duffy now started to shake slightly in the seat of the chair. He looked very sick. His head was lolling, he was losing control of his convulsing arm.

"Sir, I think you should see a doctor," Buzini said.

"I'm winnin', so I'm grinnin'. Gotta go. Gotta go. Luck's on my side. Let 'er ride."

Buzini was looking at the pile of gold chips on the table. He knew that one house roll would bring the casino back to even. He also knew this was loser's logic, but he didn't know what to do. "Get Tommy on the phone," he said to Luke. Buzini didn't want a million-dollar loss on his shift report. He wanted to be taken off point. He'd get Tommy Rina to approve the action.

Luke looked at his watch. "It's three-forty-five A.M.," he said.

"There's half-a-million bucks on the table. Call him. He'll wanna know."

Luke started to dial while they all waited.

"Gotta go, gotta go. What's the problem? Gotta go," Duffy complained, stirring the crowd, most of whom were also now betting and winning with him.

♠ ♠ ♠

"Who the fuck is this?" Calliope's sleep-filled voice said over the phone. She was in the bed in the large private villa Joe owned, adjacent to the hotel.

"This is Luke, in the casino. Gotta talk to Tommy. Put him on."

"Tommy ain't here, the little prick. God knows where the fuck Tommy is," she said, and slammed down the receiver.

Luke looked at Buzini and shook his head.

"Gotta go, gotta go. Let's do it...gotta go," Duffy started shouting. Buzini didn't know what to do.

"For God's sake, let him shoot. He's getting so excited he's gonna have a grand mal. You haven't seen anything till you've seen one of those fuckers," Beano warned.

"Okay. New dice. Let's roll 'em," Buzini said, as two Pit Bosses from ajoining tables wandered over to watch.

They brought out a new set of casino perfects. Buzini checked them, then dropped them on the table. They were pushed over to Duffy.

Duffy tapped them on the green felt then rolled a six.

"Point is six. Good point for the shooter," the Stick-man droned.

And now, under the careful scrutiny of three sets of eyes, Duffy went to the arm of the wheelchair and performed his short hand magic, switching the dice as the trained Pit Bosses stared directly at his hands. They never saw the switch, never saw it happen. He put the loaded dice in his palm, held them, heated them and rolled them.

"Six, a hard-way winner," the Stick-man said, and now Duffy had a million dollars in chips. There were so many, they couldn't lie in front of him on the green felt and still leave the table clear for play.

"Let 'er ride," Duffy wheezed and the twenty or so spectators cheered.

"Get Joe in New Jersey," Buzini said, sweat starting to form on his forehead.

Luke grabbed his phone and called the emergency number for Joe Rina.

"Let 'er ride."

"No, sir, you can't bet a million until I get an approval."

"Whatta buncha ass wipes," Duffy growled. He wheezed, his arm quivering on the table rail where it was resting.

♠ ♠ ♠

Joe came awake instantly when the phone rang. It was almost four A.M. He knew this call had to be important. Nobody would call him at four in the morning unless it was a wrong number, a disaster, or somebody looking to get his face rearranged.

"What is it?" he said.

"Just a minute, sir," Luke said. "I have Arnold Buzini from the Sabre Bay casino."

He handed the phone to Buzini, who cleared his throat and watched as Duffy and Beano argued about his medicine. "Sir, we have a little situation here," he said softly. "We have a big winner on the number three crap table. He's hit us for over a million dollars...in less than an hour. This guy is white-hot. And a buncha other players are slip-streaming with him."

"You check the dice?"

"Yes, sir. They're okay...least they seem to be."

"Tommy's down there. Get Tommy."

"We can't find Tommy, sir. He's not in your villa. We don't know where he is."

Joe sat up in bed. Sometimes Tommy's lack of responsibility was startling. He was great when it came to wet-work, great at clipping somebody you wanted to put down, but when it came to just common-sense business, he was lame. Joe stifled a flash of anger at his brother and tried to clear his head of sleep and concentrate. "Okay, this guy on any of our sheets?"

"No, sir. His name is Harry Price. Old guy in a wheelchair. He owns a car lot in Fresno. His nephew is named Douglas. Says on his credit-ap he's an unemployed oil company geologist. The Eye-in-the-Sky was watching them. They're either very good or they're not cheating."

"Okay, here's what you do," Joe said. "Put the table limit at fifty thousand. You let them roll once more to buy some time. While they're doing that, go through their room. If it's clean, plant something...dope, anything. Call the Bahamian Patrol. If your player gets angry or starts an incident, close the table for an accounting. Pay them slowly to stall them, but don't let them out of the hotel with the money. We'll bust 'em for drugs and then take their winnings. Got it?"

"Yes, sir."

"And tell my brother I wanna talk to him soon as you find him."

"Yes, sir." Buzini hung up the phone. "Okay, table limit is fifty thousand, you can roll," he said to Duffy, who started to bitch that the no-limit was off. Buzini didn't stick around to listen. He moved to another pit area, picked up the phone, and ordered Security to come to table three and to notify the Bahamian Patrol they had a possible drug problem. Then he called his assistant and told him what to plant in Duffy's High-roller suite on the tenth floor.

"Same shooter, new point," the Stick-man said. Beano bet the new lower table limit of fifty thousand dollars, grumbling at the casino Manager as he did. As they pushed the dice over to Duffy, he was quivering with anger.

"Buncha cheap fucks," Duffy muttered, as he picked up the dice.

"Come to Daddy. Seven come eleven," and he pitched the dice to the end of the table and they came up nine.

"Nine. The point is nine."

Beano could tell from the phone calls and the furtive looks that they were about to get closed down. He nudged Duffy in warning, so Duffy didn't go for the loadies and instead rolled the casino dice. After three rolls, he sevened out. The crowd around the table let out a sad collective breath and the dice were passed.

"Cash me in," Duffy growled.

"This table's closed while we do the count," Buzini instructed, but the other players stayed there and watched as the old man's chips were counted. The process took almost fifteen minutes.

"One million one hundred and twenty-five

thousand dollars. How do you want that, sir?" Luke Zigman asked.

"Cash fucking money," Duffy yelled, and the people at the table laughed.

They rolled a cart out from the cage and made a big deal of counting the money and laying the packs of bills in Duffy's lap. Beano had brought the small, blue folding bag which, had Buzini and Zigman stopped to think, would have seemed very strange. Beano packed the money into the bag. Once it was all in, he started to roll Duffy out of the casino. Security guards were everywhere now and Duffy, with the bag on his lap, was stopped from leaving just a few feet away from the casino main entrance. Buzini stood in front of them, blocking their exit. "I'd like to buy you a congratulatory drink; maybe we could get some pictures of you with the money for the newspaper. It's good for the casino to publicize big winners," he said, as thirty or so spectators gathered around.

"Don't drink. Hate having my picture took," Duffy croaked, but now he was shaking so badly that he was actually wiggling all over the chair. Several of the Security men had their hands on the arms of the chair so Beano couldn't leave.

"Harry, you're about to have one a your seizures," Beano warned.

"You sure we can't put that money in the safe for you?" Buzini said.

Then the sound of sirens could be heard in the distance and Duffy looked up at Arnold Buzini, rolled his eyes back in his head, and suddenly convulsed. His legs shot out straight and his neck went rigid. He catapulted out of the chair, onto the floor.

"Oh, my God, he's having an epileptic fit," Beano screamed, pumping the atmosphere with adrenaline and confusion. "Call a doctor! Call an ambulance!" he shouted.

Duffy was on the floor; his legs shot out, his back arched, he gagged as he inhaled.

The cops from the Bahamian Patrol now came running into the casino. Several of them were met by the Assistant Manager and led off to the tenth floor to find bags of pure heroin that were planted in Duffy's room.

Duffy was convulsing terribly. A ring of people stood helplessly with their hands up to their mouths in horror.

During all of this, Beano had managed to slip silently out of the casino with the bag full of money. He moved to the parking lot, and Victoria pulled up in the blue van. He jumped in the back. Roger-the-Dodger put his paws up on the seat and looked back at him.

An ambulance arrived a few minutes later and the attendants ran inside. When they reached Duffy, he appeared to be unconscious. When they pried open his mouth, they found he had swallowed his tongue. They cleared it out to open the airway.

"This man is in critical condition," a paramedic announced.

"Where the fuck is the other guy?" Buzini said, finally realizing that Beano had disappeared with the cash. "The guy with the bag.

289

Where's the guy with the bag?" Buzini said, in a panic.

But Beano wasn't in the casino.

The paramedics pushed Buzini out of the way. They got the rolling stretcher from the back of the ambulance and loaded Duffy aboard. They wheeled the unconscious man out and into the back of the yellow and white ambulance. Then, with red lights and sirens, they roared away, heading for the Community Hospital, ten miles to the west. Nobody noticed the van that followed.

Fit-Throwing Duffy sat up in the back of the ambulance and looked at the startled paramedics.

"I'm okay now. Feel much better. Thanks," he said. "I'll just get out here."

"Lie down, mon," the startled attendants ordered. Duffy got off the rolling stretcher and moved to the back of the ambulance, but the door was locked. Duffy tried to open it but couldn't.

"Get back on that stretcher," the young Bahamian paramedic commanded.

"Go fuck yourself," Duffy shot back.

They were now almost to the hospital. Beano could see that Duffy wasn't going to be able to get out unless they did something drastic. "Gotta stop the ambulance," Victoria said, picking up his exact thought. She gunned the van, shot around the ambulance, hit the brakes, and threw the van into a four-wheel drift right beside the ambulance. Once she was sideways in the lane next to the ambulance, she floored it; the tires caught hold, smoking and squealing on the pavement. She was now perpendicular to the ambulance, and as the Bahamian driver hit the brakes in panic, she T-boned the yellow and white ambulance, pinning it against the curb. The ambulance and van both smoked to a stop. Roger was thrown off the seat to the floor with a yelp. Beano jumped out and yanked open the back door of the ambulance. Duffy leaped out and ran for the van. Beano wasn't far behind. An ambulance attendant had jumped out and was running after them, but Victoria now had the van in reverse. She backed up and skidded the van around and cut the attendant off. The van engine was smoking, the radiator leaking water. Beano and Duffy jumped in the open door on the opposite side as the ambulance attendant banged on Victoria's locked door, trying to pull it open.

"Come back here, that's our patient," the attendant screamed as Victoria floored it and squealed away, heading in the opposite direction.

Beano looked over at her, surprised, as Roger-the-Dodger jumped back up on the seat between them.

"You okay?" Victoria asked Duffy, who nodded.

"Not my best fit but certainly in the top ten," Fit-Throwing Duffy grinned, as they roared away.

They could hear sirens coming toward

them. Beano knew that Buzini was heading toward them with the police. "Turn right, across the field!" he yelled.

Victoria turned the blue van right and crashed through a fence and drove across the soft ground. She could barely control her progress in the soft dirt but managed to keep the van slip-sliding on course, heading southwest. The van fishtailed and threw up a plume of brown dirt that was visible from the road in the lightening sky. Through the back window, Beano could see the cop cars pull up and park next to the ambulance. Several of the police, plus a fuming Buzini, got out and looked at them across the field. They had gained distance, but now the police cars backed up and gave chase, roaring out through the broken fence, across the field after them.

They arrived at the Deep Water Airfield at five past six; the morning sun was just over the rim of the hill.

"If my cousin Lee isn't on time, we're all going to jail," Beano said as Victoria pulled the van onto the runway tarmac and came to a screeching stop. Parked at the end of the runway was a red and gray King Air twin-engine plane.

"There," Duffy said, pointing.

Victoria floored it. By now the police cars were in view, coming along the airport frontage road, their sirens braying. Victoria drove the van full-speed to the plane. Beano jumped out before Victoria had even brought it to a complete stop. He ran to the pilot leaning against the wing. "Lee, get this thing up right now!"

Leland X. Bates looked off at the approaching squad cars and shook his head in dismay.

"Usually you're a little smoother than this," Lee said, moving quickly into the plane. The squad cars were now on the runway and racing toward them.

Duffy, Victoria, and Roger-the-Dodger, toting the blue canvas bag, were already out of the van and running to the King Air.

Inside the plane, Leland was looking at the approaching police cars as he set the throttles and began to start the starboard engine. "It'll be tight but let's give it a go," he said as he revved the starboard engine, then immediately started the port. "If you don't mind, I'm gonna scrap the preflight," he said, as the second engine coughed to life. He throttled up. The squad cars were only three hundred yards away as Leland shouted, "Hold on...."

The King Air roared down the runway directly at the police cars, which had come to a stop across the center of the tarmac to block him. But they had left too much runway and, just before the plane hit the nearest car, Leland pulled back the yoke and the plane lifted off.... They heard one of the tires leave a patch of rubber on the roof of the nearest police car as they skimmed over.

"Holy shit," Victoria said, her heart slamming in her chest as she clutched Roger-the-Dodger in her arms. Then she looked over at Beano, who was grinning.

"Even more exciting than my first night in jail," he said.

Duffy smiled. He was still out of breath and his chest hurt; he was pooped. Throwing a convincing epileptic fit was damn hard work.

Then the little plane turned west and headed out over the inland cut toward Miami.

TWENTY

Singing

Everybody was trying to find Tommy Rina. The Host in the High-roller casino described Dakota to the Desk Clerk, who remembered her vividly, and at eight A.M. they got a second key to her room. They opened her door to the overpowering smell of vomit. They found Tommy sprawled on the bed, face down and naked, except for his laced-up wing-tip shoes and socks. He looked like a partied-out conventioneer. When they woke him up, he groaned and rolled to a sitting position, squinting at Arnold Buzini and two Security cops. Then Tommy looked down at his crotch and his exposed howitzer.

"Get the fuck out of here," he growled at them.

"We been hit," Buzini said by way of explanation.

"Get the fuck out of here! I gotta put on some clothes," Tommy said, pulling the bedspread up onto his lap. They backed out of the room and Tommy tried to get to his feet.

"Goddamn..." he said. His head felt like it was being opened from the side with a can opener. He stumbled into the bathroom and turned on the shower. Then he got in and stood there, still in his shoes, and let it pour over him. He felt worse than afterbirth. He thought he was going to die right there, in the shower, with his wing-tips on.

Then it all came back to him...the Goddess, the trip to the High-roller casino...the fuck on the bed, which he barely remembered. "Man, that bitch can hold her liquor," he said to his water-soaked shoes. Then he remembered what Buzini had said, and he opened the shower door and called out.

"Hey, Buz...whatta you mean we got hit?"

Twenty minutes later they were seated in Buzini's tiny office, and Tommy was on the phone with his little brother, Joe, in New Jersey. The doctored dice and the wheelchair were being examined in the next room. They had found where the dice had been drilled, and they knew they'd been hit by tat players. Joe was mad but his voice, as always, was cool.

"Tommy, you're nothing but a wandering hard-on....All you think about is pussy," his little brother said to him in cold anger. "Women and clipping guys, that's your whole routine."

"Come on, Joe, it wasn't like that."

"First, the jewelry store gets hit for a hundred grand. Okay, that's small stuff; it's stupid, but I can live with it. But now this...this is over a million dollars, Tommy. You're down there and the Shift Manager can't even find you. You got that redheaded flute player stashed in my villa and you're up on eight with another hooker, while our place gets hummed for a million bucks....Nobody can find you."

"Joe...look..."

"What good are you to me if you do all your thinking with your dick? I got problems everywhere. All you do is make 'em worse."

"I don't make things worse. In Jersey last month, wasn't for me, you'd be upstate, Joe."

"Hey, Tommy, this is an open phone line," Joe exploded. "I got people listening...taps everywhere. Use your fucking head for once, will ya?"

Joe almost never lost control, almost never swore. This was one of the few times Tommy could remember his little brother cursing. It sobered him. "Whatta you want me to do?"

"You lost the million one. You either get it back or we make it up out of your end of things."

"Jeezus, Joe, what the fuck kinda deal is that? You lose money on shit all the time, and you don't have to make it up outta your end."

"When I lose money, Tommy, it's because something unforeseen went wrong, and then I study the mistake and never, never repeat it. You're losing money 'cause you can't keep your dick in your pants or your mind on business. You make the same mistake three times a week. So now, you get the money back or pay it back. Those are your two choices."

And Joe hung up in his ear.

Buzini had turned and moved to the far side of the office early in the conversation. He didn't want to witness even one end of this tongue lashing. He hated having to hear Tommy plead, because he knew Tommy would take it out on him. But he was stuck in the room.

"What the fuck're you lookin' at?" Tommy said when Buzini looked over at him after the phone was hung up.

"Nothin'...I..."

"You want a piece of this trouble? I can deal you in, asshole. How'd you let these guys pull this on you? You took the table limit off, what kinda shit is that?" he screamed at the startled Shift Manager. "Didn't you even see him pulling the loadies outta that chair arm? Whatta you, blind?"

"I...I didn't..."

"You didn't think...didn't do shit! You stood there and watched these sharpers pick our bones," Tommy yelled. His face was red and he was thinking he'd like to take a ballpeen hammer and club this greaseball casino Manager to death. "Okay, so where's the bitch, Dakota, who drugged me? Where is she?" Tommy yelled. But he figured she had to be in on it and was probably long gone.

"I don't know, sir...."

"You don't fucking know much of any-thing, do ya?" He looked at Buzini, seething with anger. Tommy's head was throbbing; his stomach was sour. He wanted to pay somebody back, hurt somebody. Sometimes that was the only thing that made him feel bet-ter. "I'm gonna go t'the villa and change. Send over something to eat. My stomach feels like piranhas're feeding in there. Send over some yogurt or something to settle it." Tommy turned to leave but spun back in the doorway and caught Buzini off guard. "You fuckin' guys can't keep your mind on business," he said, with disgust. "You're supposed t'run this shift, but you keep makin' the same fuckin' mistakes. You're supposed t'make decisions, not all the time comin' runnin', look-ing for me to tell you what to do. What the fuck else do I pay you for?"

"I'm sorry, Mr. Rina."

"You're fuckin' sorry and you're fuckin' one step back from being a dead man. You bet-ter be thinkin' how t'make this up, and how not to make the same mistake ever again," Tommy growled and walked out of the office, picturing how nice it would be to beat that fuck-ing self-satisfied Buzini's head flat with a ballpeen hammer.

Tommy cut through the lanai on his way to the villa. He took the stone footpath that led below the pool next to the beach. He had his face turned away from the sun, because the bright sunlight needled through his eyes and into his brain like acupuncture. Then he saw something that amazed him. The fantasy Goddess from last night was climbing the ladder out of the pool. Dakota walked across the pavement to a chaise lounge. She was wearing a thong bikini bottom and no top. She arranged herself on a towel and closed her eyes, the water beading on her perfect skin and dripping off her wet hair. Tommy couldn't believe she was still there. She had come to the Sabre Bay Club with the old guy in the wheelchair and his nephew. He assumed she had gotten him drunk and fucked him to keep him out of the play. He was sure she was part of the tat, so what the hell was she still doing here, lying out by the pool? He hurried down the path, got to his brother's villa, picked up the phone, and dialed Buzini's office.

"Arnold Buzini," the Shift Manager said, his voice tired.

"Hey, cocksucker, here's something you can do t'start savin' your job. That whore I was with last night is down by the pool. You go down there with two of your plastic badges and you bring that lyin' cunt to Joe's villa."

"Yes, sir."

"And, dickhead, try not to start World War III in the process. I may end up wastin' this bitch, and I don't need you to start some slapdance tournament in front of all them geeks down there. You got me? Real easy, real smooth, bring her up here."

"Yes, sir," Buzini said, his voice shaking, and he hung up the phone. What did Tommy mean, he might end up wasting her? Buzini was a hotel casino manager, not a hood. He'd actually been to hotel school. Was he now about to become involved in a murder? *How on earth did I get to this place?* he wondered.

Tommy paced in the luxurious villa. There was a white grand piano in the living room, and the villa had its own private beach off the bedroom porch. Joe had supervised the decorating and had fine oil paintings under glass, in hermetically sealed frames, so the ocean air and humidity wouldn't destroy them. There were also priceless Aztec art treasures that Joe collected and had placed out on the sideboards. Then Tommy's alcohol-soaked brain stopped slipping cogs, and he remembered Calliope. He had to get her out of there. He moved quickly into the bedroom and found her asleep on the king-size bed. He yanked her up by the hair.

"Whatta you doin'? Whatta you...leggo," she squeaked as he pulled her up and threw her dressing gown at her.

"Where the hell were you, Tommy?" she said in a sleep-filled voice, and Tommy hit her in the mouth with his fist. She flew backwards. Tommy loved hitting.

She rolled and she landed on the pillows. Blood was flowing out of her mouth.

"*Don't...*" Tommy said softly. "*Ask...*" and he walked around the bed, leaned down, and pushed his face into hers. "*Questions*," he finished.

"I'm sorry," she said, looking into eyes filled with hate and anger.

"Just get the fuck out of here. You come back before afternoon, you're gonna look worse than a Bosnian housewife."

Calliope scrambled off the bed and ran from the room, out onto the patio, and up to the hotel.

Now Tommy paced back and forth, waiting. A few minutes later, he could hear talking on the porch.

"No...no. It's for our best customers, a complimentary gift from the hotel; I keep the bottles cold in the refrigerator here," he could hear Buzini saying as the door opened and Dakota moved into the room. She was wearing only her bikini bottom and a coverup. She was barefoot and her hair was still wet.

"Hi," Tommy said from the living room. "Remember me?"

"Tommy," she said, smiling, "I thought you were still asleep."

"Come here, doll face," he said, grinning his ghastly, ax murderer's smile.

She moved toward him, and when she was only a few feet away, he swung from his heels. It was his Sunday punch. Tommy had always been a great puncher and he hit her high on the cheekbone, snapping her head around and driving her back against the wall. He charged her like a mountain gorilla as Arnold Buzini gasped in horror. Then Tommy grabbed Dakota's hair and, with a fist full of her tresses, he yanked her up and hit four more times: two chilling shots to her midsection, where he actually felt something break, then he moved upstairs for two ringing head shots. Some of her teeth were knocked out and hit the carpet. She went down, her back slamming the floor. She was quiet for a moment, then Dakota slowly struggled to prop her elbows under her. She smiled up at him weakly through bloody gums. "Is that the best you can do?" she finally whispered.

Tommy grabbed Dakota's wrist and yanked her up. Her legs were jelly, but once she was up, she tried for his groin with her knee. But he was too fast and kicked her in the stomach with his still-wet wing-tip. She went down again and curled up on the carpet.

"You're gonna kill her!" Buzini said, with pain in his voice.

"If she's lucky, she'll die. Now get the fuck outta here," he said. And when Buzini didn't move, Tommy grabbed one of Joe's price-less Aztec treasures off the sideboard and hurled it at the Shift Manager. It shattered against the wall. Arnold fled in terror.

Then Tommy grabbed Dakota up off the floor and pushed her backwards. She stumbled into the living room, leaving a trail of blood on the white carpet. But remarkably, she was standing her ground, weaving slightly, both of her fists clenched, ready to defend herself as Tommy moved toward her and stood a few feet away. It was a good punching distance for him, a distance he'd measured from the time he started fighting as a kid. "Okay, we need some answers, doll face," he said.

"About the worst piece of ass I ever had," she answered.

"That wasn't the question," he sneered. "Who are they?"

"Who are who?" she said, buying time, trying to clear her head. Without warning, he hit her again. This time she went down immediately. She had lost most of the strength in her legs. She was on the edge of going into shock, but she turned her face to him, glaring defiantly. "Better, but I'm still conscious. You can't even take out a girl, Tommy."

"You're a tough bitch," he said. "I gotta give you that."

"Or maybe you just can't hit for shit," she hissed, her voice cold as Wilkinson steel. She struggled to sit up against the back of the couch, breathing through her mouth.

"Who are they?" he said again. "The old fucker in the tricked-out wheelchair...who is he? A professional tat player? He's not in our records....He some kinda dice cheat?"

"His name is Harry Sutton," she said. "He's...not a dice mechanic, he's a...a physicist or some kinda physical engineer, an inventor."

"I see. And what's he been inventing, queer dice?"

"The dice are loaded with cellophane gas. He invented the stuff. It turns solid when you heat it, not the other way around.... Could I have a wet towel for my mouth, please?"

Tommy moved to the kitchen, turned the cold water on and ran it over a towel and threw it to her. She caught it and held it to her mouth, which was bleeding badly. When she brought it away, Tommy could tell that he'd really connected with that last shot. He'd opened up a two-inch cut on her lip. "Go on," he commanded.

"Harry lives in Fresno, on a houseboat called *Seismic Shot*. It's docked at the Mud Flat Marina there. They brought me from Vegas, told me to pick you up."

"And who are you?" he snarled. "A hooker?"

"I'm an opportunist...who used to have a great smile."

"Go on. The redhead guy, who's he?"

She hesitated for a minute and Tommy took two steps forward and now was standing in range again. "Don't fuck with me, sis....I love wrecking people. This is my favorite sport."

"He's Douglas Clark. He's a doctor of geology. Works for an oil company...the Fentress County Petroleum and Gas Company, or something like that. They just fired him and he's all pissed off about it. He's got some harebrained plan to get even. They're trying to buy the company's stock or something. That's why they were stealing from your casino, they need lots of money for stock.... Could I have some ice? This lip is ballooning on me."

He went to the bar and grabbed a few cubes out of the ice machine and threw them at her. One hit her on the head and fell into her lap. She picked it up and winged it back across the room at him, missing and hitting a glass decanter behind the bar, breaking it. He knew he'd hurt her badly, but like a gutsy prizefighter, she refused to show the pain.

They looked at each other for a long time. Finally, Tommy moved back and, with the toe of his shoe, touched her deep between her legs. She recoiled slightly and closed her legs, wrapping her arms around her knees.

"So, they're not professional dice thieves?" he said. "We got hit by a couple'a outta-work scientists? I don't believe it."

"I don't know what their story is," she finally said. "They paid me five hundred bucks, plus expenses. Now it'll all have t'go for new bridgework."

"Or maybe a funeral." He looked at her for a long time. "This turns out to be bullshit, you're fertilizer."

"You can try," she said, and began to shiver as she started to go into shock.

Tommy felt better. He turned and went to the phone and dialed a number. "Get the Challenger ready," he instructed his pilots. "We're going to Fresno in an hour." Then he hung up and moved back to Dakota. He grabbed her by the hair and pulled her up to her feet. She surprised him again when she spit in his face. The glob was bloody and filled with mucus. He didn't wipe it off; he felt it roll down his cheek. He was still holding her upright by her hair and he could feel her legs shaking under her. She was barely able to stand, but still ready to fight. She glared at him defiantly. He was impressed. She was one hell of a woman.

"You're coming with me. It's gonna be fun," he said. "Maybe along the way you can help me get that weak punch a'mine straightened out." Then he hit her again. This time it was square in the mouth and sent her flying across the room. She landed on the floor, curled up, and moaned.

"That one was a little better, don't you think?" he said softly. Then he walked into the bedroom, threw a few things into a suitcase he would need for the trip.

Part Five
THE TALE

"IF YOU GET INTO ANYBODY DEEP ENOUGH,
YOU'VE GOT YOURSELF A PARTNER."
—Anonymous

TWENTY-ONE

The Tight Hole

Tommy had his pilots land Joe's red and white twin-engine Challenger jet at the Fresno Airport. It was four P.M. They taxied up to the new Spanos Executive Jet Center where Tommy had a limousine and three "heavy bag buttons" waiting. The buttons had driven over from Las Vegas where they worked as freelance muscle. The three enforcers looked like a wall of beef leaning against the front of the car. They watched as the big executive jet turned and parked. The wheels were chocked, and as the engines wound down, they pushed their bulk away from the black Lincoln stretch limousine where they had been bending the shiny fender with their bulk. The leader was a broad-shouldered hitter named Jimmy Freeze. Jimmy had a knife scar that ran down the side of his face like a psychopathic warning and disappeared into his collar. Beside him were the Summerland brothers, Wade and Keith, also ex–pro-football jocks. At over 250 pounds each, they were straining the stitching in their 56 extra-long suits. They had once worked for Joe and Tommy as security, until Joe fired them under dubious circumstances that Tommy didn't understand. So he threw a little work their way when he could.

When the door opened and the gangplank dropped, the first one off the plane was

Dakota. Her face had swollen and turned purple where Tommy had hit her. Her split lip still needed stitches and dried blood was caked on the wound. She was in obvious pain and walked slowly down the steps, holding the rail for support. She was wearing one of Calliope's new outfits and it was too small on her. She was followed closely by Tommy. Dakota moved to the car and got in the back seat with painful care and without speaking. As Tommy approached, Jimmy Freeze motioned to her.

"The fuck happened to her?" he asked.

"Shut up and let's go," Tommy barked.

He got in the back of the car and the limo pulled through the gate and onto the Airport Highway. Tommy handed Wade Summerland a slip of paper.

"The Mud Flat Marina is the fucking name of the place. Call four-one-one and find out the address. She says these fucks are on a houseboat named *Seismic Shot*."

They sped past grain storage warehouses and freshly plowed fields alive with flying bugs, and headed toward Fresno. The sprawling city had grown up around the agriculture and the inland waterways that fed into the San Joaquin River, allowing the farm goods to be shipped cheaply to San Francisco on huge grain barges. Wade picked up the cellphone in the car, dialed Information, and got a number. He found out where the marina was and got directions over the phone. Fifteen minutes later, they pulled down the gravel road and parked in the marina parking lot. The place seemed deserted except for one or two cars parked in the lot near a closed, one-room marina office. A blue and white thirty-six-foot Winnebago was at the far end of the lot with the shades down.

Tommy looked at Dakota. "If they ain't here, ya better make an appointment with a good plastic surgeon."

"Hey, Tommy, you do what you want? I told you all I know. This is where they said they lived," she said, weak with pain.

Tommy grunted, and then he looked at Keith. "Stay with her an' cut her no slack. She'll surprise you if you ain't careful. She's got guts." He got out of the car with Jimmy and Wade. They walked over to a wood railing and looked down at the sleepy marina. As the name indicated, it sat on a low river tributary which was surrounded by mud flats. It was dusk, and the mosquitoes were beginning to swarm. For some reason they refused to bite Tommy, but vectored relentlessly at Jimmy and Wade, who swung their overdeveloped arms and slapped at themselves as they looked down at the small marina, surveying the layout. An old, decrepit wood dock paralleled the shore and served as a base for three finger docks that jutted out into the shallow water. Tied alone at the end of one of the fingers was a badly maintained, rusting houseboat. The stern said SEISMIC SHOT.

"If these fucks're here, I'm gonna chop some fucking lumber," Tommy said softly. Then he led them down to the dock.

311

They walked slowly and silently out on the tippy dock, creeping softly as they got closer. They could soon hear talking coming from inside the houseboat. It sounded like an argument. Tommy put a finger up to his mouth and they crept closer until they were just outside the old vessel. It was then that Tommy could hear Beano's voice over the sound of a top-forty radio station:

"It's supposed to be a tight hole!" Beano was protesting. "We gotta keep everybody quiet or the whole deal will get out and the U.S. regulators will be in there."

"Don't worry," Duffy responded. "You're always worrying. Nobody's gonna say shit. These guys know what's at stake."

The houseboat was about forty feet long and shaped like a shoe box. The faded yellow paint was peeling badly, exposing rusted tin underneath. There were a few tan pool chairs on the back deck that had been cooked and faded by the sun. A window air conditioner was growling loudly.

Tommy pointed at himself and then at the main hatch, indicating he would take the main door, which was opposite the gangplank leading from the dock up to the houseboat. Then he pointed Jimmy to the stern, and Wade to the bow. The two huge buttons nodded, and cracked their knuckles. Then Tommy pulled a 9mm SIG-Sauer out of a hip holster, signaled both men, then charged up the ramp, hit the door, and exploded into the main saloon....

Beano was seated in a metal chair at the

saloon table. He was wearing a striped, shiny tie and thick tortoise-shell glasses. He had a pen protector in the pocket of his shortsleeve shirt. When the door banged open and Tommy appeared in the room, Beano immediately bolted from the chair, heading out the back door of the houseboat. Duffy ran out the front, leaving Tommy, for a moment, alone in the main saloon with a small brown and black terrier, who had been asleep on the sofa and now jerked his head up to see what was happening. There was the sound of a brief struggle on both decks. ...Suddenly Beano, and then Duffy, were thrown backwards onto the saloon floor. Jimmy and Wade followed them in, filling the front and back doors with their girth. Tommy put his gun away and moved to Beano. He yanked him up onto his feet and held him by his striped shirt collar.

"Don't hit me," Beano pleaded.

So Tommy hit him, knocking him backwards into the chair. Then he stepped forward and kicked Beano in the nuts. Beano doubled over into a fetal position, still seated in the chair. To complete this brutal choreography, Tommy stepped forward and hit him with a vicious uppercut, straightening him out and knocking him to the floor. Roger-the-Dodger was on his feet, now looking at this in alarm.

"Please, please...I'm just a scientist, I have no money. Don't hurt us." Beano had now become a wimpy and very frightened Doctor of Geology.

"You ain't half as tough as the fuckin' bitch

you hired," he said to Beano, who was shaking in fear, curled up on the faded, threadbare carpet of the saloon, holding his throbbing nuts in both hands.

Duffy stood up in the center of the saloon. He tried to run again, but was grabbed by Jimmy Freeze and thrown back into the room.... Tommy took one shuffle step forward, timed his punch perfectly, and nailed the stumbling old man with a perfect left hook, knocking Duffy right out of his canvas boat shoes. "Think maybe I'm finally getting that left hook dialed in," Tommy said to himself. He was slightly out of breath from all the wood chopping he'd been doing. His knuckles were red and sore, but he was happy. He lived for moments like this.

♠ ♠ ♠

Ten minutes later, Beano and Duffy were tied to the metal chairs in the saloon with an extra dockline that Tommy had found in a forward locker.

It was dark outside, and Tommy had turned on the two old, shaded saloon lights, which were throwing an evil yellow hue on everything. Tommy had been through the boat, but he had not found his money. What he did find was mountains of graphs from the Fentress County Petroleum and Gas Company that were dated and carefully annotated. They had to do with something called the Oak Crest

Stratigraphic Trap. There must have been forty of them or more. Some were labeled "Biotherm Shot"; others, "Basal Conglomerate" or "Basal Shale Seismic Shot." There were several pen-and-ink drawings of what looked like a geographic map of the sub-soil strata in Oak Crest, near Modesto. They showed a huge underground domed area labeled "Faulted Dome and Cap Rock." There were seismic maps of things called "anticlines" and drawings of "fault traps." Somebody had written copious notes in the margins. Tommy glanced at a few before he lost interest. They said things he didn't care about or understand, like "Reshoot the 3-D seismic for section 16-B." It was Greek to Tommy, and he could care less. He threw them in a pile on the table. What he wanted was his $1,125,000 back, plus a little blood flow for his trouble.

Beano opened his eyes when Tommy threw a glass of water into his face.

"Hey, dipshit, over here," the mobster said, and Beano looked over at him. His groin was throbbing, and his face was bleeding. Tommy had loosened a few of his teeth. Duffy was still only half conscious, parked in the chair beside him.

"Ahhh," Beano finally said, trying to regain his senses. "Can't see, need my glasses. I lost my contacts yesterday."

Tommy found Beano's thick, Coke-bottle, tortoise-shell glasses on the floor and shoved them roughly on Beano's nose. Tommy knew he was menacing, and he wanted this academic twit to get a good look at who he was fucking with.

"Want my money back," Tommy said, as he pulled up the extra chair, turned it backwards, and straddled it, folding his arms over the back, now holding the SIG-Sauer in his right hand and resting his chin on his forearm. "You think we can get that done right away?" he said to Beano.

"I don't have it...I swear," Beano replied.

"Hey!" Tommy said sharply, barking the word out so that Beano, Duffy and Roger, who was still on the sofa, all flinched. "I got what they call a social disease," he said. "It's more of a psychological disorder, waddayacallit, an emotional dysfunction. My problem is I like t'kill. That surprises some people." He smiled his ghastly smile at them over the back of the chair, and Beano recoiled in horror. Tommy's chin was still on his forearm, the SIG-Sauer dangling dangerously. "These people, doctors mostly, they say that's a very serious personality flaw. But I'm not so sure I agree, 'cause I'm a student of the *Homo sapiens* species, and did you know that killing is inbred into the human DNA, just like wanting t'drive sports cars and fuck good-looking pussy?"

Beano cleared his throat again. "Actually, DNA has not yet been absolutely proven to determine behavioral characteristics. It deals only with physical genetic-code markers," he said academically.

"Don't fuck around with me, asshole," Tommy warned. "Just listen. Now, I'm sayin' this to you because I would have absolutely no difficulty goin' down to the hardware store an' buyin' a Black an' Decker, an' chain-sawin' you two pricks up a thin slice at a time. I would not cringe from this event in any way, because I have decided not to violate my natural instincts. I'm at peace with this brutal fact."

"Mr. Rina, I wish I could tell you I had your money, but it's gone," Beano said, his eyes magnified through the thick glasses.

"Gone." Tommy looked down at the floor, then over at Duffy. "Gone?" he asked Duffy, who was just coming back to the party and nodded his head. Tommy pulled the gun up and put it under Beano's chin, then he moved it up until the barrel clicked against Beano's still-sore teeth.

"Okay, okay...It's not gone, it's...well, it's..." Beano looked at Duffy.

"Don't tell 'im," Duffy croaked in dispair.

"You fuckin' guys misevaluate what is going on here. I am a fuckin' murderous psy-chopath...clinical. It's no shit! I got medical papers from Leavenworth shrinks. My dick gets hard over this shit."

"We used the money to buy stock certificates," Beano blurted.

"Don't!" Duffy screamed.

Tommy stood and kicked Duffy's chair over. Since he was firmly tied in it, he stayed aboard and hit his head on the floor.

"He's an old man," Beano pleaded. "Stop it."

And Tommy moved over and hit Beano three hard shots in the head. His glasses flew off. This time he almost went out. Fireworks exploded in his brain. When Beano finally pulled it back together and squinted at Tommy without his prop glasses, he could see Tommy had a ghastly expression of carnal pleasure on his simian face. Beano pointed weakly: "In the bedroom, under the bed, there's some loose panels....Pull them up. There's a metal lock box."

"No..." Duffy croaked.

Tommy nodded at Jimmy, who moved quietly into the master stateroom and returned a few minutes later with a metal lock box.

"The key's around his neck," Beano said and they grabbed the chain from Duffy's neck and pulled the key free, unlocked the box and pulled out ten beautifully engraved stock certificates for the Fentress County Petroleum and Gas Company. Each certificate was worth ten thousand shares. Also in the box were several color printed brochures for the Fentress County Petroleum and Gas Company. The folder that contained the press kit was a bright, glossy, rust-red color, loudly announcing the company's bright future from every page. There was an entire section describing and highlighting a great projected field in Oak Crest with helicopter photos of Carl Harper's newly painted, rust-red pipes and cisterns. There was a corporate photo of Paper Collar John. Under the picture, it said he was Linwood "Chip" Lacy, Chairman and CEO. Under that was the Chairman's message detailing the rosy future of FCP&G.

"What the fuck is this?" Tommy growled in dismay. "Where's my million dollars?" He threw aside the brochures and rifled through the certificates.

"Stock certificates. We used the money to buy them. The stock is trading at ten dollars a share. We got a hundred thousand shares, but it's not enough. We didn't win enough at craps to gain control."

"You dumb shits used my cash to buy *oil stocks*?" It was beginning to dawn on Tommy that his money was gone and the two men tied in chairs before him, despite being scientists, might also be world-class dimwits. Beano read the look and went to work.

"You just don't get it," Beano said indignantly, beginning his spiel. He always liked to hit a mark with a little attitude before selling him. "You wouldn't understand what this is all about. You couldn't understand. It's too technical for you and you're too stupid to see it." Tommy's anger flashed. A psychopathic rage swept through him that was overpowering. It obviated all reasonable thought.

Beano knew in that instant he had overplayed his hand. He could see the white-hot craziness flash in Tommy's eyes as the little mobster turned the gun on Beano and instinctively thumbed back the hammer. In those horrifying split seconds, Beano knew he was dead. He knew that he had made a fatal error in judgment. The mark had "come through" on him. Beano hadn't counted on Tommy's hovering insanity. He had always been able to read and control a mark; it was a skill he counted on. The click of the hammer filled the room. Tommy's finger went white as he started to pull the trigger. It was over.

Then something exploded off the sofa and launched itself at Tommy's neck.... Roger-the-Dodger was only twenty pounds, but he hit Tommy's throat like a Romanian bat, knocking the mobster over. Roger's jaws were firmly clamped on Tommy's throat. Tommy struggled to his feet, grabbing at the terrier, who was locked in a death grip. Blood was beginning to flow from the wound. Tommy dropped the gun and staggered around the cabin trying to get the terrier off his neck. Roger was snarling viciously and hanging off the mobster's neck like bad Indian jewelry. Tommy finally got his hands around Roger's throat and began to strangle him. The dog continued to snarl, but he was losing air, and when he was almost unconscious, Tommy finally pulled Roger off and flung him across the room. Blood was flowing down Tommy's neck, staining his white shirt collar. He screamed in fury and then grabbed for the SIG-Sauer, which was on the floor at his feet. He snatched it up and fired at the terrier, who had recovered and was now moving fast toward the rear door. The first shot was high—it broke a window and whirred away over the mud flats—but the second shot hit Roger in the hind end and knocked him down. He squealed in pain, but he rolled up and kept going out the door and across the deck. Tommy ran after him, but it was too dark outside and he couldn't see the brown and black dog, who was running and whining somewhere up the dock.

Tommy stormed back into the saloon. He grabbed the chair Beano was in, shoving the gun into Beano's mouth. "That fucking mutt tried to kill me!"

"Listen to me, that stock is worth billions," Beano slurred, his tongue tasting the gun barrel. He was desperately trying to focus Tommy on the bait. Beano's eyes were straining to see the black steel weapon that was in his mouth, buried up to the ejection port.

"Yeah? You little fucks. How is this shit worth billions?" Tommy backhanded the stock certificates off the table and then he pulled the gun out of Beano's mouth so he could talk.

"We found the biggest oil pool in North America, even bigger than the Alaskan strike. All those graphs there on the table confirm it. He and I are the only ones who know where it is," Beano said in a rush, looking toward Duffy. "The field's been proved out, but the oil company that's developing the field, FCP&G, they don't even know it's there, 'cause we haven't told them. We're buying up the company stock instead."

The crazy murderous glare that had been in

Tommy's eye now more closely resembled puzzled antagonism. "Oil?" he said. "What the fuck you talking about?"

"Shut up," Duffy yelled at Beano from the floor. "Don't tell him....Don't....Please. My whole life, my whole life I been waiting for this."

Tommy growled, already losing his patience, which was not a quality he was known for in the first place. He grabbed Duffy's coat and started to pull the chair upright. Jimmy and Wade moved to help.

"All of these graphs, all of this stuff...It proves that Oak Crest, California, is the biggest undiscovered oil find in North America," Beano continued, "and nobody but me and Dr. Sutton here, and Donovan Martin, know about it."

"Zat what all of this stuff is about?" Tommy asked as he motioned to all of the graphs and drawings on the table.

"Yes, those are seismic shots Dr. Sutton made. They were done over the last two years. FCP&G holds the mineral rights to that property in Oak Crest, they're the operator, but—"

"You're giving it all away, Douglas," Duffy wailed.

"We can't spend the money if we're dead, Harry. Can we? This man is gonna kill us." He turned to Tommy, who was now squinting again at the confusing graphs.

Duffy shook his head as Beano now looked directly at Tommy, going for the hard sell. "He's a doctor of physics, I'm a doctor of geology. We were both hired by the Fentress County Petroleum and Gas Company of Tennessee to check on a suspected stratigraphic trap near Modesto, a hundred miles northwest of here. But nobody really thought it was going to be there. All oil field exploration is a crap shoot at best, with only one in ten or fifteen fields panning out."

"A strati what?" Tommy said, his snake-mean brain struggling to comprehend.

"It's a separation in the natural rock layers in the earth's crust," Beano explained. "It creates underground caverns that trap oil. All big oil fields are a result of stratigraphic traps. Of course, the right geological substrata have to exist. We're looking for Paleozoic rock formations. Then we do what's called a three-D seismic shot. It's mildly complicated to explain, but basically, a seismic shot is accomplished when we drill a hole in the ground in the target area and then blast off a dynamite cap. The sound of the explosion travels through the rock. We trace it with sensitive geophones attached to our seismic computer; the sound waves bounce against the different rock hydrocarbons and tell us the nature of the rock and sand strata below the surface of the earth so we can graph them. Harry here is a seismic operator, a physicist; he uses his geophones to graph the hydrocarbon density to find the over-pressurized zones and then he interprets rock porosity."

"The fuck are you talking about?" Tommy finally yelled, getting angry because he didn't understand a word Beano was saying.

"What it boils down to is, we're sitting on the biggest undiscovered oil field maybe ever in the world. Bigger than Midland, Texas, or the Alaska find. It could be worth between two to five billion a year in crude E.O.R."

Tommy grabbed his arm. "Talk so I know what the fuck you're saying, you geek," he growled. "I'm fuckin' up to here with you already."

"E.O.R. stands for 'Enhanced Oil Recovery.' It's an upgraded pumping system," Beano added quickly.

"You fucking guys stole my money to buy stock in this fucking oil company?" Tommy said, returning to his first basic fact.

"But we didn't get enough money. We need three to five million. See, Fentress County Petroleum and Gas doesn't know the oil is down there, 'cause after we found it, we didn't tell them. If they did know, no amount of money could buy this company, because it would be worth billions. It's still our secret because we made a deal with the service company who was drilling the delineation well. The owner agreed to play along."

"Slow the fuck down," Tommy said, still trying to reel in the facts.

"Look," Beano said—he knew he had the hook in now and started a softer sell—"it's really simple. The oil company we work for, Fentress County Petroleum, spends millions in oil field discovery costs. People like me an' Harry are sent all over the world to find potential fields. We're sorta project managers. If we find a stratigraphic trap in the right Paleozoic rock strata, we do our seismic shots and, if we get what is known as a 'hot spot' or a 'bright spot' on our computer graphs, we notify the company and then they spend a lot of money to develop the potential field, put in pipes and cisterns. Then they hire an independent service company in the area to prove out the field. The service company drills what's called a delineation well to see what's down there. The service company Fentress hired is an outfit called W.C.P.D." Under Tommy's glare, he quickly added, "West Coast Platform Drilling Company, 'cause they also drill off-shore. W.C.P.D. drilled a bunch a'holes in this Oak Crest field that were basic P an' A's."

"Knock it off with the fucking letters."

"Plugged and Abandoned. Dry holes basically, but the core samples were promising. Dr. Sutton and I found out that W.C.P.D. wasn't getting paid by Fentress County Petroleum for their work. I complained to my boss about it and the Fentress County Petroleum and Gas Company fired me. At first I thought that was very strange, because I was running the operation out here. We didn't know it then, but Fentress is going broke. That's why they fired me. They were cutting new field development to nothing. We got together with Donovan Martin, who owns the service company, and all agreed to go ahead and try and prove out the field on our own. But because I'd been fired and Donovan's service company hadn't been paid, we agreed that if we found oil we would make it a tight hole, and not tell the F.E.R.C. We—"

Tommy reached out and backhanded Beano.

"I'm sorry." Beano winced. "Federal Energy Regulatory Commission. A tight hole is a secret oil well. You're supposed to tell the F.E.R.C. if you get positive results, but we agreed not to." He looked at Tommy. "We proved the field. Our delineation well came in. It was huge. This oil find is incredible! Fentress County Petroleum and Gas is in big financial trouble. They don't know we proved the field, they're going to go out of business, and their stock is falling. We're trying to get a controlling interest before the bank takes them over. Once the bank grabs the company we're out of luck, because there'll be an army of bank examiners and—"

Tommy held up his hand to silence Beano. "So you two assholes come to my casino in the Bahamas and steal money to buy this oil company, using crooked dice?" Tommy said, getting his next basic fact.

"It was his idea," Beano carped, looking at Duffy. "Harry used to do close-hand magic. He discovered the cellophane gas. He said we could do it, it's just we couldn't get enough money from the casino to buy the company before you shut us down."

"How can I believe all of this?" Tommy said, beginning to get interested.

"We've got the oil core drilling samples. They're at the service company warehouse," Beano said. "Donovan Martin, who owns the platform drilling company, has got 'em."

Tommy picked up the stock certificates from the floor and table, then gathered up the seismic graphs, the drawings, and the glossy printed brochure. "Let's go see," he finally said. "If this is all true...you guys just got yourselves a new partner."

TWENTY-TWO

Going with the Flow

Victoria had been crouching in the front seat of Beano's blue and white Winnebago, deep in the parking lot of the Fresno Mud Flat Marina. She had a brand-new Nikon long-lens camera on her lap and a copy of that day's *Fresno Herald* on the dash in front of her as Beano had instructed. She'd been sitting there for almost two hours, thinking about the last several days.

Her mind was a mixture of conflicting thoughts and emotions. She wasn't at all sure what she was doing there, but at the same time, she knew this was where she belonged. She was glad to be avenging Carol's death and to be a part of the plot to bring the Rina brothers down, but she resented her minor role in the adventure. So far, all she'd done was stand in the parking lot of the Sabre Bay Club *waiting* for the phone to ring so that she could give Duffy's phony credit rating, and now she was *waiting* in Beano's Winnebago with the new long-lens camera, *waiting* for Tommy to show up while Beano and Duffy told the tale in the houseboat. She could see how it worked now. The inside men were the important players in the con, there was no doubt about it. Everybody else was a shill or a lugger and performed a minor role. She was not used to the sidelines, and it bothered her. She understood that Tommy would recognize her if he saw her, but that fact didn't help. She had always been in control of everything in her life, from her pep squad in high school to moot court in law school. She had been the quarterback on the fifty or so felony cases she tried in the D.A.'s office. She was not good at holding other people's coats and was determined not to let that be her role in this situation.

Still, she had to admit that, so far, it had been the most invigorating experience of her life. She had enjoyed chasing the ambulance in the Bahamas more than she dared admit. She had re-lived it in her mind countless times, all the way up to the moment she pulled up alongside and yanked the wheel, spinning the van sideways and then slamming it into the speeding ambulance. There was something very freeing about the loss of control, like letting fresh air into a stuffy room. She knew the pictures she was supposed to take now would be critical later, and she was looking forward to her confrontation in two days with Joe Rina. It would be a chance to finally score a few points on that elegant piece of shit. As these thoughts were going through her mind, a black Lincoln limousine pulled into the parking lot. In a few minutes, Tommy and two men, roughly the same size as Texaco Phillips, got out. They dwarfed the five-foot eight-inch Tommy.... The three of them moved over to the railing and looked down at the marina. She took a few pictures, being sure that the newspaper lay open on the dash in front of her and was included in the shot. Then she watched as they walked down the gangplank to the wooden dock below. She crouched low inside the motor home, the lens of the camera pointing out of the window just under the shade. Again, she could feel the excitement bubbling. Beano had been right so far. He had gotten Tommy to do exactly what he had planned. They had controlled his movements. She wondered if Dakota was in the black Lincoln thirty yards away, as Beano had predicted.

♠ ♠ ♠

The back seat of the Lincoln was stuffy, and Dakota felt awful. She had begun to suspect she had some bad internal bleeding. One of Tommy's body blows must have ruptured something. The pain in her abdomen and stomach had become intense. It was hard for her to concentrate as the big enforcer in the front seat kept talking.

"I got lotsa stamina, I can stay hard for hours," Keith Summerland was bragging. He had turned around and was looking at Dakota in the back seat, a big wide leer on his flat, uninteresting features. "Soon as Tommy gets through with you, I'll take you someplace and give you a demonstration. Some guys don't like going down, but my tongue can do magic tricks. You're gonna beg me for more. Then you get to sit on Mr. Buffy. You're gonna get a ride you won't forget."

Dakota couldn't believe this piece of shit. The minute Tommy got out of the car, he'd started up with this. Dakota could barely talk because of the pain and he was up there bragging about his Johnson, which he'd named Mr. Buffy. She tried to get more comfortable.

"Right now, you're probably thinkin' you're gonna find a way to get out of it, but Tommy's nuts. He's not like other guys. I ask him if he's through with ya, he'll give ya to me." He grinned at her; he was twisted around in the front seat and eyed her hungrily like she had just been served to him, fully garnished, at a steakhouse. "You're gonna see a lot of me for a while."

Changing conversational topics, but not anatomical subjects, "Look, I didn't get a chance t'take a leak back at the airport," he said. "'Gonna go over t'that stand a'trees over there, and tap a kidney. I should tell you when I played football I did a four-six in full pads, in the forty, so don't try an' take off on me. You ain't gonna make it," he bragged.

"I'll be right here," she said softly.

He got out of the car and moved away from the limousine. As soon as he was gone, Dakota struggled up, grimacing in pain. She reached over the front seat, grabbed the cellphone, and dialed a number.

♠ ♠ ♠

In the motor home, Victoria was startled to hear a phone ringing somewhere. She had to go searching for it. It was on a table in the bedroom.

"Hello?" she answered.

"It's Dakota..." But Victoria thought she sounded funny. Her voice was deeper and without the "fuck you" lilt it had before.

"Where are you?" Victoria asked.

"Parked in the marina parking lot...probably about twenty yards from you. Look, I don't have much time. Tell Beano I can't control this guy. I've lost him."

"Are you okay?"

"Tell him I need to get out of here. I'm trashed. I think I'm hurt real bad. Something inside is leaking....The pain's getting worse. I don't have much left...."

"He's in the houseboat. They're in there with him." And then Victoria could see the big bodyguard coming back from the trees, zipping his fly. "Listen, Dakota, your guard's

331

coming back. I'll find a way to get you out of there. I promise. Hang tough," Victoria said, not at all sure how she was going to accomplish that feat, and then, just as the bodyguard approached the car, she heard two shots ring out. They actually sounded like dry limbs snapping off some distant tree. It took her several seconds to identify them as gunfire.

"You hear that?" Dakota asked. "Shots. This guy Tommy is nuts."

"I'll get you outta there but the other guy is right outside your car. Hang up!" Victoria said.

The line cut out as Keith Summerland turned to look down at the houseboat. He made no move to check out the shots. It was almost as if he expected them.

Then Victoria saw Roger-the-Dodger running awkwardly up the gangplank. He seemed to be limping. He moved past Keith Summerland, who turned to watch as the little terrier teetered across the pavement toward the Winnebago, barely staying upright. He got halfway there and fell over on his side. Then he pulled himself up and kept going, now almost dragging his hind end. Victoria could hear him whimpering as he got nearer. Then the heavyweight who had turned momentarily to watch the wounded dog refocused his attention on the houseboat. He started to walk down the ramp, then stopped. He was still in view of her with his back to the motor home. Roger-the-Dodger was moving very slowly now, and it didn't look like he would make it, so Victoria decided to risk going to him. With Keith's back still to her, she opened the door, ran outside, and scooped the terrier up. When she picked him up, his whole back end was wet and covered with blood. She ran back into the motor home, closed the door, and locked it. She laid Roger on the floor. He looked up at her with an expression she could describe only as gratitude.

"Rogie," she said, scrambling up to get a wet towel from the bathroom, "what happened, honey?" She returned and carefully washed his hind quarters, then examined the wound. She could see that there was a large, deep crease cut into his right flank. As she leaned down to clean it, he stopped whimpering, then unexpectedly licked her face.

♠ ♠ ♠

They came out of the houseboat and moved along the rickety dock. Jimmy Freeze had his hand on Beano, Wade Summerland was holding Duffy, and Tommy Rina was bringing up the rear. He had found some first-aid supplies aboard and had bandaged up his neck. He was moving with a long stride to keep up with the two larger men. They approached the limousine and waited for Tommy, then got in.

When Beano saw Dakota, his stomach dropped. She had been brutally beaten; she sat in the back seat, her head back, her eyes barely open. He got in with Duffy; the last in was Tommy. Jimmy and Wade sat in the front with Keith.

"Little mutt came runnin' up here," Keith said, "piece of his ass missing."

"Good, maybe he'll bleed to death. Get rollin'," Tommy barked. Keith put the car in motion and they drove out of the parking lot.

"Are you okay?" Beano asked Dakota.

She nodded, but didn't say anything. She seemed completely drained of energy.

Tommy handed a slip of paper to Jimmy Freeze. "Jimmy, go to this address. It's a service company called...what?"

"West Coast Platform Drilling," Beano said, and he looked out the window for Roger. He knew if the little terrier hadn't attacked Tommy, he would be dead. He saw blood on the pavement where Roger had fallen and prayed Roger-the-Dodger was alive. Then Beano looked back at Dakota and took stock of where they were. He knew it was up to him to keep them alive. He had to stay focused.

The plan had worked. Tommy seemed hooked, but in a good scam, the sharpers weren't supposed to get hurt. He looked again at Dakota. He didn't like the color of her complexion.´

♠ ♠ ♠

In the motor home, Victoria had tried to perform first aid on Roger. She found an Ace bandage in the bathroom. She put a clean washcloth on the wound and then tried to wrap the bandage as tight as she could to stem the bleeding. Then she carried Roger over to the sofa and carefully laid him there. "I'll take you to the vet as soon as I can," she told him, but she knew she also had to stay close to Duffy and Beano. She didn't know if the other shot had hit one of them. She couldn't lose Dakota. Victoria had been distressed by the sound of her voice.

Then she had seen Tommy and the two huge bodyguards leading Duffy and Beano up the ramp. She grabbed the camera and focused on them as they walked up under the overhead light in the marina parking lot. She got three good shots of Beano and Duffy with Tommy by the car before they got in. In one shot Beano turned toward the lens, smiled, and put his arm around Tommy. She snapped the shot before the little mobster knocked Beano's arm off.

As the limo pulled out of the parking lot, Victoria put the big motor home in gear and followed with the headlights out. She wasn't sure what she was going to do. This was not going exactly the way Beano had described. She looked back at Roger, who was lying on the sofa, his chin on his paws, looking up at her. He seemed to be asking, "What now?" A question she couldn't answer.

Then the limo turned onto the freeway and headed northwest, toward Modesto.

Victoria Hart, who had once been voted the "most organized" in her senior class, who since law school had never made an important move without planning it and mapping it out meticulously, now blindly followed the black stretch limo up onto the freeway. She knew she had no chance to plan anything. With her heart beating frantically, she gripped the steering wheel in desperation and decided this time, she would just have to go with the flow.

TWENTY-THREE

W.C.P.D.

The West Coast Platform Drilling Company was in a warehouse district in the small town of Livingston, twenty miles southeast of Modesto. The sign on the corrugated tin building was freshly painted and showed a derrick with oil shooting out of the top. In the fenced yard were rolls of cable and used parts. A roof light threw its glare across the enclosed parking lot. The limo pulled in and stopped. It was 10:15 P.M.

Beano looked over at Dakota, who had her eyes closed now and was breathing with difficulty. Her head was tilted back, resting on the back seat; her skin color was pasty.

"You gotta take her to a hospital," Beano said.

Tommy looked over at Dakota for a long, speculative moment. "Why?" he finally said.

"She looks horrible. Something's wrong with her."

"Are we talkin' about the same cunt who put something in my drink so I'd pass out, so you two fucks could run the table on me at my own club and get my brother so pissed he starts cussing?"

"She needs to be looked at," Beano insisted.

"Hey, Dr. Dipshit, or whatever your fuckin' name is—"

"It's Douglas," Beano said stubbornly.

"You called the tune, Douglas, this is the fucking music. Now let's go see this asshole." He grabbed Beano and pushed him out of the limo. As Beano passed in front of Dakota, she opened her eyes and they exchanged looks. Beano didn't like what he saw there.

They were all out of the limo. Only Keith was left behind with Dakota. They moved to a side door of the corrugated metal warehouse. Beano knocked; Duffy was standing right behind him.

"Donovan, it's me. It's Dr. Clark and Dr. Sutton," Beano yelled, and in a minute, the side door was unbolted and Steven Bates was standing there, wearing old coveralls with W.C.P.D. stitched on the pocket. He was wiping his hands with an old rag and looking warily out the slit in the door at Beano and Duffy.

"Dr. Clark, Dr. Sutton." He nodded; then his eyes shifted to Tommy and the two wide-bodies behind him. "Who are they?" Steve asked.

Tommy moved in front of Beano and stuck the automatic in Steve's face. "I'm your new drilling partner."

Steve looked down at the barrel of the 9mm SIG-Sauer and swallowed hard, dismay on his sun-reddened features.

"Inside. We ain't havin' this stockholders' meeting in the street. Let's go." And Tommy pushed Beano and Duffy into the warehouse. Jimmy Freeze and Wade Summerland came in last and closed the door.

The inside of the warehouse had been carefully dressed by Steven. He had leased the building and rented everything. Two large portable water pumps with metal derricks that were used for agricultural field irrigation were on rolling pallets in the center of the warehouse floor. Even though they were water pumps, they looked enough like oil derricks to fool the uninitiated layman. Steve had helped the deception by labeling one OIL PUMPING UNIT C, the other OIL PUMPING UNIT J. He had rolls of cable strewn around and a forklift parked in plain view. A small safe was conspicuous in the corner. Everything was on a two-week rental from a farm supply company just two blocks away. The hand props he had rented from a dive shop in Modesto.

"What the heck's this?" Steve Bates said, as he looked down at the gun in Tommy's hand.

"You ain't askin' the questions, Joe Bob, you're answerin' 'em. I wanna hear about this oil field you found in Oak Crest."

Steve Bates looked warily at Beano, then at

Tommy. "There's no field," he stammered. "That's just a buncha dry holes. Wish t'heck we'd a'hit something, by God."

"Forget it, Donovan," Beano said. "He's seen all the graphs, the seismic shots. We told him everything."

"You told him?" The betrayal in Steven Bates's voice was nothing short of Shake-spearean.

"Let's try and get past that, Donovan. The fact is we need more money anyway. We can't control this thing with just a hundred thou-sand shares. We're outta time." Beano pushed his glasses up on his nose.

Steven Bates looked at Beano and then his eyes slid back to Tommy. "I don't know what he's talking about," he said, but his voice was hesitant now.

"Then lemme put it in line for you," Tommy said. "I wanna see this field in Oak Crest and you buncha pricks is gonna take me there tonight. How far away is that?"

"'Bout an hour," Beano said.

"Dr. Clark," Steve said, "this was a tight hole. How could ya tell 'em?"

"I didn't have a choice. He followed us back from Sabre Bay. He found everything. He's got the stock certificates. Besides, I think we should take him as a partner. We're better off letting him in on this. Believe me, we can't control it ourselves anyway."

Tommy glared at Beano. "I'm not in on any-thing yet, asshole. I'm on a fact-finding mis-sion, and I'm tryin' t'get my million dollars back. So far, all you got from me is some mild interest. If I don't get a lot more info in the next few hours, I'm gonna cash in these stock certificates, get my money back, and you guys are all deader than junkie luck." He thumbed the hammer back and pointed it at Steve. "Are we straight?" Steve nodded. "Then keep talkin'."

"The Fentress County Petroleum and Gas Company stock is falling," Steve Bates said. "We bought it at ten, it's already at eight. The rumor is out that Fentress County can't make their bank payments. Their cash flow is too low. Buncha big stockholders are already calling for a meeting in San Francisco at the main office. They wanna liquidate the company. It's hit the street already that they're in trouble. Even if you cash in those hundred thousand shares, you're not gonna get back much more than seven hundred and fifty thousand dollars."

Tommy's eyes were roaming the warehouse. "You use this shit to drill them elimination wells?" he asked, motioning at the equipment, his mind already racing ahead.

"Delineation wells," Steve Bates corrected him. "Yeah, them small rigs only drill a six-eighths-of-an-inch hole that we side-cement with sleeveless piping. These units are good for slant drilling or directional drilling. Once we hit oil or natural gas, we put on one a'these," Steve said, picking up a small gauge attached to rubber hosing that had been rented from the Modesto Dive Shack. The gauge was actually part of an air-flow regulator.

Tommy took the piece of equipment out of Steve Bates's hand and looked at it. "What the hell is it?" he said.

"It's a flow meter," Steve said. "We use it to determine velocity of fluid. We use all kinds a'different ones. That one yer holdin' is a positive displacement unit, but we got turbine units and electromagnetic flow meters...depending on what we're tryin' to determine." As he spoke he was looking at the gun in Tommy's hand.

"I don't give a shit about any of that. How much oil is down there?"

"Hard to say," Steve said. "Dr. Clark thinks we got a major pay zone. I like t'keep my estimates on the conservative side."

"Like what?"

"We hooked up the PD meter, that's yer Positive Displacement meter, to the flow meter. We can estimate gross volume, using a flow rate formula. According to that test, seems like we got a pretty big pool down there. Could be half-a-billion barrels or more...maybe much more."

"The size of that stratigraphic trap is huge," Beano interrupted. "Covers almost six hundred acres. Only reason we missed it ten months ago is that our original seismics misidentified the site. We were off by half a mile. The field we were looking for is actually a little south of where we were doing the seismic shots, but by slant drilling, we got into the main trap." Beano was so excited when he spoke about it, his eyes were flashing. He was believing his con and selling it.

"You say you need more money to control the company? How much?" Tommy asked, nibbling at the bait.

"Used to be we needed maybe ten million, but I think, with the price fall on the stock, we could control it with five or six," Beano said, "providing the S.E.C. doesn't freeze the stock on us because of erratic fluctuations."

"Five million *plus* my million you already invested?" Tommy asked.

"That oughta do 'er," Steve Bates said, and took the diving air-flow meter out of Tommy's hand. The rule was you never let the mark hold a prop too long.

"How do I know this is all on the level?" Tommy asked, his eyes narrowing.

Beano looked at Steve hopefully. Steve finally exhaled and moved over to the small safe, kneeled, and dialed a combination. He pulled open the door and grabbed several long metal canisters that were stored inside on racks. Each canister had a glass window. Steve held each one up to the light, reading the label before finding the one he wanted.

"The fuck is all this?" Tommy said.

"Side core samples," Beano explained. "This is how we finally hit the pool. Take a look at this." He took one of the cylinders from Steve and handed it to Tommy, pointing at the window in its glass side. "This core sample was from sixteen hundred feet down. You can see from the brown color that we're already getting discoloration from the oil shale. That means the porosity of the top soil has absorbed the oil at the roof of the trap. That's why I think this is a full trap with a lot more than half-a-billion barrels," Beano insisted.

Tommy took the sample tube and stuck it in his pocket.

"You must leave that here," Beano said, alarmed. "It's part of the drilling record, eventually it will have to go to the F.E.R.C."

"Hey, asshole, ain't you figured out yet who's in charge? I'm gettin' my own geologist. I'm gettin' this checked. You're not dealin' with some chucklehead here."

Beano and Steve exchanged nervous looks.

"Okay. Let's say for now, I'm interested," Tommy went on, "so let's go take a look at this field."

♠ ♠ ♠

Victoria had followed them to the warehouse in Livingston and watched as everybody got out and went inside, leaving Dakota and the bodyguard in the limo. She had parked the Winnebago up the street, then checked on Roger, who whimpered when she touched his hind end. "Sorry, honey, but it's not bleeding, so that's good." Then she moved to the back of the motor home and got the spandex dress that she had worn at the jewelry store out of the small wardrobe closet. She grabbed the plastic heels and started to change.

♠ ♠ ♠

She knew she would have to find a way to disable the gorilla standing guard if she intended to rescue Dakota. The man was huge, and she was afraid that unless she distracted him, she could never control the situation. She decided that the sexy dress might give her some added advantage. She had been remembering a Trenton street villain she'd prosecuted several years ago. He was a 120-pound creep who was actually a collection agent for a loan shark. He had put hundreds of slow-pays in the hospital using a simple trick. He would wear leather gloves, and inside the palm of his right glove, he would hide a flat, curved, heavy metal sap. He would disable his victims with one slap to the side of the head. Her E.N.T./M.D. expert witness had testified that a sharp hard blow to the ear, even by a 120-pound man, could easily explode the capillaries in the inner ear, causing the victim to lose all of his equilibrium.

Victoria searched the motor home and finally found a white golfing glove in one of the drawers. She slipped it on her right hand. It was loose but it sort of fit. She kept looking in the drawers for some tool Beano might use for roofing scams or to make the wheelchair dice brackets. She found a toolbox in the outside storage compartment. Inside was a small metal rasp for filing wood. It was about four inches long and one inch wide, and it weighed almost two pounds. She shoved it down into the glove. The metal file stuck out too far, but maybe, with the purse over her arm, the huge bodyguard wouldn't notice. She hoped he wouldn't be near the car, and that she wouldn't have to use it. She'd been a state junior tennis champion and her forehand was awesome, but she'd never actually hit anybody before. Her Prosecutor's brain instructed her that this would be a felonious assault and battery. Then she remembered the troubling sound of Dakota's voice and pushed all those thoughts away, grabbed her purse, and moved out of the Winnebago. She hurried up the street until she got to the fence that bordered the warehouse. She could see that the bodyguard had left the front door of the limo open for air and that his big leg was dangling out, his foot tapping on the pavement as he listened to country music radio. Tanya Tucker was singing about a lost love.

"Hey!" she called out to him.

In a second Keith stuck his head out and saw Victoria standing there, looking through the gate. "Hi," he said, getting out of the car and moving over to her, smiling.

"My car broke down. I need a phone....Can I use the one in your limo?" she asked. "I'll pay for the call."

Keith eyed her platform heels, the micro-mini exposing her sexy legs. He grinned and moved closer.

"You're too cute to be out here walkin' around alone," he leered, turning on his NFL groupie-catcher smile. Keith was feeling horny; just being close to Dakota had got his juices flowing, but he knew if he touched her before Tommy said okay, he would end up dead. This girl was a whole other story.

"Gate's over here, come on, I'll let you in," he said.

She followed him along the fence until they got to the gate, and he let her in. "'Course, I can't really let you use the phone in the limo," he leered, "but that wasn't what you had in mind anyway, was it?"

"Yes," she insisted, "my car broke down." She was sizing him up. He was huge, six-four at least, and over 250. She wondered if the little Trenton street villain had ever used his glove sap on a mountain of gristle like the one towering over her.

"How 'bout we have some fun?" he said, grabbing her and holding her shoulders with both hands.

"Slow down, honey," she said as he pawed at her. She was within striking distance now, as he fumbled to open the front of her dress. Almost without thinking, she swung her right hand, a powerful forehand winner. The two-pound rasp caught Keith Summerland smack on the left ear. He let out a howl, went backwards, and dropped to his knees. She stepped back in horror and for a brief moment watched as he held his head, moaning. Then she stepped around him and ran across the asphalt toward the limo, pausing on the way to kick off the damn platform shoes. Victoria reached out and opened the back door and peered in at Dakota. She looked horrible: A light film of sweat covered her swollen bruised face.

"Oh, my God," Victoria whispered, "what did they do to you? Can you walk?"

"Don't know," Dakota said. "Pull me out."

Victoria reached in, took Dakota's hand, and pulled her out of the car, then walked with an arm around her, steadying her as they left the lot. Dakota glanced over at Keith. He was struggling to get to his feet, dizzy and totally out of it. He didn't see them leave.

"Let's go," Victoria said, hurrying Dakota away and up the street to the Winnebago. "I never hit anybody before," Victoria added.

"Good...start..." Dakota mumbled. Once they got into the motor home, Victoria settled her on the sofa next to the wounded terrier. Dakota was looking at Victoria with new respect.

Twenty minutes later, Victoria found the small, one-story Livingston Hospital. The E.R. attendants took one look and got Dakota on a gurney, rushing her into Emergency while Victoria picked up Roger-the-Dodger and carried him gingerly inside. She filled out the admitting slip for Dakota, using her own mother's maiden name, Barker. Then she got a nurse to take a look at Roger.

"What happened to him?" the sympathetic woman asked. "He looks like he's been shot."

"I don't know. I found him outside her house. I think her boyfriend may have beaten her and shot the poor dog," Victoria lied, wishing she was as good as Beano at spur-of-the-moment bullshit.

"I'll get Dr. Cotton to take a look at him," she said.

♠ ♠ ♠

Two hours later Dakota was rushed into Emergency Surgery. Her spleen had been leaking blood into her abdomen for at least twelve hours. Her blood count and blood pressure were so low, they were life threatening.

When the doctor came out after the surgery, he looked worried. "She lost a lot of blood. She went into cardiac arrest on the table from low BP. We removed her spleen, pumped her full of plasma. She's been stabilized, but...I don't know..."

"How long till you can tell?" Victoria asked.

"I let God sort out the close ones," the doctor said. "I've called the police. She was obviously beaten, so I'm going to need your statement. They're on their way."

"I'll be glad to talk to them," Victoria said, but she knew she had to get out of there before the police came. Once they started asking questions, they'd sense her complicity. She needed to get Roger, so she wandered the sterile linoleum corridors, asking for Dr. Cotton. She finally found a plain-faced young woman M.D. in a doctors' lounge, holding Roger-the-Dodger and talking softly to him. His entire back end was now bandaged in white adhesive.

"Is he your dog?" she said accusingly, as Victoria moved into the small room.

"No, my friend's dog."

"This dog was shot," the doctor said angrily. "A large caliber, from the look of it."

"Oh," Victoria said. She wanted to get the hell out of there, so she reached out and took Roger out of the doctor's arms.

"I shouldn't have sewn him up. I'm a doctor, not a veterinarian, but I love animals and I couldn't leave him like that. He needs a vet's prescription—some strong antibiotics for possible infection," she lectured. And then mercifully, her beeper went off. "Excuse me, don't leave," she said and moved out of the room.

As soon as she was gone, Victoria took Roger and carried him out of the small hospital and into the Winnebago. She pulled the motor home out of the parking lot just as a police black-and-white arrived. The old Victoria would have glanced away in fear, but the new emerging one waved confidently at the cops, then turned left and sped away into the night.

TWENTY-FOUR

Proving the Pasture

They heard a banging on the warehouse door and, when Steve moved to open it, he found Keith Summerland standing there with blood all over the side of his head. When Tommy saw him, he immediately moved to the door. "The fuck happened to you?"

"She hit me," Keith said, still holding his bleeding ear. He had decided not to tell Tommy he had been away from the car, trying to put a juke on a girl whose car had stalled.

"I told ya to be careful a'her," Tommy said. He moved out quickly and looked at the empty lot and limousine. There was no sign of Dakota. He knew if she had hit Keith and escaped, there was a chance she would call the law. "Let's go, alla you," he said, waving the gun.

They all moved out of the warehouse toward the limo. Tommy glowered at Keith, whose ear was still leaking blood.

"You get the fuck away from me, you dumb asshole," he shouted at Keith. "What was you doin'? Tryin' t'give her a feel?"

"No, Tommy, I just turned around for a minute and—"

"Shut the fuck up. Get away from me. Joe was right to fire you. I'll deal with you later."

Tommy pushed the huge man toward the gate. He was in a hurry to get out of there before the cops arrived.

Beano had wondered how it would be possible for Dakota to hit Keith Summerland and do that much damage. She seemed almost unable to talk, let alone knock this 250-pound monster silly. Then, as Beano was looking across the pavement, something glinted in the overhead light. When he looked closer, he saw what it was....

A plastic platform heel. He smiled to himself. *Good girl, Vicky,* he thought.

Tommy pushed him into the back of the limo next to Steve and Duffy. He made Jimmy ride in front with Wade. They pulled out, leaving Keith Summerland by the gate, still holding the side of his head and wondering what he was going to do next.

♠ ♠ ♠

In the back seat of the limo everybody rode in silence. Beano pushed his glasses up on his nose and looked at Tommy, whose expression said nothing.

"Whatta ya looking at?" Tommy finally snapped.

"Well, sir...uh...not to be indelicate, but...uh, well, the people at the field where we're going, they don't know there's oil down there, and it would be helpful if they weren't alerted to that fact. We drilled a slim hole, like Donovan said...only six-eighths of an inch, and we capped it off 'cause we don't want them to know we proved the field."

"So, we ain't gonna tell 'em," Tommy said.

"I've been fired. If I go out there with a crowd of people looking around, they're bound t'figure something's funny."

"So, you don't want me to see this field?" he said accusingly.

"No...it's not that, it's just...if I'm looking around out there, they're gonna get suspicious. If we just stayed in the car and sorta drove around, it might be better."

"I don't know yet what we're gonna do, so shut the fuck up," Tommy said. "You're givin' me a migraine."

They arrived at Oak Crest at a little past midnight, and drove around Carl Harper's alfalfa field. In the full moonlight, they could see the freshly painted pipes and cisterns, all dressed up in their new rust-red Fentress County Petroleum color. A big FCP&G shone in white block letters on the top of the large cistern by the road. Tommy turned on the dome light in the limo and got out the beautiful glossy oil-company brochure that Beano had printed. He looked carefully at all the colorful pictures of the painted pipes and cisterns; then he looked back out the window at the same pipes and cisterns in the field.

"What's all the pipes for?" he asked Duffy.

"Well, you should ask Dr. Clark. He's the geologist, I'm just a physicist."

"When you set up a Class One-A field,"

Beano lectured, "that's a field on a large stratigraphic trap where there could be a pay zone of billions of gallons, there is the possibility of a blow-out or a gusher, and the F.E.R.C.—that's the Federal Energy Regulatory Commission," Beano added quickly, "—they don't want millions of gallons spewing around on the ground for ecological reasons, so they make you set up a gathering station in advance to control the flow of oil or L.N.G." Tommy glowered. "Liquefied Natural Gas... This gathering station is a collection of pipes and cisterns like you see out there. That way if you hit a well, this mechanism is already in place to bring the oil from the pumping station, or wellhead, to a cistern where it can be stored and tested." Beano smiled at Tommy, then removed and cleaned his glasses on his tie, like any good geek scientist between academic thoughts. He slipped them back on and took the brochure. "Let me show you on the map of the field here," Beano said, showing Tommy a printed schematic drawing of the farm that was in the brochure. "We put the delineation well in right about here. It's a horizontal well on a forty-five-degree slant. We used deviation drilling techniques and a subsurface reservoir catch basin we vented with horizontal drain holes." Beano was in full sales mode now and orbiting freely over his own planet of bullshit.

Tommy was lost, but it didn't matter; he was buying it. "So, show me the well you drilled," he finally said.

"This is so fucked," Duffy muttered.

"Come on, Dr. Sutton," Beano said, "Mr. Rina has the money we need. We were going to have to try and steal more from Las Vegas. With all the security they have in those casinos, we might very well have been arrested. You told me yourself the reason we went to Sabre Bay was because it was smaller, with less security. Besides, the S.E.C. is going to shut down Fentress County Petroleum any minute. This is our best and last chance. Mr. Rina can make this happen. He puts in the cash, we buy the stock, the money relieves the company's debt, the S.E.C. and the bank go away. We're rich."

Duffy grunted and mumbled, but stopped complaining.

Beano showed Wade Summerland where to turn. Beano thought it was strange that Wade had not even protested once when his brother had been left behind alone, to deal with his ruptured ear.

♠ ♠ ♠

"The well's over here," Beano said as they moved away from the limo, down the road from the large, freshly painted cistern, and over to a small shrub area. Beano pulled the shrubs aside. They had been cut and tied to a sandbag to hide the wellhead. Under the shrubs was a small capped hole with a metal plate on top. The plate was engraved with the letters FCP&G. A small three-inch-diameter pipe led off across the field and intersected with one of the larger rust-red pipes.

"Open it up," Tommy said.

"It goes down eighteen hundred feet," Beano whined, "you can't see anything."

"Did I ask about that? I said open it up."

"Donovan, the man apparently has his heart set on seeing a hole in the ground," Beano said to Steve Bates, sighing loudly to show his disgust.

"Am I boring you, dipshit? 'Cause if I am, I can arrange to give you a few minutes of memorable action," Tommy sneered at Beano, who took a quick step back while Steve removed a tool from his belt and started to open the capped hole.

Beano started to mollify Tommy. "Mr. Rina, I'm a geologist...MIT actually, with my doctoral studies at Yale, post-doc at Stanford. I have fifteen years in satellite well production and sand control analysis. I worked my way up to Field Manager. I'm a man who analyzes rock hydrocarbons. I spend hours in the laboratory looking at complex organic molecules."

"I don't want your fuckin' résumé," Tommy interrupted.

"It's just...you keep threatening me. I'm not a brave man. I don't pretend to be a hero. I'm interested in this field on a geological level primarily, and yes, if I make some money, that's wonderful. I'm trying to say to you that I view you as a real asset in this situation, but you keep holding a gun and threatening me like I'm some kind of low-life criminal who's just on the edge of jumping you. I'm not a physical threat, I've never even been in a fight in my entire life. So can we please stop acting like little children?"

Tommy loved to hear weasels weasel, and he smiled at this concert of gutless pleading. He didn't answer, but a few minutes later, he did tuck the gun back in his pants.

"Okay, got 'er off," Steve said, as he pulled the heavy plate back and Tommy looked down the cement-walled, metal-jacketed hole. He took a quarter out of his pocket and held it over the opening and dropped it, waiting for it to hit. Since the hole went down only twenty feet, Beano had to cough loudly at about the right moment to avoid the slight possibility that Tommy would hear the quarter hit.

"We better get outta here," Beano warned.

"So, you hit oil right here, huh?" Tommy asked, ignoring him.

"That's right," Steve Bates said. "Pumped fifteen thousand gallons t'prove out the well. Took it right up outta that little five-inch hole."

"So, where's the oil?" Tommy insisted. "You said you can't leave it on the ground...so you gotta do something with it. Where is it?"

"Over there," Beano said, pointing to the large, two-story-high, rust-red cistern with the white company letters displayed proudly on the top.

"The fifteen thousand gallons is in there?"

Tommy said, squinting at it in the moonlight.

"That's right. This tank is supposed t'be
empty, so nobody even checks it," Beano said.
"We hadda put the oil somewhere. We had
the flow meter on her and we fed the spillover
into that nine-inch ground pipe and that pumps
it into the storage system over in that cistern."

"Let's go see," Tommy said.

"Huh?" Beano replied.

"I wanna go see the oil."

"The cistern's sealed, you can't get inside
it."

"Bullshit. I can get in anywhere I want.
Now, let's go."

"That tank's buttoned up airtight. I'm
telling you, you can't get in there," Beano
insisted.

Tommy grabbed Beano by the shirt collar
and pulled him up close. "I'm not getting
through to you, Doc, and that really pisses me
off. How smart can you be if every fucking question I ask, you come back with 'Huh?' or 'I can't
do that.' 'Huh?' isn't a fucking answer. You
got me? I say I wanna go see the fucking oil,
you say 'Follow me,' or 'Yes, Mr. Rina.' Any
other answer is gonna get your fucking head
punched." Tommy was spitting the words
into Beano's face and spraying his Coke-bottle glasses.

"I'm just telling you the facts. I don't see
why you insist on this violent presentation of
your position."

"'Cause I don't fuckin' like you," Tommy explained.

"O-Okay," Beano said, stuttering slightly. "Okay."

Tommy finally released him. "Now, are we gonna go get a look at that oil or we gonna stand here jerking off?"

"We're gonna go get a look at the oil," Beano said.

They moved back to the car and then over toward the main cistern. A full moon glinted on the fresh paint as they climbed the small ladder to the top of the cistern. Only Wade stayed behind with the car. Once they were on top of the two-story metal container, the entire field could be seen spread out before them in the moonlight....Acres of rust-red pipes criss-crossed the field, punctuated by three other rust-red cisterns; it was all very impressive. Across the road was the abandoned office building that Beano had found, which was now also painted in the company colors. A big sign out front read:

FENTRESS COUNTY PETROLEUM AND GAS DEVELOPMENT FIELD 32

Tommy had brought a crystal glass and one of the decanters from the limo. "Open this fucking thing up," Tommy said to Beano, pointing at a three-foot-square hatch in the cistern, which was held in place by twenty rusting bolts.

"How? We'll never get these bolts off and it's gonna be rank in there. Crude oil is very rich, organically speaking. It smells terrible."

"Open it up," Tommy repeated. "I wanna see the oil."

Finally Steve stepped forward. "We can get these here bolts loosened, I think. They're three-fourths of an inch. I think most tire irons is three-fourths. We could use the lug wrench outta the trunk."

They sent Jimmy Freeze down to get it. He returned a few minutes later with the lug wrench. He and Steve went to work unbolting the hatch. It was slow going, but they all took turns, except Tommy, and twenty minutes later they had it off. It was now three-thirty in the morning. They lifted the metal plate off the big cistern and set it to the side of the opening. Tommy leaned over and sniffed at the hole. "Don't smell nothin'," he said.

"You'd have t'climb down," Beano said nervously.

"If there ain't no fucking oil down there, you're one dead fucking geek."

"Maybe they found it and drained it," Beano stuttered. "You can't just kill me if it's empty."

"Watch me," Tommy promised.

"The tank's ladder is right here, inside to the right of the opening," Steve pointed out, to change the subject.

Tommy looked at Jimmy Freeze. "Go down there an' get me some oil, Jimmy."

"Ahhh, Tommy, how come it's gotta be me?"

"'Cause I said so, and I wanna keep my eyes on these assholes."

Jimmy took the decanter and the glass and slowly lowered himself over the side and found the ladder with his toes. They watched while he disappeared down into the cistern. There was a deep bonging every time he kicked the side of the cistern with the toes of his shoes. They could hear him coughing and then they heard him swearing. A few minutes later, Jimmy Freeze reappeared at the opening of the cistern. "There's a bunch of it down there, filled almost halfway up." His eyes were watering from the fumes.

"This is a thirty-thousand-gallon reservoir; that's fifteen thousand gallons in there," Steve said.

Then Jimmy lifted the crystal decanter up and set it down by Tommy's feet and climbed out of the cistern. Tommy picked up the decanter and looked at it in the moonlight. It was half filled with crude oil.

"Son-of-a-bitch," he said, looking at the black gold.

"I told ya. When are you gonna believe me?" Beano said.

"Right after I get this analyzed," Tommy said.

The oil in the cistern had been brought up from Santa Barbara. Steve had bought it from an offshore rig. When Tommy sent it to a lab, he would be told it was high-quality, 90 percent pure crude with no shale content. Of course, there wasn't fifteen thousand gallons in the cistern. There was only fifty. Since oil is lighter than water, all they had to do was float the fifty gallons of crude on top of Carl

Harper's water supply. There was only six inches of oil floating on top of fifteen thousand gallons of water.

They put the stopper on the decanter and climbed back down to the ground. Once they were all back in the limo, Beano looked over at Tommy. He could see it wasn't going to be necessary to take him to the little oil office in the morning and run him through that maze. The ugly mobster was hooked. He kept looking at the oil in the decanter. He would pick it up out of the decanter rack every few minutes, hold it in his hands, look at it again, and smile. "Okay, you guys, I'm in."

"How much of this is ours?" Beano said. "We still haven't discussed an equitable stock distribution."

Tommy looked over at him as if the thought hadn't even occurred to him. "How's sixty-forty?" Tommy said, a small smile on his face. "Of course I get sixty, you guys run the technical stuff and get forty."

"This is fucked," Duffy said.

"No, it's not. We'll get forty percent of billions of dollars," Beano said. "Come on, Dr. Sutton. This is better than we could have hoped for, trying to make it the other way, stealing from Las Vegas." Beano shoved his glasses back on his nose. "You got a deal," he said to Tommy, but then added, "You better hurry though. The S.E.C. could shut this stock down and freeze trading on the company any day."

"I can be back here with the money in less

than a day," Tommy said, stroking the decanter of oil on his lap like it contained a magic genie.

"Good," Beano said.

Tommy nodded to Wade, who put the car in gear, and they headed back to Fresno where his jet was waiting. On the way, Beano looked at Tommy intently again.

"The fuck you always starin' at me for?" Tommy growled.

"I know all about you and your little brother," Beano said. "You probably have to go ask his permission to take his money."

"I don't ask nobody's permission for nothing."

"I heard he was the boss," Beano insisted. "He makes all the decisions."

"You heard fucking wrong," Tommy snarled.

Duffy thought Beano had played it perfectly, by being reluctant to do what the mark wanted and then being forced to agree. Tommy was sure he was getting the truth. When Tommy finally ended up with the oil in his hands, he was convinced because his own insistent questions and demands had led him to it. Now he was sold and ready to plunge. In the old days once a mark was hooked on the con, the sharpers would always send him home to get more money. It was called "The Country Send."

Part Six
THE COUNTRY SEND

"The Devil can quote scripture."
—An American Proverb

TWENTY-FIVE

Much Closer Than Before

They left Tommy at the Fresno Airport. He got on the big red and white, three-engine Challenger jet. Beano and Duffy watched with Wade and Jimmy Freeze as the plane thundered off the runway and lifted into the pale morning sky.

Beano took off his glasses again and wiped them on his tie. He turned his geeky smile on Jimmy. "Said he'd have the money in a day," Beano said happily and slid his glasses back up on his nose. "Very exciting. Very exciting, indeed."

Jimmy grunted, turned, and along with Wade got back in the limo and pulled out, leaving Duffy and Beano standing there. Beano immediately bagged the goofy grin and the thick tortoise-shell glasses which had been giving him a headache. He dropped them into his pocket.

"Tommy fell for the moose pasture hook, line, and decanter," Duffy grinned, watching the plane until it was out of sight.

"Come on. We've gotta see about Dakota and Roger." They called for a rental car to be delivered to the Spanos Executive Jet Center. A yellow Caprice arrived twenty minutes later, and they drove it back to the houseboat at Mud Flat Marina.

Victoria and Roger were sleeping in the

Winnebago at the far side of the parking lot when Beano knocked on the door. She let them in, and Roger-the-Dodger wagged his tail, even though he was too weak too stand.

Beano moved over to the dog, kneeled, and patted him gingerly on the head. "You got him. I was afraid he was dead," Beano said. "Where's Dakota?"

"Hospital in Livingston," Victoria answered. "Tommy really beat the shit out of her. They had to remove her spleen."

Beano winced as he listened to the rest of the details.

"You can pick him up," Victoria said, pointing at Roger after they'd finished exchanging information. "He likes being held. Just watch out for his right hind end. He's missing a few centimeters back there."

Beano picked the little terrier up into his arms and cradled him. "Thanks, buddy," Beano said to the dog. "I screwed up on Tommy. If you hadn't taken a piece out of his neck and bought me a few seconds, I'd be one dead grifter."

Roger tried to wag his tail as Beano cradled and hugged him gently.

Victoria had her hands in the back pockets of her jeans. "We could drive up to Livingston and see how Dakota's doing," she said.

"Yeah," Beano said, "I'd like that."

"And I got an address for a vet. I told him I found Roger this way and he wants to see him. We can drop him on the way."

They took Roger to the vet, who, once he

examined him, said he should keep him for twelve hours just to be safe. They kissed Roger good-bye and drove to the little hospital in Livingston. Victoria explained to Beano that she should stay in the car because she had left before the police arrived and hospital Security might try to hold her until the police returned. Besides, she couldn't take the chance that Tommy's thugs might see them together. Beano nodded and got out of the rental car. She watched as he and Duffy moved into the hospital.

Victoria suddenly felt tired, and something else hovered around her, beating dark wings of despair.

♠ ♠ ♠

The hospital room was filled with metal C-stands, all draped with dripping fluid bottles. Dakota was awake, and she looked up at Beano and Duffy for a long time without talking. Her face was still badly discolored from the bruises. Her lip had been stitched up, but it was going to leave a bad scar.

"You gonna be okay?" Beano asked, worried.

"That's what they tell me," she replied softly, trying to talk without moving her lips.

"You weren't supposed to get beat up."

"Just get those two assholes, Beano. If you get 'em, it'll be worth it."

They talked for a few minutes, and then Duffy kissed Dakota and told her that his part in the hustle was over for a while and he'd stay here in Livingston to look after her and Roger.

"You're a doll," she said, smiling up at him, her luscious black hair fanned out on the pillow, her body taped up under her hospital gown.

"You'll be glad to know Fentress County Petroleum has full dental and medical," Beano said, reaching for her hand. "We'll take care of all this."

Dakota smiled weakly, exposing her broken teeth, then she closed her eyes.

"We better get goin'," Duffy said and they started to leave.

"Beano, I need to tell you something," Dakota said, and Beano stayed behind as Duffy moved out into the corridor. "What happened in the Bahamas," Dakota said, talking slowly, "this beating, was partly my fault. I mishandled it...but Tommy isn't right. He...he snaps. Loses it completely. And when he does, he's got no control. It's scary. I've never seen anything like it. He loves hurting. You can see it in his eyes. Be careful of him. He doesn't bounce right."

Beano already knew that. He'd seen that look when Tommy shoved the gun in his mouth. "I'll be careful," he said, and leaned down and kissed her gently on the side of her face. "You did great. You got him here. He's in play."

"I'm sorry about us, Beano," she said. "Y'know, I thought we could work. I really did. But I don't know how to love a man, only how to take one."

Then she smiled. Her two missing front teeth devastated him. She had been so beautiful. The effects of this beating would never completely vanish.

"All this great-looking equipment," she continued, "and they left out one important ingredient. No desire to make a nest...to share a dream. But I want you to know I tried with you, I really did. I wanted it to be you, and when that didn't happen, I decided it would be nobody."

He looked down at her and nodded.

"One other thing," Dakota said, "that lawyer, Vicky..." She paused and Beano wondered what Dakota would say. "She's okay, she stepped up. She put it on the line for me. She lured that rapist who was guarding me away from the car and hit him with a sap. The docs here said another hour and it would have been too late. Wasn't for her, I'd be dead right now."

Beano said nothing as he looked down at Dakota.

"What you need is somebody like that...and under it all, she wants to settle down."

"You're trying to fix me up?" Beano smiled.

"Don't laugh it off, buddy. Sweetheart scams are my bubble. Opposites attract. That's why you and I could never be happy. We'd keep looking into each other's bag and hating what we see. We both have the same sickness." Dakota closed her eyes. "Gotta sleep. Feel like shit. Be good, baby," she whispered.

Beano squeezed her hand, and after Dakota squeezed back, he left.

They dropped Duffy at the houseboat and then, since Beano was hungry, he took Victoria out for a late brunch. They found a small but romantic restaurant on a man-made lake off the inland waterway. They got a table out on the wood deck and ordered eggs Benedict and champagne cocktails, and when the drinks were delivered, they clinked glasses. Beano felt strange sitting opposite her on that deck, boyish and almost awkward, as if he were on a first date. Dakota had opened his eyes to something he'd been feeling. A few days ago, he'd viewed Victoria Hart as a necessary evil, somebody he needed to accommodate to get information so he could run the con. But she had transformed herself into something more important. He marveled at her energy and her organization. If he'd thought about it, he could have predicted these skills. What he hadn't been prepared for was her courage.

They sipped champagne cocktails, looking at one another, as the sun began its trip down the afternoon sky, turning the small, man-made blue lake to glittering gold.

"Thank you for helping us," he finally said.

"You don't have to thank me," she said. "I'm here because of Carol...same as you."

"Dakota thinks a lot of you...."

"And what do you think?" she said softly.

"I'm not sure. I'm still trying to figure out what I want to be when I grow up."

"Not a con man?"

"This is my last hustle...if I survive it. I think I want more for myself."

She looked at him and then added, "So do I."

He wasn't sure whether she was talking about herself or about him, but either way, he thought it was a promising remark.

They ate their brunch, and she told him about her parents and her life growing up in Connecticut. She told him that she had never before known the thrill of these last few days, that he had taught her things about herself she never would have learned any other way.

He told her about his life on the road, traveling around with his parents, doing roofing scams, tent hustles, and Gypsy blessings. He told her about his gnawing loneliness.

She listened to this and tried to envision his childhood....She couldn't, it was so different from hers. But it was the loneliness that struck a chord in her....This was what had been depressing her and pulling her down.

They left the restaurant at four, and as they were driving back toward the marina, Beano saw a small rental-boat dock and stopped unexpectedly.

They picked out one of the electric launches with cushioned benches and a blue fringed top. Painted on the stern, in blue letters, was its name: TREASURE HUNTER.

He bought a cheap bottle of wine in the little market and they boarded their tippy vessel for an afternoon excursion, neither of them knowing where they would go or what exactly was happening.

Beano piloted the boat up the river tributary as Victoria opened the bottle and poured the wine into paper cups. The boat's electric motor whirred softly as they adventured along at a stately five knots, the water lapping against the sides.

Sometime later that afternoon, with most of the wine gone, they found themselves with their arms around one another in the bottom of the small boat while it drifted with the motor off.

"Is this what we really want to do?" Victoria asked, her one last caution light flashing.

"It's what I want to do," he said. "But it's up to you...."

And then she kissed him. In a strange way, that kiss released her. He wasn't everything she wanted. But he was more important to her right now than any other man in her life had ever been. She wasn't sure she could even describe why, but she knew her feelings had finally overtaken her structured and cautious mind.

They lay in the bottom of the small boat, holding one another. He started to slowly undress her, and then, after only a moment of hesitation, she reached for the buckle of his belt and undid it. In moments they were naked. The late-afternoon sun peeked under the fringed awning and played on their bodies, heating their skin and emotions.

When he entered her, she felt another moment of pure release, and then, slowly and gently, together, they brought themselves to climax. When it was over, they lay in the boat, breathing heavily.

"This could be a mistake," he said, softly.

"Probably," she answered him.

They lay there in each other's arms till sunset. The little boat's name, *Treasure Hunter,* was appropriate because that afternoon, under its blue-fringed awning, they had discovered treasure.

TWENTY-SIX

The Big Brother

The three jet engines whirred softly as Tommy "Two Times" Rina sat in the richly appointed cabin of his brother's Challenger and thought. Tommy had never spent much time thinking. That had always been Joe's end of things. Tommy was the hammer, the enforcer. Even when they were just ten and twelve, his little brother, Joe, got the best ideas, and Tommy let him do the planning. But there were times, especially lately, when Tommy hated the way Joe treated him. He was, after all, the big brother. He had let Joe take over the role of leader and for years hadn't even thought twice about it. They had both risen in the criminal world of La Cosa Nostra—Joe to the level of Boss; Tommy, his trusted Consigliere. They had money and power. But lately, Joe had lashed out at Tommy as if he didn't think Tommy even belonged. It was as if Tommy were just excess baggage that Joe had been saddled with, forgetting all the street work Tommy had done, all the guys Tommy had clipped to help get them there.

Tommy looked at the seat across from him, at the decanter of oil wrapped in a towel and seatbelted in, along with the drilling core sample cylinder with its glass window that showed the dark oil shale. Tommy had called Beau Taylor in Texas from the airphone. Taylor had been a frequent high-stakes player at Sabre Bay and he and Tommy had become friends. They had even shared a few showgirls. More important to Tommy right now was the fact that Beau Taylor was a wildcat oilman in Dallas who had made millions finding Texas crude. Tommy had described to Beau the little he could remember about the stratigraphic trap and the delineation well. He told about the exploratory field without telling Beau where it was or the name of Fentress County P and G. He didn't want to trust anybody with that secret. The thing that immediately impressed him was that Beau seemed very excited about the information Tommy gave him. He confirmed to Tommy that all of this information was accurate, that the Federal Energy Regulatory Commission required a gathering station be built over large stratigraphic traps before punching down a delineation well. And Beau was alive with questions about the field and the drill site, the side core samples and the fifteen thousand gallons of crude that had been already pumped. Tommy would not tell him much more than the general facts. He lied and said the well was off the Northern California coast. Tommy asked if Beau knew a geologist, and his friend gave him the name of one in Midland, Texas.

Tommy next called the geologist on the airphone and made arrangements to get the oil sample analyzed. Tommy would divert to Midland and drop the sample off. He was sure it would turn out to be exactly what the geek geologist, Dr. Clark, had told him it was. He was sure he was about to show his brother he could do more than clip guys and be a wandering hard-on. From now on he was being the big brother; he was going to check things out, do the planning, make sure things were what they were supposed to be. He was going to drop the oil sample off in Midland, Texas, and then fly on to Nassau and, when the oil sample checked out, Tommy Rina was going to take five million dollars out of the SARTOF Bank and buy control of the Fentress County Petroleum and Gas Company. He had decided not to tell Joe. Even that geek Dr. Clark had heard Joe made all the decisions. Well, that was going to stop. If this oil deal was what it promised to be, if this field was the largest oil strike in North America, then it was going to be Big Brother Tommy, not Joe, who was going to bring it home for the family. He would tell Joe *after* the deal was complete, after they were all drowning in Black Gold. Then his little brother would finally give him the respect he deserved.

They landed in Midland, and the geologist was waiting there at the Executive Air Terminal. Tommy had scraped the label off the core sample cylinder, removing all of the West Coast Platform Drilling Company decals so there was no way the geologist could find out where this sample had come from. Tommy was playing it smart. *This is exactly the way Joe would do it,* he mused silently to himself.

Tommy handed the samples to the geologist, who stood in the door of the Challenger with the starboard engine still running and screamed at Tommy through the opening. He was dressed exactly like Dr. Clark, his tie was blowing over his shoulder, his horn-rimmed glasses glinting in the sunlight. Even the same plastic pen protector. They were a breed, Tommy thought.

"Shouldn't take more than a few hours!" the geologist yelled. "You have my number?"

Tommy nodded, held up the sheet of paper, and handed the geologist a thousand dollars in cash, which they'd agreed upon for the work. Then Tommy closed the door and they taxied back to the end of the runway.

Minutes later, the Challenger was airborne again and Tommy was looking down at the aqua-green water of the Gulf of Mexico. The pilots estimated three hours to Nassau, and Tommy settled back. A new sense of energy and purpose enveloped him. He was much more than a wandering hard-on; he was a businessman with a plan. He went over the details once more, looking for holes: He would arrive at Nassau at five P.M., just before the SARTOF Bank closed. He would have Tony Vacca, who ran the bank for the Rinas, open the safe in the dead-drop room, which contained money that had not been laundered yet and wasn't on the bank's books. Tommy knew that there were no records of this cash....Technically, as far as the U.S. tax records were concerned, it didn't even exist. He would get a little more than he needed, just in case. Five mil in cash. He estimated that would be a couple of suitcases' worth. He would tell Tony Vacca that if he said anything to his little brother, Joe, Tommy would come back to Nassau and beat his head flat with a hammer. He planned it carefully in his small, simian brain. He thought out every detail, keeping his mind focused on business just like the big brother should. Only occasionally did he think of Dakota. Only twice did he conjure up the memory of her silky-smooth skin and protruding nipples. And only then did he reach down and rub his hard-on and wish he'd had a chance to fuck her one more time.

Almost the same time that Tommy was landing in Nassau, Victoria Hart got on the red-eye connecting flight from Chicago to Atlantic City, which was where Joe Rina was. Beano had kissed her good-bye at the Fresno Airport loading ramp and told her not to overplay her hand. He told her about his moment of pure terror in Duffy's houseboat when Tommy had lost it and almost shot Beano with the automatic, before Roger-the-Dodger saved him from the Grifters' Hall of Fame and a place under a cemetery stone.

"Don't worry," Victoria said. "I spent almost six months in pre-trial with Joe Rina. I know exactly how that handsome little shit thinks. He's not like Tommy. He doesn't lose his temper...for him, that's a sign of weakness."

They stood in the jetway for a long moment, holding hands, while the rest of the passengers streamed by them. Victoria had the developed photos, of Tommy with Beano and Duffy, under her arm. Beano kissed her a second time; he could smell her fragrance, and she could feel his heart beating under his shirt. They held on as if they were afraid to let go, until a flight attendant touched Victoria, and she pulled away and moved down the jetway and onto the L-1011.

She found her seat in Business Class and settled down, stuffing her overnight case under the seat, then opened the Foto-Mat folder. The shots of the Summerlands she tore up. Then she studied the six or seven shots she had of Beano, Duffy, and Tommy coming up the houseboat gangplank by the limousine. In one, Tommy seemed to be smiling, and Beano had his arm almost around the little mobster. Beano had posed for that one, turning toward the camera and smiling, to give Victoria a better shot. She selected the four photos she liked best and destroyed the others. She could read the slightly out-of-focus *Fresno Herald* on the dash in the foreground. The blurred headlines, barely discernible, announced: CONGRESSIONAL BUDGET CUTS IN DEFENSE FUNDING. It would be enough to establish the date of the pictures.

The plane took off and she laid her head back on the seat rest. Tomorrow she would lay the trump down. That should be the beginning of the end for the Rina brothers. Finally, she was going to confront the little monster with the wavy hair who had killed Carol Sesnick, along with her friends Tony Corollo and Bobby Manning. She could hardly wait for revenge and retribution. Then she thought of Beano and about all that had happened in the last ten days. It was almost too much to contemplate. Her emotions were rolling, her senses struggling to hold on to her shifting feelings. She could still feel the afternoon sun on her skin.

Beano left the Fresno Airport and headed back to the parking lot. He got into the Winnebago and looked at Roger, who was curled up on the sofa in his white bandages, looking like a molting caterpillar. He stared at Beano with wise eyes.

"I never felt like this before," Beano told the little dog, who wagged his tail in expectation of something more.

"Don't give me that look," Beano said. "I can barely take care of us. How will I be able to take care of her? Would she even *want* me to take care of her?"

And then he got behind the wheel and, while his mind worked on that problem, he put the motor home in gear and began the three-hour drive to San Francisco.

TWENTY-SEVEN

Knocking the Mark

She moved into the Hancock Building, which was on the Strand in Atlantic City. The Rinas had built it with Organized Crime proceeds four years back. It was known in the D.A.'s office as the Pasta Palace because every crooked union official and trucking boss had his office there. The building was one-stop shopping for syndicate bag men. A huge bronze statue of John Hancock was on display in the lobby. Victoria took the elevator up to the twenty-third floor.

She expected to be stopped by Security, but

she sailed right past watchful cameras, down the hall, and into the executive offices of Rina Enterprises. In another startling lapse of security, there was nobody in the reception area. The check-in desk was empty and Victoria waited with her manila folder under her arm, not sure what to do next. Then a mail boy buzzed the electric lock and came out through the inner office door. Victoria rushed and caught the door before it closed. It was almost noon, and she wondered if Joe Rina was still in the office, or perhaps had left for an early lunch. She moved down the hallway, where several secretaries were typing. They never looked up at her as she moved to the end of the hall, where she could see a magnificent pair of antique doors which, she assumed, fronted Joe Rina's office. She opened the doors without knocking and walked in.

The room was magnificent. It had picture windows that overlooked the Boardwalk on the south, and the Atlantic Ocean on the east. She could see the famous Atlantic City Pier jutting into the raging surf two blocks away. She quickly surveyed the office. The mandatory grip-and-grin photographs dominated the west wall: shots of Joe Rina with sports celebrities and movie stars; two Presidents were up there, grinning stupidly in the presence of a known Mafia Boss while Joe had his handsome face turned toward the camera, his electric smile lighting every shot. The art in the office was priceless, some of it under glass. A few pre-Columbian Aztec treasures dating back to the thirteenth century were on the antique sideboard next to a golfing trophy. She moved over and looked at the trophy. The plaque said BEST BALL FOURSOME, GREEN-BOROUGH COUNTRY CLUB, 1996. Victoria moved to the desk and laid her best photo there, front and center. Then she moved over and sat in the high-backed wing chair and waited.

Twenty minutes later he hurried into the office, rolling down his sleeves. He seemed late for something and was moving fast, carrying his suitcoat. He moved to his desk, saw the picture, and picked it up.

"That was taken by an FBI Electronic Surveillance Team yesterday in Fresno, California," she said.

He spun and saw her partially hidden, sitting in the huge wing chair. She got up and faced him.

"What are you doing here?" he said, his voice surprisingly soft, considering the intrusion her presence in his office represented.

"I came here to see if I could wreck something." She moved to the table with the Aztec treasures and picked one up.

Joe moved protectively toward the tiny statue but stopped short of trying to grab it.

"Don't worry. What I want to wreck has more value than this." And she put it carefully back down on the table.

"I asked you how you got in here."

"The place was empty. I just walked in. You need to get a few more Indians up on the rocks."

"I'll give that some thought."

He was still holding the picture. It was the one where Beano seemed to be smiling at Tommy with his hand on Tommy's shoulder. They were beside the limo at the Mud Flat Marina. "What's this supposed t'be about?" Joe said, indicating the picture. His eyes were hooded. Victoria surmised he recognized Beano as the card cheat Frank Lemay. She knew it bothered him to see Tommy with the man Joe had beaten with a nine-iron, but Joe knew he could not be tried for that crime again. Victoria let these thoughts simmer before moving on.

"I've been let go from the D.A.'s office or I'm quitting....We're still arguing about which it's gonna be."

"Good news from an unexpected place," he grinned.

"Here's the bad news from the same place," she grinned back. "I went by there this morning to clear out my office and I got those photos from the FBI team that's been covering Tommy's activities...."

"Tommy's being followed? I wasn't aware there were any pending prosecutions. He's not wanted for anything."

"Maybe they just got tired of him beating up every hooker he's slept with and dealing drugs outside of all those high schools. I don't know, but the Feds have a three-man Weedwhacker team on him. They took these pictures. They also told me that Tommy financed that card cheat in the picture there.

They tell me he's been stealing from you for years. The Feds think that's funny. Supposedly, he's into you for millions but since I'm leaving the office, and since I know firsthand you're a hard guy to get a conviction against, I thought I'd just come over and dump that fact on you and let you deal with it yourself. Might be more fun to watch this way."

Joe smiled at her. "Tommy's stealing money from me? That's the angle?" he said; his gorgeous movie-star smile was widening. "He tells me you're the thief....He tells me you scammed a hundred thousand dollars from our jewelry store here in Atlantic City."

"Think about it, Joe....Does that make any damn sense at all? That sounds exactly like some kinda dumb thing your brother would come up with while he's the one doing the stealing."

"Why would he need to? Half of everything I own is his."

"Why?" she shrugged. "Why do male timber wolves eat their young? Why did Cain murder Abel? Why do pigeons shit on statues? Some things have no answers, Joseph."

"I see. And this picture is supposed to upset me in some special way?"

"That's right, because aside from being the guy who cheated you six months ago, those two guys your big brother is yucking it up with are also the two dice cheats that knocked down your casino in Sabre Bay for a million dollars two days ago."

"How do you know?"

"Because the Feds were down there taking

pictures. They're everywhere your psychotic brother goes." She smiled. "I'm sure your casino has pictures of all the big players, especially the cheaters. Have your casino Manager fax one up to you. These are the same two guys. You can see Tommy's having a pretty good time with them in that shot."

The office door widened and two men came into the office; one was a tall accountant named Bruce Stang, the other one Victoria had never seen before.

"Hey, Joseph," Bruce said, "we gotta go. They'll only hold the table for twenty minutes."

"Leave me alone for a minute, Bruce," Joe said softly.

Bruce looked over and saw Victoria. He hesitated. "Want me to call Gerry?" he asked. "You shouldn't be talking to her without an attorney present."

"Get out of here for a minute," Joe said more forcefully and both men left, closing the door. "So these are the two who hit the Sabre Bay Club. That's the story?"

"That's the fact, Joe. That picture was taken the day before yesterday. You can read the headline on the paper. According to wire taps we've been getting, your brother hates your guts for pushing him around."

"So this picture, which could have a lot of other explanations, and your word, are supposed to get me all lathered up?"

"Yep, that's the idea." She got to her feet and moved to the door. Then she turned, "Oh, yeah, there was something else....I'm not supposed to know this, but I have a few friends in Justice and, since I have more than a passing interest in you and your family, I cashed a few chits."

Joe stood waiting.

"According to the FBI surveillance, your brother was down in Nassau last night. He took four or five million dollars out of your SARTOF Bank. Got it out of the dead-drop you've got down there. You might sweep that bank if you get a chance. It's got more bugs than a flea circus."

"And just what, exactly, is a dead-drop?"

"Call the lizard you've got running that French laundry....Ask him if your big brother didn't just rob you of millions yesterday." She took the rest of the photos and dropped them into the chair. "Some of these others aren't bad either, but basically, they're the same shot." And she turned and walked out of the office, past Bruce Stang and the other man, through the door and over to the elevator, her heart pounding and adrenaline flowing. She knew she had sunk her hook deep.

Before she hit the lobby, Joe Rina had Tony Vacca on the phone at the SARTOF Merchant Bank of Nassau.

"I'm gettin' word that my brother Tommy's been down there," Joe said softly.

"Uh...how? Who told you?" Tony Vacca said, and then he fell silent. The sub-Atlantic phone cable crackled.

"I'm gonna say this once," Joe said, slowly and without anger, to the bank President he had hand-picked and put down there at a quarter-million dollars a year. "I want t'know...was my brother, Tommy, down there? Simple question: yes or no?"

"Yeah, Joe, he was here."

"Did he remove any money from the dead-drop?" Joe asked.

"Uh, Joe, you know I'm loyal t'you...you know that?"

"Tony, I'm asking this once more, for the last time! Did Tommy take any money out of the dead-drop?"

"Yes."

"How much did he take?"

"Five million dollars," Tony Vacca said.

"And if I could inquire, why did you see fit to give it to him?" Joe asked reasonably.

"Uh, well, Joe...you know Tommy...."

"Okay, I know Tommy. But I'm wondering why you gave it to him. I gave you strict instructions...that money is never to leave the dead-drop until it's been washed, and then only by my instructions. So, why did you give Tommy the money?"

"Joe, he threatened me. He said he'd kill me with a hammer, said he could do it so it would take three hours for me to die. I've heard the stories. I was scared."

"I see. And so you gave him my money, because you were scared?"

"He said it was his money too."

"So you gave him *our* money, but you didn't even call me and tell me."

"He said if I told you he'll kill me, Joe.

387

What'm I supposed t'do? You know how Tommy can get."

"You're fired. Put Carlo in charge and pack up and get out. I ever see you again, you're gonna need medical attention. Good-bye." And he hung up the phone as Bruce Stang brought in the pictures that Arnold Buzini had just faxed up from the Sabre Bay Club. Buzini had already moved the pictures of Beano and Duffy off the Deadwood Players' Board and had put them into the Tat Cheaters' Book in the Security room.

Joe held the black-and-white fax of Duffy and Beano up next to the pictures that Victoria had just left. They were the same two men. He could read the newspaper headline and he knew that Congress had cut back Defense funding just a couple of days ago. That meant the pictures were current. He looked up at Bruce Stang.

"So, what the hell is Tommy doing?" Joe said softly. "Looks like he's hanging with this guy I beat up, and who stole a million from us at Sabre Bay. Then he forced Tony Vacca to give him five million of my money and not tell me. What's he doing?"

The pungent question hung in the room like the painful smell of death.

Bruce shrugged. "You know Tommy," he said weakly.

"Everybody's always telling me I know Tommy. Well, y'know something...? Maybe I don't know Tommy at all."

TWENTY-EIGHT

Bleating to the Heat

When Victoria left the Pasta Palace in Atlantic City, she was being observed by two FBI Agents in a gray sedan. The lead man was Stan Kellerman. He was five months from retirement with over forty in. He'd seen it all...but the thing he hated most was when "one of ours" turned bad. He had his binoculars up as Victoria hailed a passing cab.

Seated beside Stan Kellerman was Sheila Ward. She was in her rookie year at the Eye. She and Stan had nothing in common, from their opinions about the job to the music they listened to or the movies they liked. She had been hoping to get some experienced training from Stan, but he was a miserable son-of-a-bitch who barely ever spoke to her unless he was ordering her to do something.

"Get Greg on Tac Two," he barked. "See if he got her."

Sheila picked up the mike. "This is Red Dog to Lazy Boy. Did you pick up the female target in there?"

"Roger that."

The FBI Electronic Surveillance Team had cut into the Rina office video security and had been using Joe Rina's own security system to watch him. They had an E.S.T. man in the basement watching three pirate TV monitors. Tommy and Joe Rina had been priority targets

389

since the blown state trial. The FBI had been startled when Victoria Hart, the Prosecutor who screwed up the case, walked into the Pasta Palace and showed up in Joe Rina's office suite on the video monitors. Unfortunately, they didn't have a way to see inside Joe's office because he would never allow a security camera to be placed there, but they had the hall camera that showed her going to his office, carrying a folder, and then they saw Joe hurry in carrying his coat. Ten minutes later the cameras showed Victoria leaving without the folder, a very strange and troubling occurrence.

Stan reached over and snatched the mike away from Sheila, who gritted her teeth in anger but said nothing.

"Whatta you think, Greg?"

"I don't know. You tell me what the Prosecutor who was trying this shithead is doing paying him a visit and leaving off a package. I think we got runny poo here."

"Me too. I'm on her. Let's see what happens."

They followed Victoria to the Atlantic City Airport and watched as she went to the United counter and bought a ticket. After she left they edged to the front of an angry line of customers and badged the agent. They found out that Victoria was on the next direct flight to San Francisco. It was scheduled to leave in an hour.

It was then that Stan Kellerman called Gil Green's office and found out that the D.A. was in Albuquerque, at a law enforcement conference. Stan was Federal and Gil was State, but Vicky Hart worked for Gil, so Stan stayed jurdisdictionally in bounds by making the call. They got through to Gil's hotel room and caught the colorless D.A. just as he got back from a round of golf. After they filled him in on what was happening, Gil Green remained silent, his mind weighing the potential downside possibilities.

"What do you want us to do?" Stan asked. "I can't leave Atlantic City without a district transfer approval, but we could have some guys pick her up on the other end. We've got her flight number. We can fax an I.D. photo to the agents out there. They can pick her up in San Francisco and run a tail."

"Hang on a minute," Gil said, and he put the phone against his chest and tried to analyze the situation: It was hard for him to believe that Victoria Hart had gone sour, but then he would have bet a year's salary that she wouldn't have gone on TV and accused him of job malfeasance either. Maybe that on-air threat against Joe Rina wasn't as stupid as he'd originally thought. If you had just given up your own witness to a mob hit, what better way to cover your tracks than to attack Rina publicly? Technically, Victoria still worked for his office. That could be politically embarrassing. He had finally maneuvered his way onto the "short list" for Lieutenant Governor. A scandal in his office would be devastating, unless somehow he could make it look like he had orchestrated the investigation to uproot the corruption. Then he could go wide with it. Play it out in front. He could already hear himself reading the press conference copy: *"This is not about politics, it's about clean government."* There could be great TV exposure here if he could control the spin.

He put the phone back to his ear and cleared his throat. "Okay, put a tail on her in California and keep me posted. If she does anything illegal, pick her up and notify my office immediately. And thanks for putting me aboard."

"You got it."

Victoria boarded the United Airlines flight. Stan and Sheila watched her all the way onto the aircraft, then Stan put on a UA flight attendant's jacket and walked down the passenger ramp and onto the plane with a clipboard to see if she was seated with any K.A.'s. She was alone, no one in the seat next to her. He checked the passenger manifest and walked back out to the gate.

"Any Known Associates aboard?" Sheila asked.

Stan didn't even look at her. He just grunted and Sheila clenched her teeth again. The guy was truly pissing her off.

Beano Bates met Victoria at the airport in San Francisco. Another FBI surveillance team watched as they kissed. Victoria and Beano held hands as they headed out of the airport. The two suits followed at a discreet distance.

The lead man was Grady Hunt. He was short and compact with a flat top and flat face. His nickname in the Eye was Hammerhead, and it fit him. Walking next to him was Denny Denniston. He was tall and fair and usually dressed in light-colored suits with pastel shirts. He was soft spoken, but also had a violent temper, which had earned him the nickname Vanilla Surprise.

"You make the guy?" Grady asked, as they followed Beano and Victoria through the terminal.

"Looks kinda familiar. I think I know him from somewhere. Maybe a local pinch report."

Since Victoria had no checked luggage, they moved right out of the terminal into the parking area. Grady and Denniston had their car parked at the curb in the red zone and they eased it up near the exit of visitor parking and waited. A few minutes later, the targets drove out in a yellow Caprice. Grady put his sedan in gear and followed.

"I seen this guy somewhere. Maybe on the wall, downtown. I think we got a posting on him," Denniston said, racking his memory.

Then Grady snapped his fingers. "He's not on the wall, he's on the list!" Grady said. "Bumbo...somebody."

"Beano Bates," Denniston corrected him. "He's a Ten Most Wanted. Fuck me." Denniston had been in the Eye for ten years and had never even seen a Ten Most Wanted fugitive. "No wonder I recognized him. I get this asshole's picture in the mail once a month."

He smiled at Grady. "Whatta you wanna do?"

"This is supposed to be a Watch and Report Surveillance. We better call it in."

When they called New Jersey and talked to Stan Kellerman, he put them on hold and contacted Gil Green in Albuquerque.

"Tricky Vicky ain't so tricky, is she?" Stan said limerickly, after filling Gil in.

"She's consorting with a known felon. She's guilty of half-a-dozen Class-B felonies, maybe one Class-A beef. This could be big; I'm on my way to you." Gil was already adding up the political points.

"What do you want my team in Frisco to do?" Stan asked.

"Something more is going on here. I want to find all the edges before I pounce. Wait till Victoria is alone and pick her up. Take her to the Federal Building. Stay on Bates, but don't arrest him. I'll be on the next flight."

♠ ♠ ♠

Grady Hunt and Denny Denniston were on point and followed Beano and Victoria to a small but neat two-story motel next to the Golden Gate Marina. Within five minutes they had the Marina Motel staked out with five back-up units. Everybody was "jacked and flaked."

They watched as Beano drove out alone at three-thirty in the yellow Caprice. He turned right and headed down toward Market Street; two units followed him and then the rest moved in on the the motel room.

Victoria was in room 22 and they hit the door without warning. "Freeze, FBI!" Grady Hunt screamed as he pinned himself against the inside wall, his 9mm Beretta cupped in his hand, his heart lunging, his finger on the four-ounce trigger. Denniston took a shooting stance from a cover-fire position outside. Both agents held Victoria in their sights.

"On the floor. Now!" Grady shouted as Victoria, who was unpacking her overnight case, looked up, startled.

"What are you doing?" she stammered.

"On your face. Now!"

She kneeled down, and before she touched the floor, Grady landed on her and cuffed her quickly and brutally. They pulled her up and out of the room, jammed her into the back of the plainclothes sedan, and pulled away, smoking tire rubber as they left.

The whole apprehension took less than three minutes.

The Federal Building downtown on Flower Street was like Federal Buildings everywhere: Hand-me-down furniture squatted in overcrowded case rooms, with fly-specked windows that looked out onto brick walls, and coffee-stained Styrofoam cups filled with cigarette butts floating filter-deep in sludge.

Victoria had been put in a holding cell with a one-way mirror. She sat there alone for an hour, wondering what the hell to do. Obviously she had stumbled into a surveillance trap, but she didn't know how much they knew. She hoped she could bluff her way out. She'd been a prosecutor for five years, so she knew that there were basically two reasons why cops cool out a suspect like this: Guilty arrestees, when left alone, often would relax and even go to sleep, because once caught, they were prepared for the worst and gave up to it. Only the innocent would fidget and pace, because they knew they were innocent and they tended to panic. She knew that on the other side of her one-way mirror she was being closely observed, so she spoke out loud to the hidden mike she knew was somewhere in the room: "I know this routine, guys. I pulled this cool-out a hundred times myself. I'm not gonna take a nap, so can we get on with it?" When nobody came, she contemplated the other reason cops held somebody like this. It was usually because they were waiting for the principal interrogator to show up.

Gil Green arrived at the Flower Street Federal Building at five-thirty-five. He asked for a polygraph operator to be put on standby, then he asked that Victoria be brought down from her holding cell.

He was dressed in a conservative gray suit with a charcoal tie and matching handkerchief. His nondescript features were arranged in a placid expression as Victoria was led through the door and seated in a wooden chair in the sterile, windowless interrogation room.

"Victoria, I wish I could say it's a pleasure to see you," Gil opened dryly.

"Aw, go ahead and say it anyway, Gil. Insincerity always seems to work for you."

"We're already at ground level in two sentences," he smiled. "I can't tell you how happy I am to see you in such trouble. I'll never forgive you for that interview on 'New Jersey Talking,'" he said softly.

"I'd like to know why I've been arrested."

"Do you want the charges chronologically or alphabetically?"

"How 'bout just so they make sense?" she said.

And then he told her about the surveillance of the Pasta Palace, about the fact that they had witnessed her meeting with Joe Rina and dropping off a package. Then her consorting with Beano Bates, a known felon, which, if she had prior knowledge, made her an accessory-after-the-fact in all of his crimes. When Gil got through, she continued to look at him, trying hard not to let her face give her away.

"So far I can't see the crime," she said. "Joe Rina isn't wanted for anything. I can meet with him without facing indictment. As for Mr. who...?"

"Bates."

"Bates. Well, he said his name was Curtis Fisher, so there goes your prior knowledge. I met him in a bar five days ago. He seemed nice. You say he's a criminal? Well, can you imagine that?" She looked at him and they locked hostile gazes.

He was so bland, she couldn't, for the life of her, read him. His thin lips and wispy hair all seemed to blend together on his pale, featureless face.

"Victoria, you are in major trouble. Let me run a few possible scenarios for you."

"Please do," she said agreeably.

"I think it went like this....You had a case that could put Joe Rina in prison. Maybe he threatened you or threatened your family or maybe he just offered you a helluva lot of money, or maybe you went to him with a For Sale sign. Either way, I think you cut a deal and you sold him the location of your witness. Carol and two brave cops got murdered. Your case got pitched and you ran off to San Francisco with the money to hang out with a Federal criminal."

"Lots of 'I thinks' and 'maybes' in that brief, Counselor. You might want to harden it up before you file it. And it's always nice when you have evidence. Can you document a shred of this?"

"I have you on video in Joe Rina's office yesterday, dropping off material." He smiled without humor. It was a strained, ghastly smile, almost as if he were shifting gas. "Tell me what was in the folder you dropped?"

"Family pictures," she said evasively.

"Beano X. Bates is a con man on the FBI Ten Most Wanted List. That list has been circulated through your office once a month for the five years you've been there. Bates has been on it for twenty-six months; his picture is on the wall in the coffee room, downstairs."

"I don't pay much attention to those lists, Gil; I was a very busy little girl, what with all the bullets I was taking for you and everything."

"Beano's here in San Francisco. We have a surveillance team set up on him right now. When I snap my fingers, he's dust. I could have picked him up with you, but I thought because of our association, I owed you this meeting first. If you insist on playing hardball with me, then he goes away."

He watched her closely and could see her flinch ever so slightly when he said that. He knew he was on the right track.

"You don't owe me a meeting, you're just trying to turn me."

"I don't need to turn you, Vicky. I got you dead bang. I got him dead bang. I'm hardly out looking for a charge to pin on Bates. I've got a shopping list of felony warrants I can use."

"Okay, then what *are* you looking for?"

"I'm not a great attorney, I'm sure you know that."

She held her comment.

"But I'm a pretty decent student of human nature and I know how the game is played. So, I say to myself, 'Why is this happening? Why is Victoria pulling such a harebrained stunt?' And you know what the answer is?"

"Too many Hostess Twinkies?"

"Something else is going on. There's a piece of this puzzle that I'm not seeing...and what I want from you is that piece. You're way too smart for any of the scenarios I just got through running. I figure if you level with me, then maybe I'll help you. Maybe we cut a deal and minimize the damage to you and Bates."

She looked at him for a long moment. "What kind of deal?" she finally said.

"You come clean and then we'll figure something out."

"Hold on by letting go?" she smiled. "Not with you, Bucko; that only works when the sharper's running the game."

"I don't understand what you're talking about."

"I'm sure you don't," she said, and then sat silent for a long moment. "Don't think we can deal, Gil. Hit me with what you've got and let's see what happens."

He sat there for a long time, looking at the razor-sharp pleat on his pants as if somewhere in that perfect crease was his answer. "Not totally unexpected, but still a shame," he finally said. Then he turned and rang the bell on the door. In a minute it opened. Grady Hunt, in full Kevlar body armor, stepped in. "Take Bates. Use S.I.S.... If he runs, use extreme prejudice and put him down hard."

"Be a pleasure," Grady said, then turned and closed the door.

"You're not gonna kill him in cold blood?"

"S.I.S. ain't short for 'sister,'" Gil said softly.

Victoria knew all about S.I.S.; it stood for Special Investigative Service, and they were notorious for the way they did business. They held court in the street by targeting a habitual criminal and, instead of picking him up when they found him, they would follow him, wait until he did a robbery or some other crime, then shoot him in cold blood as he came out of the liquor store with a bag full of cash. It was legalized execution. If S.I.S. was on Beano and he ran, which she assumed he would, then S.I.S. would drop him, no questions asked. It was the operational M.O.

She tried to hold her bluff but she kept thinking of Beano lying in a pool of blood, dying alone. All the while Gil was watching her, meticulously picking invisible lint off his gray suit. Time lapsed until she could bear it no more. "Okay, stop," she said softly. "You've got a deal."

He reached over and hit the button on the door and another cop looked in. "Tell Agent Hunt to put a hold on that order. We may go in another direction," Gil Green said.

Victoria negotiated the best deal with Gil that she could. It included his promise to let her plead Beano's case to the U.S. Attorney after his arrest. Gil insisted she make her statement hooked up to a polygraph machine. She was taken to the next room and connected to "the Box."

During the next hour she told the entire story. She explained the tat, and the moose pasture, and told all about the Big Store. Gil Green and the two FBI Agents listened quietly as the polygraph charted her veracity. When she was finished, she felt tired and dirty and sick. She had given up the con. She had rolled over, and ratted them all out. And her only excuse was she couldn't bear the thought of Beano being killed. The men in the room said nothing as the machine was turned off and she was unstrapped from it.

"I like it," Gil finally said.

"I beg your pardon?"

"I like it. If this con works, Tommy will give us Joe. We get Joe, and I win."

The two FBI men in the room didn't understand his change of pronouns. Only Victoria knew he was talking about his chance to become New Jersey's Lieutenant Governor. "Run the scam anyway?" she asked.

"Yeah. Only we're your partners. You keep us informed. Once it goes down, *we* bust everybody."

Victoria looked at him, not sure what to do. Finally she shook her head in disgust. "You constantly amaze me, Gil. You keep setting one new low after another."

"I'm not the one sleeping with a felon," he prodded her. Then he gave her a satellite vibrating beeper, and told her she had better call in every twelve hours or when they beeped her, whichever came first. If she failed to comply, they would fall on the scam, bust everyone, and all deals would be off.

Then Gil drove with her in the back of a government sedan to the Marina Motel. When they were a block away, he let her out of the car, but he stopped her before she could walk away. "Of course, you understand that regardless of how this goes, I'm going to see that you're disbarred for this."

"See you at the hearing," she finally answered and walked away into the night.

TWENTY-NINE

Inbred Insurance

Beano had left Victoria at three-thirty in the afternoon and had driven the yellow Caprice across town to pick up Paper Collar John at his hotel; then they headed toward the Red Boar Inn two blocks off Market Street down by the harbor. Beano could hear them even before he and Paper Collar John pulled into the large asphalt parking lot. The Inn was an arched, two-story, stucco, Spanish-style structure with a red tile roof. There were ten wide-tire trucks parked in the lot, all of them sporting Arkansas license plates, mud flaps, gun racks, and tuck-and-roll upholstery. For some unknown reason each radio antenna had a red feather taped to the tip. The trucks were pristine, and glistened with chrome wheel rims and lacquer paint. The sound of laughter and catcalls was pouring out into the early evening through the open door of room 15.

"Shit," Beano said to Paper Collar John, "they're gonna end up getting busted for noise pollution before we even get them in the lineup."

"I already came down here twice yesterday and talked to the Manager of this place. Gave him an extra five hundred not to call the cops."

"Who's in charge a'these hillbillies now?"

Beano asked as they got out of the Caprice and moved toward the room where a huge, three-hundred-pound albino man in overalls was tipped back in a creaking metal chair.

"Hard to tell," John answered. "None a'these Hog Creek Bateses have IQs higher than the Arkansas speed limit. I think it's either the skinny one, Cadillac Bates, or maybe it's the fat guy, Ford."

Beano remembered that more than half of the Hog Creek Bateses were named after their vehicles. The reason for that, he'd been told, was because most of them couldn't read. They chose names they could copy off their trucks for hospital birth certificates.

As they got nearer, they could hear Travis Tritt singing on the full-volume radio, but still barely cutting through the wall of Hog Creek noise. The Albino in the chair, whose skin and buzzed hair were both snow-white, finished a beer and burped at them.

"Hi, cousin. I'm Beano. Cadillac Bates around?" Beano asked and smiled at his huge, inbred relative.

The Albino didn't answer but turned and bellowed over his shoulder, "Yankees comin'!"

"Thanks for that kind assessment," Beano said to the Albino, who blinked pale eyes at him, missing the sarcasm. "Which one are you?" he added.

"Bronco Bates," the young man said, and burped again. End of conversation.

Beano nodded and moved past Bronco into a motel room that had been cleared of all furniture. The king-size bed had been dismantled and stacked up against the wall. The rest of the furniture was piled up in the hall. There were twenty Bateses and two roosters in the room. The men were in a circle cheering, while the game cocks in the center of the room were tearing the shit out of each other. Money was on the floor everywhere, and the men, who ranged in age from twenty to fifty, were yelling obscenities at the two warring roosters. The spectators looked like refugees from a monster truck tournament.

"Jesus," Beano said to John in disgust as the two cocks went at each other.

Finally, one of the birds went down, and the owner of the defeated rooster yelled, "Done," and grabbed his game cock before it was ripped to shreds by the winner. Then a scramble for money took place and finally, after several loud arguments, the gambling seemed to be over. While Tammy Wynette took possession of the radio and started warbling another country favorite, the room full of Bateses seemed to finally notice Beano and John standing in the doorway.

"I'm Beano!" he yelled loudly, just as another huge Arkansas inbred came in from the bathroom with a rooster under his arm and started to unleash him for another bout.

Beano stepped into the circle. "I'm Beano Bates," he repeated, "and I've got money for you." That seemed to get their attention.

"Hey, Echo, turn that fuckin' radio down," Bronco yelled.

Echo Bates was an identical albino twin to Bronco. Born ten minutes behind his brother, he escaped being named after his mother's Studebaker, getting the marginally better name Echo. He got up, lumbered over, and turned the radio down.

"I'm looking for Cadillac Bates," Beano said again.

They all sat there and looked around at each other like contestants on *Jeopardy!* until finally, a tall, skinny man in his forties stood and walked over to him.

"You ain't paid us what you owed, cousin."

"That's why I'm here."

"Blazer and Wrangler, you come on with me. Rest a'you hold 'em birds. I want in on this next 'un."

He moved out of the room with Beano and John and across the parking lot. Finally he turned and stood by the row of shiny trucks, leaning his skinny ass on the bug protector grill of the closest one. He folded his arms and looked at Beano.

"Nice t'see you again," Beano smiled. The last time he'd been around the Hog Creek Bateses he'd been about ten and had gone with his mother and father up into the Ozark Plateau mountains to hide from the law. They spent two weeks with the family in Hog Creek. Back then there were only two brothers and their wives and families. About fifteen people. They lived in a remote valley, miles from the nearest neighbors. It seemed they'd done a lot of serious inbreeding since then. "Lotta new family," he grinned at Cadillac Bates, who seemed in no hurry to speak. Or maybe, Beano mused, he just hadn't been able to form a complete thought yet. "'Bout half this many boys in the family back then." Beano continued trying to fill the awkward silence. "Bronco and Echo and lots of these cousins probably weren't even born yet; 'course, it was over twenty years ago."

Then Cadillac furrowed his brow. A thought pushed its way out of his constipated brain. "Most Bateses ain't been born, they's squeezed outta bar rags," he said, without smiling.

"That's pretty good, very funny," Beano said.

"We come all the way out here 'cause you called, but we got no deal yet. You owe us travel money."

"I didn't know you were gonna bring twenty people," Beano hedged. "I only need five or six."

"Know the trouble doin' business with kin?"

"No."

"Y'all think we got a family discount."

"Don't we?" Beano grinned, trying to lighten the mood.

"Come all the way from Hog Creek, Arkansas, 'cause you said you wanted a posse." He dug into his pocket and handed a sheet of paper over to Beano. Somebody had obviously taught Cadillac Bates how to read and write because he had all of their expenses itemized. "That there's what it cost us t'git ta this place an' back. I'm puttin' three cents a mile fer wear an' tear on them pickups. Rambler an' Dodge lost a tranny on their Ram truck in Oklahoma an' I stuck that on there."

Beano took the sheet of paper. It came to almost two thousand dollars. "Lotta money," he said, handing the sheet to John, who examined it.

"Is what it is." Cadillac jerked a thumb toward Paper Collar John. "The other job he told us about gonna cost ya fifteen thousand plus ten percent of the takedown. Dental and medical is extra if we need it. That's the deal, no bargaining. Pay it now, otherwise Church is out an' you can deal with this mess yourself." John handed the accounting back to Beano.

"Guess we need the back-up," Beano said and John nodded, so Beano walked to the trunk of the Caprice, opened it and took seventeen thousand dollars of Sabre Bay money out of the blue canvas bag, walked over, and handed it to Cadillac Bates. The skinny geezer hillbilly counted it and stuffed it into his overalls, way down into his crotch, where it would be safe, next to his shriveled nuts.

"Listen," Beano said, "you gotta knock off the cock fights and hold it down. You're gonna get turned in by another guest. Fighting birds are against the law. You get arrested, you're no good to me."

"Cousin Beano, you jist bought yerself a Hog Creek solution. We ain't too citified and that's a fact. Them boys in there, they ain't all quite right an' sometimes they tend t'eat supper 'fore they say grace. But that ain't gonna ever change, an' if anybody calls the *po*-lice, then we'll just hafta clean that plow when it gets here." He was still leaning against the truck, squinting at Beano through slate-gray eyes.

Beano finally nodded his head. He was already regretting this choice. This branch of the family had been inbreeding for fifty years. Most of them were dumb as dirt, and tough as nickel steak. It was a dangerous combination. He didn't remember them quite this way, but he'd only been ten and maybe hadn't been paying very close attention. He did remember that his mom and dad had packed up the Winnebago and left weeks before they'd planned. The men in the motel room just a few yards away were a couple of notches down on the evolutionary chart. Their eyes betrayed a huge intellectual emptiness; their speech was born from a culture of moonshine and Confederate flags. But Beano had no choice. Tommy was on his way to San Francisco, and the final stage of the con was ready to be played. Tomorrow morning they would walk Tommy into the Fentress County Petroleum and Gas Company and try to separate him from Joe's five million dollars. Beano hoped this collection of yahoos could step up and save him at the blow-off.

He left the Red Boar Inn and headed back to the Marina Motel, where Victoria was waiting. Periodically, he had an unsettling feeling, almost like he was being watched, but each time he checked his rear-view mirror he could see nobody following.

He got back to the motel at seven and Victoria wasn't there. Her overnight bag was half unpacked and he stood in the room while an unreasonable panic washed over him.

She was still not back at eight.

He called John, but he had not seen or heard from her.

At eight-thirty she opened the door and came into the room.

"Jesus," he said, both angry and relieved. "Don't do this to me. Where were you?"

"Law school girlfriend of mine lives here, we met for a drink, I lost track of time," she lied. Then she went to the curtains to close them. She looked out at the street. She couldn't see the FBI van, but she knew they were out there waiting to pounce. She felt so guilty, she could barely look at Beano.

"Tomorrow we do the sting," he said.

Part Seven
THE STING

"CAVEAT EMPTOR."
LET THE BUYER BEWARE.
—Roman Proverb

THIRTY

The Hurrah

Tommy was flying back to San Francisco in the Challenger, looking down at the two tan leather bags he'd brought from Nassau. They were on the floor before him and contained five million in banded cash. He had never before done something like this without his brother's permission, but despite that, he couldn't help himself, he was smiling. He could hardly wait to tell Joe what he'd done and how he'd done it. He had been fantasizing about that moment since they took off from Nassau. He kept visualizing the scene: He'd call Joe up, make him come to Tommy's apartment in Atlantic City. Joe wouldn't want to come, but Tommy wouldn't beg....He'd laugh and say something like *"Come on over, I think it just might be worth your time."* He'd have the graphs and the oil core sample, which his Texas geologist had told him was called O.C.M.—Oil Cut Mud. Tommy would show his geologist's report, which indicated the sample shale was over 90 percent pure. "Incredible," the Texas geek had told him over the phone in Nassau. Tommy would throw in some of the oil terms he'd been learning to show his brother he wasn't just some dumb street hitter with no brains and nine inches of lumber between his legs. He'd tell Joe about the high G.O.R.—Gas-to-Oil Ratio—and talk

413

about how they would use water-induced B.H.P.—Bottom Hole Pressure. He'd scribbled all of this stuff down while the geek from Texas explained what he needed to know. Once he parked this huge deal in the family's driveway, Tommy was absolutely, for damn sure, through taking shit off of Joe. From now on, his little brother would have to admit that it was Tommy who had brought this good fortune home.

He leaned back in his seat and adjusted the air nozzle over his head. He closed his eyes....Being smart wasn't all that difficult, he mused. He had let Joe convince him that he'd always fuck things up if he didn't let Joe run things, but he was about to prove that piece of horseshit wisdom wrong. Anybody could be smart. Doing deals was a lot like clipping guys. All you had to do was be careful, make sure you had good accomplices, and get rid of all the Dixie cups. He had decided that the two geek doctors from Fresno were definitely Dixie cups.

In the cockpit of Joe Rina's Challenger jet, the phone rang, and the pilot, Scott Montgomery, picked it up immediately. It was a new airphone that got its calls off of the *Satcom 9* geosynchronous satellite. The calls cost twenty dollars a minute, and the only person who ever used this phone was Joe Rina.

"Yes, sir," Scott said into the receiver while his co-pilot, Daniel Rubin, looked over.

"Is Tommy aboard?" Joe asked from his house in upstate New Jersey. He was looking out through the windows of his den at a shallow man-made lake that was beginning to freeze in the unusually early winter.

"Yes, sir, he's on board. We're headed to San Francisco."

"I don't want you to tell him I've spoken to you," Joe said firmly. "I want you to give me an estimated time of arrival in San Francisco and the name of the F.S.O. you're going to use there."

"We're scheduled to land at Pacific Aviation Flight Service Organization in two hours, at about ten P.M.," Scott said, wondering what the hell this was all about. Tommy and Joe never worked behind each other's backs. Their trust in one another was legendary.

"Okay," Joe said, "if that changes or if Tommy diverts you to another field, I want you to call me. And Scott, I'm warning you, if you tell him anything, I'm going to deal with you harshly and personally—you understand?"

"Yes, sir," Scott said, and hung up the phone.

In New Jersey, Joe stood in his den, seething. It was a little past eight as he looked out at the last glimmerings of twilight playing across the glistening gray body of landscaped water. He couldn't believe that Tommy had turned on him. Black anger churned like boiling asphalt.

Then Joe extinguished these emotions. He would deal with this methodically, not emotionally. So far, all he had was some pictures given to him by Victoria Hart, who was, after all, a mortal enemy. She could be trying to fool him. He still wasn't convinced she hadn't played a role in the jewelry store scam. Tommy said she had, that it was on tape, but Joe hadn't been able to see it yet and now Tommy was making some very spooky moves. Maybe there was another explanation. He would give Tommy a chance to explain. If the explanation made sense, then he would have Victoria Hart killed for her treachery. But if Tommy *had* been stealing from him, if he'd arranged to put the card sharp into the game in Greenborough, like Victoria had said...if Tommy had been involved in the tat at the Sabre Bay casino and had stolen money from the dead-drop without an overwhelming personal reason, then Tommy would have to pay the Sicilian price. He would no longer be Joe's brother and would die in agony.

Joe was now moving impatiently around his den as these thoughts consumed him. He was waiting for a phone call from San Francisco. His mind played across the facts once more, searching for a plausible explanation he might have missed: He knew for sure that Tommy had taken the money from the bank in Nassau. What possible reason could Tommy have for stealing five million dollars? Why would he do that? If he needed money, Joe would give it to him. No matter from which angle he surveyed the question, there seemed to be no answer except one: Tommy must have done it to show disrespect. Tommy had broken their bond of faith, and that fact tortured Joe. He could not excise it from his mind. It seared the edges of every other thought.

Then the phone rang and he snapped it up. "Yeah?"

A voice he knew well said, "You get the info?"

"He's landing at San Francisco at ten. They're using Pacific Aviation. Let me know."

"Done," the voice said and then they both disconnected, providing very little, if any, information to a potential government phone tap on Joe's house.

The man he had just talked to was named Reo Wells. He was not a made guy, but an independent contractor that Joe used when he had to do sanctions outside the family. Reo was government trained, a Delta Force commando, who had once done unauthorized wet-work for the CIA.

Joe paced in the den for several more minutes. The sun was down now and he had not turned on the lights. He couldn't seem to control his emotions. Anger swelled. He couldn't just stay caged up here and do nothing....He snatched up the phone and dialed an air charter service and booked a private jet to San Francisco.

"The Hurrah," Beano explained to Victoria, "is that point in the confidence game where the mark has completely committed himself. From this point forward there's no way he's going to pull out. He's got the bit in his teeth. He can smell the gold."

They were driving to the Penn Mutual Building two blocks east of Market Street, where Paper Collar John had dressed the top three floors to be the Fentress County Petroleum and Gas Big Store. Beano parked in the parking garage next door; then he and Victoria rang the security buzzer out front. She looked around, sure there would be a government sedan with two buzz-cuts somewhere nearby watching, but she saw nothing. After a few minutes, an aging security guard came down from the mezzanine. They showed their driver's licenses through the thick glass door and the guard found their names on a list John had left; then he let them in.

"Lotta people up there. You havin' some kinda do?" he asked.

"Yep," Beano said nonchalantly. "It's some kinda 'do,' all right." They left the guard and took the elevator up to the twenty-fifth floor.

When they walked out, there were fifty members of the Bates family standing around, or sitting on desks or in chairs. A few were sitting on the floor. They were all dressed about the same, mostly jeans and T-shirts. When Beano walked into the room they started to applaud. He was their famous cousin and the acknowledged best sharper in the game. He was the only member of the Bates family to ever be known as "King Con."

The top floor of the office building, which would serve as the Fentress County executive floor, was magnificent. John had really done his job in the last three days. Rented antique furniture, computers, and beautiful statues on pedestals dominated the carpeted floor. The blond, matched ashwood walls were now decorated with beautiful paintings in gold leaf frames. This was a setting that reeked of class, money, and success.

Steve Bates came up and shook Beano's hand. "John had everybody put on name tags 'cause I figured you ain't met some of these family members," he said.

Beano smiled and nodded. "That's great," he said. "Where's John?"

"Don't know," Steve said. "He was supposed to be here, but we should get started. He'll show up."

Victoria wondered if the FBI Agents might have broken their promise and picked up John, but why would they? It would ruin everything. She'd given Gil her word, which was her bond...and then she remembered that Gil's word was worth almost nothing.

Beano stood in front of the group. "I'm Beano," he announced unnecessarily, as they all nodded and grinned. They'd seen him on *America's Most Wanted.*

"Thanks for being part of this Big Store," he began. "The mark, as I'm sure John has told you, is Tommy Rina. But there's something that he probably hasn't told you." He paused to make his point. "Tommy is, in my opinion, certifiably insane, a homicidal maniac who can't control his temper. When he loses it, you can't steer him. He's an unguided missile. If he comes through hot, he'll shoot up the place. You should all know this, and if anybody wants out, now's the time, no hard feelings."

They all looked down, shook their heads, and waited for him to go on.

"Whatever we take from him, we split evenly."

An old man named Theodore X. Bates, from San Francisco, stood up. He was handsome, with a closely trimmed white beard and full white hair. "That's real nice, cousin Beano, but Carol was our family. We talked it over 'fore you got here, and we don't want no money. We're doin' this for her, same as you. Don't seem right to take money for it." They all murmured their assent.

Beano took a moment with that, and then he nodded. "Thank you, that really means a lot," he said, looking out at them. "Okay... here's how we're gonna run the bubble." Then he told them about the sting, explaining in detail what they were supposed to do and how they should act. He showed them a computer disk that Victoria had programmed, which would replicate the falling stock price of Fentress County Petroleum and could be interfaced with the on-line Quotron business report, which ran the real New York ticker at the bottom of the screen. "Remember, those of you who haven't played inside on a Big Store, the idea here is this has to be so realistic and so flawless that it would never even occur to the mark that what's going on here is not real. Never for a moment come out of character, no matter what happens."

They nodded and murmured and fell silent as Beano continued: "This Big Store con we're running is a variation on 'The Magic Wallet.' It was originally developed by a sharper named William Elmer Mead at the turn of the century, but it works just as good today. It basically gets the mark to invest in a dying company to save it. His magic wallet will buy the failing company at the last minute and make him rich. We have to convince Tommy that Fentress County Petroleum is on its last legs, that the float on the stock is so thin that his five million could control a hundred-million-dollar company." They nodded. "This isn't like running a short con. On this we have to be ready to move in any direction to head off the mark's questions. He's gonna be nervous about laying out five million dollars. He may even bring an accountant or attorney. He may get balky at the last minute. If that happens, I have a stall and a red ink close-out set up. We're gonna do the play-off somewhere else. The play-off is against the wall."

"Isn't that kinda dangerous, cousin Beano?" Theodore Bates asked.

"Yeah, but it's the only way that Tommy is gonna get the message. We gotta take him right to the edge. That means we gotta go to the edge with him." He looked at them and smiled.

421

"Okay, now here's the gaff: Fentress County is a watered-down company that we actually own. It's listed on the Vancouver Stock Exchange. It hasn't been traded much in years, except for stock swaps John and I make twice a month to keep the stock active. Tomorrow the price is going to drop, courtesy of Victoria's disk." He held it up. "This will show that Fentress County Petroleum stock is falling out of bed. It's about to go bankrupt. You're all about to lose your jobs. You all have to play the situation, lots of nervous activity, strained looks, hopelessness. This is the *Titanic,* and we're sinking, okay?" He looked at them and they nodded. "Who has John picked to be the point-outs?"

Six elderly men and two women held up their hands, and Beano nodded.

"We'll have a separate point-out meeting in a minute, then I want you to run rehearsals. I'll walk you through the first one, then you can run two or three more when John gets here. We need to have this down pat by tomorrow, at eight A.M. The Vancouver Stock Exchange closes at one-thirty P.M. This whole 'stock reload' has to take place before the closing bell. We keep the pressure on so he doesn't have time to re-think it."

Beano took the six men and two women who were point-outs into the President's office and talked to them for about twenty minutes. A point-out in a Big Store con is an inside player who is pointed out to the mark as a person of power or influence. The eight

Bates point-outs would be identified as big stockholders—disgruntled heavy hitters who wanted their money back.

By nine-thirty, it was time for Beano to leave. He had to be at the airport when Tommy showed up. He wondered where the hell Paper Collar John was. He was supposed to be here to do the rehearsals. None of the shillabers in front of him had ever done this kind of sting. "Okay, let me quickly run you through this," he said, afraid to leave until he knew John was there.

Beano led them from room to room, explaining what each area was for. He showed Theodore X. Bates, who was one of the point-outs, where he would do the cross-fire, which was a point in the con where, if the mark lost his nerve, he would "overhear" an important conversation. He demonstrated the speaker phone in the secretary's office. He showed them the Board of Directors' room, one floor down, where the rest of the point-outs would gather prior to the sting. He coached the "stock-holders" on their lines. It was well past nine-thirty when he finished, and if he didn't leave now, he would miss Tommy.

"We'll keep rehearsing," Victoria said, and Beano looked at her skeptically. "Come on," she said angrily. "How long have I been in on this? How many times have we talked it through?" she argued. "I've run complicated felony murder trials. I know how to perform in front of a jury....This isn't all that different."

423

"There's a huge difference between talking and doing," he countered. "And a manacled defendant in court isn't a maniac like Tommy with a gun in his pocket."

"I know what's supposed to happen. Go on, go to the airport. Steve and I will keep this moving till John shows up."

Beano finally nodded; he had no other choice. He looked at his watch one last time, then kissed Victoria and left.

♠ ♠ ♠

John showed up twenty minutes later. When he stepped off the elevator, Victoria knew immediately something was very wrong. He looked awful. His face was pale and his eyes were rimmed in red. He'd been crying. Victoria took him by the hand and led him into one of the beautifully appointed offices and closed the door.

"What's wrong?" she asked him, fearing the worst.

"I've been on the phone to New Jersey," he said, his voice quivering. "The hospital called. Cora's not going to live much longer."

"Oh, John, I'm so sorry," Victoria said, reaching out for his other hand.

"I can't stay," he said. "She's awake. The doctor said they can keep her alive for maybe seven or eight hours. If I ever want to see her again, to say good-bye, I have to leave now. I have to go home....She's been asking for me."

Victoria looked at him, her mind racing. "But

John, Tommy's seen the brochure we printed. You're in there as the President of this company. You have to sell him the stock. Without you, we can't do this."

Paper Collar John stood there, tears running down his cheeks. "I'm sorry," he said. "Cora and I, we've been married for fifty-five years. She's been my best friend for my whole life, Vicky. I hate running out on you, but she's my wife. If Beano was here, he'd tell me to go. I won't let her die alone...."

Beano would know how to figure something out, save the sting, Victoria thought. The way it was planned, from now on Beano had to be with Tommy. There was no way to even reach him and warn him. Tomorrow at eight A.M., Beano would walk in here with Tommy and the play had to go down with or without John. It was up to her and Steve Bates to make it happen. Steve was a short-con expert who'd never done this before. She was a State Prosecutor, a lawyer. Even though she could perform for a jury, she found strength in solid facts. Beano was right... bullshit was her weakest category.

"Is there anybody here who can play inside for us?" she finally asked John.

"I don't know. Most Bateses do short plays, house hustles and the like." Then he looked at her very carefully. He wrote down a number on a piece of paper and handed it to her. Then he told her what to do. After she heard his solution, her knees were weak with fear and excitement. "It will never work," she protested.

"Call him. He can help," Paper Collar John replied; then he turned, and with tears still on his face, he walked out of the Big Store and took the elevator to the street.

Victoria Hart stood there with her heart pounding. The FBI was outside and fifty Gypsy roofing sharpers were inside. She was caught in the middle and left to deal with the sting alone.

THIRTY-ONE

The Buildup

Beano was ten minutes late getting to the Pacific Air Private Jet Terminal. The Challenger was already chocked and Tommy was standing out in front of the Pacific Aviation Flight Service Company, looking pissed at being kept waiting. He had rented a tan Lincoln Town Car and the two leather bags with the five million dollars were already in the trunk.

"The fuck you been?" Tommy said. His anger at seeing the geek physicist brought up bile he could taste.

"This entire experience is so nerve racking. I can't find Dr. Sutton. I've looked and looked," Beano whined, as he pushed his tortoise-shell glasses up on his nose and squinted through them. He had changed his clothes in the car and was now wearing a short-sleeved pink shirt with a plastic pen protector and a clip-on bow tie and was carrying a scarred brief-case.

Tommy looked at him and remembered that, when he had first seen him in the bar at Sabre Bay, he had actually thought the geologist was handsome, a threat to his campaign to fuck Dakota. That was before he'd heard him wimper and plead. Once you got to know Dr. Clark, he was about as sexy as leather pants on an insurance executive.

"Who the fuck cares about Dr. Sutton?" Tommy said angrily.

"Well, uh...how to put this...uh..." Beano took off his glasses, pulled up his shirttail, and cleaned them before slipping them back on his nose. "Dr. Sutton was never, as I'm sure you remember, all that excited about your inclusion as a financial entity," he stammered weakly.

"Who the fuck cares what that bag of bones thinks?"

"Well, I'm not saying this is really going to happen, but...well, Dr. Sutton took all the graphs and three-D seismic shots. The biotherms and the anticlines, along with his geophone resonance material, and he...well, he left."

"So he left. Fuck him. Who needs him? We got what we need from him."

"Well, you see, Mr. Rina, I don't think he took all that material with him because he wanted to frame it and hang it on his wall, so to speak...."

"So, why did he take it, shithead? I'm tired

of playing twenty questions. Spit it out," Tommy barked, thinking this fucking geek was beginning to annoy him worse than Calliope Love. At least he could park his Johnson in Calliope's mouth occasionally to shut her up.

"I'm very concerned that maybe he decided to seek out another partner. You see, if he could convince one of the major stockholders of the viability of our find at Oak Crest, well then, there'd be a competitive bidder."

Tommy's hand shot out and grabbed Beano by the throat. Beano was yanked forward, letting out a little squawk as he was pulled into Tommy's face. "You fucking people amaze me. I'm not some dink you can cut outta the play. I'm a real fucking sore loser. Don't you get that yet?"

"I get it," Beano squeaked. "Please, please...can't breathe."

Tommy let him go. Beano took several deep breaths and straightened his glasses.

"I'm not saying he did it; it's just he didn't like the sixty-forty split, kept complaining about it. I argued with him but he took his stuff and left. At first, I just thought he was going to drive around and pout and would come back. Now, I wonder. He might try and make another deal on this information."

"Get in the fucking car," Tommy demanded.

"I have my own car."

Tommy backhanded him.

Beano got in the car. Tommy drove, and they pulled out of the parking lot.

A few seconds after they left, Reo Wells

turned on the headlights of his midnight-blue Lexus. He put the car in drive and followed Tommy's rented Lincoln Town Car out of the parking lot and down Airport Drive toward San Francisco. Nobody saw the FBI surveillance team on the roof of the American Airlines building across the street. They radioed their chase car, which was two blocks up the street, waiting.

♠ ♠ ♠

Tommy and Beano pulled into the Ritz-Carlton Hotel on Stockton Street. Tommy's attorney was waiting for them under a huge crystal chandelier in the ornate, richly appointed lobby. Tommy checked in and was directed up to a large suite on the fifteenth floor. Tommy dropped the two bags next to the bed. He had refused to let the bellhop carry them or show him up to the room.

Beano found himself standing opposite Tommy's lawyer, whose most distinguishing feature was gray-black wisps of hair that were growing like ragweed out of all the wrong places on his face. It poked in bushy clumps out of his ears and nose. It crowned his eyebrows, which seemed to trumpet constant surprise as they curled in bushy splendor up on his forehead. To make things worse, he had dressed funereally. His name, Beano learned, was Alex Cordosian. Alex now pulled a huge folder out of his bulging briefcase and laid it down on the table. Beano looked at the tab and saw that it was marked "Fentress County P&G." Beano hoped that getting past Mr. Cordosian wouldn't be hard. He was banking on a proven fact: Once a mark was hooked, it was usually impossible to knock him off the con. The mark's greed and dreams of riches made him throw away all caution. Beano only had to fill in whatever holes needed filling and keep reminding Tommy of the billions of dollars at stake. Tommy wouldn't want reason from his attorney. He would want to be told he was right. At least, that's what Beano hoped.

"To begin with, I just found out about this three hours ago, so I've had almost no time to research," Cordosian complained. "I've tried pulling the Ten-K's off the computer for this outfit, but they haven't filed any recently. They're on the Vancouver Exchange, which has very lax listing requirements. They've been quite inactive as far as trading. Four years ago they were a penny stock and now they're almost up to nine and a half."

"Who the fuck cares?" Tommy said, as he fished in the mini-bar for some Scotch and ice.

"Well, sir, the float on the stock is very thin. Only four or five hundred thousand shares outstanding. You start buying it up in quantity and the stock is going to go up like a Chinese rocket. You'll be chasing it...paying more for each new share because of the pressure your own buying is putting on the stock. Furthermore, they haven't filed a Ten-K for years. It could even be a shell company that somebody has been buying back and forth to push the price up."

"Shell company?" Beano piped up from over by the window. "It's not a shell. What are you talking about? It's a closely held company, that's all. I worked there for six years. They own a pile of land in Fentress County. Here, look at this," he said and pulled some papers out of his briefcase.

"The fuck is that?" Tommy demanded.

"Stock analysts' reports," he said, handing them to Alex and reeling off the big broker-ages' names. "Morgan Stanley; here's the Goldman Sachs report." The reports were all counterfeit on stolen letterhead. They all said the company was for real, but had been doing poorly of late. "The principal stockholders have taken the major position in the stock," Beano continued. "They control all of the Class-A Preferred so they don't have to file Ten-K's." He looked over at Tommy. "Where'd you get this guy? Gee, it's always like this. I get something really good and then attorneys come in and screw everything up."

"I'm just saying there's some due-diligence stuff to do here. We don't want to throw five million dollars around without looking at this company a lot more carefully."

"Is it currently active on the Vancouver Exchange?" Beano challenged.

"Yes," the narrow-shouldered attorney answered.

"Are the outstanding shares registered?"

"Yes, but that's not the point."

"Why don't we just let Dr. Sutton and his partners have it? Let the whole deal just slide away," Beano said, sarcastically. "Let's just waste time asking a million dumb questions and let the other guys have the oil and billions of dollars of profit."

"I've been hired by Mr. Rina to analyze this transaction. That's what I intend to do," Alex said hotly.

"'Cept I agree with him," Tommy said, pointing at Beano. "Attorneys fuck everything up." He filled his mouth with Scotch and bar ice. "I got you here to document the transaction...okay? Nothing else. You start asking all these dumb fucking questions about S.E.C.'s and Ten-K's or whatever, and I'm gonna jam all this paperwork so far up your ass you'll need fucking Roto-Rooter to take a shit."

Alex Cordosian looked at Tommy, shocked. *What kind of talk is this?* he wondered. He had done legal work for Joseph Rina in San Francisco and Las Vegas. Joe was a refined and astute businessman. Alex never had to deal with Tommy before. Tommy had already told him downstairs that if he let anyone know what he was doing, including Joe, he'd kill him. *Kill him!* It was absurd...like a bad movie. But Alex didn't like the look of Fentress County Petroleum and Gas. Something was strange about it, and he needed time to do the due diligence. Yet this little thug across the room from him was threatening his life for trying to do his job! Even so, he was determined to pro-

432

tect his client. He would do the best he could to dissuade the ugly mobster from making an expensive impulse buy.

They talked for almost an hour. Beano answered Alex Cordosian's questions slowly, claiming ignorance on most of them because, after all, he was just a geologist. He frequently interrupted the lawyer, repeating, "There's a huge pay-zone under the Oak Crest field. End of story." He insisted they buy Fentress County in the morning, before Dr. Sutton could make a competing move. Alex kept explaining it was going to be very hard, if not impossible, to get his due-diligence answers in such short order. Beano sure the hell hoped Alex was right. Luckily, during the hour or so of questioning, Tommy was getting more frustrated and angry.

"Are you fucking through yet?" he asked the harried little lawyer more than once.

At midnight, Tommy threw Alex out with instructions to meet him on the twenty-fifth floor of the Penn Mutual Building tomorrow at eight A.M.

Tommy had decided not to let Beano out of his sight. He told the geologist he would have to stay in the same room with him. He said he didn't want Dr. Clark to take a powder like Dr. Sutton. Tommy moved into the bedroom, kicked off his loafers, and turned on the TV. "Whatta you wanna watch?" he asked politely, "*Goldilocks and the Three Chicago Bears,* with Ashley Lynn, or *Video Cum Shots,* with Donna Dare and Toluca Lake?"

"Tough choice," Beano said dryly. "Maybe you oughta pick."

Tommy pushed in his selection and flopped down on the bed. Beano went into the other room and lay on the sofa. He looked up at the ceiling and tried to run through the sting one last time, while the sound of Donna Dare's moaning and sighing came in from the bedroom. When he glanced over at Tommy in the next room, the mobster had his zipper open and his hands down in his pants.

"Another opening, another show," Beano mused to himself. He closed his eyes to shut out the ghastly sight. He was stuck with Tommy till morning.

THIRTY-TWO

The Sting

At eight A.M., they parked in the side lot next to the Penn Mutual Building. Tommy locked the two suitcases full of cash in the trunk and walked briskly from the car, not waiting for Beano. He headed directly to the front of the building.

Tommy hurried through the double glass doors as Beano followed.

"When's this stockholders' meeting?" Tommy demanded as they rode up in the elevator.

"It's supposed to be at eight-fifteen," Beano said.

The doors opened on twenty-five to a bustle of activity. A young man with an armful of folders dove into the elevator before they could get out. He was chased in by a young woman, who held the door but didn't enter. "Tell Mr. Munroe the stock just ticked down an eighth of a point to five and seven-eighths," he said desperately to the girl, who looked harried and confused.

"I can't bust in there with that kinda news," she said. "You go run the Eastern and Southeastern fields' B.P.D. reports for Miss Luna like she wanted. I'll see if I can get Mr. Hatcher to slip a note to Mr. Munroe."

"Barrels per day," Beano told Tommy, who looked angrily at him for a translation as they got out of the elevator. The doors closed, whisking the young man away.

Beano wondered who the hell Miss Luna was. He knew the sharpers were trying to send him a message, a warning. He was on full alert, but he didn't know what had happened yet as they moved into the main secretarial area of the executive floor.

There was bustling activity everywhere: Bates family sharpers, dressed conservatively, were working on their computers or running folders of oil reports back and forth. Phones were ringing; there were pages over the sound system. Beano heard his own name: "Beano Bates, line two." He looked at Tommy, who, he hoped, didn't know who Beano Bates was. Tommy was devoting his limited powers of concentration to all the frenzied activity. He seemed impressed by the expensive art and the multitudes of scurrying, well-dressed yuppies.

Beano stepped away from him, picked up the phone, and hit extension two. "Go," he said.

"We got problems," Steve Bates said. "We got a mess here. Victoria is trying to set—" Suddenly, a hand reached in and disconnected the phone. Beano looked up and saw Tommy standing there, glaring at him.

"The fuck you doing?" Tommy demanded.

"I was going to page Dr. Sutton, see if perhaps he was here. I thought it would be nice to know what he's up to, since he might scuttle the whole deal," Beano said, his voice dripping snotty sarcasm. He was taking a chance that Tommy wouldn't backhand him here, and though Tommy's eyes flashed crazy, Beano got away with it.

"Get the President a'this outfit, this Chip Lacy prick," Tommy said, flipping open the brochure and pointing to Paper Collar John's picture, under which was the name LINWOOD "CHIP" LACY. "Let's go brace this motherfucker."

Tommy grabbed one of the sharpers who was flying past and spun him around roughly by the arm. "Wanna see Chip Lacy," he said.

"Mr. Lacy isn't here."

"Isn't here?" Beano asked, startled.

"No. He had...Mr. Lacy had a slight coronary last evening. He's in the hospital."

"Who the fuck's runnin' this show?" Tommy growled.

"That would be Miss Luna."

"Miss who?" Beano said, his mind reeling. He couldn't figure out what was going on.

"Miss Luna, the Chief Financial Officer from the Knoxville home office. She flew in for the stockholders' meeting. Excuse me, I've got to get these wildcat-well asset sheets for Mr. Stuart," and the grifter pulled away.

Beano called after him, "Where's Miss Luna?"

"In Mr. Lacy's office, getting ready for the stockholders' meeting," the yuppie said, as he turned the corner down the hallway and disappeared.

Tommy looked at Beano and then at the flurry of activity, phones ringing, people running here and there...

"I've only been here once," Beano said, "but I think Mr. Lacy's office is in the corner, over there." He pointed and headed off.

"Wonder where the fuck Alex is?" Tommy growled, looking around for his attorney. "We don't need him," Beano said, moving off toward the corner office, glad the hairy Armenian hadn't shown.

Seated in the President's outer office was Ellen X. Bates, Steven's wife. Beano knew from the dinner they'd had in Oak Crest that before she married Steve, she'd been an experienced telephone yak and had worked bucket shops from New York to L.A. She had a good gift of gab and a breezy intelligence. He and John had picked her to be a point-out stockholder. It surprised him that she was playing the lesser role of the President's secretary. Something was definitely up.

"We'd like to have a moment to talk to Miss Luna," Beano said.

"I'm afraid that's out of the question," Ellen snapped and continued dialing her computer phone.

Tommy reached over and depressed the switch-hook. "Nothing is out of the question. Is she in there?"

"She is preparing for a very important stockholders' meeting," Ellen said huffily, pulling his hand off the phone.

"That's gonna work out fine, because I just happen to be a very important stockholder," Tommy growled.

"I...I...I'm still..."

"Who fucking cares?" Tommy said, and walked right past her and into the office without knocking. Beano followed.

Standing in the center of the room, holding a large sheaf of papers, her back to them, was Miss Laura Luna. She was talking on a speaker phone when they burst in: "...no other explanation, Alan? One of our major stockholders must be selling for it to drop like this." And then she stopped and turned around.

Beano had never seen her before. She was a middle-aged, overweight, Janet Reno–sized woman, about five foot eight. Miss Luna was wearing a black pant suit that failed to disguise her immense girth. She had a double chin, and her half glasses were hanging from a chain around her neck. Her stout legs bulged in the loose-fitting pant suit. Beano wondered who the hell she was; then she spoke again and he recognized her. His heart sank. *There's no way we're ever going to pull this off.*

"Get out of this office," she said. "I'm preparing for a shareholders' meeting. You can't be in here."

"I'm the only fucking meeting you got that counts," Tommy said and he closed the door behind him, cutting off the noise of the busy office outside. Then he moved to her desk and disconnected the phone.

After John had left to go home to be with Cora, Victoria called the number he had given her. It belonged to a family member named Stuart Bates, no X. He was in Los Angeles working on a TV show. Stuart Bates, like Carol Sesnick, was one of the few Bates family members who wasn't on the bubble. Stuart did special-effects makeup for a Space Odyssey television show that was being made on a soundstage in Hollywood. When Victoria told him what she wanted, he had said it was impossible. He needed to make body molds and cure them; he needed to get the correct skin tone to do the makeup. "Two days, working round-the-clock at the very least," he told her...besides, he had a TV show to do. "What time does this have to happen?" he finally asked.

"Eight-fifteen, tomorrow morning," she said. "Beano Bates is running the sting."

"King Con?" Stuart said; his voice seemed to hesitate, slightly in awe.

"That's who's running it. We could sure use the help. One of our main inside men just went down."

"Okay, I'll do the best I can," he'd said.

He phoned in sick and chartered a plane, which she said she'd reimburse him for. Stuart had flown up to San Francisco with all of the equipment he could carry. Victoria had next phoned the FBI. "Let me talk to Grady Hunt," she said, and in a minute he was on.

"So far so good," Grady bragged. "Everybody's in town, Tommy and your boyfriend are at the Ritz. Whatta you want?"

"You said I had to call, so I'm calling."

"Then gimme something I don't know, like where's the old duck with the gray hair going? He got on a plane for New Jersey. I got a team set to pick him up in Atlantic City."

"John Bates is going home. Don't follow him, his wife is dying. He's out of the play."

"Boo-hoo and whoop-de-do," Grady said.

"Don't follow him, okay? He's just going to sit at the hospital with his wife. I'm meeting a guy tonight named Stuart Bates. He doesn't know what's going on either. He's doing me a favor, so don't jam him up. He's not part of it."

"Nobody seems to be part of it," he said. "We got a first here, a crime with no criminals."

"I'll call you in the morning before it goes down," she said, and hung up on him. *What a jerk.*

She'd picked Stuart Bates up at the airport at eleven-thirty, and they had gone directly to a motel that was a few blocks from the Big Store. He'd asked for a room with a bathtub. Once they were inside, he had insisted that she take off all her clothes. She had hesitated, but then thought, *What the fuck*, and threw caution and her clothes away. She stood naked before him. He looked at her beautiful body and tried to decide which areas to pad.

"I'm gonna give ya the cellulite transformation, a big stern, and thunder thighs," he said. Then he handed her a robe. He poured three bags of plaster of Paris into the tub and had her sit on a chair in the bathroom with her head tipped back in the sink while he made a face mold.

"Okay," he said, "I'm going to give you body padding. I brought some in the huge suitcase. Try it on; we'll probably have to tailor it, but you'll wear it under clothes so it should work. Your hands are going to be tough, a real giveaway. Hopefully, he won't look at them too closely. We'll get a pant suit for you to wear, with pockets. Keep your hands in your pockets to hide them. I don't have time for the hand appliances. I'll do chin, cheeks, and neck. You can look through that suitcase for a wig."

They had started at twelve-fifty in the morning, and seven hours later the sun was up, and he was just applying the finishing touches. She was sitting in a motel bathroom four blocks from the Penn Mutual Building while he fine-tuned the eye makeup and powder-dusted the glued-on appliances. She watched in fascination; he had transformed her into a fat, middle-aged woman with three chins. In high school, Victoria had developed a very funny imitation of her history teacher, Miss Laura Luna. She had been rather large and had a breathy but slightly squeaky voice. Victoria needed a new persona so that Tommy wouldn't recognize her. She decided to resurrect Miss Luna.

Stuart had picked up some size 15 clothes and she had selected a dark blue pant suit, with pockets. It also hid the leg and stomach padding, which were held on with Velcro. The whole contraption weighed over thirty pounds.

She was sweating under it as she cabbed the four blocks to the Penn Mutual Building and took the service elevator up to the twenty-fifth floor. Her FBI tail didn't recognize the woman who hurried past them to the cab stand. Instead, they stayed and watched the empty motel room. She dashed into the President's office just two minutes ahead of Beano and Tommy. Now, with almost no time to get set and settle down, she was face to face with Tommy Rina.

"I'm sorry, I can't meet with anybody right now," Victoria told the ugly mobster.

"Hey, lady." Tommy took a menacing step forward. "Who the fuck you think you're talking to?"

"I haven't the slightest idea," she said, in her breathy soprano. "I've never seen you before in my life. But I'm going to insist you leave my office or I'll have to call Security. I'm preparing for a meeting with our million-dollar shareholders and I only have a few minutes to review Mr. Lacy's notes."

"I own a million dollars' worth a'this oil company," he said, and he yanked open his briefcase and thrust the stock certificates at Victoria.

She looked at them. "This is only a hundred thousand shares. The stock is trading at just under six. That means the market value of these certificates is only about six hundred thousand."

"The fuck," Tommy said, "y'mean I'm still losing money?"

"Please leave my office," she said insistently.

Beano pulled Tommy aside and whispered to him, "If the stock goes down, that's good for us. Means we can buy more for our money. Forget the first million," he whispered, "we're talking about *billions*."

Tommy pulled back and looked at Beano. Finally he seemed to connect to that. He nodded.

Beano thought he needed to slow the pace

slightly. He had never played a mark who had less understanding of business. "We're interested in buying control of this company," Beano said to Victoria.

"And just who might you be?"

Beano thought Victoria's makeup was a bit too heavy. At one spot, it looked like it had been put on with a trowel to cover the neck appliances. Then Tommy said something to Victoria that jerked him back.

"Don't I know you?" he blurted. "We met someplace before?"

"I'm sure not," Victoria asked.

"Yeah...yeah, I'm sure. Florida? You ever been to Florida?"

"What do you mean, you want to buy the company?" she said, abruptly changing subjects. "That's hardly possible at this point."

"Miss Luna, is it?" Beano said and she turned to him. "I know you've got a bunch of angry stockholders convening here this morning. These people want their money back. I happen to know they all hold Class-A Preferred Stock, same as Mr. Rina here. And somebody, some insider, must be selling it fast to push the price down like this."

"I can't discuss insider business," she said.

"Now the other stockholders can't sell without flooding the market and driving the price to nothing. Since they're all stuck holding this plunging stock, I think they're going to want you to liquidate assets. If they vote this morning to do that, then you're going to have to start selling stuff like the Tennessee land,

444

and if that happens on top of this falling stock price, even the Vancouver Stock Exchange is going to panic and freeze everything, maybe even de-list the security. You're in a horrible fix, Miss Luna. You should be treating us like saviors. We happen to be the only buyers in a market full of sellers," Beano grinned.

"I still don't know who you are," Victoria said.

"This is Mr. Rina, a respected businessman. I used to work here until I was fired for doing my job. I'm a geologist, Dr. Douglas Clark."

"Oh, yes. Seems to me I read that termination slip. So now what's your story? You trying to buy the company and teach us all a lesson?"

"I'm trying to offer a solution, not a lesson."

"I'm sorry, but I don't think selling you the company at a distressed price is a very good business solution...at least, not this morning. As the corporate CFO, I'm empowered to negotiate deals for FCP&G, but I hardly intend to take advantage of that power until Chip Lacy gets better and can offer his opinion."

"What's she saying?" Tommy asked, leaning forward in his loafers like a railbird at the Aqueduct finish line.

"I happen to know this company is falling apart," Beano exploded at her, losing his temper. "You people haven't been bringing in new wells. Your field development costs are killing your cash flow. You haven't even been paying your bills. Don't stand there and preach to me about good business solutions."

445

"I think you need to get ahold of yourself, Dr. Clark. You were fired for meddling in a financial matter that was not your concern. Now, obviously, you're harboring the fantasy of buying us and firing everybody to get even. Revenge and retribution? Is that the plan?" she said, her voice rising in indignation to match his.

"The West Coast Platform Drilling Company was hired by me!" Beano screamed. "Donovan Martin was my friend. We had a contractual obligation to him, and all I did was—"

Then the door opened and Teo X. Bates entered the room. He was tall and broad shouldered. He had been doing land scams in the Phoenix area and flew in to work Beano's sting. Following Teo into the room was a driveway specialist from Simi Valley, California, named Luther X. Bates.

"Everything okay in here?" Teo said, looking suspiciously at Beano and Tommy. "We heard shouting."

"Perhaps these gentlemen would like to leave now," Victoria said.

"I own a hundred thousand shares a'this company," Tommy said. "I ain't goin' nowhere."

Victoria looked at him unpleasantly, then seemed to relent. "Maybe if you'd wait in another office for a minute. Perhaps I can arrange for you to be included in the preferred stockholders' meeting."

As Tommy turned to leave, Beano gave Victoria a lingering look. She held it for a minute, then winked at him and shrugged.

446

Tommy pulled him out of the office. It was then that Beano saw Alex Cordosian standing there, out of breath. He had just arrived.

"They're gonna let us in the stockholders' meeting," Tommy grinned.

"The reason I'm late is I've been making some calls. You can't just walk in here and buy this place. I can't get any banking information on this outfit. You don't know what the debt obligation of this company is....What if they owe a hundred million against a bunch of devalued assets? You're gonna be liable for all their loans." Tommy blinked his lizard eyes at the Armenian attorney. "What if there are outstanding claims by other subs?" Alex continued. "What if there's hundreds of millions in lawsuits pending? You don't know what you're buying. You could be buying a long-term headache. I'm determined to point these things out to you," he lectured. "You can threaten me, but I owe you my best judgment. Your brother would never plunge blindly like this, believe me." That sentence, more than all the others, snapped Tommy's eyes wider.

"Did you check on all that Tennessee land, did you call about that?" Beano asked hotly.

"Yes, I talked to the Clerk in Fentress County. The company does have a land grant title for the acreage, and I did feel better when I confirmed that, but there's no current value for the land listed. The land grant goes all the way back to the Civil War."

"There's more value here than they even

begin to suspect," Beano whispered intently, turning Tommy so Ellen seemingly couldn't hear. "Don't forget all that oil in the ground. The largest stratigraphic trap ever located." He led Tommy away from the secretary's desk and out of earshot.

But Alex kept following and buzzing, "How much is the oil field really worth? You don't know, nobody knows. You don't even really know there's crude down there, you just have this guy's word for it. What if it's just a pocket well?"

"A what?" Tommy asked.

"It's no pocket well," Beano corrected. "Are you kidding? I've worked the seismics on this acreage for eighteen months. We've got at least a six-acre pool down there. The flow pressure tests were incredible."

"I saw it. I saw the oil," Tommy said.

"How much?" Alex asked. He was cooking now, he could see indecision clouding Tommy's narrow thoughts. "Did you see a billion barrels' worth, like he said?"

"You don't have to see it. I know it's there. That's what geology is about," Beano hissed angrily.

"I didn't see it," Tommy said, "but I got a decanter full."

"Oh, a decanter. Well, great, that's gotta be worth about two bucks. You can't do this."

"Look, you," Beano said, leaning in on the lawyer, who pulled back in fear. "I don't need all this sarcasm from you. I worked to prove that field for almost two years. You don't know what you're talking about. In half an hour this opportunity goes away."

"I've been in a few oil deals in my life, and they're not done like this. This is nuts. I called some friends of mine back east this morning. They think this company went bankrupt in the late seventies."

"Bankrupt in the seventies?" Beano sputtered.

"I'm not saying you shouldn't buy this eventually, just slow down. Joe never buys stuff quick. He always says, 'If there's a clock anywhere in the deal, then let the buyer beware.'"

"Joe says that?" Tommy asked.

"If this is an up-and-up deal, it will be for sale tomorrow or next week. You don't have to buy it now. If you insist, we can negotiate an option today, preserve all your rights, and then, after I've checked it out, we can let go of the cash."

It was a solution that would never work for Beano. Alex would surely discover the fraud if given enough time to investigate. Beano had to up the stakes....So, he moved back to Ellen's desk, borrowed a pencil, and wrote a note for her while Alex was slowly getting Tommy to reconsider.

"What's it matter if you buy it today? Look, big purchases don't happen like this. You don't roll in with a suitcase full of cash and plunk it down. That's insane. Do it the way Joe would do it. Do it smart." Alex had finally found the right tune to play, and Tommy was listening and nodding.

449

Beano handed the note to Ellen. She read it and stood up. "You can wait in Mr. Spencer's office while Miss Luna gets the approval for you to attend the meeting," she said, as she showed them to a nearby office.

They entered and looked out of the huge plate-glass window. Across the street, the Exxon double locking *x*'s were shining. Ellen left them in the office and closed the door. Then she handed Beano's note to her husband, Steve. *Rig a chill and play the cross-fire,* the note read.

♠ ♠ ♠

There was a computer in the office where they were waiting. Tommy watched as Beano turned it on and booted it up.

"I'm telling you," Alex went on relentlessly, "we can hold our dirt. If they're really in cash trouble, time is working for us, not against us."

Beano had the Quotron stock report up, and he motioned to Tommy and Alex.

"Look't this," he said, and he punched in FCP&G and they watched the stock ticker report. "This stock was trading at ten yesterday, this morning it's down to five and seven eighths and whoa, no...look't this..."

Tommy leaned in and, as they talked, he saw the stock drop from five and seven-eighths to five and three-fourths. Again, Victoria's program had overridden the real Quotron ticker, and Fentress County fell right before their eyes.

"This fucking thing is dropping faster than a bad tit job," Tommy said, glaring at the screen.

"Mr. Rina," Beano said, "I don't mean to stand here and argue with Mr. Cordosian, brilliant in legal matters as I'm sure he is, but I've been in the oil business for fifteen years. This stock is about to get frozen by the Vancouver Exchange. An insider is obviously dumping stock without notifying the Board. They've gotta be looking at this. A stock goes from ten to five and three-quarters, loses almost half its value in one day, and you don't think the Exchange is gonna stop trading and de-list it? Once that happens, we are absolutely out of the game. Maybe your brother thinks if there's a clock in a deal there's a problem, but I'm sure he wasn't contemplating a foreign stock exchange taking the whole transaction out of our hands. We have one hell of an opportunity here. But we've gotta suck it up, be a little brave, and move now."

Then the door opened and Ellen Bates stuck her head in. "Miss Luna says you can join the stockholders' meeting. It's on the floor below, in the big conference room. I can show you down."

Tommy picked up his briefcase and they all followed her out of the office to the elevator.

♠ ♠ ♠

The stockholders' meeting was more of a shouting match than a meeting. Miss Luna,

451

a.k.a. Victoria Hart, was trying to maintain some control, but the Bates point-out players were screaming at her and each other.

"You can't be serious!" Leonard X. Bates was shouting. "If we don't make a move now, take this into our own hands, we're going to get frozen. One or more of us is selling and killing the market for everyone else. We have to move now, Laura. Sell the Tennessee land, dispense the assets. I understand we have a buyer on that property."

Everybody started talking at once.

"Mr. Lacy had very strong opinions about liquidating that asset, and the offer on the table is ridiculous," Victoria yelled out. "Once we do that, we're basically out of business. That property is leveraged against our bank loan. Besides, we feel we have certain development fields that show wonderful promise. We're not in a crisis situation here, at least not yet."

"If we're not, I'd sure as hell like to see your definition of a crisis!" Theodore Bates barked.

"I'm holding way too much of this paper. I'm not gonna stand here and eat it, sheet by sheet," another sharper yelled.

"This is the worst quarterly P and A field report I've seen in twenty years," another interrupted.

And then everybody in the room started shouting over one another and Victoria was clapping her slender, out-of-proportion hands to get them all to quiet down. "If we can please speak one at a time," she yelled, but arguments were raging all around the table.

Beano leaned toward Tommy. "This thing is so ripe. We won't even need the whole five mil. Make an offer."

Tommy looked over at Alex, who shook his head, and Tommy leaned back. He was going to wait, like he thought his brother Joe would do.

Beano was stuck, so he flashed a sign at Theodore. It was time to play the cross-fire.

"Miss Luna, I want to adjourn for a while. I have partners in Texas I need to speak with. Could we have a few minutes, please?" Theodore yelled.

The din in the room lessened with planned orchestration, so Victoria could give her line. "Okay, I think we all need to cool down. We'll take five."

"I know this fat broad from someplace," Tommy said. "I fucking can't pin it down, but when it comes to pussy, even ugly pussy, I got fucking unbelievable instincts."

"Let's go find a room to talk," Beano said.

He moved with Tommy and Alex out of the conference room. All of the sharpers were growling and arguing at the turn of events, cursing the falling stock and the stockholder among them who was selling. They filed out into the hallway. Beano led Tommy and Alex to an empty office.

All the offices on twenty-four were less impressive than the ones on twenty-five. The offices had half-walls with decorative, frosted glass up to the ceiling to create an open feeling.

Beano motioned them into an office, then hesitated. "I gotta take a quick leak," he said. "Be right back." He closed the door, counted to ten, then opened the door and quickly re-entered the office.

"Fuck! I knew it!" he exclaimed, turning Tommy and Alex around. "He's here. He's fucking here. I knew it!"

"Who's here?" Tommy said.

"Dr. Sutton. He's talking to that old guy, Theodore Lanaman, the guy who called for the recess. They just went into an office across the hallway."

"You think he's making a deal with that guy?" Tommy said, concern crossing his feral features.

"Of course. Whatta you think? He's not at this stockholders' meeting to give a geophone report. We're fucked," Beano said, totally defeated. He pointed at Alex. "If you hadn't listened to this guy, we could've already owned this thing."

"Where is he? Let's go see," Tommy said, then opened the door and walked out. Beano and Alex followed.

Beano pointed to the office across the hall; then Tommy saw that there was a door right next to it. He opened it. It led to a secretarial area which was between two executive offices. One was the office that Duffy and Theodore were in. The other was empty.

They walked into the secretarial area and looked through the frosted-glass dividing wall that separated them from Duffy and Theodore. They could see Duffy talking animatedly, but his voice and image were muffled by the decorative glass partition. Beano finally found the secretary's speakerphone and hit a button. Immediately they could hear the conversation, because Beano had connected the speakers between the two phones:

"...I been doing it just like we planned," Theodore was saying, and through the distorting glass they could see him holding up a piece of paper. "These are the trading slips."

Duffy was standing facing him, his Einstein hair frizzy in the distorted backlight. Beano grabbed a miniature tape recorder out of his pocket to record the conversation.

"I'm telling you, Mr. Lanaman, they won't find out you're the one selling....The price is going down. It's already in the mid-fives."

Beano, Alex, and Tommy were hunkered over the speakerphone, eavesdropping, while Beano recorded the "betrayal."

"I'll call my broker and dump the rest of my stock. That should drive it down to the mid-fours and then they'll be desperate to sell. It gets me out at an average price of about six, which is not all that bad."

"Then let's get to work," Duffy said, as they left the office and Beano turned off the recorder.

"If Sutton told him about the field and all

the oil, why is he selling his stock?" Tommy asked, his brow knit. Business had always been hard for him. It wasn't like clipping guys where you just stepped up and did it. In business you tried to fool them or bluff them. Sometimes it just didn't make sense.

"It's very simple," Beano said slowly. "He wants the stock price to fall so these other stockholders will panic and sell him their stock right now. He'll pick up control of the company for bubkes."

Tommy looked at Alex. "Zat sound right?" he asked. Alex thought for a second then nodded. "Yeah...it's probably exactly what he's doing," he agreed, beginning to be a believer himself. "By buying it here at the stockholders' meeting, he doesn't have to buy it over the counter and create a higher and higher market as he goes. He also avoids the five-day stock exchange clearing procedure. Pretty damn smart," Alex said grudgingly.

"It's fish-or-cut-bait time," Beano said. "It's us or them or it's the V.S.E. in Vancouver. This time tomorrow this company and that billion-dollar field is gonna belong to somebody else. I'm saying it should be us."

♠ ♠ ♠

Victoria reconvened the stockholders' meeting, and as they sat at the now more subdued table, Duffy walked into the room and sat behind Theodore Bates.

456

"Who is this gentleman?" Victoria asked in her breathy Miss Luna voice.

"He's my assistant," Theodore said in his authoritative Mr. Lanaman voice. "And I'd like to make an offer to everybody in this room. I understand you want out, but I think it would be nothing short of criminal to sell that Tennessee land grant for what's being offered. I always believed in this company and in Chip Lacy, so I'm willing to buy your stock certificates, the Class-A as well as the outstanding Class-C, at one point over Close of Market today."

Immediately the room broke into a flurry of discussion. Finally, the buzz died down and the stockholders looked over at Theodore.

"Why would you do that? The stock is dropping like a rock," one of the point-out sharpers asked Theodore.

"Frankly? Because I've been semi-retired for a year and I'm bored. I'd like to give running this place a shot. Gimme something to do, but I'm not gonna spend that much time and energy unless I own it."

Beano looked over at Tommy, and now Tommy nodded, so Beano exploded to his feet. "He's not trying to own it. He's trying to steal it! It's Lanaman who's been selling his stock and knocking the price down so he can buy it for nothing."

"That's patently absurd," Theodore thundered.

"Is it?" Beano asked rhetorically, as he

turned on the little tape recorder and set it on the polished mahogany table.

Through the speaker they could hear Theodore's voice: "I been doing it just like we planned. These are the trading slips." Then Duffy was saying, "I'm telling you, Mr. Lanaman, they won't find out you're the one selling....The price is going down. It's already in the mid-fives." Then Theodore again: "I'll call my broker and dump the rest of my stock. That should drive it down to the mid-fours and then they'll be desperate to sell. It gets me out at an average price of about six, which is not all that bad."

Beano turned off the tape and the room exploded in anger.

"My offer still stands," Theodore shouted.

"You get the hell out of here," one of the sharpers yelled at Theodore. "I wouldn't sell you my stock at gunpoint!"

"Get out of this meeting, you son-of-a-bitch," another yelled, and he was on his feet grabbing for Theodore X. Bates, who, along with Duffy, made a hasty exit from the room. Once he was gone, they all sat there looking at one another.

"Too bad," one of the sharpers said. "I was hoping I could sell. I wish we could find another buyer."

Beano looked pointedly at Victoria. "Tell him, Miss Luna," he said. "You've a fiduciary duty. You can't withhold that kinda information."

"Well, I just...It seems to me we're all panicking."

"Tell him!" Beano said firmly, and then Victoria turned to the room full of sharpers.

"Well, there was another offer this morning, but I think—"

"Another offer?!" they all said, before she could finish. They were astounded.

Now it was Tommy who rose majestically to his feet. He felt exactly the way he knew Joe must feel when he was closing a well-planned deal.

"I'm willing to pay cash money, one point over C.O.M."

"Over what?" one of them asked.

"Over C.O.M., Close of Market," Tommy said.

"They don't call it C.O.M.," Beano whispered. "It's just called Close of Market."

"Oh," Tommy said. "Well, I'll buy all your stock up to five million dollars."

"You gotta deal," one sharper yelled.

"Count me in," another yelled, rising to his feet, pulling his prop stock certificates out of his briefcase.

Tommy smiled. He liked doing business on his terms. He decided it was just like clipping guys, only your dick didn't get quite as hard. Then he left Beano to sort out the sellers, while he and Alex went down to get the two suitcases of cash out of the trunk of Tommy's car.

They returned to a selling frenzy. Each sharper

handed over his certificates, and Tommy gave him the appropriate amount of cash. It was in banded packages of hundreds, right out of Joe's dead-drop room in Nassau. In less than two hours the transaction was complete.

Once the sharpers had left with their money, Tommy was seated with fifty or sixty stock certificates in a pile in front of him and a satisfied smile on his face. He told Beano it was time to have a party and celebrate.

"I hope you're happy," Miss Luna said angrily to Beano. "You own the company. It'll probably kill Mr. Lacy." And she moved out of the conference room in a huff.

"I know that cunt from someplace," Tommy said after she was gone. But, for the life of him, he still couldn't remember from where.

While Tommy was packing up the stock certificates and Alex was instructing him that they should be immediately placed in a safety deposit box, Beano found Victoria in the President's office.

She was looking out the window at the oil buildings across the street. Her stocky legs were spread wide to balance the heavy load of padding. She was in a pensive mood and, with a delicate hand up to her mouth, was looking down the street. She wondered how many Feds were down there. Beano came in, and she spun around as he locked the door.

"Great job," he said, and she nodded without enthusiasm. "What's wrong?" he said, picking up her mood.

Victoria could not lie to him for another

moment. As she stood there, a completely disparate thought hit her. She knew in that instant she really loved him. Strange as it was, he had crept into her every waking thought, coloring all her values and perceptions with his personality.

"Beano...the police know all about this," she said slowly, hating every word she uttered. "For all I know they're outside the door right now."

"How could they?" he said, still smiling, but looking at her closely. It was hard to read her expression behind all of the makeup.

"Because I told them."

"You told them?" The smile died slowly on his handsome face. "Why?"

"They picked me up in Jersey coming out of Joe's office. I stumbled into a Federal stake-out." Then she sat on the edge of the desk, and while he listened in utter disbelief, she told him about everything that had happened since her return to San Francisco.

"Why didn't you tell me earlier?" he said after she finished, his feelings hurt.

"I was ashamed, I guess. Now I know it was a mistake. I know I can't trust Gil Green to keep his word. He'll double-cross me. He only cares about one thing and that's getting into the Governor's Mansion. If I didn't do what he said, they would have killed you."

Beano looked at her for a long moment.

"Whatta we gonna do?" she said, after long moments of uncomfortable silence. She was feeling utterly helpless and totally responsible.

"I guess we better start a fire," he finally said.

461

THIRTY-THREE

Playing Against the Wall

The call came from the hysterical executive at exactly twelve-thirty-five in the afternoon.

"This whole place is on fire!" Victoria screamed through the receiver and then, while the Fire Department dispatcher was talking, the call came in from the building's Direct-Dial Sentry Fire Alarm System. They had electronic confirmation of the blaze at the Penn Mutual Building. "We're trapped up here! We can't go down, the stairs are filled with smoke."

"Go to the roof," the dispatcher on the phone told the panicked C.E.O. "Get everybody up there."

Grady Hunt saw the smoke billowing out of the twenty-fifth-floor windows from his surveillance position across the street. He immediately sensed he was in trouble. He and Denniston ran inside the building just as the first Fire Marshal's unit screeched up.

"Hey, you can't go in there!" the Fire Marshal yelled, but Grady ran in anyway, with Denniston right on his heels.

The building lobby was clear of smoke, but the elevators were full of people from all floors, pouring out in a panic. The alarms were ringing loudly. Grady was knocked down on his way into the elevator, and then run over like a calf in a stampede.

The Fire Marshal grabbed Grady, pulling him to his feet. "I'm not gonna tell you again! We have a three-alarm on the twenty-fifth floor."

"Get your fucking hands off me, Smoky," Grady said, pulling out his badge and pushing it in the fireman's face.

"I don't care if you're President Fucking Clinton. Get the hell out of this building, asshole!" the Fire Marshal screamed.

Then Grady and Denniston grabbed the startled man, knocked him down, and jumped into the elevator. They made it all the way up to the twenty-fourth floor, where the elevator computer-locked and prevented them from going any higher. They jumped out, found the fire stairs, and ran up to the top floor of the building. Smoke was billowing down the staircase at them, and when they got to twenty-five, they could see why....There were two huge wastebasket fires burning on the top landing.

"This fucking guy," Grady said, as he burst through the fire door onto the twenty-fifth floor, which was almost completely full of smoke. Several of the plate-glass windows had been broken on the east side and smoke was billowing out into the afternoon air. Under each broken window was another raging trash can fire. Nothing else on the floor was burning. The cans were full of stuffing ripped out of the office chairs and they were putting out thick, black smoke.

Then they heard an approaching helicopter. "Roof!" Grady yelled. He and Denniston pulled guns and ran back to the fire stairs.

As they were climbing to the top, they could hear the chopper landing. When they broke out onto the roof, Beano was waiting. He delivered a solid right cross to Grady's square jaw. The Fed catapulted back onto the landing and was out.

Alex, Tommy, and Victoria were running to the chopper, which was just setting down.

Beano looked over at a shocked Denniston, who was now holding his pistol, half-pointed at him. Beano kicked at the gun and it went flying out of Denniston's hand. He and Denniston faced off. Beano didn't think this blond pastel prince was going to be much trouble. Then he got the Vanilla Surprise: Denniston lost his temper and exploded in a rage, charging Beano and taking him down.

Tommy saw this from the helicopter and looked over at Beano, who was now rolling around with some guy in a tan suit he'd never seen before.

Tommy had thought the building was on fire and wanted to get the hell out of there. He had not seen the trash can fires because Beano had lit them and let the floor fill with smoke before breaking the windows and steering a shaken Tommy out of the conference room, where he had just finished packing up his briefcase with stock certificates. Victoria shouted, "Up on the roof!" and he'd gone without asking questions, lugging his briefcase with him. Now, he looked out of the helicopter and saw his personal corporate geologist getting pounded. He climbed down to help.

"Only got room for one more!" the chopper pilot yelled, so Tommy, who didn't want to lose Dr. Clark just yet, got out, walked over to where Denny Denniston was choking Beano, and calmly kicked the Vanilla Surprise in the head. He helped Beano up and they moved to the chopper....

"What about that other guy?" the pilot said, pointing at Denniston, who was sitting with his head in his hands.

"He said it's okay to come back and get him on the next trip," Tommy said.

The helicopter lifted off and away. They flew to a chopper pad five blocks down and were let off. Beano, Alex, Tommy, and Victoria got out, then the helicopter pilot lifted off to return for the last man on the roof. Alex was shaken. He'd had enough and wanted to go back to his office. Tommy, Victoria, and Beano cabbed back to the Penn Mutual Building and slipped into the parking garage, where they got in Tommy's rented car and sped away without being seen in the commotion.

♠ ♠ ♠

"Here's to the fucking oil," Tommy said, as he raised a glass of Scotch and drank it down. He already looked half in the bag, grinning at his captive audience of Beano, Miss Luna, Wade and Keith Summerland. Keith still had his left ear bandaged from where Victoria had hit him a couple of days before. "Where're these fucking girls?" Tommy asked Wade, who had

465

made a deal to have some strippers brought over from the Pussycat Theater in the Tenderloin District.

"They oughta be here any minute, Tommy," Keith said, and Tommy poured himself another glass, then looked over at Victoria.

"You say you've never been to Vegas?" he asked her, and she shook her head. "This broad looks real familiar. This is like fucking drivin' me nuts, but I'm gonna pin it down."

They were in Tommy's suite at the Ritz. He had the stock certificates in his open briefcase on the table. "So here's the deal," he said, turning back to business and looking at Beano with a lopsided grin. "Since Dr. Sutton turned out to be a fucking hemorrhoid specialist instead of a physicist, I ain't giving him his end. His twenty percent goes to me. And as for your twenty percent, Dr. Clark, I'm thinking it's way too much. What the fuck did you do?"

"Mr. Rina," Beano said. He had lost his prop glasses on the roof in the struggle with Denniston and was now squinting at Tommy, pretending he could barely see him. "I did everything. I found the field. Without me, we wouldn't have the oil company at all. We made a deal, and a deal is a deal," he said lamely.

"You got our deal on paper?" Tommy asked, grinning maliciously.

"Well, no," Beano said, "but we have a verbal agreement."

"We do? Got any witnesses to this fucking verbal agreement?"

466

"Dr. Sutton—"

"He don't count. Anybody else?"

"No sir, but surely you remember—"

"No, I got no recollection of no deal with you, douchebag. And since that makes it your word against mine, I sure hope you ain't calling me a liar, 'cause if you are, I'll fucking ballpeen your geeky ass through the floor." And then he smiled and looked at Wade and Keith, who were smiling with him. "This business shit ain't so tough. Everybody makes it sound tough. Not tough at all." The two ex-linebackers' smiles were strained and unnatural, like the grille of a fifties Buick. Tommy was only five-eight, but he scared the two ex-linebackers to death.

♠ ♠ ♠

Joe Rina pulled up to the front entrance of the white alabaster Ritz-Carlton Hotel on Stockton Street. He got out of his chartered limousine and walked on the balls of his feet into the lobby where Reo Wells was waiting for him. They moved without talking into the bar and sat at a table in the back. It was five-thirty in the evening, and the bar was beginning to fill up. The sounds of clinking glasses and laughter masked their hushed conversation.

♠ ♠ ♠

"What've you got?" Joe said softly.

"I don't know what the hell's going on here, Mr. Rina, but something sure is."

"Lay it out."

"Tommy is definitely hanging with the guy whose picture you faxed to me. They been all over the place. Right now he's upstairs with the guy and some overweight woman named Laura Luna. He's also got two of your people from Las Vegas, Keith and Wade Summerland."

Joe flinched slightly. He had fired the Summerlands for doing a chip skim in the Bahamas two months ago. He had told Tommy to take care of them; now he was hanging with them instead. He pulled his emotions back. "What about my five million?"

"Never saw it, Mr. Rina. But that doesn't mean it's not in his briefcase or in his luggage."

"Right. How many people do you have here?" Joe asked; his anger was burning, the ash from that emotional fire making his eyes black, his voice brittle.

"Five guys, including me. All graduates of John Wayne High. Event-trained, ex–Delta Force incursion specialists."

"Okay, let's go find out what my big brother is up to." They got up and walked out of the bar right past Theodore X. Bates, who picked up the house phone and dialed Tommy's suite, letting the phone ring once and hanging up before Tommy could answer. The call would signal Beano and Victoria that Joe was on his way up.

Joe and Reo Wells took the elevator to Tommy's floor and met up with two specialists in gray suits, with eyes like licked stones.

They were standing in the fire stairs. Reo referred to them only by their mission names, Doughboy and Reefer.

"Okay, you know the S.I.O.P. Get the whole unit on standby," he told them.

Doughboy, who was the unit XO, started to whisper into his walkie-talkie. After a minute, a door opened down the hall and another man in a gray suit, with an earpiece, stepped out and waved Reo over. They walked down to the door where the man was standing and entered the room without talking.

Joe found himself looking at two men and a lot of sophisticated equipment. Three tubes attached to a junction box and computer were sticking through the wall into the adjoining suite.

"What the hell is all this?" Joe demanded.

"Anti-terrorist wall scope," Reo said. "Your brother is next door in that room." He pointed to the wall with the cables through it.

Joe looked at him flatly, his expression demanding an explanation.

"If you want, we can take out his back-up right through the wall."

"How? You can't see them," Joe asked, amazed at all of the equipment that was stashed around. It had come out of four large suitcases which lay open and mostly empty on the floor. There were two large helmets with full-face-plate visors lying on the bed. Each helmet was hooked up to an assault rifle by flexible metal cable that ran from the huge sophisticated gunsight into the left side of the helmet. Another cable ran out of the other side of the helmet and was connected to the computer, which was attached to cables stuck into the wall.

"All this stuff was developed to use against terrorists in hostage situations. That wand over there reads and catalogues exactly where all of the metal or concrete support beams are in the wall. Then, with high-speed drills, we go through the wall and insert three miniature video cameras. We then computer-key each person in the room by color and bulk. The 'hits' are green, the 'no-hits' will be on the face-plate visor screen in red. The computer over there references all of the input and blends all the components together. The result is you can see right through the wall, including all the structural elements, so when you fire, you won't deflect off an interior wall support. Put on the helmet there and look through the gunsight."

Joe went over and put on one of the helmets, snapped the visor down, and picked up the gun.

"Gotta stand on one of the X's we drew on the floor. That's so the computer won't get screwed up on the sight lines."

Joe stood on one of the X's they had put on the carpet with adhesive tape, then pulled the gun up and looked through the sight. "Don't see anything but the wall," he said.

"Turn on the power," Reo said; one of the team flipped a switch and instantly Joe was looking down the sight of the assault rifle right into the room next door. It was green-tinted magic.

The five people in the room were all color-keyed. Three of them were red; the two wide-bodies were green. As he moved the gun from right to left, he could actually pan through the building wall supports, seeing the concrete pillars and metal cross structures inside the wall.

"The soft green targets are Tommy's gun-bunnies, the two linebackers, Wade and Keith. They're cut-downs. Your brother, the woman, and this guy who hit your casino, we marked in red. They're no-hits on the S.I.O.P."

"What the hell's S.I.O.P.?" Joe asked, as he watched the fat woman move out of the suite's living room and into the bathroom. Since they didn't have a camera on the bathroom, she walked out of frame.

"S.I.O.P. is Single Integrated Operation Plan," he explained. "Wanna hear what they're saying?" and he flipped another switch and Joe could hear Tommy's drunken voice:

"...like he's the only one knows shit about anything. Like if it weren't for fuckin' Joe, we wouldn't even have a fucking pot to piss in."

It took all Joe's self-control to keep from squeezing off a shot right then. He'd never talked bad to anybody about Tommy. Their relationship was the Sicilian bond of brotherhood, and here Tommy was putting him down to a roomful of strangers. He wanted his five million back or he would have pulled the trigger and ended Tommy's life on the spot. He lowered the gun and took off the helmet, unable to listen to any more.

"You gonna hit the Summerland brothers?" Joe asked.

"This is all quiet ordnance." Reo nodded. "Nobody will hear anything. Those two are packing, and they're main line resistance. If we take them out first, it eliminates any possibility they'll bring smoke during the action."

"Okay, let's go. Let's do it," Joe said impatiently.

And the two sharpshooters put on their helmets while Joe and Reo went out in the hall to meet Doughboy and Reefer. Doughboy was carrying a room service coat and an empty champagne bottle he had removed from a cart outside one of the rooms. He shrugged off his jacket and put on the white coat with epaulets on the shoulders, then knocked on the door.

It opened a crack and Tommy stuck his face out. "Yeah?" he said.

"Complimentary champagne from the Manager," Doughboy said, holding up the dark glass bottle.

When Tommy unlatched the door, Reo and Reefer hit it hard, knocking Tommy backwards into the room. He stumbled and fell. "Take this fuck," Tommy yelled as he was going down.

Wade and Keith pulled their guns and, simultaneously, two holes appeared in the wall. Both of the linebackers went down from the kill-fire, like head-shot buffalo. Immediately blood started to stain their white shirt collars.

Joe walked in and looked disdainfully down at his brother, a black mixture of anger, betrayal, and disappointment filling his eyes. "Yeah, without Joe we sure wouldn't have a pot to piss in. You sure got that right, Tom."

Tommy was up on his elbows, astonished by the presence of his brother. "What are you doing here? I thought you were in Jersey."

"I thought you were in Sabre Bay till I found out you were robbing my bank in Nassau."

"Joe...you ain't gonna believe this. We're rich!"

"Where's my money, Thomas?" It was cold the way he said it. He had never called Tommy "Thomas" before. It was almost as if he were addressing somebody he didn't know.

Then Victoria came out of the bathroom. She had removed the body appliances and she wasn't wearing the wig. She looked like herself now as she swept into the room, laughing. "Tommy, honey, there's no toilet paper in the..." And she stopped to look at Joe Rina and the room full of strangers holding silenced automatics.

Tommy finally realized where he'd seen Laura Luna before, but it was too late.

It's you...you're Victoria Hart," Tommy said.

"You're actually fucking the bitch who was prosecuting me?!" Joe was so mad, he was actually shaking. Tommy had never seen him like this. "Where's my money, Thomas?"

"It's gone, Joe. I bought us an oil company. Look't this," and he moved to the table and grabbed for his open briefcase to show his brother the stock certificates, but they were gone. They had been printed on flash paper, which bookies used to keep their betting records. Victoria had scooped them up on her way to the bathroom and dropped them in the toilet....They'd disappeared in seconds.

"You cunt! You took them. They were here a minute ago, I swear, Joe. Tell him!" he screamed at Beano. "Tell him about the oil company."

"I don't know what the hell you're talking about, Tommy. What oil company? There's no oil company. Just give him his money back. Please, we shouldn't a stolen it in the first place. I knew it," Beano pleaded.

"Whatta you mean, there ain't no fucking oil company?" Tommy said. "Whatta you talkin' about? We used the money to buy the stock."

As Tommy started to get up, Joe kicked him in the face with his shoe, sending him back against the wall. Tommy flashed his anger, jumped to his feet, and started to charge his brother, but two guns were pointed at his face and he froze.

Joe had the hammer back on a nickel-plated revolver and now, slowly, he moved the barrel toward Tommy's eyes. "Where's my money?" he said.

"It's gone but we own the company," Tommy said.

"The money's in the trunk of his car," Beano corrected him.

Tommy looked over, confusion and panic in his beady, lizard eyes.

"Let's go see," Joe said coldly.

They took the elevator to the underground parking area and Tommy was forced, at gunpoint, to give up the keys to his rented Lincoln. Joe popped the trunk open and there, in the back, were the two suitcases that Tommy had brought from Nassau. Joe reached in and opened the suitcases and pulled out several stacks of money, still with the Nassau bank bands around them.

"How'd that get there?" Tommy said, unable to believe his eyes.

"Let's just end this," Joe said to Reo, who waved an arm. A van pulled up with the two sharpshooters in the front seat, then parked next to the Lincoln.

Then Reo produced riot-control plastic wrist cuffs and put them on Beano, Victoria, and Tommy. Reo pushed them toward the van.

"I'm your brother," Tommy said, looking into the hate-filled eyes of Joe Rina.

"I don't have a brother," Joe said. "I used to, but he died."

THIRTY-FOUR

The Blow-off

It was ten-thirty Friday night and Grady Hunt was in an FBI satellite van on Fillmore Street, just off of Geary. It was hot in the back of the van and Denny Denniston had just stepped outside to have a smoke.

Victoria and Beano were somewhere inside the Ritz-Carlton. Grady had several two-man jump-out teams in sedans parked in strategic locations around the hotel. He had placed an agent in a doorman's coat out front. Every time that unlucky agent had to lift luggage off the valet cart and pack it in a guest's car, he would swear at his FBI teammates in low tones over the mike on his lapel.

The paging unit that was in Victoria's purse was sending a very nice signal up to *Satcom 6* and bouncing it back to the Global Positioning Satellite Dish on the top of the blue minivan. Grady could follow Victoria, watching her movements on the lighted electronic map on the screen in front of him. The pagers had been developed by the FBI field operation lab and were actually miniature tracking units. He loved giving these special pagers to snitches. He would always page them a few times to let them know he was thinking about them, but the real reason was to activate the satellite tracking in case they took off or got out of pocket. Victoria and Beano thought they had lost Grady on the roof of the Penn Mutual Building, but the beeper gave him back their location in less then five minutes.

The phone in the van rang and he snapped it up. It was Gil Green from his hotel room at the Fairmont, downtown. "Give me an update," the colorless D.A. demanded without preamble.

"They're still cooped. When they leave, I'll call."

"Still at the Ritz?"

"Yeah."

"I wonder what they're doing there. Makes no sense."

"Yeah." Grady was trying to get the politician off the phone. Then his satellite track went hot. "They're moving. Gotta go," and he hung up.

He banged on the back door for Denniston. Seconds later the Vanilla Surprise jumped back into the van. Grady Hunt yelled at his driver, "They're headed down Stockton, just took a left on Broadway," he said, as the driver put it in gear. "Get on the air and tell Larry White this Mobile Command Post is in motion," he said to Denniston, who picked up the mike and switched the scanner over to Tac Two.

"This is Operation Brushfire, M.C.P. We're hot. Target was heading down Stockton, took a left on Broadway."

"Roger that," the voice said back.

Grady leaned forward and tapped the driver on the shoulder. "Put a little oomph in it. I'd like to make visual contact, see what they're riding in."

"Okay," the driver said, and he put the pedal down and the blue minivan accelerated.

Grady grabbed the mike and triggered it as he watched the blip turn on his video map. "He's making a right on Van Ness. He's on Route 101, everybody. I'm going to move up. Intersect point is in two blocks. Hold your pattern," he said.

The others all waited.

♠ ♠ ♠

In the ex–Delta Force van, one of the sharpshooters was driving, the other rode shotgun. Tommy was seated, his hands cuffed behind him in a backwards seat facing Joe. He was looking into his brother's hollow, cold eyes. Beano and Victoria were in the tan Lincoln just behind them with Reo, Reefer, and Doughboy.

"Joe, you gotta listen to me," Tommy finally said.

Joe didn't respond. His eyes were looking right through his brother.

"We own a fucking oil company. It's the largest stratigraphic trap in the Northern Hemisphere. I bought it for both of us. I found out about it from these two guys who hit the casino in the Bahamas. The old guy, he's a physicist; the young guy is a geologist.

They worked for this Fentress County Tennessee oil company. Stop fucking staring through me and listen to me, Joe!"

But Joe Rina said nothing.

"They found this huge oil field. I'm talkin' a fucking monster, Joe. Six acres. Now, I know that don't mean nothin' to you, but if you knew geology, you'd know a six-acre pool is like, unheard of. It's not like some fucking little pocket well with fucking anticlines an' shit. It's a full, shale-roofed stratigraphic trap or some damn thing. That's where the big oil finds always are. And these two geeks worked for FCP&G and they proved the field with this well...called a delineation well and..."

"You bought the company?" Joe interrupted. "Is that your story? But the money was still in your car. You think I'm stupid?"

"I don't know how that happened, they musta—"

"What were you doing hanging out with Victoria Hart?" Joe interrupted again. "She tried to put me in jail for attempted murder. We had to kill three people to shake her off. Now she's in your hotel room calling you 'honey' and 'darling.' You make me want to vomit."

"She was in makeup, Joe. I didn't recognize her. She was pretending to be Laura Luna, the company's Financial Officer. See Chip Lacy, he's the President of the company, but he had a heart attack and..." Tommy stopped because Joe rubbed his forehead in disgust.

"Listen, this whole thing sounds stupid, I know...but if you'll fucking listen, Joe, just listen to me, I'm sure you're gonna—"

"You know why I quit clipping guys and started letting you do it?" Joe interrupted for the third time.

"Look, Joe, this whole fucking thing...I can explain it."

"Reason I quit was I couldn't stand listening to dead men whine. You *used* to be a man; don't go out whining. Not that I care about memories anymore...but why don't you help me here and stop it? You're nothing but a walking piece of yesterday. A disappointing part of my personal history."

"Joe, how can you say that?"

"Only reason I don't put you down right now," Joe continued, "is this suit is raw silk, and at this range, I'm gonna get pieces a'you all over me from the back spray."

Tommy looked into Joe's eyes and saw such cold clarity that he knew his brother wasn't kidding.

"Joe, please listen...just let me..."

But Joe thumbed back the hammer and fired a shot. The driver of the van jumped and almost ran off the road. The bullet tore through Tommy's chest, puncturing his lung. He jackknifed forward from recoil and landed on Joe's lap, pouring blood all over the black, raw silk suit.

"Nuts," Joe said softly, then pushed his stunned and bleeding brother back into a sitting position. "Now shut up, will ya? I don't wanna hear any more."

They arrived at the Presidio entrance on Lombard. Reo pulled the Lincoln around in front of the van, got out, and, using a padlock key he had in his pocket, opened the gate of the old, abandoned military base. It sat on fourteen hundred acres of prime waterfront land and used to be the military command center for the eight Western states until it was closed because of budget cuts. The site was magnificent, with its wood-frame, turn-of-the-century architecture. The clapboard structures were built in the 1870's, with large bay windows that looked out on the Golden Gate Bridge. Reo opened the large gate in the fence and stood aside as the Lincoln, driven by Doughboy and containing Reefer, Beano, and Victoria, pulled through the gate, followed by the sharpshooters in the white van with Joe and Tommy. Once they were through, Reo locked the gate. Then he got in the Lincoln and they pulled up Presidio Boulevard, past the deserted Letterman U.S. Army Health Clinic with its low eaves and slanting roof. They passed the old wood-frame Army Headquarters, which was closed up and abandoned. They turned left on Arguello Boulevard and headed up into the hills, leaving the base and the road lights behind. They drove south on the old rutted road, climbing toward the wooded hillside where Reo and his squad had done their LURRP training years before.

♠ ♠ ♠

"They're in the Presidio," Grady said into the mike as he hunched over his GPS unit in the back of the van. He had a slight tinge of annoyance in his voice. "They could get lost up there. Let's move in. I'm gonna take the Lombard gate, you guys go in on Presidio Boulevard. Don't fuck with the lock, break it off if you have to."

Denniston was already out of the van and had taken the tire iron and busted the lock on the Lombard gate. He got back in the van, and they drove up into the Presidio....Following the GPS, they turned south, heading up into the hills that overlooked the old military base and San Francisco Harbor beyond.

♠ ♠ ♠

The sharpshooter parked in a wooded area and set the hand break on the white van. An unusual gale wind several months before had blown trees down in this area of the Presidio. It was dense with fallen trees and thick underbrush.

They got Tommy out of the car, still handcuffed. His legs were weak, and he stumbled in front of his little brother. He didn't look like he would last much longer or make it much farther. Blood was running down the front of his shirt and also out a large exit wound in his back.

When Beano saw him, he knew they were

in trouble. The entire con depended on keeping Tommy alive to testify. He hadn't thought Joe would shoot him in the van. With Tommy dead, they didn't have a witness. Joe Dancer would get away clean.

They moved through the underbrush, and Reo found a foot trail that led into a clearing. This was the place where Reo's weapons team had done Long Range Reconnaissance Patrol training. Reo and his crew knew every inch of this terrain, especially the underground network of caverns that had been built to prepare them for tunnel fighting. Reo's S.I.O.P. called for them to kill Tommy, Victoria, and Beano, then drag their bodies down into one of the abandoned tunnels and, using a physics package made up of C-4 and a radio detonator, collapse the tunnel, burying the three bodies fifty feet down under tons of soft earth. They would never be found.

The group of nine moved along the footpath, and finally out into the clearing. Reo kicked back a big piece of wood that had been covering a man-sized "spider-hole" trap door just like the ones Charley had used in Vietnam.

"On your knees," Joe said to the three of them.

Tommy was coughing blood now. He half dropped to his knees, and the loss of blood was making him dizzy. It was all he could do to stay upright.

Beano knew they were all just seconds from oblivion.

♠ ♠ ♠

Doughboy had set up down the road to guard their backs. He heard cars coming, so he edged up on the ridge and looked down at the road below through a Starscope. He could see a blue van with a satellite dish, being followed by several cars full of men. He made them instantly as Feds, and grabbed his mike.

"I got a number ten situation here," he said.

Reo had his Heckler and Koch MP5 submachine gun out. He slowly lowered it and triggered the walkie-talkie instead. "Whatta you need to fix it?" he said.

"Send Reefer with a Zippo unit. I've got less than a minute."

"Wilco," Reo said. Then he turned to Reefer. "Get the flame thrower out of the back of the van and set up down the road with Doughboy. Unfriendlies coming."

"Shit," Reefer said, and he took off running toward the van. He opened the back, grabbed a small flame-thrower unit, and started running down the road, shouldering the two tanks as he went.

♠ ♠ ♠

Grady didn't know what hit him. They were driving up toward the woods at the top of the hill when, all of sudden, the entire satellite van was awash in fire. Then almost immediately, and without warning, the gas tank exploded, and he was shot through the roof of the van and was dead before he hit the underside of the metal satellite dish.

"Holy shit!" the FBI Agents said in the sedans behind, as the van, billowing smoke and fire, rolled out of control toward a sheer drop and tumbled off, taking all three men with as it fell.

The FBI Agents in the follow cars hit reverse and squealed backwards as Reefer, carrying the flame thrower, ran across the top of the hill and down the opposite bank, then took up a fire position on the road below. The cars full of FBI Agents roared past him, still in reverse. He pulled the trigger and let them have a stream of liquid death. The cars both caught fire. The Agents all dove out while the cars were still moving. Some men were burning and rolled in the dirt to extinguish themselves; the others came up pulling their weapons. They laid down a cover fire and chopped Reefer down with a hailstorm of hollow-point Devastators. One of the rounds hit the Zippo tank and Reefer exploded in a rolling orange cloud that singed everybody and lit the sky above them in a ball of raging rocket fuel.

In the clearing, they all heard the thundering explosion as Reefer was blown to cinders. Joe pointed his gun at Tommy.

"Joe, don't do this," Beano said. "He's been telling you the truth. It's all been a scam." Beano was on his knees, his hands cuffed behind him.

Victoria was on her knees beside him. "It's true," she said, also trying to save Tommy's life. "The whole thing was a con."

But Joe aimed his gun right in his brother's face. "Hey, go fuck yourself, Joe," Tommy coughed at his little brother.

Victoria wasn't prepared to die, but it seemed like there was nothing she could do to save herself or any of them. She was strangely calm, almost as if this were not reality. Then a remarkable thing happened. She looked over and saw that Beano was looking at her. In that moment, through his startling blue eyes, she could see right into his soul. Despite the situation, it was a beautiful sight.

"Light 'em up," Joe said.

Beano heard the two sharpshooters pull the slides on their assault weapons. Tommy looked up into the deadly bore of Joe's revolver. It was, for a moment, as if time had slowed and was almost standing still. They heard the click of Joe's gun as he pulled the hammer back and aimed at Tommy; this was followed by a distant rumble.

"The fuck?" Reo said, as the ground started

to shake. It got louder and stronger, followed by some kind of ungodly screaming....

A shiny, red, three-quarter-ton Chevy Silverado four-by-four exploded over the rim of the hill from below. It flew into the clearing, all four tires spinning loose dirt in the air. It landed hard and the whip antenna, with a red feather taped to the top, swayed back violently, almost touching the back fender. And then three more shiny lacquer-and-chrome trucks, with red feathers and Arkansan license plates, came right behind: two Dodge Rams and a Dodge Dakota Club Cab. There were albino Bateses tied with rope to the roll bars in the backs of the trucks. All of them were holding pump shotguns. Simultaneously, four Ithaca over-and-under shotguns with hand-carved stocks fired in the darkness. Red feathers whipped and swayed in the night as more trucks raced around the clearing.

Reo's two sharpshooters started firing at the trucks. Then three more crew cabs came from the other side, roaring into the clearing. The sound of hillbilly music and Confederate war cries filled the night, along with the reports of shotguns and automatic weapons fire.

During all of this, Joe turned to finish off his brother.... Beano lunged at him just before he pulled the trigger. Beano's hands were pinned behind him by the plastic cuffs, but he hit Joe in the stomach with his shoulder, driving him back. They both fell in the soft dirt, but Joe scrambled up and aimed his pistol at Beano. Then, as he was seconds from death,

Victoria lunged at Joe, hitting him mid-shin. He went down again, firing the gun in the air. The gun flew from his hand and skidded near the spider hole that was to have been their grave. Beano jumped up and kicked the gun down the hole. He heard it land in the darkness fifteen feet below.

Beano lost track of the commotion behind him as he lunged again at Joe, hitting him with a head-butt, letting all of his adrenaline complete the follow-through.

Joe was finally on his back, dazed. When he tried to lift himself up, he didn't seem to know where he was. There was still gunfire going on in the clearing, but it was mostly mop-up.

Doughboy had taken up a position on the high ground, but didn't count on the Hog Creek Bateses, who drove their shiny trucks right up the hill after him. He was badly out-numbered and finally threw his weapon down and surrendered, lying down on his stom-ach, looking up at three plastic bug shields on the trucks' shiny grilles. Bronco and Echo Bates pounded on him gleefully.

"Say uncle," Echo yelled, as he repeatedly hit the commando.

"Uncle..." the bleeding man finally said.

Beano could see that Tommy was in deep shock. "Let's get him outta here. He needs a hospital," he said, as Chevy and Cadillac Bates cut the plastic handcuffs with their skinning knives.

Beano and Cadillac lifted Tommy into the rear of the Ram truck. He was delirious now, losing consciousness. Suddenly, there were the sounds of sirens approaching from far away.

"I think we better throw the chairs in the Buick and get rollin'," Cadillac said. "Picnic's over."

The Bates family members ran to their trucks. Beano yanked Joe to his feet and handed him over to Cadillac Bates. "Sit on this movie star till it's time for his curtain call." Cadillac Bates put Joe Rina in the Silverado crew cab, next to him. Echo Bates got in beside the mobster, who now looked over at the huge albino, wondering what planet they'd all come from and who the hell they were.

"You're so gad dum pretty, I might just have ta fuck ya right here, Boy-oh," Echo Bates said and grinned, exposing two empty spaces in his gum line.

Joe feared it actually might happen.

They all left the clearing, going in different directions, not using the road. The four-wheel-drive trucks churned in low gears down the rock-strewn hillside. Beano was holding Tommy as they roared past the burning FBI satellite van. They slowed, but Grady Hunt, Denny Denniston, and the driver were all dead. The remaining FBI men were running toward them, so they didn't stop, but roared on. They had to save Tommy's life in order to save the bubble.

THIRTY-FIVE

Holding On by Letting Go

Nobody knew what had happened to Tommy or Joe Rina. They had completely disappeared. Both had been missing for almost two days when Victoria walked into Gil Green's office in Trenton, unannounced and uninvited, and stood across the oak desk from the bland District Attorney.

"Victoria," he said, without warmth, "surprised you had the nerve to show up. You're, of course, guilty of half-a-dozen or more crimes...not to mention possible complicity in the death of several Federal Agents in the Presidio."

"I had nothing to do with anybody's death, Gil. If you had me followed, then maybe it's your fault. As I recall, tailing me was not part of our deal."

He sat and looked at her, and then he started to fidget with the pen on his desk. "I suppose we could argue that indefinitely," he finally said softly.

"Sure we could, and I'd win. I wasn't wanted for anything. You can't prove I had prior knowledge of Beano Bates's record, so cut the bullshit."

"I suppose you had some reason to make this visit." His vacant expression was all-consuming.

"Maybe there's a way we can still save a few

490

parts of our original deal, Gil, but it's gonna have to change in a few key areas."

"Yeah? Why's that?"

"Because you aren't holding good cards anymore. Matter of fact, your cards are terrible, especially if you factor in the political aspects. You fumbled this investigation badly. You lost three Federal Agents by screwing up your end. You tried to frame your own prosecutor. The list of 'Oh shits' is awesome," she said.

"I see."

"Do you?"

"And what is it you're proposing?" he said, knowing she hadn't come here to spit this furball up on his desk.

"What if you could still have most of it? What if Tommy Rina is still willing to come forth and testify against his brother?"

"You're harboring Tommy Rina?"

"I'm not 'harboring' anyone; he's not wanted for any crimes, Gil, despite the fact that he's been committing them all his life. But he knows his brother won't rest till he's dead. He'd rather do seven years for second-degree murder than an eternity for profound stupidity."

"Okay, so Tommy comes forward. But nobody's seen Joe. He won't be anywhere around if Tommy is gonna testify against him."

"I can have Joe dropped off on your doorstep."

"And what is Tommy going to say?" Gil asked.

She reached into her briefcase and withdrew a sheaf of papers and handed them to Gil. He looked at them quickly, skim-reading the pages. "It says here that Tommy declares under penalty of perjury that Joe gave him direct orders to kill Carol Sesnick, Bobby Manning, and Tony Corollo," he said, laying the papers down on his desk. "But this confession isn't signed."

"I have the signed copy in a safe place."

"I see...."

"I also have Tommy ready to testify, but you're going to have to do a few things to earn all this political good fortune," she said.

He let some time tick off the antique grandfather clock in the corner of his office. It tick-tocked the seconds loudly and Victoria sat and looked out the window, trying not to show any concern for his decision.

"Okay. So what's the price?"

"Three things," she said, reluctantly shifting her gaze back to him. "One: You promise to try Tommy Rina on second-degree murder, not first, and you arrange with the court for him to have a sentence with a seven-year cap."

"He's the one who pulled the trigger."

"I know, but it's the only way I can get him to play."

"He's a murderer."

"He also has an enemies list longer than Qaddafi's. Tommy's killed too many players. He probably won't even survive the seven-year jolt."

"And what's number two?"

"If he lives out his sentence, you guarantee him the Federal Witness Protection Program."

"And the last?"

"You arrange for all of the Federal charges pending against Beano X. Bates to be dropped."

"I see. Of course, I'm only a New Jersey District Attorney. The Federal Government doesn't generally do what I tell them."

"Hey, Gil, stop fooling around. You and I both know the FBI Organized Crime Strike Force is all over the Rinas. How much do you think they spent last year building a case against Joe and Tommy?"

"I haven't a clue."

"Four hundred and fifty-nine thousand dollars, not including expenses and overtime. Let's round it to half a million in surveillance costs per year. They've been swinging at those two curve balls like Little League outfielders and haven't even hit a pop-up. They'll deal, Gil. They'd like to drop both these bad boys and you get to be the hero. You get to take the bows at the press conference. It's your party. All you've gotta do is broker the deal."

"Beano Bates is on the Ten Most Wanted List. They aren't gonna deal on him."

"He's a white-collar criminal. He's not violent, and besides, that's what it's gonna take to get this done." She looked at him for a long moment and he studied her back, without expression.

Finally, Victoria stood and clicked her briefcase closed. She headed to the door.

"You know I've filed a brief with the New Jersey Bar to get your license yanked. I'm surprised you don't want to trade on that."

"I'm through being a lawyer, Gil. It's no fun anymore, because I figured something out...."

"What's that?"

"I always wanted the law to be about right and wrong, but it's not."

"Then what's it about?"

"It's about legal and illegal. That's a whole different concept that deals with fine points of law that get confessions thrown out of court and evidence inadmissible on technicalities, and I'm just not interested in that game anymore. Call me before close of business today. If you don't call, I'm taking this deal to the Feds. Only reason I brought it here first is, I know once you think about it, you'll fight like a son-of-a-bitch to get it for me... because after all, Gil, once you boil it down, it's still just politics."

Victoria left his office, got in her car, and began the three-hour drive to Wallingford.

When she arrived and saw her parents, she couldn't believe how good it was to be home. She hugged her mother and father and sat in the kitchen with them while her mother made peanut butter and jelly sandwiches. Her wheelchair was parked up next to the counter and she reached up to cut off the crust.

"'Ut the 'ust off, way you li'," she slurred to Victoria, who took the sandwich and ate it pensively. All her life she had cut the crusts off sandwiches, just like she had cut the crusts off most of her experiences. She wondered why; what event had put her on such a careful and precise path?

Her father was looking at her from across the room, smiling, almost as if he could read her thoughts. "What're you going to do, Sweet-pea?" he asked. He was wearing plaid golf slacks and a pink shirt and socks. Silly as that was, she thought he looked absolutely darling. Her heart went out to both of them.

"I don't know, Dad," she said. "I had some plans, but I'm not sure now."

She told them everything that had happened, ending by explaining that she had cashed her last ticket at Justice to get Tommy checked into the hospital at Lompoc Prison under an assumed name. Tommy's lung had been punctured, but the bullet had not hit anything vital. He'd been sewn up and filled with bottled blood and was glowering at the prison nurse when she left, but he'd agreed to cooperate. Victoria had gotten Tommy's signed confession and his promise to testify against Joe.

The rest had been mop-up. After Victoria got Tommy checked in, Beano told her he was going to go pay off the Hog Creek Bateses the percentage they'd agreed on, and that he would call her as soon as he was through.

It had been John who called a day later and said that Beano had taken Roger-the-Dodger and disappeared for a while. He had taken the $4.5 million in cash with him. She couldn't help herself; she was disappointed that Beano had talked a good game, but in the end had taken the money and run. That he was just a charming rogue who could never change...So that chapter in her life was closed. She could never love a criminal, anyway. She hadn't come *that* far, but she still felt a sense of loss.

Before she hung up, she had asked John about Cora. "Cora's paintin' number nine oil on the driveways and roofs up in heaven." And even though he meant it to be lighthearted, his voice cracked over the phone when he said it.

Now she felt tired. Victoria went up to her bedroom after lunch and lay on the bed. She looked at the ballerinas, only now she thought she could see, for the first time, what they were really doing. They weren't dancing at all. They never had been. They were simply expressing themselves in the best way they knew how, just as Victoria had always been trying to do. Maybe she had to come all this way to discover that one basic fact.

"Hold on by letting go," she said quietly in the empty room. She had let go and now she was waiting for the right things to happen in her life. She wouldn't force it anymore. She wouldn't bowl everybody over with dedicated energy, but rather nourish herself with the joy of her accomplishments.

Gil called her at seven-thirty. His voice was soft on the phone. "I can't promise Murder Two for Tommy, but I can get him First Degree with no special circumstances."

"Hey, Gil, I want you to listen to this very

carefully; speaking for Tommy and using his exact idiom: Go fuck yourself." And she hung up. In seconds, the phone rang again. She let her father pick it up and call for her.

"It's Mr. Green, sweetheart," he called from the bottom of the stairs.

She came back out of her bedroom and picked up the phone again. "Look, Gil, this isn't even tough. You get Tommy Murder Two and you give him the Protection Program after he's out, or I'm gonna just let him go and you can worry about him coming after you, which he might do because he's insane."

"Okay, Murder Two, and I can get him the Protection Program. But I can't drop the Bates charges."

And she hung up on him again. She waited for the callback, and when it came this time, she snapped up the phone. "Don't waste your money calling me again, Gil. This is a package. Make the deal or watch the Feds make it."

"Okay, I can get him probation. Bates pleads guilty and he gets five years' probation. But he's gotta take the felony bust, Vicky. I can't absolve him of that."

"Okay, set up the deal and paper it. Once it's done, I'll arrange for you to get both Tommy and Joe."

♠ ♠ ♠

Two more days passed, and still she hadn't heard from Beano. She hoped he would call. She had to tell him he was no longer wanted by the law, but had to show up at Gil's office. Now, she was beginning to suspect she would never see or hear from him again. He was probably in Rio living it up on his millions. She took long walks and played canasta with her mother. She tried to contemplate a life without the man she had fallen in love with. It seemed odd that she would find the missing pieces of herself in such a strange place.

She completed her negotiations with Gil and got the deal on paper; then she told Gil where Tommy was. Last, she called Paper Collar John in Atlantic City. She told him the deal was done and that the Hog Creek Bateses should drop Joe off at the police station in Trenton. There would be no questions asked.

"Okay," he said.

"You hear from Beano?" she asked at the end of the conversation, her heart pumping with expectation.

"Y'know, Victoria, I seen him change over these last three weeks. He ain't the same as he was before. But I'm not sure that's good. You can't take his kind and turn him into something he ain't...."

"I guess you're right," she said, "but it would sure have been fun to try."

That night Victoria and her parents went to dinner at the country club. The TV at the club was on, and everybody was full of the story of Joe Rina's arrest and how the tabloid star's brother, Tommy, had come forward with the testimony to indict Joe for Murder One. Gil Green was on every news station. She listened while one reporter commented that these two brothers had been very close, and then asked rhetorically how it was possible that Tommy, who had once allegedly killed a man to protect Joe, would now testify against him.

"Because," Victoria said, repeating Beano's words, "the relationship had never been adequately tested."

She slept fitfully that night and woke up with a start when something jumped in bed with her. She sat up straight, feeling blindly for it in the darkness. And then, Roger-the-Dodger lunged up. He wagged his tail and licked her face.

"Roger, baby," she said, and she turned on the light and hugged him. There was a long crease in his hind end where the bullet had hit him, but brown and black fur was beginning to grow over the pink wound. She gathered him up in her arms and walked downstairs. She knew Beano was around somewhere, and then she finally saw him sitting in a chair out by the kidney-shaped pool in her parents' backyard. She moved over and sat in the chair beside him. He looked over at her and smiled.

"Hi," he said, "remember me?"

"Vividly," she said, still holding Roger. "He woke me up." She handed the dog over to him, but Roger jumped right back onto her lap.

"He's got good taste," Beano said. "I didn't mean for him to wake you. He must've gotten in an open door," he lied.

"You were just sitting out here?"

"My second night," he said, and looked at

her. "If you were David Letterman, you could get a restraining order."

"I've missed you," she said. "I've been thinking about you a lot."

"Me too," he said. "I'm sorry I ran, Victoria. I'm not sure what I am anymore. All the things I believed in have changed."

"So, everything doesn't have to happen at once," she said.

"So many questions...like what should I do from now on, what kind of life should I live, what should I do with the rest of Joe's five million?"

"You still have it?"

"Yeah, all but the ten percent I gave to the Hog Creek Bateses, but something tells me if I spend this Rina blood money, I'll ruin what I've found." He looked at her. "Silly, huh? I sound like a real sucker."

"No, I think it makes a lot of sense. You can't hold on without letting go."

"Then we have to do something. Get dressed," he said. "I'll need a lot of moral support."

They drove back to Trenton. It took only two hours at that time of night. Beano pulled up in front of the Trenton Children's Hospital.

"What's this?" Victoria said.

"Carol was a pediatric nurse here, gave a lot of time and money to this place. She'd work like a dog, then hand half of it back. I thought she was being a sucker with these people, like she was trying to make up for the rest of the family."

He got out of the car, opened the trunk, and pulled the two tan suitcases out. "I can't

500

believe I'm doing this." Then he walked into the building with Victoria.

"I want to make a cash donation," he said to the nurse behind the counter. "Who do I talk to?"

The nurse led them to a man named Dr. Foster, who was the Assistant Hospital Administration. It was past midnight, but he was there, working on the annual financial report. Beano put the suitcases up on his desk.

"I want to make a charitable contribution. I want you to invest it, and I want the annual proceeds to be spent on child cancer research."

"I see. And in whose name would you like this gift to be made?" he asked.

"In the name of Carol Sesnick," he said. "She used to be a nurse here." And then he filled out the paperwork.

When the man opened the suitcase and saw all of the banded cash, Beano put a finger to his lips. "Nobody is looking for this money. It's not stolen," he told the man. "But it would probably be better if you didn't talk a lot about it."

They filled out the paperwork and left the hospital and got back into the car. Dr. Foster was watching them from the front steps of the large hospital, wondering who they were. He only vaguely remembered a round-faced, freckled nurse named Carol Sesnick.

Beano drove Victoria to the main street in Trenton. They cruised the boulevard of dead-end dreams. Finally he pulled the car to the curb and turned off the engine. "Come on," he said.

She got out of the car. He had a strange smile on his face.

"What is it?" she asked, wondering where they were.

He walked with her down the seedy street and finally entered a tattoo parlor called The Black Angel. Standing there was Paper Collar John, along with Dakota Bates. Dakota was still wearing the after-effects of Tommy's beating as Victoria hugged them.

"What are you two doing here?" she asked.

"They wanted to be here to see this," he said. And then he took off her wristwatch and she knew what he was about to do.

The tattoo artist began to work in the painted shop full of the colors of sunset and dawn. She looked away as the bearded and beaded man performed his artistry.

Roger-the-Dodger had jumped up in her lap and sat there, looking up at her, until the man was finished and had wiped the tattoo clean. When she looked down at her wrist and saw it for the first time, she smiled. It read:

$$\mathcal{B}$$

6-17-97

It was a strange badge of honor and meant more to her than her law degree. "But I'm not a Bates," she finally said, her voice shaking in anticipation.

"We've got a best man and a maid of honor," Beano said. "If you want, we can even take care of that."

So two days later they did.

If you have enjoyed reading this large print book and you would like more information on how to order a Wheeler Large Print Book, please write to:

 Wheeler Publishing, Inc.
P.O. Box 531
Accord, MA 02018-0531